REGALLY BINDING

Rebecca Chase

Copyright

This ebook is a work of fiction. Names, characters, businesses, places, events and incidents are either the products of the author's imagination or used in a fictitious manner. Any resemblance to actual persons, living or dead, or actual events is purely coincidental.

Copyright 2024 Rebecca Chase

All rights reserved

Published by Rebecca Chase

Cover design © seajart

All rights reserved. No part of this publication may be reproduced, distributed, or transmitted in any form or by any means, including photocopying, recording, or other electronic or mechanical methods, without the prior written permission of the published, except in the case of brief quotations embodied in critical reviews and certain other noncommerical uses permitted by copyright law.

To the people from our past who inspire our stories and those from the present who inspire our love.

Chapter One

Liss checked her mobile from under the bar as she wiped down the worn wood. Still no message from her latest Tinder match, although there was a breaking news notification about the Royal family. Liss swiped the notification away without reading it. She just wanted a response to the underwear picture it took all her courage to send. She shouldn't have done it, but she wanted to feel attractive and carefree and like her best friend, Isla, who wouldn't hesitate to send something like that.

"Have you heard from Hugo today? He's checking in a lot," Greg, the pub's regular, whose ear hair was longer than his eyelashes, said through a yawn before supping the head of his pint. His dog, Joyce, was propped on his knees, eyeballing Liss.

"Not yet," Liss replied with a shrug. Hugo, the pub's owner, used to be happy with Liss running the place, but now, there were rumours that he was selling the pub to a chain, which would leave Liss without a job.

"You could do better than this place, you know," Greg added, tipping his head in the direction of the two university students who were sucking face. "You could run a bar where your boss doesn't take credit for your ideas."

"A smile from you is worth the stuff I have to put up with," Liss said, her gaze flicking to her phone, where another breaking news notification flashed up. She swiped it away without reading it as Greg grunted. It was probably about the royal wedding happening later in the year.

Steve, one of Liss's closest friends and the pub's deputy manager, was making the most of the late morning lull, reading a newspaper while occasionally glancing at Liss above it. "Liss won't leave us. She always says this place is her family."

He had a point. It had been like her family since her mum died.

"We all know why you stay, Steve, even though you spend too much time judging the people who drink here," Greg grumbled as he fed Joyce bits of sausage. "Especially when your middle-class parents with upper-class judgements visit."

"I don't know what you mean," Steve retorted with a huff. But he did. Liss and Isla had spoken to him about it before. He grumbled that he could work in any city job.

Liss stared at her phone, willing the guy she'd sent an underwear pic to respond as she rejoined the conversation. "Why do you stay he—"

"No phones while working," Steve mumbled, cutting off Liss.

Liss dropped her grubby cloth onto the bar and glared. "I'm well aware. I was the one who came up with the rule."

"Who are you waiting to hear from?" Steve replied, dropping the paper and collecting glasses.

The one thing Liss refused to talk to Steve about was her dating life or, rather, lack thereof. He always got weird about it but never explained why. And besides, it was humiliating telling anyone that she'd messaged a sexy picture to a man she'd not yet met, and he hadn't replied. She tucked her phone in her pocket. "Oh, it's nothing—"

"BBC1! BBC1! Give me the remote, Liss!" Isla ran into the pub, saving Liss from the awkward conversation.

"Isla, chill." Liss paused at the till, pushing back strands of her brown hair before surrendering to the frizz and tying it into a ponytail. The humidity wasn't helping the frizz, nor were the hoodie and jeans she'd thrown on that morning.

Isla dived onto the bar and fumbled for the remote they kept near the tills.

"Isla, no." Liss slapped Isla's hand away and popped the remote into the back pocket of her jeans. This pub was her kingdom; not even her best friend controlled the television. "You have no say on the channel the pub is watching."

Isla did a dramatic look behind her. "You're the only one of the five people here who cares."

"We're fifteen minutes from the lunch crowd coming in, and they'll want to watch horse racing," Liss countered, hands on the curve of her hips. "Tell me what's so important, and I'll consider changing the channel."

Isla huffed before throwing her arms in the air.

Liss stood on the step behind the bar she used when she needed to meet customers' stares, which was tricky at her five-foot height. She eyeballed her bestie.

"Liss has more attitude than the King's corgi," Greg said with a chuckle.

He was kind of right. If you put her in front of anyone but her friends and punters, she turned into her latest date, running for the door with no intention of returning. But in the bar, she controlled her anxiety.

"The King, the actual King, is doing a live broadcast in two minutes," Isla ranted.

"And that's important because?" Liss wiped the bar with the damp and oddly smelling cloth. Maybe she should consider moving on, but this was the only place she'd worked since dropping out of university five years ago. And her only skills were pulling pints and cleaning toilets.

Joyce walked around the bar and sniffed the spilt beer on Liss's dirty Doc Martens. Even the scents from her mango moisturiser and vanilla and strawberry shower gel weren't strong enough to overwhelm the beer smell. Liss's raised eyebrows were enough to send the pup back to its owner, though not before Liss sneaked her a biscuit from her pocket.

"This never happens." Isla's leg bounced.

Liss moved around the bar and started moving chairs to prepare for the lunchtime rush. Isla followed her around the pub.

"Kings don't do live broadcasts," Isla continued. "Every year, he makes a Christmas speech that's filmed weeks before and has a carefully managed script. He doesn't do anything like this because it's not allowed.

My media colleagues have messaged our networks for the last hour, and it's all over Instagram."

"So I'm asking again, why is this important?" Liss's voice echoed around the pub.

Steve collapsed into a chair and propped his feet up on a table, commentating, "The big fight resumes, Liss Granger in one corner and Isla Redding in the other."

Liss raised her eyebrow, and he dropped his feet to the floor.

"You don't have social media, so you don't get it. But this is massive. No one talks about the royals on social unless they're in court, doing something controversial, or getting married. The royal media team is streaming his announcement everywhere. This is epic. Please, Liss. I'll come to yours and do your washing up for a week," Isla begged.

The teenagers watched the action from their worn wooden chairs before resuming their kissing. Oh, to be that desperate for someone else that you didn't care about the shitty décor and bad furnishings. This pub needed work. If her mum were still around, she'd have helped Liss improve the place herself with little touches. But she wasn't and never would be again.

Liss shook her head and stepped closer to Isla, crossing her arms over her chest. "You don't do your own washing up."

"Fine. I'll cook for you for a week." This broadcast must have been significant. Isla's career, and climbing the ladder in the PR firm she'd joined out of university, were everything to her. Although they were best friends, they were painfully different. While Isla was conquering the PR world, Liss was still trying to find her purpose.

"A month," Steve called out.

"Shut up, you," Isla called back, swatting his presence away with her hand. "Please, Liss, I need to see this. It might help my career."

"And you can't watch it on your phone because…?" Liss stared at Isla, who was looking anywhere but at her.

Steve jumped in, "She's run out of data watching all those dodgy videos her Tinder dates send her.

"There's nothing dodgy about sexy videos, Steve. Stop being judgemental."

Liss winced. This wasn't the first time they'd had this argument. At least Isla was getting videos. No one sent Liss videos of what they'd want to do with her. But then again, she'd probably freak if they did. She had to focus on finding a good guy; that was what being around her lonely mum as a teenager had taught her.

"Fine." Liss switched to BBC1 and stood with Isla to get a good view of the television—anything to stop Steve and Isla from arguing. Isla hugged her tightly.

Her phone buzzed with a call as the announcer appeared. Surely, the guy she messaged wouldn't call. Still, she glanced at the phone screen with hope.

"I bet it's Nana Bets," Steve said, sidling up to Liss. Only Liss's two friends, work and her grandma called her, although her grandma only called when she wanted something. "Tell her I won employee of the month again."

Liss glared at him as she answered the phone. Hugo awarded Steve that honour every month. Hugo went to school with Steve's parents, although he denied that had anything to do with his choice.

"Hi, Nana. Is everything okay? I can't talk right now. The King is doing a live broadcast, and we're all watching," Liss whispered as Isla snatched the remote and increased the volume with exaggerated presses of the remote control.

"You can't watch that broadcast until you see me. Come outside," her grandma ordered. She had a lot of audacity for a woman who was usually swanning around the world visiting her former dancer friends. "I'm waiting in a Bentley."

"But—"

"No buts. Right now, Felicity," she snapped.

Liss winced before mumbling, "Everyone's so bloody demanding today. I don't like stressy people."

"And yet you're friends with us." Steve chuckled. His skin turned pink when she shot him a look.

Isla grabbed her hand giddily. Liss liked to see her pseudo family happy. They were the only family she had aside from her nana.

"Hello. I am sure this is a surprise for you all." The King stared into the camera, his chin raised in pride. There was that charisma the country loved.

"He looks a bit off. He should be wearing a tie," Steve mumbled.

Isla shushed him.

The way the King slouched slightly in a grey woolly jumper ticked the "break from protocol" boxes.

The King continued, "It's unprecedented for a monarch to speak to his country like this, and I realise you are all waiting to hear what I have to share. But first…"

"Felicity, you'd better not still be listening to the King. My only grandchild is usually so obedient when her poor grandma needs her," Nana Bets whined down the phone. Liss ground her teeth. Her nana's guilt-tripping tactics were legendary.

"Don't worry about the lunchtime rush," Greg said, understanding her reluctance. "Mr. Employee of the Month can cover it."

"I'm not doing toilets," Steve grumbled. Liss stared at the two of them. She always cleaned the toilets. Her job used to make her feel valued, but not recently.

Isla gasped. "The King is talking about abdicating in the future because he's unwell."

"And I have something further," the King continued. "I believed this would remain private my entire life, but I'm nearing death due to a complicated illness, and I must share something personal because it has implications for the country."

That one statement stopped the teenagers from kissing. They stared at the screen as people drifted through the doors, instantly drawn to the news.

"Felicity," her nana pressured.

"Fine," Liss grumbled, hanging up and sauntering around the bar, locating her bag and keys.

Liss tiptoed to the door, stalling to catch the King's announcement. Since Liss's mum died four years earlier, she always responded to her demanding grandma when she called, but Isla's enthusiasm about the announcement and her grandma's command she not watch it had piqued her curiosity.

Liss grabbed the edge of the door as the King said, "Nearly forty-five years ago, while I was a prince and

"So that's a yes then, Bear. Do you know where we're going? Give me my phone back, Bear." Every time she said his name, she overemphasised it. The B was like a poke.

Bear's only movement was widening his legs as if hinting at the package in his trousers while squishing her limbs tightly. With broad thighs and taut trousers, she couldn't stop staring, even as he disregarded her space. It turned out her message to Isla was wrong. He did look bigger than she'd suggested. But the size of his package was irrelevant. She shouldn't be attracted to this knobhead. She licked her lips and fisted her hands. Her body was intent on embarrassing her.

She side-eyed her nana, who was busy staring out the window while speaking on her mobile. In her faux upper-class accent, she was giddily telling someone called Sergio about the King's announcement. She was so involved in her conversation that she was unaware of the drama next to her. Why was she allowed her phone?

Liss needed to get her phone back and control her growing lust. If asked, she'd explain her next tactic was because, once, her mum told her after a detention, "You catch more flies with honey than vinegar." But in truth, Bear's widening thighs pressing against hers were doing things to her. She desired a reaction from him and couldn't stop herself.

"Look, Bear. Maybe we can come to a deal." She slid her hand down his thigh. His leg shuddered so subtly that she would have missed it if she hadn't touched it. Liss fought the temptation to squeeze it to get a bigger response. She was supposed to get her phone back, not seduce a stranger.

He cleared his throat, and there was a teeny twitch to his right eye as he picked up her hand and popped it back on her lap. His hand was hot and coarse, like she fantasised a night with him would be.

Liss leaned into his ear. He smelt of aftershave, something with notes of wood and citrus. She was tempted to breathe him in and imagine his scent on her skin after a night of decadence. Fuck. It was too long since she had sex. Maybe that was why she was acting so out of character.

"Okay, so I need my phone. I don't want my grandma to know why." Liss sneaked a look at her nana, but she was still engrossed in her phone call, cackling loudly.

"I'm listening," Bear grunted.

"The thing is, I sent this guy a picture of me in underwear an hour ago, and he hasn't replied," she confessed in a rush of words to the brooding stranger. She wasn't this confident with strangers, yet his impenetrable persona made her want to poke the bear.

"Does the photo include your face?" His voice was gruff, and it made her skin tingle. She added his voice to fantasies she didn't need to be embracing. Her throat dried at the idea of sharing the image with him.

"No," she replied quietly. "I never include my face, and I don't normally send underwear pics, but my potential date asked, and he's really hot, and he probably hasn't replied because—"

"I don't care how hot he is. I was asking for security reasons." He refused to make eye contact, as if she wasn't worth his attention. Seeds of anger threaded through her desire.

"Rude much?" Liss folded her arms and stared at a spot on the windscreen. Her skin heated, and she ran through everything she should say. Usually, with strangers and out of her comfort zone, she'd sink into the seat and hide away.

"And for the record," he whispered in her ear before slowly looking her up and down. Liss clenched her thighs under his inspection. "If he hasn't replied to an underwear picture within five minutes, he doesn't fancy you."

Again, she was reminded that he was too big for the back seat when the driver took a corner too quickly and his entire body pressed into hers. She avoided the need to release the moan tickling her tongue. Liss shifted, which made his thigh slide against hers. She stilled suddenly, processing his words. How dare he suggest the guy didn't fancy her. But the statement gripped her fears about her Tinder match, who hadn't appeared as keen as she hoped and bruised her further. Bear had no right to say that to her. She hissed, "He's busy, and he's working—"

"I don't care what he's doing." Bear's voice was like thick, sweet honey, and his breath as he leaned in close made the hairs on her skin rise. "Once, my fuck buddy sent me a photo of her in a couple of dresses. They weren't fancy, but she wanted help to decide what to wear before seeing me. I excused myself from a meeting, feigning that it was an urgent work issue. Then I called her immediately and told her what I would do to her in my favourite of her dresses while she played with herself in the changing room. I only returned to my meeting when she came from my words. Her moaning climax made me hard as a rock. And I have a big rock."

Oh shit. He'd seen her messages to Isla.

His dick juddered as if remembering, and Liss fisted her hands, sinking her nails into her palms. The pain from her nails in her skin and the silver ring that dug into her flesh was almost satisfying. Anger and arousal blistered as she imagined his thick London accent telling her to touch him while he stroked between her thighs. Liss shifted awkwardly in her seat. *Don't let him in your head.*

Bear leaned in again, and his scent filled her once more. Her whole body quivered. Her fantasies were suddenly more vivid, filling with colour as she memorised every aspect of him. His full lips parted. "If your date hasn't replied by now, then bin him off, because he doesn't want you. And buy better underwear, because that must have been a shit photo for him not to respond even now."

Anger won, and she snapped back, "Fuck off. I looked great. I'll show you."

"No, thanks and you're not getting your phone back. Besides, the last thing I want is to see you like that."

Liss reared away from him, but there wasn't enough space. Her lips were tight, and her face burned.

"I've got to go, Sergio. My granddaughter is being a drama queen." She hung up the phone and handed it to Bear. "Stop wriggling, Felicity," her nana reprimanded, making the fire in Liss's cheeks from Bear's insult grow further. Her nana reached up to touch Liss's hair. "And do something about your hair. You look like you work in a pub."

Liss batted her hands away as her insides flamed. "I do work in a pub."

"Yes, but not as a cleaner."

Bear chuckled, and Liss glowered, but he smirked before mumbling something towards the window.

Liss rallied at Bear. "Is it 'have a go at Liss' day? And you still haven't answered my questions. I don't know where we're going or why you're talking to yourself, Mr. Meathead."

"We're here," the suited stranger in the front passenger seat announced. Camera flashes penetrated the windows from outside the car as they slid through a set of gates, and the driver spoke to someone from his open window.

"Where's h—" But she was cut off by the front passenger getting out and opening the door for her nana. Bear had said earlier that he needed her phone for security reasons, but she'd been too distracted by his body to ask what he meant.

Bear dived out his door before holding it for Liss. She huffed as she slid across the seat and climbed out. He offered her his hand, but she ignored it, instead sticking up her middle finger at him. At his chuckle, she barely resisted the temptation to claw out his eyes.

"The ladies are out of the car. We're coming in now," he said with a quiet grunt.

"Who are you talking to?" she snarled. Bear pointed to his earpiece with a roll of his eyes.

Everyone was rushing around the car, noises coming from all angles. Strangers walked out of what appeared to be an old building into the courtyard before them.

Questions about the past and present flooded her consciousness. Her ears pounded, and she planted her feet firmly on the ground. "I refuse to go anywhere until someone tells me what's happening. I've had enough of being forced here and there. Someone tell me something, or I'm going back to my pub. And you"—Liss jabbed a digit at Bear—"you give me my bloody phone, or I'm coming for it myself."

She reached into his jacket, but he wrapped his hands around her wrists with lightning-quick reflexes and pinned them mid-air. Her legs quaked, and her skin blistered as arousal filled her veins. *Why does that do it for me?*

"I will pick you up if I have to," he grunted. "There's very little stopping me from throwing you over my shoulder and taking you to the—"

"I can't apologise enough," a male voice called out in the classiest accent she'd ever heard. Even that couldn't stop the heat burning between her thighs at the idea of being popped over Bear's shoulder. It was so caveman, and yet fuck, it was hot. None of the preppy guys from her past would have considered it, let alone dared to do it. "The secrecy is all my fault, darling Felicity."

Liss spun and gasped loudly. She was in the presence of King Archibald.

The King opened his arms, and a measured smile covered his face. "Please come in and have coffee with my family, Miss Granger, and I will explain everything. And security, unhand her. Felicity Granger is a princess now."

Chapter Three

Liss's mouth gaped as she glanced around the morning room for the umpteenth time. Opulence glittered from the chandeliers that seemed to drip light delicately into the space to the baroque-style chairs with gold edges and red velvet cushions. Liss teetered on the sofa's edge with quaking limbs as she desperately tried to keep her boots raised millimetres off the antique carpet.

"It was a gift from a Danish count," King Archibald announced, his voice strained as he talked about the sofa. When he gave Liss a brief tour of the morning room, he moved gingerly, and his finger quivered when he pointed out art pieces. Liss recalled what he'd said about nearing death in the video. "The wood was handcrafted, and the feet are gold. It took many men to lift it when it first arrived."

"Be careful not to mark it. It's priceless," the beady-eyed blonde fiancée of the prince muttered. She held her swanny neck high, emphasising her string of pearls and immaculate chignon without a strand out of place.

"Marianne," the King's son, Alex, who sat poker straight beside her, uttered with a stiff smile. "These are our guests."

Liss quickly pulled on her hair to flatten the fuzz, but it was pointless. She bet she looked like frizzy candyfloss compared to Miss Upper-Class Universe. Marianne wore a cornflour blue suit that brought out the colour of her eyes, and she sat with her legs next to each other and her feet tucked into the side. She was a cross between a genuine princess and Jackie O, or would have been if she'd unpursed her lips for a second.

"Not just our guests, Son," the King said with a beaming face aimed at Liss. He occasionally glanced softly at her grandma but nothing more. It was difficult to believe they were first loves now reunited. Archibald's eyes were the same almond shape as her mum's. Their hazel hue matched her own, too. "Felicity is my granddaughter."

Marianne clasped her hands tightly.

"We can't say that 100%. Felicity needs to agree to a DNA test first," Prince Alexander said. His politeness didn't disguise his judgement. He squinted his eyes into little black peas every time he spoke to her, and his knuckles were white as he gripped the dainty china cup he sipped out of. Now, they were getting to the real reason for dragging her to Clarbon House. "Which she has no reason to avoid."

The King started his official family late, marrying Queen Beatrice at thirty-seven. Sadly, she died three years later in childbirth. Liss and Prince Alexander were both twenty-four. Liss spun the ring on her finger as she stared at him.

"She is the King's granddaughter. There is no doubt about her," Nana said, nodding profusely. Her greying hairstyle was pure hairspray. It moved perfectly in time with her head. When did everyone else get the memo about having perfect hair?

"A DNA test will tell us for sure," Marianne sneered.

Liss winced from the ache in her thighs. She'd kept her boots off the perfect carpet for the last fifteen minutes of faux niceties, fearing muddying their pristine rug.

Liss spun her ring quicker, remembering Bear's hands around her wrists. It was as if his fingers were still pressed against her skin. The fantasy of his hands pinning her wrists above her head as he slid a leg between her ankles to widen her stance continued on a loop as Marianne made accusations. She had to be fantasising to take her anxious brain out of the situation.

She busied herself by glancing at the carpet, using the opportunity to stare at Bear out of the corner of her eye. He stood straight and still at the edge of the room with his hands by his sides. They were enormous hands. It was as if they were still pressing against her pulse points. The weird lust that she'd never experienced before brought on by the day's trauma was intense. Liss held her breath, and her skin tingled as he stared straight ahead. Occasionally, his gaze flickered around the room as if he were reviewing every risk. Liss took deep breaths to distract herself from her fascination with Bear. He'd made it clear in the car that she was insignificant or, worse, a joke.

And yet, I might be a bloody princess.

"You look uncomfortable, Felicity, and you haven't touched your tea," Prince Alexander commented. Small lines appeared on his forehead as he studied her over his teacup. She spun her ring faster. How would he react if she told him she was terrified she'd break the cup or find another way to embarrass herself? But there was something else that was making her flick her finger to spin her ring faster. She didn't trust any of them. The silver ring glinted under the chandeliers as it turned. It was nearly hypnotic.

All eyes stared at her with suspicion, confusion, and judgement as she continued to flick her finger like it was a lighter that refused to light. These strangers weren't interested in learning about her, and she wasn't sharing. She was like a spore on a petri dish. She wanted to be back at the bar, serving pints and laughing with drunk Greg as he fed treats to Joyce.

The scent of lilies from the vases of bouquets around the room nearly made her gag. The silver ring was hotter each time she flicked it, climbing to the tip of her finger as she skimmed it. But she couldn't stop. It was the only thing grounding her in the unfamiliar situation. It was on the edge of her finger as Prince Alexander suddenly caught her attention with a snide smile.

"Surely you're not scared of a little DNA test," he said with an arched eyebrow.

Liss fumbled for words as her ring spun off her finger and rolled across the perfectly varnished floor. As one, the group watched as it sped to Bear before hitting his foot and coming to a halt.

Bear's gaze burnt into Liss as he bent to pick it up and walked over to her. "Princess, I think you dropped something," he said as he neared her. As he helped her put it on, he whispered in her ear, "Now calm down. You're as important as these people, if not more. Don't let them railroad you. Pretend you're at your pub and they're no more than rude punters." He placed a hand on her knee and pushed down, forcing her dirty boots onto the carpet. Embers lit in her belly at the touch. "And for fucks sake, put your feet down. Even your thighs can't last this long."

Bear strode back across the room before resuming his position at the wall. It was as if nothing had happened, but she remembered what he'd said. Need turned the embers to fire as she ground her feet into the carpet, and her confidence appeared like a cheeky gremlin on her shoulder.

"Of course I'm not scared of a DNA test," she said witheringly to Alexander. "But I also didn't ask to be part of this bloody circus, so we'll do it on my terms."

"Felicity," Nana scolded. "You can't swear in front of the royal family."

Bear's words gave her the confidence she needed as the day's frenzy collided with her fury at the judgement the family were tarnishing her with. "Nana, don't start that bullshit. You have the mouth of a Peaky Blinder on a bender. Apparently, I'm a royal now if I accept it and don't renounce my place or whatever the phrase is."

Liss settled back on the sofa, confident that its embroidered material hadn't been soiled by someone like her before.

"Renounce your—why would you renounce your title?" Alexander stuttered. "If we have conclusive proof that you're the King's granddaughter, it will transform your life."

"She is the King's granddaughter." Nana's cup rocked on its saucer.

"As I said, if she is, her life will be glorious." Prince Alexander raised his voice. "She won't be slumming it anymore. Instead, you will live a life of luxury. You will—"

"Firstly, Alex,"—Liss jumped to her feet—"no one speaks to my grandma like that, so put your polite face back on. You know, the one you save for opening a supermarket or a politician's toilet."

Liss's heart swelled and her shoulder gremlin growled when the corner of Bear's mouth rose temporarily in a smile.

"Secondly, I don't slum it in my world. I enjoy my life. At least I can leave the house looking like me and not Royal Barbie." She looked Marianne up and down. "Finally, I will have the DNA test, but only because I want to prove my grandma right. Once we get the result, I'll make a decision. Just because the King wants to admit he has a second family doesn't mean I agree to be part of this shitshow."

Dropped mouths and wide eyes faced her. Liss fiddled with her ring again. The King's chest shuddered with each breath. She'd gone too far. Maybe she shouldn't have brought the fire-filled pub version of herself. She usually saved her attitude for greasy drunks grumbling about the condom machine in the toilets, but this was the royal family, and she didn't want to make the King's health worse.

A cough from Bear drew her attention. He winked at her, fanning the fire and replacing her anxiety with pride.

"Right, well, if we're done with this *Princess Diaries* shit, let's get this DNA test over with," she sassed with a smile.

Chapter Four

"That was eventful," Liss announced to her grandma, who sat by her side, leaning as far away as possible. The bodyguard, who was in the front passenger seat when they'd arrived at Clarbon House, was driving, and Bear took his seat. They said a few indistinguishable words to each other, but the rest of the journey was in silence.

"I preferred the Bentley to this," Nana commented as she stared out the window of the black Range Rover. At least she'd stopped waving to strangers. "I feel like I'm in a police corruption television show."

"Are we seriously not going to talk about what happened, Nana? That whole thing was surreal. You've had sex with the King. Why didn't you mention this sooner?" Liss turned in her seat, but her nana avoided eye contact.

"I didn't think you'd find out." Nana shrugged.

"Are you fucking kidding me?"

"Language," Nana replied, her neck snapping as she stared Liss down.

Liss narrowed her eyes. What she said in front of the King about her grandma's language was true, and if he'd spent time with her when she was young, it shouldn't have been a surprise. "Did Mum know?"

Nana yawned.

Liss took deep breaths, although it didn't stop her

chest from tightening. "Did mum know who her dad was?"

Nana huffed and briefly touched her hair as if checking if the hairspray was still holding. It was her tick. She learnt as a dancer not to show anxiety, but Liss recognised the action from the brief parts of her childhood spent with her. "Stop being so dramatic, Felicity. None of it would have interested your mum. She was happy with her life."

"I'm trying not to lose my shit with you, Nana, especially as I don't know what will get back to the King. Yes, Bear and Bear's mate, I know you're listening," Liss declared to the front seat. Bear shifted, but he didn't say anything. "But I will be as dramatic as I want to be. Mum died a hideous, slow death from cancer—"

"I was there."

"No, you weren't." Liss's voice cracked, and she fisted her hands. "You were swanning around the world with your friends. I gave up university to be with her because she only had me. You didn't fight the doctors daily to give her better support. I did. She could've received the best medical treatment as a member of the royal family. We wouldn't have been alone."

Flashbacks of her mother crying out in pain as she neared the end of her life stabbed at Liss's heart, and tears brimmed her eyes. All that time, she had been alone, and her grandma knew it.

"Stop shouting at me. I'm an old lady." Liss bit her tongue. Her nana only called herself old when it worked for her narrative. She was sprightly and adventurous when travelling the world. "Besides, if I'd told the King, I would have had to fight the royal family like you fought them today. That Marianne doesn't like you, does she?"

So that was it. Altercation over. Liss learnt long ago

that her nana didn't discuss anything she didn't want to. She was the queen of ignoring the bad, hoping it would disappear. Liss would let it lie for now. A heaviness filled her limbs. She was usually slow to anger unless she perceived injustice, but pain wasn't unusual for her. However, she kept it locked in a box so as not to remember the sadness of her childhood before watching her mum suffer as she became an adult.

"No, I guess she doesn't," Liss replied with a slow sigh. Her body sagged as the last hours took their toll. "But I'm not sure why. Alexander will have the throne no matter what. The lineage is set even with this news of Mum.

"Make sure you tell the King that we've worked that out, Bear," Liss shouted. Too many emotions were rushing through her body now that fatigue gripped her, revealing themselves without warning and at the wrong people. She should be taking this anger out on her grandma, not a stranger who'd helped her with the royals. "I'd hate for him to think a pleb with dirty boots and shit hair wanted to usurp Alex."

"You could have made an effort," her grandma retorted.

There was no point reasoning with her and explaining for the fifth time that her nana hadn't told her where she was going or that she needed to make an effort.

"Your hair isn't shit," Bear grunted from the front. He didn't look her way, but she knew what it was like to have those deep brown eyes staring at her. "And Strike and I are freelance."

"I'm Strike," the tall blond from the driver's seat said, eyeballing her through the rear-view mirror. He was beautiful and reminded her of Thor. But it was Bear who held her attention.

"Hey, Strike. I won't ask where you got your name. I will presume you're also a naturist in your spare time and that it's related to your baseball bat–sized meat."

Bear coughed like he was choking. *I'll take that as a win.* The all-seeing bodyguard was fun to surprise.

"If you could drop me in that parking bay there, that would be very kind," Nana proclaimed. Her accent changed from cockney to clipped and faux posh during the day.

Liss glanced out of the window. "Why are we at the airport?"

Nana unclipped her seatbelt as Strike pulled over to the curb. "I'm flying to Italy to visit friends. Do you remember Sergio? He suggested I stay at his villa while this blows over. I'm afraid the invitation only included me."

Liss's heartbeat raced. "But—"

"Let me stop you before you get dramatic again. Bear and Strike will protect you for the next two weeks. I called in a favour, as my contacts helped them grow their business." Her nana kissed her on the cheek before getting out of the car with Strike's help. "I'll be in touch. I love you, Felicity."

Liss slumped against the seat as her grandma waved goodbye. "Love you, Grandma." But Strike closed the door.

Alone again.

A tear slid down Liss's cheek. She'd been unable to rely on her grandma, even when her mum was dying, and she was foolish to hope it would be different after the day's chaos. She wanted to cling to her grandma, but every time she did, she got hurt. Liss's head dropped, and her lips trembled.

Bear cleared his throat, reminding her she wasn't completely alone. Just alone while sitting with a stranger.

That was worse. She swiped at her tears, but they were falling quicker now and harder to hide.

"It will be okay, Felicity," he said, his gruff voice soft. "Strike and I will keep you safe."

Liss covered her face with her hands. She was used to being deserted but didn't want strangers to witness her humiliation. She knew how to do pain alone.

"There will always be at least one of us with you. We'll follow you everywhere."

"If this is your way of comforting upset women, you need practice," Liss stuttered between sobs.

"I don't tend to do a lot of comforting when I'm with women." Liss dropped her hands and eyeballed him. "I mean, we're safe people. You don't need to worry."

"I don't know you." This version of him was different from the earlier version and equally fascinating. Maybe crying women scared him.

He fumbled in his pocket before turning to look at her. Small lines appeared around his eyes as he held out a tissue. It smelt so heavily of him that she wondered how long it had sat in the jacket. She dabbed her eyes with it before blowing her nose loudly. Bear offered her a smile that barely lifted his lips. "Well, I'll tell you, I'm not a naturist. Although, I don't have time for hobbies. Maybe I am a naturist and don't know it. You could imagine me naked if you get nervous about things."

Liss's eyes bulged from her head, and she choked on her breath.

Bear's ears pinked. He added quickly, "Because that's what they say when you're doing speeches, right? Do you need some water or something?" She shook her head as he fumbled with his words. One tear and the badass bodyguard was all over the place. "Anyway, it will be okay.

I expect you'd prefer to be in an Italian villa with your nana, but at least you'll be safe with us."

"It depends if the Italian villa also involves you being naked," she joked, smiling when his eye twitched, and he cleared his throat. Strike returned to the car. From the rear-view mirror, she glimpsed his brow furrowing in Bear's direction. Bear dropped his head as he studied his phone.

"It's Liss, by the way. Only Nana calls me Felicity," she said to Bear. He nodded subtly as his back flattened against the seat, but he didn't look at her again. "Can we go back to my flat?"

"Certainly, Felicity," Strike replied.

"By the way, I wouldn't want to go to Italy," Liss said to the front seat as she pulled herself up, unsure if they were listening. "I'm not going to run away from this. I'm not leaving my friends and home. It's only a small flat, but it's mine."

"Okay, Liss," Bear said, the gruffness returned.

Liss imagined Bear trying to fit through her doorway as the car sped through the city. Goosebumps covered her arms, and anxiety coiled in her belly as she gripped the tissue he'd given her.

Chapter Five

The four-by-four vehicle with tinted windows and an air of mystery suddenly stopped outside the pub. Liss's rented flat was across the road above a garage. It was called a coach house, but that was a fancy name for a tiny shit hole.

But it was her shit hole.

"They're here already," Strike murmured to Bear. Neither spoke to her the entire ride. Energy flowed out of her like air, bleeding out of an inflatable rubber ring as she looked where they were staring. Even through the Range Rover's tinted windows, the odd camera flash intruded on her space.

"Who are here?" Liss asked, but no response came.

Liss bit her nails. She should head to the pub first and tidy up from the lunchtime rush. It was an excellent place to hide away from her life like she always did. Steve was probably tearing out his curly hair while managing the place in her absence.

The flashes increased rapidly, and strangers shouted. Liss gripped the door handle. Maybe something had happened to the pub. She should get in there. Liss tapped her pockets before she huffed loudly. She needed her phone. "Let's get her in her flat," Bear replied. Strike nodded.

"Her has a name," Liss replied before wincing. That made no sense at all. She unsnapped her seatbelt and leaned forward to force her presence on the pair, although the movement removed the last of her energy from the strenuous day. She checked her watch, and her mouth fell open. It had only been four hours since she'd left the pub. "You need to share whatever you're talking about with me or… or…."

"Or what?" Bear asked. The edge of his lips twitched as if he was concealing a smile.

"Or I'll probably fuck it up," she conceded.

"There's a bunch of paparazzi outside. We need to get you into your flat," Strike said. There was no twitch to his lips or softness to his voice. Strike was business only. "I want your keys and for you to explain the route. I will stay in front, and Bear will remain behind you. We'll flank you the entire way."

Why did being flanked by Bear make her blush? *Get a grip, Liss.* The situation sounded serious.

"How did they find my flat?" As she took in the view out of the windscreen, she gasped. Crowds of people swarmed around her front door, with others by the pub. She glimpsed through a gap between paparazzi the pub's shut front door. The closed sign was in place. With this much custom, they could have a bumper evening.

"Keys," Strike grunted.

"You don't need to be a dick about it," Liss snapped. Again, Bear's lip twitched.

"Give me your keys now, Felicity," Strike said between gritted teeth. "I'm not in the mood to piss about."

"Mate," Bear reasoned.

Strike glared at him. "Be careful, Bear. We can't have more mistakes."

What did that mean?

Bear glowered. "Fuck you, Strike."

Liss fumbled in her bag for her keys. "There's only one door. It's the blue one next to the garage. It leads up the stairs and into the flat. The door only leads to my flat."

"Right. And will there be anyone else in the flat? I know you don't have a partner. Boyfriend?" Strike asked as she threw her keys into his lap.

Her emotions were smacking around her body like balls on a pool table whacked hard with a cue. One minute, she was scared and, the next, ready to rip the heads off her so-called bodyguards. "How do you know I don't have a partner? I could be polyamorous or be fucking the entire local rugby team. You don't know nothing."

"I researched you when your grandma contacted us this morning. You spend all your hours at the pub and don't have much social life. Your only family is your nana," Strike replied as Liss's eyes twitched with tiredness. She spun her ring. "Although you're not on social media, your digital footprint is extensive. Our IT support will sort it out and get you a burner phone. I couldn't find a boyfriend or girlfriend, but they might be new. Do you have anyone?"

"You're fucking rude, and I don't see what any of this has to do with you. You can get stuffed. I'm not answering any more of your questions." She folded her arms and flopped back against her seat.

Silence filled the car. Paparazzi were congregating around them. The palace hadn't conclusively declared she was a princess, so the newspapers shouldn't care. Liss toyed with her ring as her eyes flitted around the vehicle.

"She doesn't have a boyfriend, and her only potential date still hasn't replied to her earlier message. Her friend Isla is in the flat, as is a guy called Steve who works at the pub. I'm guessing he fancies her. She doesn't have anyone else."

Liss's mouth dropped open as her stomach muscles tightened. She wasn't safe with these guys and needed to return to her flat. She needed Isla. Her breathing was so noisy that it crowded the space of the vehicle.

"And before you ask, I've been monitoring the notifications on your phone." Liss's nostrils flared as Bear's eyes snapped to Strike. "For work purposes."

She jumped out of the car and slammed the door. How dare they research her, go through her phone, and make judgements about her friends. She opened her mouth to scream when suddenly a microphone was shoved into her face.

"Felicity, what did the King say when you saw him?"

"Felicity, when do you move into the palace?" another voice shouted.

There were so many of them that it was impossible to distinguish features. They crowded Liss like demons in the underworld, each clawing for a piece of flesh.

"How does it feel to be rich?" a woman with a microphone screeched.

"Are you going to steal the throne from Prince Alex?"

The voices were coming thick and fast. Liss was jostled against the car as strangers propelled cameras in her face. She looked left and right, but they'd surrounded her. She took deep breaths as flashes blinded her to anything but shapes. She blinked rapidly, but there was no gap to flee through.

"Has your grandma left the country because she's ashamed?" asked a perfectly tailored blond Liss recognised from breakfast television.

She shrank as bodies closed in on her, but it didn't stop the onslaught. The questions and comments took a darker turn. Tears brimmed in her eyes, and her body shook. *Don't cry. You're fucking strong.* But there was no escape.

"What would your dead mum say about you meeting the King dressed like that?"

She pulled her arms in and squatted like she did when the bullies at school cornered her before laying into her. Suddenly, an arm thrust through the crook of her right elbow. "I've got you."

Bear pulled her against his side as Strike pushed through the baying crowds. "Move," he roared without apology.

Liss took deep breaths, but the air was thick and didn't reach her lungs. They were getting her to safety, yet her chest tightened and her pulse climbed. People moved as the two beasts of men manoeuvred through the crowd. They paused as they neared the door, where a pair of photographers refused to budge.

Bear didn't let go of her even as he stood alongside Strike, and they used their presence to make them back down. "Get out of my way!" he shouted, but Liss was distracted by a small voice whispering in her ear.

"Are you scared for your safety? You should be, Felicity." She whipped her head around to locate who'd threatened her. But all she saw were faceless strangers, her vision still blurry from the flashes of cameras.

"Wait," she tried to shout to Bear, but the crowd swallowed the word before the bodyguards shoved her through the door.

Bear dragged her up the stairs as Strike locked the door. Her legs wobbled at each step, but the air of her home was easier to breathe than the suffocating atmosphere outside.

"Don't you ever do that again," Bear snarled as he helped her up the stairs. "We're here to protect you."

His face burnt redder than the sunset picture from a holiday with her mum that hung behind him, and he refused to make eye contact as they reached the top of the stairs. She implored him with her stare, unsure what reaction she wanted from him. Suddenly, Isla and Steve rushed her with open arms, but Strike stepped between Liss and her friends.

"Isla and Steve," Bear said simply.

"Is there anyone else here?" Strike growled.

"Let me hug my friend," Isla snapped, attempting to push him out of the way.

Strike's posture was rigid, and he widened his stance.

"Isla, is there anyone other than you and Steve here?" Liss asked so quietly that Bear side-eyed her.

"No. There's only us two." She stood on her tiptoes, but she couldn't eyeball either bodyguard. "You can check if you want, you nosey bastards."

"We will. Don't worry about that." Strike was curt.

Steve hung back as Bear checked the bedroom, bathroom, and tiny kitchen in about twenty seconds before re-joining them. "It's just us."

Strike stepped to the side, and Isla pulled Liss into a hug. The tension barely eased as she took the love and support she needed. Liss held on tight, squeezing her eyes shut as if the day could fade into a forgettable nightmare. Isla was her only real friend and had stood by her even when she dropped out of university and throughout her mum's illness. Yet Liss continued to fight the tears as Isla dragged her to the plush sofa. It cost more than the rest of the furniture combined, but it was Liss's haven. Steve perched on a chair as the women let the cosy sofa envelop them.

"Shush, you're okay," Isla whispered as she stroked Liss's back. "Take slow breaths." But the questions from the strangers outside played on a loop.

"We'll decide on a plan for where you're staying, and we will do it properly with you following our instructions this time," Strike declared before he led Bear out of the communal space and into the kitchen.

"What does that mean?" Steve stuttered once the three were alone.

His golden curls shone under the spotlights that brought little pools of light to the room. Liss considered what Bear had said in the car about Steve fancying her. The guy was a lovely friend, but there hadn't been any suggestion of attraction between them. Most days, he was like an annoying little brother. Liss shrugged to hide the gag that came with the image of Steve kissing her as Isla grabbed a blanket and tucked it around her.

Steve stared towards the kitchen. "Do you want a drink or anything?" As lovely as Steve was, he'd never offered to get her a drink and usually preferred to be waited on. He probably wanted to question the bodyguards.

She shook her head as her punishing thoughts returned to her present dramas. It left no space for words.

Her life had transformed within hours. She pulled the blanket higher and hid her eyes as if creating a fort removed her from the situation. Liss wanted her mum to hold her close and make all the problems disappear. Even with their struggles when Liss was a child, her mum magically made things better with a smile or a story. The grief of losing her rushed her as it often did. Liss withdrew further under the blanket as she shivered.

Suddenly, Liss was aware of a shadow above her, and she peaked above the blanket to find Bear's looming body. A mug of coffee and a chocolate bar looked tiny in his hands. He knelt beside her and popped the coffee on the table next to her. The action forced him to lean closer, and a woody citrus scent accompanied his movement. It was already familiar, and she breathed it in as his hand rested on the blanket above her knee.

"It's milk one sugar like you asked for at the palace. I would've added whisky for medicinal purposes, but I can't find any alcohol," he said quietly. The heat of his hand penetrated the blanket, warming Liss's skin as her knee trembled beneath his touch.

"I don't drink much," she replied. Bear raised an eyebrow, giving his ordinarily stoic face an unexpected cuteness.

"You're shivering because of the adrenaline."

She stilled, mesmerised by the rosy hue of his lips. It was as if his presence filled every space of her flat and mind so that nothing else existed. Liss sat on her hands to stop herself from reaching out to him for further comfort. What was it about his brown eyes that held all her safety within them?

His tongue brushed his lips as he fixed her with an unwavering gaze. His Adam's apple bobbed as he swallowed, and the fingers beneath her body trembled as she fixed him with her stare. She was cocooned within promises he hadn't uttered.

"Hand, please," he commanded. Something gentle hid behind his request, and she pushed her closed hand out of the top of the blanket and presented it to him. He ripped open the chocolate with his teeth. He didn't break eye contact as he opened her hand with his thumb and placed the open chocolate bar into it. He held his thumb there, warming her hand.

He stared at her mouth as she slowly licked her lips. Liss dragged her lower lip into her mouth while he held her knee down. It stopped her trembling temporarily.

"Bear, in here now," Strike shouted from the hallway, breaking the spell between them.

"Keep wrapped up and drink your coffee, Princess," Bear said before striding out of the room.

"Fuuuuuuuck," Isla said, elongating the word until it was longer than a Bronte novel.

Chapter Six

"The flat was a strange place with all the bodies crowding it. Bear was gone from her living room, although Liss couldn't stop thinking about the heat of his gaze and the power behind his touch.

Steve's foot tapped repeatedly against the carpet as he waited until there were three of them. Suddenly, he bombarded Liss. "Are you really a princess? Is something going on between you and the ugly guy?"

Liss destroyed the chocolate bar with a few bites. *I wanted him to look after me.* But no one looked after her. She'd cared for her and her mum before she got ill. Her mum worked three jobs and picked up extra cleaning work, as did Liss, to ensure they survived. Yet, when Bear gave her coffee and implored her to eat, she wanted that. But she was independent, not someone who relied on others, especially not strange men who had no business making her skin blister and her belly flutter. And where did he find a chocolate bar? She barely had any food in the flat, as she ate most of her meals at the pub. She spent her life there.

"Ugly guy? As if. Liss was right. He looks like a young Tom Hardy," Isla said, handing Liss her coffee. Maybe that was it. A sexy man and an overwhelming day forced her to find solace in a bodyguard who was there to protect her, nothing more. She cradled the mug in both hands, letting it warm her bones. "And I suspect he wants to be in Liss's—"

"He's got shit hair," Steve snapped.

"It's a dark buzz cut with that extra bit on top that Liss can run her hands through." She didn't hear the rest of Steve and Isla's back and forth.

Instead, she relished the scalding heat from the coffee that filled her mouth and flowed through her throat. From the moment she returned from university to care for her mum, she'd learnt an independence and resilience she hadn't wanted. As her thoughts continued to spiral, she closed her eyes and focused on Bear, who'd kept her safe.

"Was she, Liss?" Steve distracted her from her daydreams.

"What?" Liss asked, blinking.

Isla nudged her. "Someone on TikTok said you visited the King, and Steve is obsessed with Prince Alex's fiancée, Marianne. He's wondering if she was as beautiful close-up."

"She's stunning."

The trembling stopped, but its absence brought a new issue. She needed the toilet. Liss pushed the blanket off.

"I knew Marianne would be beautiful in person," Steve proclaimed, his hands flat in front of him. "I bet she's looking for a strong man like me. I could beat Prince Alex in a duel."

Liss chuckled as she exchanged a look with Isla. "You're kidding yourself. She's more opinionated than you, so you two wouldn't work, and out of the three of you, she'd kick yours and Alex's arse simultaneously. Neither of you would stand a chance. She's terrifying."

Isla's cackles echoed behind Liss as she left the room and attempted to creep past the kitchen. The door was closed, but Strike's shouts reverberated through the solid wood. She froze at the sound of her name.

"Stop fucking around with Liss. You've only just met her, and yet you're acting like—"

"She's going through a lot, and we're pretty much all she has after her nana left her stranded," Bear explained. There was an assurance behind his voice that made her pause. "But fine, have it your way. She's just a client."

"Wasn't the last one *just* a client? And look how that ended. You nearly cost us the whole business. We're lucky that we stopped the story from getting out."

Liss leant closer to the door as Bear mumbled something, but he was too quiet.

Suddenly, Strike's booming voice started again. "You're acting like you don't remember what happened. I know what you're like when you want someone. She's out of bounds. She's a bloody princess. We can't get involved in her life, and I don't need you bringing your saviour complex because you're triggered. You owe me for what happened before, so no more of this shit, or both our careers are over."

Liss itched to find out more, but suddenly, the door handle went down, and she bolted so they wouldn't catch her eavesdropping.

Bear had history with his clients. Why would her life trigger him? Her attraction for him was undeniable, but he was probably like that with all women.

As she exited the toilet, she heard her name again. "Where is Liss?" Strike shouted.

"I'm here," Liss murmured as she returned to the room. Bear stood at the side, looking anywhere but at her. "What now?"

"We're taking you somewhere private where we can keep you safe."

Liss folded her arms and stared Strike down, or at least she would have if he wasn't nearly two feet taller. "This is my home, and I'm not going anywhere. Besides, I'm working at the pub all day tomorrow, so I'm staying."

Her skin heated as she caught Bear staring at her. She glowered at him, and he quickly looked away.

"Coward," she mumbled under her breath.

"Deal with her," Strike said. "I'll sort out a safe location."

Bear pulled up his shoulders as he stepped closer. He was using his bulk to intimidate her.

"Listen," Bear said, standing close enough for Liss to see a chocolate bar poking out of his suit trousers. He was a modern-day Willy Wonka. "What happened outside is not how we do things. The lack of briefing from your grandma about what this entailed and that everyone knows where you live and work was a risk to you and us, too. We scope out places and know exactly what we're facing, Felicity."

Liss attempted to glare him into submission, but her neck ached as she craned to look at him. He was close enough to touch her, and as his dark eyes shone with power, a heat grew between her thighs. She fisted her hands and scowled.

"It was a shitshow that we won't be repeating. You need a secure place that has more than one exit. You'll brief us on your life and what information about you might be available besides what we already know."

Bear had already embarrassed her with his comments about her date and underwear picture. He'd pour more scorn onto her embarrassing lack of social life and abysmal dating experiences. She needed to delete that underwear picture. A thickness filled her throat at the memory of sending it to someone who cared so little about receiving it.

"Are you listening to me?"

"I'm not telling you about my life." Liss spied her phone on the dining table. She strode towards it. "But I will check my messages."

Bear was right behind her. His heat was like a wall. Anger radiated off him. There was something satisfying about denying this man and making him lose control. She wasn't like this with anyone else, yet with him—this virtual stranger—the temptation was too much.

As Liss picked up her phone, a message from an unknown number flashed on the screen.

She gasped, and the phone slipped out of her hand, clattering on the wooden floor.

Isla and Steve looked at her, but only Bear held her wide-eyed stare. Pain radiated through her stomach as if a stranger had reached through the phone and punched her. Liss struggled to pull in a breath.

"Liss?" Isla whispered.

Steve attempted to reach where the phone, now with a cracked screen, lay, but she snapped it up and thrust it at Bear with a shaking hand. "Okay, I'll do whatever you say."

Bear rubbed his forehead as he read the screen out loud.

> Unknown: Your life is in danger. Give up the princess title, or there will be serious consequences. How do you want to die, Felicity?

Chapter Seven

Bear's movement filled Liss's blurring vision as he shouted for his colleague. Strike returned swiftly for a big man whose gait suggested, until now, that he carried himself slowly and purposefully like a killer from a nineties slasher movie. From their grunts and mumbles, the men appeared to be making a plan.

Liss's legs barely held her up as she stood at the side of her sparse dining area even as Bear instructed her, "You need to pack now. We have a location that we've used before."

Liss swallowed noisily. The temptation to argue was akin to eating a sugared doughnut while being told that you couldn't lick your lips, but she resisted. Her safety was paramount.

"I'll call when it's safe. And I'll get a car sent around, too," Strike said to Bear. They weren't consulting her. The latest punch of adrenaline dissipated into nothing, and exhaustion quickly replaced it. Liss slipped down the wall to collapse on the floor. Strike turned to Isla. "Can you come with me?"

Isla looked warily at Liss before stepping out of the room with Strike.

Bear knelt at Liss's feet. "I know you've had enough, but either you can pack your stuff, or I can. I'm guessing you don't want me in your belongings, and I don't understand what women need when they're away for two weeks or more. One pair of really thick socks and a pair of joggers should do it."

"Two weeks?" Liss lifted her head to find a wry smile on Bear's face.

"I was expecting an argument about the socks."

"I can't leave the pub for two weeks. It can't run itself, and I need the job."

He sat down in front of her, although he was bulky and there wasn't enough space for him to recreate her cross-legged position. "Princess, I'm sorry to say this," he said softly. His eyes were bigger than she remembered, and it took all her remaining effort to listen to him and not study the myriad of colours swirling around them. "You might be away for the rest of your life. We'll find out about the DNA match in several days, but after that, you may decide you want to live in one of the royal residences or somewhere else. It's unlikely you'll return here for a long time. Your life is going to transform."

Tears brimmed her eyes. Bear took her hands in his impossibly large ones and cradled them. He had a couple of patches of yellow where bruises had nearly disappeared, and on the one hand, she spied tiny cuts around his knuckles.

"I don't know if I can do it." Her voice cracked.

Steve stood behind Bear. "You don't have to. You could stay with Isla and me and tell them you don't want to be a princess," he said, repeatedly stepping from one foot to the other. She'd forgotten he was in the room.

Bear said to Liss in gentle tones that she appreciated, "You don't have to decide your future now. But you do have to pack and come with me. We promised your grandma we'd keep you safe."

As if Liss's grandma gave a shit about her safety. She'd ditched her at the first opportunity. But Bear was right. She needed to stay safe until they knew the DNA results.

"You're thinking hard, Princess," Bear said, his face creasing like she imagined hers was. With one hand, he held both of hers and, with the other, reached up as if to touch her forehead. But suddenly, he stilled, as Strike came bustling through the door.

"Bear, a word," Strike said, pointing his thumb toward the hall. Was he angry all the damn time? Bear stood immediately, although his gaze lingered a little longer on Liss before he followed Strike into the hall. Isla took his place and sat in front of Liss.

"You're going to be okay, honey. They know what they're doing," Isla said. "And can I borrow a jacket? I need to be a decoy."

"This must be serious. You once told me all my clothes needed burning."

The memory made both of them smile. It was a couple of years ago, and Liss's wardrobe and style had improved recently, although it was still seventy-five per cent yoga pants, jeans, and hoodies.

Liss let Isla help her weary body off the floor.

"I can help you pack if you want," Steve said.

Liss shook her head. She didn't want him rummaging around her underwear drawer. "Thank you for the offer, but I'll be okay." She also wanted to ensure she packed the heart keepsake from her mum. It was a silly item she kept hidden in her bedside drawer, but she couldn't stay anywhere indefinitely without it. It carried memories she didn't want to explain to Steve, especially not now.

Isla tucked her arm through Liss's. When they needed someone on their side at university, the other one knew when to offer grounding and love. Isla held her tight as she spoke. "As much as those two mean machines annoy me, they'll keep you safe. And you have me and Steve when you need us."

They passed the kitchen, where Strike and Bear talked in hushed tones. She nibbled her lips as she searched for an explanation as to why she wanted to frustrate him yet make him smile. It was the adrenaline and the drama. She wouldn't have looked twice at him any other time. Well, not openly.

She glanced briefly at him through the crack in the door. He was hunched over a pad, making notes as Strike nodded. Liss worried her lip as Isla explained how she'd dress like Liss and then run to the car with Strike. The hope was that the crowd would follow them and that Strike would lose them on his drive while Bear took her to the hotel. Bear locked eyes with her briefly before returning to his notes. The heat behind his stare made the hairs on the back of her neck rise and filled her belly with a pleasurable ache.

She hadn't felt like this in a while, but then she hadn't faced such drama.

Fucking monarchy bullshit.

"Are you nearly ready?" Bear filled the doorway.

Of course he chose the moment she was deciding which pairs of knickers to take and was holding up a pair of her everyday function ones and her expensive lacy blue ones.

His focus dropped immediately to the delicate material in her right hand. His lips slowly parted as he stared.

"Yes. Only a couple of things left to pack," Liss squeaked. He still didn't look up. A pink tint touched his ears, and she shivered at what he might be considering. A fantasy of Bear slowly pulling those knickers down her legs as he knelt before her was as vivid as the material she held. "Give me a moment. Unless you want to see the entirety of my underwear drawer."

He locked her gaze. "Is that an option because…" His eye twitched briefly, and he cleared his throat. He was chewing something, which gave his jaw a slow up-and-down motion. It highlighted the chiselled jawline that she ached to run her fingertips across. Something as unimportant as her underwear drawer made a man like him pink. The memory of his comments about his fuck buddy obliterated her fantasy, yet the temptation to needle him remained.

"Because?"

He shook his head and pulled on the back of his neck. "It doesn't matter. You've two minutes, and pack light." Before he turned away, she fixed his gaze and dropped the sexy blue knickers into her case.

He continued to shake his head as he walked away while mumbling "fuck" under his breath repeatedly.

Chapter Eight

The plan to make Isla a decoy for Liss worked.

Steve also helped by drawing attention to "fake Liss" while pretending that was the opposite of what he was trying to do.

As Liss and Bear slipped out of her flat with a case and a couple of rucksacks, Liss reflected on her destiny. Suddenly, everything she understood was different. Bear held her back until he'd checked there were no paparazzi in sight. Greg, the pub regular, and his terrier, Joyce, were the only ones near the flat.

"Give me a minute," Liss said to Bear as he tossed her bags into the back of the new black vehicle that Strike had arranged for them. It was a copy and paste of the last one.

"Liss, we have to—"

"Joyce," Liss shouted, calling the dog over as Bear tapped his foot restlessly. She sneaked a dog biscuit out of her pocket and giggled as Joyce pirouetted before sitting in front of her. Greg had named the grumbly terrier after his dead wife, but even after all these years, Liss didn't know if it was out of spite or respect.

"Are you okay?" Greg asked as he hobbled closer.

"Yeah, all good. And sorry, the pub is closed," she replied. "I'll get Steve on it." Liss fumbled for her phone before remembering Bear kept it for his tech colleague to investigate. She couldn't run the pub remotely without a phone.

"I saw him after the other big black car left, and those shouty camera people followed it." Greg's big eyebrows bounced.

"Yeah. A lot is happening," Liss replied, conscious of Bear turning his head from side to side, presumably checking for risk. She spun her ring.

"Liss," Bear demanded. "We need to go."

Liss huffed. He had her best interests at heart, but there was much to come to terms with.

"I'm worried about you," Greg confessed. "Promise me you'll be okay."

"I promise." She hugged Greg quickly and slipped a ten-pound note into his hand. "Take care, and I'll see you soon, yeah?"

"Okay, Liss." Greg pointed a bony finger at Bear. "And you protect her, or we'll come for you. Joyce may look like an angel, but she'll take a chunk out of your ankle."

Bear raised his eyebrows. "Liss is safe with me."

Liss gave Joyce a quick cuddle before she and Bear jumped into the car. As Bear headed down the road, she waved at Greg and Joyce out of the back window. It was pointless because the vehicle had blackout windows, but she was waving goodbye as much to the life she knew as she was to her two favourite pub regulars. A lump filled her throat as Bear turned out of the road that held her sanctuary.

Hunger or the day's activity must have wiped her out instantly because she was next aware of movement beneath her as someone jostled her in their arms. It was Bear. She held a sigh as the scents of his natural musk and aftershave filled her. The rhythm of his heart tried to lull her back to sleep as she rested her head on his chest, but she forced herself awake. The heat from Bear's body and the gentle way he cradled her against his broad chest caused her to sigh softly. She nuzzled into his neck as she pretended to sleep.

"I know you're awake," he whispered, his breath tickling her skin. "But we can pretend you're not if it's easier. Stay quiet for now, Princess. I've got you."

He juggled her slightly, and she opened her eyes a crack as he carried her through metal doors and into a lift.

"And so you know, you make the cutest moans when you're asleep." His mouth was against her hair. Tingles criss-crossed her body, and goose pimples covered her arms. Then he shook his head and mumbled, "Be professional with clients, Bear. Remember what Strike said. You can't risk the business again." Maybe he thought she genuinely was asleep, or maybe he was testing her.

Liss stilled in his arms as she recalled what she'd overheard in the kitchen. Strike stated that Bear had a reputation with clients. Maybe this was his way of keeping himself entertained on jobs before he moved on to the next one.

Bear jostled her around again, and she wrapped her arms around his neck to keep from falling as his palm pressed against her bum. Thank God she was still wearing her jeans and not a dress.

"Stop squirming, or I'll drop you," he said gruffly. "Now, be a good girl and hold on tight."

Her stomach flamed. *What I'd do to be his good girl.*

Her eyes widened before she snapped them shut. She tightened her hold around his neck and bobbed against his arms. The temptation to ask him to repeat "good girl" or to palm her butt teetered at the edge of her lips. Was she so desperate for a connection with everything going on that she was throwing herself into his arms?

The lift stopped, and they were on the move again. Bear's steps thudded less now as if he were walking on softer ground. She refused to open her eyes and converse with whoever was around. Bear leant down, and suddenly, a supple mattress and soft material replaced his touch. He slowly removed her hands from around his neck and pulled a duvet over her.

Liss's eyes remained closed as she sank into the mattress. She didn't want to know where she was or what was happening. Maybe if she fell asleep again, she'd wake up in her bed and everything would be a dream.

"You'll be safe here. I'll be outside your room all night. I won't leave you or let anything happen to you." His baritone timbre brought a heat between her thighs as he tucked a strand of hair behind her ear and walked away. "Sleep well, Princess."

But it wasn't a dream. None of it was. Liss was in a mysterious place, and as much as Bear stayed around, she was alone, but not in the way she controlled. As soon as the door clicked shut, she shoved her jeans off, kicked them away, and tossed her top to another part of the room until she was just in her underwear.

As much as she longed for sleep, she couldn't fight the day's drama roaring through her. Suddenly, the text from earlier and the words from the stranger in the crowd flooded her memories. She let the tears fall. Silent sobs held Liss prisoner as she accepted how isolated she was.

She couldn't crawl into her mum's comforting arms. Isla would come if she called, but she had her job and life to lead. Liss had no one.

Tears wetted Liss's pillow, but she sobbed quietly as exhaustion from the day and the muffled voices of Bear and Strike dragged her closer to sleep.

Chapter Nine

"Where the fuck am I?" Liss croaked.

Was it the light barely finding space under a door she didn't recognise or the unfamiliar springs of the bed that woke her?

She reached underneath her pillow and fumbled for her phone, but it wasn't there. Squinting, she caught the shape of a lamp next to a glass of water. She downed the entire glass before reaching for the light.

"I wouldn't do that if I were you." Bear's familiar growl made her jump and ache all at once.

"Why not?" she replied, switching on the light. Although groggy, she was in no mood to be controlled by a burly guy with the same name as a woodland animal.

Light flooded her vision temporarily. White spots appeared before her eyes as her duvet flopped down, and suddenly, Bear's comment made sense. Sitting in the corner of the room, still wearing his suit though the jacket was gone, was the man she wanted to defy. His hands covered his eyes as he grimaced.

"Because you're just in your underwear," he stated. "And I'd rather not see you like that."

"Rude," she mumbled, although her face burnt as she sneaked a look to confirm he was right. She grabbed the edge of the duvet in both hands and dragged it up to her chin. "Did you two undress me?"

"No, you must have done it after I left the room last night," he replied. She breathed deeply as she remembered tossing her clothes off before crying herself to sleep. "Can I open my eyes now?"

"Yes," she stated, grabbing the duvet so tightly her knuckles hurt.

His dark brown eyes eased open as if he were expecting her to streak across the room while screaming his name. His gaze fixed on hers, but momentarily, it dropped to the duvet covering her chest.

"Making visual checks, Mr. Bodyguard?" she teased.

"I was ensuring you're not lying to me." He ground his teeth as he locked eyes with Liss. "You've not been the best client so far."

"I didn't ask for this." Her life had transformed in the last twenty-four hours. The grogginess that accompanied waking made her tetchy, and each word from him reminded her of how trapped she was.

"I aim to keep you safe. You've not made it easy. I need you to do exactly as I tell you."

"You're not my boss, and you're not in control of me." Bear remained silent, but his eyes darkened as he stared at her. "I'm not going to obey your every whim. I won't say 'yes, sir' or 'where do you want me, sir?'" Her snorting laugh was cut short by his animalistic grunt. "Please, Bear, tell me where you want me next. Make me your good girl." The last part slipped out, and she slid the duvet higher to cover her mouth.

He raised his eyebrow and shifted in his seat. "You want to be my good girl, Princess?" Her face burnt as if flames licked at her cheeks. "And what sort of things does a good girl do? I'd like to know when to reward you."

Her thighs trembled, but the duvet hid it, much to her relief. How, with everything going on, was she this horny? It had to be misplaced anger or because she didn't want to revisit her tears from earlier. But as the heat between her bare thighs grew, she knew it wasn't that simple. "Well, I'm happy that you didn't undress me. The idea makes me want to puke."

"'Course it does." He winked. The sun was rising and forcing itself through the gap in the curtains and lighting the bedroom. Liss resisted hiding her face even though Bear could see her heated cheeks and bitten lips. Life was getting complicated, and that was without the princess thing. *Don't think about the princess thing.* It was too much to deal with.

A knock at the door broke the thick tension in the room. Strike entered without waiting for a response.

"I heard voices," Strike grumbled before looking at Liss. "You're awake then."

She nodded.

"Isla called. She's going to visit tonight and will bring Steve too," Strike informed her.

Strike glanced at Bear, who was scowling but not at anyone. "Get some sleep if you can. The next two weeks will be heavy."

Bear nodded as Strike left the room and clicked the door shut.

Liss glanced at Bear.

She'd always hidden a thing for bad boys, although the only two guys she'd slept with were men your mum would love and your dad would invite to play golf. Although she didn't have her mum anymore and she'd never met her dad. Bad guys were her kryptonite, so she kept as far away from them as possible. But how did you control the distance between you and your bodyguard?

"Tell me something about you," she said. If she knew more about Bear, maybe the attraction would die. The intensity was due to the mystery alone. It had to be. She shouldn't be this attracted to someone she'd only just met.

He shrugged. "All you need to know is that I'm your bodyguard and will keep you safe."

He wasn't going to make this easy. "Where did you grow up?"

"Here and there." His face was blank, although his jaw twitched.

Liss threw her hands in the air before grabbing the duvet in time to stop it from revealing her bra. "You're impossible." The less he told her, the more she wanted to know, and the mystery wasn't helping the heat that was continuing to crawl through her aching body. Her tongue darted out, and she licked her lips. "What made you want to be a bodyguard?"

He shrugged again. "Something to do." If Liss had more clothes on, she'd stride over and slap him to get a reaction.

"Fine," Liss snapped, lying back down and tucking the duvet around her. "You might as well get some sleep, because the next two weeks 'will be heavy,'" she said, repeating Strike's comment.

Little dots on the ceiling made a shape like a cloud. It reminded Liss of when she and her mum used to laugh at the funny images clouds conjured up. She gritted her teeth. Her mum could have had a chance. And what if the royal family announced Liss as a princess? On top of that, someone wanted her dead. Her arms trembled. Her grandma should have said something sooner. Nana had disappeared to stop the questions, but in her typical way, she'd cared for number one with no thoughts for the situation she'd put her granddaughter in. Her grandma was always selfish. She hadn't been around when Liss's mum was dying, but she could have stayed for the aftermath of the bomb she'd dropped. Liss squeezed her eyes closed tightly, but the thoughts kept coming. And in two weeks everything would change again. Who would protect her then?

"Why did you have dog biscuits?" Bear's voice, softer than before, made her pause.

"Huh?" Liss asked, opening her eyes.

"You gave that dog near the pub a biscuit from your pocket. It seemed weird for you to be carrying them. Did you have a dog when you were younger?"

Liss fought the temptation to stare at Bear. It was nice to just chat when so much of their interaction was confrontational. She found a little dark mark on the wall and focused on that instead. "No, I wasn't allowed pets growing up because of the places we rented. I found a stray cat once and hid it in my bedroom, but the landlord heard it and kicked it out. Our neighbours took it in, so I'd sit with it occasionally, but then we moved."

"I wouldn't have put you down as a cat person," Bear replied.

"Hey!" The noise carried in the semi-dark bedroom. "Are you judging female cat owners?"

Bear chuckled. "Calm down, Princess. I meant I thought you'd be more of a dog person. I have met many a sexy women with cats. No judgement here."

Liss's smile curved on the side of her face. She needed

to stop seeing every comment he made as fighting talk. "I like dogs too. One day, I want a puppy and a kitten, and then I'm going to make videos showing their friendship because they'll be besties."

"I don't doubt it with you as their mum. Everything about you is chill," he teased, the smile threading through his words. "So, you carry a dog biscuit for your future pets?"

Liss giggled. "No, it's for emergencies."

"Dog emergencies?" His voice reached a higher pitch.

Liss curled under the duvet and shuffled into the foetal position. A strip of light from around the door highlighted how he gazed at her with his head tilting to one side.

"Kind of. More like pub emergencies." She scrunched her nose up. "One afternoon at the pub, one of the local neighbourhood cats swaggered in and sidled up to Joyce with the confidence of an Alsatian. Then the cat, Bert, jumped at him like he was starting a fight."

"Cheeky fucker. We all need the confidence of a badass cat," Bear said. His grin made her body feel lighter than a feather.

"True. We keep dog treats in a jar on the side, and if I hadn't grabbed one and got Joyce's attention, I swear the animals and the pub wouldn't have survived."

"That's some quick thinking, Princess. You'd make a great bodyguard," he replied, leaning back in the chair and resting his foot on his thigh.

"As if. I'm only five foot tall. Although that night wasn't the first or only time I've thrown someone or something out of the pub for bad behaviour, there's been fur flying and wee on the floor. Pub life is not glamorous."

Bear chuckled. His eyes never left her face. "Neither is being a bodyguard. I once fought with the paparazzi to get them away from my client. The client insisted on leaving the hotel for meet-and-greets. The thing about being a bodyguard is preparation and anticipation. You need plans to stop you from getting into difficult situations. You're not doing your job properly if you keep getting into fights."

"I thought it was all kicking ass. What did you do with the client?"

He cocked his head. "I told them if they kept causing trouble, then I'd let the paps know which cage fighter's wife they were sleeping with and make them deal with it alone."

"You didn't, though, right?"

"I didn't need to. Strangely enough, he started behaving after that."

Liss smirked. "Well played."

They fell into a comfortable silence.

"I'm sorry for being difficult," she said tentatively after several minutes. "I'm not used to being told what to do or being with people all the time."

"But you work in a pub, and you have Isla."

"Yeah, but at the end of the day, I come home to my flat, and it's only me. It's always been just me since Mum died," she continued quickly, not wanting to chat further about her mum. "What can I do to make your job easier?"

"Trust me. Listen to me. And try not to rebel too much. You're not stupid, Liss, and you've not got a death wish. I'm pretty sure you're good at following orders when necessary."

Although he'd said it without inflexion, an image of him telling her what to do as she lay beneath him flashed in her mind. He observed as she tugged her lip between her teeth.

"And I'll call you a good girl if you behave," he added with a wink.

"Fuck you," she replied with an eye roll, but she pressed her thighs together to stop the arousal owning her body. "I will do what you say as long as it's not stupid." Or too filthy.

He laughed a deep laugh that filled her limbs and eased the tension.

"I'm sorry for the way I've acted too. Me and Strike usually do security for people who've been in the limelight for years. They're accustomed to the risks. But you were shoved into something massive so quickly, and from everything I've seen already, your life was pretty normal, in a good way."

"It's weird to think I was just running the pub a day ago."

"Exactly. So, I'm sorry because I treated you like our other clients. Some of them crave the drama, and that's not you. I'm going to try harder to respect that and be less of a dick," he added.

"Thank you. That means a lot," Liss replied with a sigh. "What time is it?"

"About half past five. You should sleep."

She murmured her agreement.

As she began to drift off, she asked, "Why are you in my room anyway? Are you scared someone is going to get in and attack me?"

"I heard you crying, and I didn't want you to be alone," he stated so simply that she almost didn't believe him.

"Oh. Thank you," Liss said, staring at him as a mixture

of emotions threatened to overwhelm her. She didn't know what to say, so instead, she replied softly, "Sleep well, Bear."

"Sweet dreams, Princess," he said with a gentle smile before she turned over and snuggled into the duvet.

Chapter Ten

Liss slunk around the bedroom and squeezed her talisman heart before slipping it into her toiletry bag. It was the last present from her mum, a plastic fast-food chain toy from their final meal together. Her mum hadn't been able to eat much, but she'd been giddy at the idea that she, a grown woman, could order a Happy Meal. It was the last time her mum smiled before she died, so that little plastic heart meant more than all her possessions combined.

Liss had slept until the early afternoon and followed it with the longest shower. Waves of honeysuckle filled the air whenever Liss fluffed her hair, and a heady combination of flowery citrus covered her soft skin.

She glanced down at her clothes. Her yoga pants were worn at the knees, and her vest had seen better days. If the DNA test revealed she was the King's granddaughter, she'd have to dress differently. Everything would change. It was bad enough that she was forced out of her home and couldn't visit the pub. She checked her watch for the umpteenth time. Maybe she should make the most of her free time. But time was a luxury she'd never been allowed.

A knock sounded at her door. "Can I come in?" Bear said from the other side.

She opened the door wide and stood back. Her

handsome bodyguard filled the gap in the doorway. His ruffled hair and the dark rings around his eyes made her want to reach out.

"You okay?" she asked.

His brow furrowed, and he stumbled over his words. "I was going to ask you that."

"I feel better after my sleep and shower. Are you okay though? You look tired."

He turned away, and she followed him into the main bit of the suite. "No one asks me how I am," he grumbled. She'd not seen this part of the suite when he'd brought her in the night before. The room was plush and yet understated, with a mixture of beige and white furnishings. Generic landscapes hung on the walls. It had everything she expected: a state-of-the-art television, mini fridge, tea and coffee-making facilities, and the sofa that now held her grumpy bodyguard, who still hadn't said how he was. "You should eat."

She stared back at him, tilting her head. His softness from the early hours had gone.

"You haven't eaten in nearly a day," he grunted. But she continued to stare at him. Finally, he relented. "Please."

She remembered her promise from the night before about making things easier. "Okay, but you too. I can't see anywhere to cook."

"Can you cook?" She raised her eyebrows and he added quickly, "I meant because of your kitchen yesterday. You know, no food."

"No, I can't unless you count tinned spaghetti on toast with grated cheese. Can you?"

His mouth formed a sullen pout, and he shrugged. "I ordered brunch when I heard you moving around. It should be here soon."

"Thanks." She fiddled with the pocket of her yoga pants as he prepared drinks. "Is Strike around?"

The lift beeped to announce someone was on their way up.

"No, we're taking turns in shifts with another client. We're tying up loose ends with them. He'll be here tonight."

"Cool." She put her hair in a ponytail, needing something to do with her restless hands. "I don't know what to say to Strike. You're grumpy, especially when you're tired." *Like right now.* "But you have moments when you can be kind, like you were while I slept."

His face softened as he turned to stare at her. Her body still fizzed with excitement when he was near. She'd hoped learning about him last night would have obliterated her attraction, but she now wanted to know more.

The room prickled with their connection. Why did being around Bear feel different from anyone else? It had to be lust from their first meeting. It would soon disappear.

"I'm a dickhead. Trust me, Princess. But let me know if you ever need someone in your room while you sleep."

"Do you do that for all your clients?"

His shoulders hunched.

"No." The revelation made her words stick in her mouth. The lift doors opened, and a statuesque blonde rolled out a trolley. His tightness released immediately. "But if you don't believe I'm a dickhead, just ask Mel." He pointed with his thumb, and the model-like stranger in a tailored suit laughed.

Liss bit the inside of her mouth. Her fizzing turned to pinches in her stomach as Mel rolled the trolley over.

"Don't believe him. Bear is a gentleman...until he's in the bedroom."

Liss choked on a gasp.

"Mel," Bear warned with a raised eyebrow.

"It's the truth." She giggled. "At least that's what I remember until you dumped me for another assignment."

Bear rolled his eyes, but there was a twinkle in them too. "She's joking," he said to Liss. "I didn't dump her, because we were never dating."

"Because the darling Bear here doesn't do relationships. Anyway, here's your brunch." She pulled up the silver plate covers to reveal a full English breakfast. Bear grinned. But was it at the sight of Mel or the food? Suddenly, Liss needed to get far away from Bear and his former conquest.

"I don't think I'm hungry right now." Her stomach rumbled loudly, drawing a cocked head from Bear. She gritted her teeth. "I might take it in my room and have some later. But thank you for bringing it."

Bear stood directly in front of her and fixed her with his stare. His hands cupped her shoulders. "Liss, are you okay? Let me get you that coffee."

"I'm fine. Maybe I need to top up my sleep. A lot has happened in a short time." Including her weird ass feelings. But it wasn't jealousy. She never got jealous, and Bear was just some random guy she barely knew. In fact, after meeting Mel, she knew more about him than she wanted. He didn't do relationships.

He brought her a coffee. "Milk one sugar," he said, handing it to her. "How you like it."

He'd remembered from the palace. It was the same as yesterday when they were in her flat. It didn't mean anything.

"Thank you," she replied. Her hands brushed his. Tingles caressed the nape of her neck. Suddenly, she was aware of Mel staring.

Liss shoved cutlery in her yoga pants pocket and grabbed a plate of food with her free hand. "Catch you both later. Enjoy reminiscing." She turned and winced. That sounded so bitter. She was embarrassing herself.

"Isla and Steve should be here in a couple of hours," he said as she slid out of the room, her plate barely balanced on her hand. "Shall I send them in?"

"Thanks. That would be great." She kept her back to him and closed her bedroom door with her foot before opening her mouth in a silent scream.

"Come in," she said when Bear knocked at her door a while later.

Liss had eaten in the bathroom to drown out the sound of Mel's and Bear's laughter, but she'd returned to bed an hour ago. Their familiarity made her want to rage, and as much as she knew why, she refused to admit it.

"I brought you another coffee and a bottle of water too. It's good to stay hydrated." He put both on the bedside table next to her.

"Thanks," she replied.

"Isla can't come over now. She left a message that she's swamped at work but she and Steve will be over tomorrow."

"Okay." Bear looked a little less tired. Maybe Mel's visit energised him. "Mel seems nice."

She hated her masochist side even as she said it.

"She is. We hung out as 'friends' before she met her husband. She was going through a bad life situation." Liss's shoulders eased at the word husband. "She's the manager here now, which is one of the reasons we use the place. She keeps things discreet."

She kept her head ducked, still embarrassed by her earlier attitude. "That's helpful."

"Yeah, your safety is key." Bear sat in the seat where he'd rested as she slept. If a heart could blush, that was what hers did at the memory. He'd cared for her. She needed to keep reminding herself that it was his job.

"Do you look after everyone, Bear?" She lifted her gaze, and his eyes met hers. It was as if he was staring into her soul, searching for the meaning behind her question.

"Only those who need it and deserve it." He shifted in his seat. "Don't get me wrong, I do my job and ensure people are safe, but for some, I go the extra mile. Strike calls it my saviour complex."

So that was all this chemistry was. Bear was going the extra mile for her for whatever reason, probably because he'd seen her cry. Lust and a saviour complex. "That's good of you." Her reply sounded flatter than she intended.

"And how about you? Do you let people...go the extra mile for you?"

Liss shrugged. "No one has since my mum; even then, it was mutual. Isla cares, but it's not the same. Why?"

Bear shrugged and stood. "No reason." As he reached the doorway, he turned. "Mel questioned if something was going on with us because I remembered how you take your coffee."

"Right," she replied. The subtext of the comment was lost on her.

Gruffly, Bear added, "Don't mention it to Strike

though."

Liss tipped her head in a nod, and he walked out. Bear was the ultimate mind fuck, and she had enough to think about.

Thankfully, the next day of cabin fever and feeling unproductive was broken up by a visit from Isla and Steve.

"Hugo is speaking to the chain that's considering buying the pub. It's not rumours anymore. He says he'll put in a good word for me. He reckons I could skip the manager stage and go to head office." Steve's laugh was giddy.

"But I thought you liked being at the pub and didn't want a corporate job. You could have got one at any point." Liss's chest tightened. She'd only been gone from the pub a few days, and everything was changing.

"I know. I said I didn't want it. So what if you're a princess? You'll still come back to us," Steve reasoned. "The pub will always need you."

"Of course. But Bear said if I'm a princess, it will be difficult to return. But I will, no problems." She took a deep breath. She sipped her coffee to hide how her conflicting emotions scratched at her.

Steve chewed his lower lip. "Bear said that, eh?"

"How long until you get the DNA tests back?" Isla asked. Steve spied her warily.

"I spoke to King Archibald today," Liss uttered. "He said it could be a couple more days."

"A couple more days stuck with a sexy bodyguard in a beautiful hotel room. You poor thing," Isla teased.

Steve rolled his eyes. "What Isla means is, how was it

speaking to the King? You've always said your family is the pub, but you could have a real family, a real grandad."

Liss swallowed as she considered her answer. "It felt nice. It was like we had this connection even though we were virtual strangers."

Steve smiled. "We've watched you long for a family since we've known you."

"But I have you guys."

"And we'll always be here for you, but it's nice that you might have family too."

"But does that mean you'll have to ditch your old life?" Isla asked.

"I don't think I have to be a princess where I leave my life completely. But I don't want to do anything that might cause problems in this relationship with Archibald." It was like Liss's lunch was curdling in her stomach. She was desperate for a family, but saying she didn't want to be a princess might ruin that.

"No matter what, you'll have an awesome time going to balls and meeting all sorts of people as well as various duties, like opening…toilets?" Isla's legs jiggled.

Liss laughed. "I didn't tell you everything that was said when I was at the palace."

Steve leaned in closer.

"Make sure you describe everything Marianne was wearing for Steve here."

Steve glared.

It was nice having her friends visit, even if it made her more anxious about her future.

Liss hugged Steve and Isla hard. Steve whispered, "I want

the best for you, Liss. I know I'm an arse sometimes, but I care about you."

Liss chuckled. "I know you do. Friends forever, yeah?"

"Forever," Steve replied, squeezing her extra tight. "And I'll look after the pub for you."

Bear had returned, and she could feel his eyes on her back.

"I nearly forgot," Isla exclaimed as Steve reached for the lift button. She dragged a plastic bag out of her handbag and shoved it in Liss's hands. "That should help your boredom."

As Isla and Steve entered the lift, Isla's eyes twinkled. Steve waved. He'd been the friend she remembered. The three of them had shared memories of their favourite nights out and some of their best pub stories all afternoon.

"What's in the bag?" Bear asked when they were alone again.

Liss handed it to him as she sipped another coffee he'd made for her. "It feels like a book. It's nice to have a distraction from the royal stuff." She added "and from you" in her head.

He cleared his throat noisily. "Hence the yoga. Will you be doing that again?" Bear said, referring to the yoga video she'd attempted that morning as he worked in the suite. He opened the bag. "Oh, hello. This book should keep you busy."

Liss's eyes were wide and her mouth dropped open when he held up the book like a prize. On the cover was a semi-naked guy. As she read the title, she squealed. Liss yanked the book out of his hand and rushed to her room. Suddenly, she stopped. "I'm not running to my room because I need to read it."

"Of course not, Princess." Her body flamed with need and embarrassment. "What was the title? I wasn't sure if I saw it before you had to bolt to your room to read it or whatever else you might need to do there."

"It doesn't matter."

"Tell me anyway," he said. His voice was gravelly, and Liss turned around even though she knew it would do more harm than good. His eyes twinkled as they dipped to the book and then back to her flushed face. "I want to know what you might read alone in that bed."

She looked at the book even though the title was seared into her memory. Her mouth was dry as she replied, "It's called *The Princess's Sexy Bodyguard*."

"Don't suppose you also want to read the blurb to me?" His voice was so deep that it made her body vibrate.

"No, I don't," she replied as she ran to her room to the sound of his chuckles. Fucking Isla and her sexy books.

Liss walked around her room as the afternoon sun filled the bedroom. The day had been quiet so far, but she refused to read any more of the book Isla had left her.

She'd managed half last night, and it had given her a memorable Bear-related sex dream. Desire careered around her body. All this time, with nothing to do but fantasise about her bodyguard. She needed to be productive.

Liss let out a huff and stalked around the room, rummaging through every drawer she passed. They were all empty because there was no point in unpacking if she wasn't staying long. She smacked them against the backboard as she closed them.

"What are you doing?" Bear bellowed from the adjoining living room.

"Nothing," she shouted back, opening the wardrobe. Liss slammed the wardrobe door. Maybe she wouldn't revisit last night's dream if she kept doing this.

A loud yawn preceded Bear's shout. "I'd rather you didn't break the furniture. We like using this hotel for work. Maybe you should get in here."

"Maybe you should fuck—" The shout died on her tongue. Bear watched her from the doorway.

"Maybe I should fuck what?" He yawned again. "You moan a lot when you dream." His gaze locked with hers in a challenge. "Are you always so vocal in your sleep?"

She folded her arms and glowered. "I don't moan in my sleep."

Bear tipped his head back, and a breathy moan left his lips. "That's how you sound. What were you dreaming about, and how's that book working out for you?" Bear offered a pouty smile.

Liss stared at him as she banged another drawer. The bodyguard-related sex dream flashed in her mind. She couldn't stop the memory of Bear's fingers deep inside her as he pulled her orgasm closer. He'd then placed her hand against his dick. At the vivid memory of his erection, she glanced down.

He cocked his head and thrust out his chest. "Enjoy the view, baby."

She glared at him.

"Maybe you make noises in your sleep too, if you ever sleep. You look knackered," Liss replied. Dark circles settled deep under his eyes, and the smattering growth of hair around his lips and chin gave him a rugged look and proved he hadn't shaved.

He returned to the living space, saying over his shoulder, "I learnt a long time ago not to sleep soundly. You have to be aware of your surroundings and not trust strangers." Did he mean as a bodyguard, or was there another reason he needed to be aware of his surroundings? His dig cut into her thoughts. "Something you don't understand, seeing as you send pictures of your naked body to guys you haven't met."

"Everyone does that." She followed him into the living space. "Don't try and shame me. Are you telling me you've never been sent a photo like that or sent one?"

"I've never sent one but received a few." He shrugged half-heartedly before giving her a smile that made her hips roll of their own volition. *Keep still, you traitorous bastards.*

"Whatever," she said between pinched lips.

"More than a few, but that's what happens when you make someone come several times in one afternoon. Add that to your dreams, and maybe the whole hotel will hear you moan next time." He sat back in his chair and checked his phone while yawning.

Liss stood directly before him and waved her hands in the air. "How come you get to have your phone and I don't?" she snapped. Maybe that would distract her from her boredom.

Bear tipped his head and folded his arms, drawing her eyes to the rolled-up sleeves of his crumpled shirt. Hints of a tattoo she couldn't decipher peeked from beneath the white cotton. As her brows furrowed, he pushed his sleeves down and hid his forearms.

"My phone is secure. I'll give you one that our IT person has secured for you, but it hasn't any numbers or messages saved. I'm afraid your non-date won't be able to message you."

Liss shoved her hands on her hips. "I don't care about him." She'd forgotten about him after days with a man too sexy for his own good.

"Of course you don't." Bear returned to his phone. "And you don't care why he didn't reply to a picture of your naked body either. You are so above that."

"You're a dick." She attempted to shove his legs apart with her knee. They didn't budge an inch.

"You're not the first to call me that, and you won't be the last. Now, if you don't have anything interesting to share, maybe you should exercise. Your strength is pitiful." He didn't look up at her as he dismissed her. He was so touchy when tired.

"Did you see the photo?" Maybe if she got her phone back, she could delete the photo from it for good.

"Of course I didn't. I may be a dick, but I'm a respectful one."

"Maybe you should look at it."

His head snapped up. "You want me to see you naked?"

"Scared you can't handle it?" Did she want him to see it, or was she trying to get a reaction out of him after the lingering sensations from her dream?

Bear shifted in his seat and fumbled in his pocket. "Maybe you should call your grandma. She must be worried about you. I've got a spare burner." He stood abruptly and turned away. He seemed to spend an age rummaging through his bag.

Her naked body made him think of her grandma! No wonder guys didn't want her. Her skills in bed were probably as bad as her body.

Chapter Eleven

"Hey Nana, how are you?" Liss asked with a singsong tone. She stretched against her headboard with the phone on speaker in her lap. The bed was like a cloud. If she were the King's granddaughter, she'd be able to buy her perfect bed rather than the half-price one she got from her landlord. The sun streaking from the window warmed her arms, and she pulled her ponytail forward and twisted her hair around her fingers.

"I'm having a ball, darling. Sergio's summer home is delightful. The sun is shining, and life couldn't be better." Liss's false upbeat tone was a joke compared to her nana's genuine joy.

Liss dropped her hair and flicked her ponytail back. "So you're not coming home soon? I presumed you'd be back within the week."

"I've barely been here three days and have a tan to top up. You know what the British weather does to my complexion. You're sounding a bit desperate. Stop grinding your teeth."

Liss forced her mouth closed and counted slowly to ten. Her grandma was impossible when it came to anything meaningful. As a teenager, her grandma sneaked her into clubs and bohemian bars where men shared poetry while swirling whisky around a glass and ageing creative types bemoaned the modern world while smoking dubious substances. The night Liss came home smelling of scotch and weed, all hell broke loose. Her mum was under the impression her grandma was showing her culture, not a "den of iniquity." Her grandma stormed out of the house, declaring her family was the ultimate disappointment and that her friends were embarrassed her daughter was such a bore. She vowed she'd never see either of them again, but Nana crawled back within a month when she ran out of money and owed a card shark a hundred pounds.

"Why are you calling? Talking twice a month is a bit much for us, let alone twice a week."

"I was worried about you." Liss lied. Her grandma looked after herself, but Liss was nervous about sharing her truth. "And I thought you might be worried about me."

"Are Bear and Strike not protecting you properly? I'm surprised you don't fancy them. You always develop crushes on the most unattainable men," her grandma said matter-of-factly. "Do you remember that nurse who cared for your mum? He was engaged to a man, but you hung on his every word when he visited after her funeral."

Liss snatched up the phone and turned the speaker off. "I listened to him because he cared for Mum, and I was grateful. I was nineteen years old and supporting a dying woman. He was my only help." Liss tried not to snarl.

"If you say so. I'm not worried about you. You've always been able to deal with everything life throws at you." It would have been a compliment from anyone else, but her grandma knew she had no choice. No one came to her rescue. Liss was alone, as always. But she didn't want to be considered resilient when her trauma wasn't her choice.

Liss attempted to count to ten but didn't reach three when her grandma yawned. "Are we done?"

"Could we talk about this situation you've got me in?"

"That's a funny way to describe a future of fame and fortune. Darling, you're one of the luckiest women in the world. All little girls dream about being a princess. Trust you to find a negative." Her nana huffed. She was overly pronouncing her T's and speaking with a cut-glass accent. "And you get the perfect family you've always said you were missing."

"Did Mum know?"

"Know what?" Liss caught a laugh in the distance before her grandma cackled to someone at the end of the call. "Be quiet, Sergio, you rogue."

"Did Mum know that the King was her dad or did you lie to her about her past too?"

"Stop being so dramatic. I didn't lie to either of you. I failed to tell you the entire truth. It's not like it would have made any difference."

"Mum could have received the best treatment. She wouldn't have died." Liss's voice rose, and her chest tightened.

"You can't know that."

"It's cocktail o'clock, Bets," a male voice sang.

"I have to go, darling. I have a lot going on here."

Liss pushed on, desperate for her grandma's support. "I received a threat on my phone, and someone in the crowd outside my flat said something nasty to me. Bear and Strike moved me to a hotel."

"Thank goodness I hired the boys then. I am clever. Anyway, take care and have fun. I'm sure you will be fine. Give my love to the King." She laughed gaily before hanging up.

Tears stung Liss's eyes. It was impossible to believe she was the same person who'd argued with the King days before. She couldn't stand up to her grandma, and most others railroaded her.

"Don't let it stress you. You make your own family in life."

She jumped at Bear's gruff voice coming from the doorway.

"I'm not stressed," she replied sullenly. Unable to look Bear in the eye, she busied herself, picking at the puffy white bedspread. "And you shouldn't listen to private conversations."

"I'm not getting into a fight with you, Liss."

She did look at him then. He leant against the doorway. He'd changed into a long-sleeved T-shirt. The cobalt blue of his top added intensity to his brown eyes and made his skin glow a deep brown. Her belly flipped, and her heart thumped in her chest. He'd heard what her grandma said about Liss's crush on her mum's nurse. She pulled the duvet higher. He'd laugh about that with Strike when they joked about the silly princess. Bear's face was blank as he tracked her movements.

"Of course you won't get into a fight with me. God forbid you might be anything other than Mr. No Emotion. So tell me more about this family of yours that you've made. Or about why you don't do relationships or why you hid your tattoos from me or anything about you," she snapped, raising her voice.

He stared her down. She pushed the duvet off and walked towards him.

"No? Have you got nothing helpful to say?" She lifted

her chin high. It was like her whole body throbbed as she confronted him. "Don't give me your advice and little words of wisdom. You're only here because someone's paying you to be here, and if you cared one bit, you wouldn't have suggested I call my grandma. You would have done something useful that helped me with this crap situation and the future waiting for me."

He raised his eyebrows as they stood toe-to-toe. His body crowded hers, and Liss fought the temptation to step down. Her body thrummed, and goose pimples rose on her arms as he watched her. "Are you done, Princess? Because I have something in mind."

She chewed her lips to avoid recalling her dream. She hated herself both for wanting Bear and for shouting at him.

"Is it more of Bear's great wisdom? Because I can't be arsed with that." She shoulder-barged him, hoping to make an impact, but she bounced straight off his body. She ducked around him and entered the living space with a flick of her ponytail. He was so fucking strong. He could pin her anywhere he wanted, and she wouldn't complain. The mixture of anger and attraction made it impossible to stay in her bedroom. She might beg him to take her mind off things, inevitably filling her with shame if something happened. She dropped onto the sofa and shouted while turning on the television, "You should write a book of all your wise sayings. Maybe you'll find at least one person who gives a shit."

He laughed, but the darkening eyes suggested he was anything but happy. Bear took the remote from her hand and turned the television off.

"I want you to come at me," he said. The way he'd overemphasised "come" had to be more than her imagination. She flexed her hips as she sat back on the sofa.

"You what?" He loomed over her like a feral animal, yet the gentle way he'd removed the remote made her want to find out what sort of guy he was when he desired someone.

"I want to teach you self-defence. Three reasons," he said brusquely. "One, it might come in useful in the future. Two, it will distract us while we wait for the DNA result."

"And three?"

"You're being a real brat at the moment, and I want nothing more than to pin you to the floor and show you exactly what I am capable of."

He revealed his teeth when he smiled. Liss's body burned as she imagined those teeth ripping off her underwear.

How was she going to think about anything else now?

Chapter Twelve

Bear's grey joggers hung low on his hips. They were barely into their sudden self-defence class, yet her need for him touched every part of her body with heat waves. As he stretched to show her how to deflect him, he revealed some of the perfect V of his pelvis that acted as a pointer to his dick. Thank goodness she wore a baggy vest, or her hard nipples would give away her thoughts.

Liss sucked hard on her lower lip as she stared. Her fingers tingled as she imagined tracing his body with her lips and making his cock judder as he groaned her name.

"Liss," he growled through the fog of desire. "Oi, Liss, pay attention. Or would you rather die when I attack you?"

"There are worse ways to go," she mumbled.

His eyebrows jumped, and she winked in response. Where did this confidence come from?

Bear let out a loud sigh as he pushed his sleeves up before pausing and shoving them back down again. "Come at me."

She attempted to punch him in the stomach, but he stuck his hand out, and she shook it.

"What the fuck was that?" she shouted. "I'm not going to shake hands with my attacker."

"And yet you just did." His chuckles were endearing. Bear's mask slipped, and dimples appeared on his cheeks.

"The shaking hand thing isn't really for attackers but for anyone who confronts you in an argument. I learnt long ago that if someone wants an argument with you or confronts you and you stick your hand out, they automatically shake it like you did there. It takes the wind out of the situation."

She tilted her head and nodded. "Does it always turn to cute giggles too?" His laughter stopped abruptly, and she kicked herself. He'd offered her a viewing platform for the adorable and worry-free version of Bear. She wanted his eyes to sparkle again.

"Let's try something else. I'll walk towards you like I intend to attack you. This is an expected attack, which is rarely the case, but it's good to know how to react. It's one-to-one, and something is about to kick off. You strike to the neck, giving you time to walk away," he said.

He strode towards her, and she attempted to hit his neck. Even with a little jump, she struggled to reach. "You're too tall. Not everyone who attacks me will be an extra from *Jurassic Park*!"

"Fine," he replied with a half-hearted shrug and got on his knees.

Surely, Bear didn't want every part of the class to be sexual, and yet, with this powerful man on his knees before her, the fantasies were intense.

His cheeks turned red as he looked from her eyes to her chest. He ran his tongue across his lips and pulled on the back of his neck with his hand. "Let me show you how the neck thing works," he said with a raspy voice. "Then you try it, and we'll get on with a different position that puts us both on our feet."

"Okay. A different position sounds good," Liss replied,

although it was more of a squeak.

"I didn't mean position," he replied gruffly before clearing his throat. "A different movement, not position."

"Stop saying position then." If she ignored the heat between her thighs, she might be able to focus on how adorable his vulnerability was.

"What you were trying to do was grab like this," he said as he went to punch, but suddenly Liss flinched and fell. His hand gently wrapped around her neck. He froze and whipped his hand back quickly while righting her.

Isla told her once about a guy she slept with in her first year of university who tried to grab her there as if it was a sexual act everyone was into. Not all women were into the same thing.

"Sorry, I shouldn't have held my hand there, even momentarily. You didn't consent to being touched like that."

He struggled to meet her eyes and dropped his chin to his chest. He yanked his hand back from her body quickly.

"Bear?" she said softly. His head remained low, but beneath his delicate eyelashes, he met her gaze. "It's okay. You were showing me a move."

Hurt creased his eyes, but he didn't look away. Liss wanted to pull this beast into a hug, but she feared he'd rear back. "I've had someone grip my throat before, and I hate it. I can't talk about it. You might be into it, but that's not a thing I do."

He started to walk away. Liss took a deep breath. She reached for his hand and held it. He stilled, but as he turned, she could see his pulse thrumming in his neck. "It was a mistake. You and I keep making mistakes with each other. I know I joke around a lot, but I'm scared too. Please, can we keep on with the class?"

"I am sorry," Bear replied with a sad smile. His chin trembled slightly. "Okay, where were we? Oh yeah, punching to the neck and not grabbing. You should make a fist like this." He demonstrated with his hand almost as if he was too scared to touch her. That moment of vulnerability and honesty was a surprise. Was he grabbed through his work or something else? "Show me how you make a fist, Liss."

They attempted it several times before changing to a couple of simple strikes she could try. He was demanding yet patient and relaxed as they tried different moves. He was at his best when instructing, touching her without the fear she witnessed previously. The impromptu class while hanging out with Bear and doing something that took her mind off her new dramatic life improved her day, and her smile was reflected in his eyes.

"Come at me again," he said, making her practice the moves like army drills.

"Were you in the army?"

"Focus, Liss," he said as he braced himself for her attack.

She pushed her hands against her hips and refused to move.

He rolled his eyes but grinned. "No, but Strike was. He doesn't talk about it, but he was in an elite part of the army. It's given us good contacts, and with that and his skills, it's enabled us to work the diplomatic and business section." He'd finally gifted her something, although it was a shame it was about Strike and not him. "But don't tell him that you know."

Liss cocked her head as she positioned herself to hit. "If you weren't in the army, what did you bring to the business?"

"Punch a little higher," he said, moving her arms to help her with her hits. "You're getting nosey, Princess."

"If I'm going to trust you with my life, then I need to know your credentials."

His eyes met hers, and his forehead wrinkled. "You make a good point. I'd want the same. Hit me again." He moved from foot to foot.

She attempted to grab his arm, and he cut her off with a dip and a push. He was sprightly and a little hypnotic with his twists and turns.

"Right, your turn. I'll come at you, and you need to push my arm out of the way and elbow me. Not too hard though." He went to grab her, and she swiped for his hand but missed. "You've got quick reflexes, but I need you to be thinking the whole time. Watch me."

He demonstrated the move on her again. "Got it?"

She nodded, and he went for her again.

This time, she deflected his arm and elbowed him in the shoulder. "Good. Much better, but next time, I need you to elbow me harder. We'll try doing it faster once you know how to do it. Okay?"

She nodded, and as they practised the move, he talked. "I worked the celebrity bodyguard circuit. Initially, as a doorman, but as the places I worked got more prestige, so did the people, and through that and other stuff, I ended up specialising with different clients."

"Do you miss the club scene?" she asked as her elbow caught him unexpectedly. Quickly, he dived away, and his hands turned to fists in front of his face in a boxing defence stance.

"No, it was fun, but it was dangerous too. I did things I'm not proud of, but sometimes it felt like kill or be killed."

Before she followed up with more questions, he changed the moves.

"Pinching an attacker can fuck them up. It won't seem like it. Kids pinch others at school all the time," he explained. "But trust me when I say that if you pinch an attacker, you can bruise and debilitate them before you run."

She squinted at his covered forearms. "Okay, where do I pinch you?"

"Are you enjoying hurting me?" He backed off slightly before cautiously showing her the points on the back of the knee and the bicep. "Once you've pinched, you rotate slightly and pull. Trust me when I say it fucking hurts."

"You're not going to let me do it?"

"I bruise easily. Like a peach." His cheeky smile made her heart swell. The softer side of Bear was going to destroy her. "You'll have to practice your pinching on Strike. His skin is like leather. I swear he sneaks off to sunbeds once a week."

She appraised Bear's skin with a slow smile.

"Now you need to kick me in the nuts," he requested with his arms wide.

"I didn't know you were into that," she quipped.

"Less of the jokes. Let's see if you're as quick with your tongue as you are with your hands."

"Now you're setting me up to be a smart arse." She chuckled.

He grinned like a naughty schoolboy as he shook his head. "Nuts, Liss. Let me show you what you need to do. Run at me." She backed up and squatted slightly. "For fucks sake. You're not preparing to sprint in the Olympics. Run at me, woman."

She rushed towards him, but in her haste, she caught her foot on the side table and face-planted into the sofa.

His giggles turned into belly laughs, and she moaned with a mouth muffled by the cushions, "I should have known your nuts would be too much for me."

"Baby, you didn't stand a chance. Now show me your blocks."

He attempted to tap her around the face once she stood, but she blocked his hands easily.

"You're the Tyson Fury of the princess world." At his wink, her belly flopped. "Let's go again."

He was oblivious to the effect he was having on her. They worked on blocking a little longer. Each time she did well, he praised her. She tensed her thighs to ward off the arousal, but the deep timbre of his compliments was a reward she couldn't ignore. If he knew he was affecting her, he didn't show it. But then he was Mr. No Emotion.

Bear checked his watch. "We've got time for one more move, but we should probably get this coffee table out of the way. I don't want any more injuries."

She gave him a half-hearted shove as he slid the table to the side.

"I'm going to turn my back on you, and I want you to come at me from behind." His eyes locked with hers, and she rolled her hips. He stared at her with an intent she didn't understand. "Really go for it."

She sighed inwardly. His shoulders were so broad. Her gaze slid down to his arse, and she teased her lip with the tip of her tongue. His bum muscles flexed.

"Stop staring at my butt and get on with it." Busted!

"Maybe my plan is for you to get bored, and then I can pinch your biceps," she said, wriggling her eyebrows.

He chuckled. "I've dealt with more dangerous and

savvier attackers than you. I know all the tricks you might pull, so get on with it."

Liss jumped on the sofa like she was performing a parkour move. She bent her knees and swiftly leapt onto his back. The action was accompanied by her hands high in the air as she screamed like a warrior bursting with adrenaline.

"The fuck?" he grumbled.

She slammed onto his back and held on tightly. The leverage from the sofa gave her an unexpected angle, and she wrapped her arms around his top half while her legs gripped him at the waist. Instantly, he turned and flipped her onto the sofa in a move worthy of a martial arts movie.

She couldn't stop laughing even as he dived onto the spongy seat beside her. His laughter was the most beautiful sound. His face lit up with a joy that floored her. He wasn't just handsome; he was the most attractive man she'd ever seen. All muscle and beauty with a laugh that made it impossible not to join in.

She gasped for breath as he leaned his head against the sofa. "I needed that," he said with a sigh. The action forced his T-shirt to ride up. The sight of rippling abs gave her an idea, and she dove onto him.

"And now for pinching time," she shouted and aimed for a bicep, but of course, he was quicker than her. In another move she wasn't prepared for, he picked her up and dropped her so that she lay the length of the sofa, her legs wide where he'd settled. She was no match for his strength and experience.

"You're terrifying, you know that?" he growled, his arms on either side of her head, crowding her in a way that made it nearly impossible not to flex against him.

"That means a lot coming from the hulking bodyguard resting between my thighs," she replied, panting from the flip and the need she couldn't deny.

Suddenly, everything stilled as he fixed her with his gaze. Joviality was sucked out of the room and replaced with a heat that filled her veins. She wetted her lips with the tip of her tongue. His gaze tracked every movement before returning to her eyes.

"We really shouldn't do this," he murmured. His features were pinched as if an internal debate was raging, squeezing his crucial organs and reminding him of his responsibilities.

Sound rushed through her ears as her heartbeat thudded.

"I'm supposed to be professional. I should be acting like a bodyguard."

She didn't respond for fear that her desire would force her to make a decision she'd overthink for days or that her sensibility would fill her with regrets. All the touching and laughing turned Liss into a ball of molten arousal, but she couldn't admit it to him. She swallowed repeatedly.

His eyes were impossibly dark, and his jaw set with an intensity that blistered every inch of her skin. Time stood still as he loomed above her.

"I won't tell anyone. It will just be one kiss." She didn't recognise herself when she was with him. "I don't understand what you do to me," she whispered, panting and trembling. "I barely know you."

"I want to understand, too, Princess." His fingertips feathered across her face, and she pressed her cheek to his touch. His hot breath caressed her neck, and she shivered against him. "You're so fucking beautiful, Liss. And you're funny and intelligent and feisty and sexy and…" His pause was painfully long. He closed his eyes, squeezing them tightly.

"Bear?" she whispered, pressing his hand against her cheek. Electricity sparked from his skin to hers.

"Fuck it." His lips crashed into hers with an almighty force. Her eyelashes fluttered, and she moaned against his mouth. "I love your moans."

His mouth opened, and she slid her tongue in. He met her kiss with less ferocity. Bear's hands slipped to her hair, stroking the strands as she pressed her lips harder against his. His gentle touches slowed her hunger, and their kisses were softer.

They stayed like that for minutes, losing themselves in each other's touch, not pushing it beyond the delicate kisses of two people wanting to immerse in the pleasure of lips and feathering touches.

He pulled away slightly and pressed his forehead against hers. His pupils dilated, and he licked his lips like he savoured her taste.

She held her breath and closed her eyes, silently willing for something.

"We shouldn't have done that," he said. His voice was so gravelly. So that kiss meant more to her than him? She opened her eyes, refusing to show emotion. His face was as blank as she hoped hers was.

"Mistakes happen," she murmured. Bear's stare was penetrating. She needed to return to her room before she let on how crushed she was. "Best get off, Bear."

He lifted himself gently off her, holding his hand out to help her up. "You okay?"

"Totally. You're not the first guy I've kissed," she replied with a laugh more hollow than she liked. He was the first to make her feel things with just one kiss. That was something she needed to hide from her features too.

The lift dinged. Strike was on his way up.

"Let me make you a coffee."

"Seriously, Bear, I'm fine, and I've already drank too many of your coffees," she replied between clenched teeth. She didn't want Strike to catch her with swollen lips. "We kissed, it was nice, but it was a mistake. Just leave it."

As she stepped into her room, the lift opened. She kept her bedroom door ajar.

"What have you done?" Strike snapped. Through the gap in the door, she spied his stance stiffening and a scowl appearing on his face.

"We were practising self-defence," Bear snarled with his head high as he moved the furniture back to its original position.

"Get downtown. You need to answer messages and take a break." Strike glowered, and his eyes narrowed. He slammed his fist against the wall. "When will you fucking learn, Bear?"

Power and anger filled the room. Liss's muscles quivered, and nausea swirled in her belly.

Liss attempted to close her door quietly, but at Strike's mutterings, she froze. "Stop thinking with your dick, and remember how much we need to do well on this job. We can't have a repeat of last time."

Although not aimed at her, Liss stung from Strike's reprimand. All they did was kiss. She closed her door just as she heard the lift doors opening again.

"I'm out here," Strike announced to Liss. "It's probably best if you stay in your room. Some of us have work to do."

Liss climbed under the duvet and prayed for sleep. Shame quickly replaced the arousal that'd died when she heard the words "repeat of last time." If she never saw either of the bodyguards again, it would be too soon.

Chapter Thirteen

After tossing and turning for an hour, Liss screamed her annoyance into a pillow. She tightly closed her eyes and attempted breathing exercises, but the memory of Bear's touch competed with the shame she felt at being caught by Strike. It crowded her mind each time her eyelids fluttered closed.

She waited for Bear's gruff London tones to replace Strike's muffled voice from the other side of the door, but they didn't come. Her stomach knotted at the idea that he'd already forgotten their kiss. He was probably downtown, laughing with a colleague that Liss was one of many women into him. He was a bad boy and a player. He probably entertained a fuck buddy in every country while she lived like life's rejected nun.

She needed Isla's words of wisdom. The burner phone Bear lent her winked from where she'd tossed it after calling her grandma. Liss grabbed it, but there were no numbers on it. Her grandma might have Isla's number, but nothing could make her repeat that call.

Liss turned the phone over in her hand before flicking through her options. It was a basic phone without internet capabilities. Suddenly, Liss face-palmed. She knew the number for the pub. Steve was managing the place in her absence.

"Steve will have Isla's number," Liss mumbled as if she needed to hear other sounds in her bedroom to reduce her isolation.

Liss crept to the door and peeked through the tiny gap. Strike's back was to her as he tapped away at a laptop. Even with the muscles that pushed against his white shirt, she wasn't attracted to him. Bear's kiss played on a loop in her head. She remembered the way her moans had carried between them. His gentleness left her flushed.

"Fuck," she grumbled. She needed to speak to Isla before her bodyguard crush made her do anything else stupid.

Liss tiptoed to the bathroom and shut the door firmly before turning on the taps to drown out her call. Her gaze flicked to the door as she quickly tapped the number of the pub. Suddenly, the phone rang at the other end, and she released the breath she was holding. Each unanswered ring bashed her in the chest, making it tighter as the knots in her belly squeezed and twisted. Strike would lose his shit if he heard her calling work. And she promised Bear she'd behave.

But then he kissed her like no one ever had.

She stamped her feet. The rings continued. It would go to the answering machine after seven. There was an answer within five rings policy. This was number six, and—

"The Bell End," a voice that wasn't Steve's shouted. Someone chose the pub's name hundreds of years earlier in all innocence, but now the employees loved announcing it at every opportunity. It was its own marketing tool, and many people wanted to spend time at The Bell End. "How can I help you?"

Liss wrung the hem of her vest. "Ewan, is that you?

Where's Steve?"

"Boss—or should I call you Your Highness now?" Ewan, the pub's self-proclaimed sex god snorted, and Liss clenched her jaw. "Steve didn't come for his shift. But I've got this, and nothing is going wrong."

Ewan was usually too busy trying to seduce the female clients to serve drinks. When not chatting them up, he shared stories of his conquests and reminded everyone that the condom machine was running empty due to his exploits. With him in charge, Liss's pub, which had survived two world wars and several football riots, would be destroyed within a day. She worried her lip as she considered rushing to the pub to sort things out. If she got hold of Isla, she'd check on Steve.

"Ewan, have you and Isla hooked up?"

Over the last few months, Ewan ducked in the back every time Isla visited. It was a familiar move for him after he'd slept with someone. He usually ghosted the women he no longer needed until the next time he was "lonely." Isla often picked the wrong guys when she was hornier than a homemaker at a Dream Boys concert, and she rolled her eyes every time Ewan hid.

Ewan stuttered, "I wouldn't say that." Liss slammed her fist down on the sink. Suddenly, there was a sound outside the bathroom door. "I mean we've never—"

"Ewan, did you sleep with Isla two months ago? It was a Thursday, and you were on closing," Liss hissed while glancing warily at the door.

"How did you know that?" he blustered. It was the next day he started hiding. It didn't take Sherlock Holmes to decipher it. "Fine. We had one intimate night together."

Liss held back laughter. She'd heard enough comments from his former conquests to know that intimacy was not one of his bedroom skills. But she couldn't talk. Her hookups were regretful, and her recent Tinder possibilities were embarrassing.

Liss shook herself. She didn't have time to consider all her failures. "Do you have her number? And don't give me the runaround."

"Yes, but, Boss, we're not meant to have our phones on us when we're behind the bar," he stuttered.

A knock came at the bathroom door.

"Felicity, come out, please?" Strike asked with an edge to his request.

"You spend more time swiping apps than pulling pints, so give me the number," she hissed before shouting, "One minute, Strike."

"Hold on. I've got to remember what I saved it under."

Liss tapped her foot incessantly against the tiled floor.

"Felicity, I need to speak to you now," Strike called more urgently.

"I'm taking a big dump," she sang.

"What?" Ewan asked, his voice climbing several octaves.

"That wasn't meant for you," she whispered as Strike continued to knock on the door. "The number, Ewan, now."

"You're a rubbish liar, Liss," Bear called out. He'd returned! The knots in her belly fluttered, and she grumbled at their betrayal. "And why have you got the taps on if you're on the loo?"

"Because I don't like people listening while I'm on the toilet like you two knobheads are doing right now," she thundered back.

The heat from the hot tap created enough steam to

write on the mirror, but time was running out, and Strike's knocks were turning to door-wobbling bangs.

"I'd saved it under 'Screams BallBags When Cums'. I guess you knew that about her."

Of course she didn't know that. Before she told Ewan how much of a dickhead he was, he read out the number, and she used her finger to write it on the mirror.

"Thanks," Liss replied, hanging up.

"If you don't come out, then we're coming in. We need to know you're safe," Strike shouted.

Liss flushed the toilet. "I'm fine." Her fingers flew over the phone as she messaged Isla. She needed another minute to get the number in.

"I'll count to ten, and then the door is coming down," Bear shouted. Every time he spoke, her body scorched. "Whatever you're up to, I'm sure it's something you shouldn't be doing."

Liss hit send.

"One...two...three!"

Quickly, she wiped the number from the mirror. Goodness knows how many random people would send Isla messages whenever the bathroom steamed up in the future.

"Six, seven," Bear shouted. She imagined a sexy game of hide and seek with him hunting her down. She suddenly flicked off the taps.

"Nine," he shouted as she deleted the message and the call history and unlocked the door to a snarling Bear.

"Can't a lady use the bathroom in peace?" she said with a hand on her hip. Bear snatched the phone.

He scrolled the history. Liss silently begged Isla not to reply yet. "Why do you need a phone when you go to the toilet?"

"Haven't you sat on the toilet with a phone? Aren't you cultured? I was searching for a game."

"You've played enough games," Bear grunted.

"Bear and I have to go. We're leaving one of our staff with you." Strike pointed to someone who looked the same age as Isla's teenage brother.

"He's a bodyguard?" she asked incredulously before wincing at her rudeness.

"He is our IT specialist. He can hack anywhere and is only with us, not in prison, because he promises to use his powers for good. Right, Luke?"

Luke nodded.

"We won't be long. Something has come up with another job," Bear grunted. "Don't do anything stupid, and stop hiding in the bathroom."

They strode away, but she couldn't resist a dig. "Maybe I was hiding because I was scared I might make another mistake."

Bear's shoulders tensed, and he pulled on the back of his neck.

"Bear, now. We've already wasted enough time," Strike hollered.

The doors slammed, and Liss sunk to the floor. At least Bear left her phone on the bed. If Isla replied, she might make it through the day without pushing any more of his buttons.

Chapter Fourteen

After a short workout that consisted of the five stretches Liss could be bothered with and painting her nails with the dregs of a bright pink varnish she found at the bottom of her washbag, Liss paced the living space of the suite. Bear and Strike had been gone an hour, and Luke had his head buried in his two laptops the entire time. The cute geeky guy with a slogan T-shirt who fit every stereotype of a hacker hadn't said more than three words.

He'd look at the door and then at Liss every few minutes before continuing his work. His fingers never rested, and if he wasn't tapping incessantly at his keyboard, he was pulling at his earlobes or poking at the hole in his jeans. He reminded her of one of her flatmates from the year she spent at university who always wore his headphones to help his concentration.

"Do you want to listen to music? We could put a music channel on the television."

Luke looked up, wide-eyed.

"We don't have to," she said, coaxing a response from the silent stranger. Liss fumbled with the hem of her vest. "But it might be better than the silence."

Luke's brow furrowed as his fingers tapped. His mouth opened, and nothing came out.

"I'll go then," she mumbled and walked to her room,

picking at the varnish on her freshly painted nails.

"I really want to listen to my headphones, but I'm not allowed," he replied quietly. His Irish accent was a surprise. His shoulders remained hunched, and he pulled at his earlobe again.

"Says who?"

"Bear. He told me to stay fully aware and check that you were behaving, as you're trouble."

Liss held back her grin. Most people thought she was dull, but she was trouble for Bear.

She tilted her head. "What else did he tell you?"

"That if I touched you, he would break every finger on my right hand and then use the left to slap me in the face." Luke blinked rapidly.

"Are you the type to randomly touch a woman, Luke?" Liss's back was poker straight as she ran through the defence techniques Bear taught her.

He winced as his eyes darted around the room. "Bloody hell. No. Not at all."

"Good. Can I sit next to you then?"

Luke nodded before moving wires out of the way.

Liss tucked her legs to the side, seated at the edge furthest away from him, but Luke was still stiff as if he feared accidentally touching her. "Does Bear normally make requests for you not to touch clients?"

"I'm not usually left alone to watch over clients because I'm busy with the tech, but you're a favourite job, and they were already supposed to have finished the last job. You're different. Bear's never said this to me before, even when I saw Mazdy to sort out her electronics."

"Mazdy the popstar? Bodyguard Corp was her bodyguard firm?"

"Yep, but never again. She's chaotic and nearly ruined the firm. Something happened between her and Bear. Strike hasn't shared the specifics, but there was a risk the whole company would tank. I deleted photos off her electronics of her and Bear kissing. If it got into the press that we were, you know, with the clients, no one would trust us again. You're a critical job for us. If we can't display professionalism and keep you secure, our reputation will explode, and the diplomatic clients won't want us again."

There was too much information, but one comment forced itself into her brain like a worm burying deep, leaving its eggs to hatch and cause more hell later. Bear had been intimate with a client. It was what Strike had suggested.

Liss's thumbed her knuckles. Whatever Bear's past, Liss needed to keep her distance. She wouldn't be another notch on his bedpost or risk the business for Strike, who was doing everything to restore the organisation's good name.

Luke stared at her. "I shouldn't have told you all that. They don't let me spend much time with clients, probably because once I start talking, I can't stop. I'm too awkward."

Liss smiled and stopped scratching. This guy was endearing. "You're not awkward. Maybe music will help. We can keep it quiet so that if the guys return, we can turn it off in time."

Luke smiled back at her. He was young, but the lines in the corners of his eyes suggested her earlier guesstimate of a teenager wasn't right. Maybe he was in his early twenties and only a couple of years younger than her. "Thanks. Music helps me concentrate."

She flicked on the television and found a generic pop channel. "One of my university friends said something similar. With headphones on, he calmed his exhausting brain and dealt with one thing at a time."

Luke's smile lit up his whole face, and his body relaxed momentarily. "I get that. The music stops the intensity of my thoughts. Sometimes, I put headphones on and listen to white noise. But don't tell the guys. They wouldn't get it."

"It will be our secret."

Luke grinned wider now. "Does your friend have any other techniques?"

Liss shrugged half-heartedly. "We lost touch when I left university to care for my mum. I didn't have time for anyone then. Isla, my best friend, stayed in touch though."

"Is she okay now, your mum?"

Liss's face dropped. Although she'd mentioned her, she hated telling people this part because their questions hit her hard. No one got to witness her sadness, not even Isla. Her pain was for her alone because that was what she was: alone, always and forever. "She died within the year."

"I'm sorry." His blinking was rapid again.

Liss shook her shoulders as if she was shaking off the memories. "Don't be. It was a while ago, and we must dust ourselves off and get on with life, right?"

She didn't believe a word she said.

"And now you're a princess," Luke added, as if her new life would make a difference. She was still alone.

"Yep, lucky me." Her smile didn't reach her eyes. Maybe she should find the positives about the princess thing. Suddenly, an old One Direction song, "Best Song Ever," played. "Let's turn this up and dance. We'll turn it back down as soon as it finishes."

Luke smiled and jumped up. "I love this one, but

don't—"

"Tell the guys?" Liss asked with a smile. Luke nodded exuberantly. "Your secret is safe."

Liss pushed the sadness to one side, but it refused to depart even as she remembered her crush on Harry Styles and her posters of him in her room. Her mum laughed about her crush, telling her he reminded her of Morten Harket and showing her photos. They giggled a lot that day. A tear slipped down Liss's cheek, but she swiped it. Luke bopped in the corner of the room, his hands in the air as he mouthed the words, oblivious to the torment Liss couldn't escape.

Suddenly, a vibration at her leg where the phone sat in her yoga pants pocket refocused her attention. She turned to hide her movements as she grabbed the phone, but Luke's back was to her. He shook his bottom to the chorus.

The text forced her eyes wide.

> Unknown: It's Steve. You need to come to the pub immediately. There's been a crisis, and we need you.

Isla must have given him the burner phone's number. But why, if she still hadn't replied to Liss's texts? Liss slid the phone back into her pocket as Luke shouted about how heartbroken he had been when Zayn left the band.

Liss nodded. She should get to the pub. There was nowhere more important to her, and she refused to let anything happen to that place and its people, even if some corporate chain was buying it. Steve, Isla, and the punters were the closest things she had to a family. Ewan the fuck bunny was like a horny cousin who brought his latest conquest to family parties before dumping them as the pudding was served. She planned her escape as her belly knotted at the guilt of ditching a happy Luke and getting him in trouble with the lads.

Chapter Fifteen

Ten minutes later, she was jumping in a taxi and directing it to the pub. Luke would be devastated that her request that he visit the front desk to get her "lady things" was a wild goose chase. But the pub came first.

Maybe the crisis was nothing and she'd return before the lads found out and Luke got into trouble. Either way, he'd never trust her again. The idea of his dejected face when he returned to the room, his mouth turned down and his eyes droopy, twisted her stomach and left her sweating.

It was only a twenty-minute journey, and she promised the driver an extra tenner if he got her there in fifteen. He gave her a wink as he sped through side streets and nearly broke the suspension over speed bumps. She redialled the number Steve texted her from for the entire journey, but he didn't answer.

Suddenly, the taxi came to a flying halt outside the pub. Liss yanked cash from her purse and thrust it at the driver.

"Don't worry," he replied in an accent that reminded her of Bear. She couldn't think about him, not with her pub family in crisis. Liss vowed to be chill as fuck with him next time after what Luke had said about Mazdy. "Driving like that is the most fun I've had in ages."

"But—"

"Anything for a princess," he added with sparkling eyes.

She must be in every newspaper if the local cabbie recognised her.

Liss offered a wincing smile. As she flew out of the car, her departing wave suggested she'd broken her wrist rather than resembling regal pizzazz, but the driver's grin was pure delight. She barely had time to return it before bolting for the pub.

Her life was changing already. She couldn't run a pub anymore as a princess, but the DNA test wasn't in. Her grandma was adamant that Liss was the King's granddaughter, but she could've lied. She wasn't a massive fan of the truth, and Liss's mum hadn't known. Surely, if her mum were the King's daughter, Nana would have told the King when she was ill?

The pub was rammed with people, but it was a Monday.

"Ewan," she shouted over the crowd.

Faces turned her way, and people pointed at her.

"Alright, Boss? I didn't expect to see you. Did you get hold of Isla?" Ewan asked, pulling a pint.

"She hasn't replied to my message. Is this chaos why Steve messaged me? Where did all these people come from?" she stuttered, pressing her hands by her sides to stop shaking.

Ewan shrugged. "We've got this covered. I called in extra staff. You're a local celeb, and everyone wants to drink at your pub. In the nicest way, we don't need you." This could be the making of Ewan. He managed two sentences without swiping his phone. "We wouldn't let anything happen to your baby while you're gone."

The pub was important to her, but she wouldn't call it her baby, although she'd called it her family. Without the pub in her life, she didn't have anything. That wasn't healthy, and it was even more reason to embrace the princess thing if the DNA test came back positive. Liss froze until several strangers held up their phones to take photos of her. A group of ladies looked her up and down and whispered behind their hands before giggling.

Liss's shoulders slumped forward as if she could hide her worn vest and leggings before pushing through the crowds to the bar, slipping behind it. "So why did Steve message saying I needed to come in urgently?"

"You'd best ask him. He's in the cellar sorting out the barrels." Ewan pointed at the back but was quickly distracted by a new line of customers. "Yes, sir. What can I get for you?"

Liss stormed out to deal with Steve and escape everyone's stares. She shivered from the sensation of eyes following her as she walked into the back corridor of the pub. With a glance behind, she confirmed she was alone, but the feeling refused to leave her.

"Steve," she hollered as she continued walking.

The Bell's corridors were a rabbit warren, but that was nothing compared to the hidden passages beneath the bar area. Most days, Liss ignored the rumours that they were haunted. In the past, rebels used them to escape from the castle, but they were a tourist attraction now that the pub's owner occasionally opened up for tours. An unexpected chill descended as she shuffled along the misshapen stones that made up the floors of the rebel hideouts. The musty smell that always accompanied her on her walks to replace barrels seemed stronger this evening.

As dizziness hit, she touched the wall, the stone cold beneath her fingertips. Her stomach rumbled. Hunger, when in the pub, wasn't unusual for her because she was usually too busy to eat, and even now, it was comforting. It was as if nothing changed, and she was still a fraught pub manager with no worries other than what film she and Isla would watch at the cinema if they could both get time away from work.

Her belly's grunts and grumbles echoed through the low-ceiling corridors. Many companies asked to run ghost hunts in the pub late at night, but Hugo drew a line there, much to Liss's relief. She didn't want them to find any truth in the haunted rumours as she was often the last to leave at night.

"There's no such thing as ghosts," she mumbled.

A murmured voice swam through the passage, bouncing off the walls. Was Steve talking to himself while sorting out barrels? She'd had a fondness for him since he'd started working in the pub and pushed himself into her friendship group with Isla.

Murmurs reverberated around her.

"Steve," she called out. At that moment, the corridor plunged into darkness. The only light switches were at the beginning and end of the passage.

"For fucks sake, Steve," she shouted, but the response was her echoing expletive followed by an indecipherable whisper. "Is someone there?"

The voice came again, but she couldn't distinguish the words. Her teeth chattered as she bellowed, "Steve, this isn't funny. Stop playing one of your dumbass pranks. I can't see."

Her breath rasped as she recalled the time school bullies locked her in the toilets at the end of the day. She was ten years old and supposed to get herself home, but to avoid the bullies who waited for her at the gate, she hid in the toilet. No one was home because her mum worked two jobs with only an hour between them. The neighbours usually kept an eye on her, but they were on holiday, and she was her grandma's responsibility.

"Can someone please turn on the lights?" Her panic echoed around the passageway.

Liss shortened her steps as she felt her way along the wall. She was close to the cellar. As she reached the switch and the edge of the cellar stairs, a hand shoved at her back. She grasped for anything to stop her fall, but her hands swam in the air as she lost her footing and tumbled down the stairs into the inky black depths of the pub.

Chapter Sixteen

Loud voices fought to infiltrate the darkness around her.

"Where the fuck is she?" Bear shouted. He should be working and not at the pub. "Ewan, mate, if you don't tell me where she is, then I will rip your fucking hands off and beat you to death with them. Are we clear?"

A squeak sounded.

Liss opened one eye and then another. She lay at the bottom of the stairs of the cellar. Big barrels surrounded her.

Her head felt like she'd gone several rounds with two Anthony Joshuas. Pain stabbed above one eye, forcing it to close.

"Stop squeaking at me, Ewan, and tell me where she is."

She giggled at the idea of Ewan dressed like a cartoon mouse, but she instantly regretted it when her head throbbed and bile rose in her throat. What was the lump underneath her?

"Liss, where are you?"

At the panic in Bear's voice, a sob rose in her throat and tears caught in her eyelashes. She shouted, but her voice was a rasp.

Come on, Liss, you can do this.

She worked her tongue to bring some saliva to her dust-dry mouth. "Bear, I'm here." It was a bit louder. She took a breath and tried again. "I'm in the cellar."

"Did you hear something?" Bear asked. His footsteps stopped.

She flashed to the moment the lights went out in the school toilets. The bullies told her they'd locked her in the school all weekend, and no one would notice because no one cared about her. They'd laughed so hard, and Liss's tears fell because they were right. Hours later, her mum's shouts woke her. Her grandma was drunk at a party and had forgotten about her. The neighbours had returned home early from their holiday and noticed her missing. They called her mum, who immediately demanded the headmaster take her to the school.

"Bear, I'm here. I'm at the bottom of the cellar stairs," Liss called out. It was more like the whisper of a librarian than the scream she was aiming for, but suddenly, Bear's thudding footsteps echoed around her.

Her head swam, and she rested it against the sandy cellar's floor.

Suddenly, he was next to her. "Princess, are you okay? Where does it hurt?"

She mumbled incoherently.

"You're not making sense, baby. You've banged your head. Did someone attack you?"

"I don't think so. But I'm safe now because you're here."

Bear let out a deep breath. "Yes, you're safe. I got you."

She tried to move, but Bear held her still.

"We might need an ambulance," Bear hollered up the stairs. He ran his hands along her legs, carefully squeezing and watching her closely. Although he appeared calm, his hands trembled. Yet his touch created little sparks throughout her body as if the sensation had returned. "Do you think you've broken anything?"

"You're going to have to start higher if you want to get me off," she whispered to calm him.

He sullenly glanced at her. "You're delirious, Princess."

"Not yet, but keep moving that hand and I might be."

He huffed, but his shoulders eased. "Alright, smart arse. I guess your head isn't too bad after all. But stop moving until the ambulance comes."

"No ambulance, Bear," she said flatly.

"But—"

"No ambulance," she pressed. "Your business doesn't need bad publicity. Ewan is a trainee paramedic, so if you stop terrorising the poor guy, he can check me over."

Bear raised an eyebrow but shouted for Ewan anyway.

Ewan's feet made quick tapping sounds on the stone as he came close.

"Liss says you're a trainee paramedic. Please look over her. And don't get too handsy, or you know what I'll do."

"Beat me to death with my own hands?" Ewan squeaked.

"Exactly." While Bear was distracted, Liss attempted to move the arm twisted beneath her. "Princess, if you move one more time, I will carry you to the hospital myself. Yes?"

"Yes," she conceded before mumbling, "You must have eyes in the back of your head."

"I also have acute hearing, so less of the cheek," he said close enough to make her shiver. "I was so scared, Liss."

"Me too," she said, and he held her good hand in his. She'd already broken her vow to distance herself when she saw Bear again. Something about being rescued by a distressed Bear overwhelmed her heart and sense.

He chewed his lower lip. "Just stay still while Ewan uses his professional skills to make sure you've not broken anything." He added louder, "I'm going to stay here and watch that you don't do anything dodgy. Aren't I, Ewan?"

Ewan nodded like a bobbing-headed dog before bending down and asking Liss questions to check she wasn't incoherent or disorientated. He gauged where her pain was and if her vision was okay. After that, he checked her limbs and worked with her to ensure she moved relatively painlessly. Eventually, Ewan helped ease her arm from behind her. It wasn't broken, but he'd strap it in a sling.

Bear's eyes never left her, and he never dropped his hand. At various points, his brow furrowed, and he shook his head. He placed his spare hand on his heart, and his chest moved slightly slower as if it was calming his breathing. He didn't speak all that time except when he called the ambulance to cancel it. Ewan focused on his task. It was unusual to see him so professional. He didn't notice the occasional moments that Bear opened his mouth to interject based on where Ewan was touching her, but every time Liss squeezed his hand and shot a warning glare at Bear, he shut his mouth without speaking.

Eventually, Bear's patience ran out. "How's it going there, Ewan lad?"

Ewan jumped up. "It's all good. Help me get her to the side room off the bar so I can put her arm in a sling. It's best to avoid the punters, as they'll want to see the princess."

"Good point. You get the first aid box, and I'll get her to the side room."

"Okay, Mister..."

Bear's jaw was tight. "Call me Bear. Now move. That box isn't going to collect itself."

Ewan nodded and ran off.

Bear tucked his hand beneath Liss. It was hot against her thin vest. Slowly, he eased her off the floor and hooked his arm under her good arm to support her. "You good, Liss? Because if you're not, we'll get you straight to the hospital. I'm not keen on this plan of yours."

She nodded and fought the tears that brimmed in her eyes. The realisation of how bad the fall could have been kicked in. Her body shook with a mixture of terror and the cold that settled in her bones as she lay alone at the bottom of the stairs.

"Come here, beautiful," he said softly before pulling her close. Her tears flowed freely, and she sobbed against his chest. He whispered into her hair, holding her, "It's okay. I won't let anything happen to you. I won't leave you again."

She fought the temptation to wrap her arms around him. Instead, she sagged against him and let his heat and strength heal her as an earthy and spicy aroma made her nostrils twitch.

"You smell different," she said as the tears eased. "Like a teenage boy that's doused himself in Lynx."

He pulled her away from him. He wriggled his eyebrows. "You cheeky cow. I smell like a sexy man who's returned from exploring the depths of foreign countries."

"Excuse me?" She giggled while wiping the last tears away with her hand.

"What? That's what it said on the back of the bottle. I found it at the office. I guess Luke used up all the good stuff during one of his late-night geek-outs and left his crap stuff instead." Bear looked down at his shirt, now soaked through with tears and streaked with dirt. He didn't complain though.

Fear settled in her heart, and she wasn't sure how to make it leave. "Smelling like that, you could rival Ewan when he's priming himself to chat up a punter. He's a massive fuck boy."

"He's not going near you again then. I'll do the sling myself," Bear said gruffly.

"He's a trainee paramedic," she replied, fighting the temptation to smile at his jealousy.

"And I've been in enough scrapes to know how to put a sling on someone. Ewan doesn't need to get his hands on you again," Bear pouted. His voice softened again. "But seriously, are you okay? Because we can go to the hospital or wherever else you want. I know you're worried about the business, which is sweet of you, but your safety is paramount. We don't even need to leave this cellar today."

"I don't want to stay here any longer." Her voice wobbled.

"As you wish, especially as the dirty floor has made you scummy as hell." Bear lifted her into his arms as effortlessly as if she was a toy. "But when you're feeling better, I have loads of questions about what the hell you were doing in the pub after I told you to stay where you were. I'm very interested in how you ended up in a crumpled heap at the bottom of the stairs. I'm seriously pissed off."

She winced against the pain but didn't dare tell him in case he called the ambulance again.

"Now, let's get you out of here."

Fear twisted in her stomach. Liss hugged Bear and breathed him in again. It didn't matter that he didn't smell like himself anymore because she was safe with him. Yet, as Bear carried her, she still felt that hand pushing against her back and forcing her to a place she was scared to go.

Chapter Seventeen

Bear eased her into the car like a priceless jewel at risk of harm. "Comfortable?" he asked, locking eyes with her.

"Stop staring at me with your human lie detector techniques," she replied, shifting her bum. The car smelt of leather and the body spray Bear was wearing. "I know what you're doing. Just because you stare at me like that doesn't mean you can tell if I'm lying. Also, I'm fine."

He huffed, but there was a twinkle in his eyes too. "I'm checking that you'll be okay until we get you to the hotel. I don't want you in too much pain and for me to be the cause of it. Is that really too much to ask?"

She side-eyed him as the heat of his stare penetrated any lies she might offer. "My arm hurts, and I'm sore all over, but the sooner we get back to the hotel, the sooner I can get some painkillers," she grunted.

He gave a nonsensical response and grabbed her seatbelt, leaning over her to click it in. His arm barely touched her, but at his proximity near her chest, she sat up in her seat. "Stop rubbing your tits against me," he said gruffly.

"You're the one touching them," she sassed.

"If I were touching your tits, then you'd be moaning my name and begging me to touch every part of you," he replied, still across her. He used humour to deflect anxiety too.

Liss pursed her lips. "That's what they all say until you're underneath them and they're giving you the dullest five seconds of your life."

He cupped her face and locked eyes with her. He could have kissed her in a dramatic Hollywood style, but he held her face gently and said, "Princess, I never do five seconds. When I'm with a woman, I take it slowly. I seduce her with words and then touch. I test and tease until I learn what she likes and what gets her soaking. I brush kisses to her neck." He brushed her neck with the tip of his finger. "I run my tongue over her nipples and take her to heights she's never experienced."

Liss gulped as he ran his fingers carefully across her body. Maybe he used seduction to deal with anxiety too. She should try that the next time someone pushed her down the stairs.

Bear paused briefly where her vest dipped above her chest before running his fingers to the waistband of her leggings.

"Then, when I've brought her to the edge, I stop and leave her writhing and begging before I start again. I want her to come on my fingers, my tongue, and to play with her until she can't take anymore." His voice was deep enough to make her legs quiver.

He paused longer than the five seconds other men had pleasured her. Her previous words about mistakes flashed into her mind. He'd given her too long to think.

She shook her head, and he backed off. "Sorry," he mumbled. "I need to learn better coping mechanisms for when I'm freaking out internally."

Instead of asking if that was what had happened with Mazdy, she replied, "It's okay. Let's get back to the hotel." She cradled her arm against her body.

"Liss?" Steve called from behind Bear. His eyes were wild with panic. "Are you okay?"

Bear turned to face Steve, holding him back with a hand against his chest as he tried to poke his head through the open door. Steve's lips pinched as he attempted to push past him, but the strength behind Bear's hand was enough to stop a tsunami.

"I'm fine, Steve," Liss replied, shaking her head to push away the myriad of Bear-related thoughts that clambered for her attention. "Where were you? Why did you message me to tell me to come to the pub?"

Bear's head whipped around, and he scowled at her with a fire she hadn't seen before. He spoke slowly and clearly. "That's why you came here?"

Liss pulled herself back up in the seat and took a deep breath.

Steve held his hands up in surrender. "I didn't text you."

"Yes, you did. You texted the burner Bear gave me. You put your name in the message," she argued. Bear's eyes narrowed in her direction.

Steve's arms flailed as Bear continued to push him back. "How would I know that number?" His feet stuck in the ground as he tried to get traction, but it would take a truck to get past the might of an angry Bear. "Get off me, mate!"

"I'm not your fucking mate. You and me need to have words." He turned to Liss and ensured her legs were tucked in the car. His chest rose and fell with rapid breaths. "And you, don't you go anywhere."

He slammed the door shut.

From the window, she watched as Bear pushed Steve back. It wasn't hard enough to hurt him, as he'd have been on the floor if Bear decided so. Bear didn't rant or scream, but his shoulders were tight and unmoving. Liss pressed the button to push the window down, but the car's power was off.

Steve shook his head, and his arms danced. Every time he stepped further away, Bear stepped closer. Suddenly, Bear turned and glared at Liss before striding to the driver's door. He opened it as he shouted at Steve, now frozen in place, "I'll tell Liss that you were worried about her, but let me make something clear, I don't fucking trust you."

He slammed the door.

They'd made it halfway to the hotel before she spoke. His knuckles were white where he gripped the wheel, and even from her side-eye, she saw his skin was mottled.

"Get out of my fucking way," he shouted at an old lady in a little red car.

"She's driving within the speed limit," Liss replied in defence of the stranger.

"Don't you dare talk to me." He turned to stare at her before yanking the steering wheel and turning left. Cars beeped at his lack of indication. "Why would you go to the pub because Steve messaged you? How little do you care about your safety?"

Liss stared at him. Occasionally, he'd glance at the road before returning to face her.

"Well, answer me then!"

Liss folded her arms and huffed exaggeratedly. "You told me not to 'dare talk to you,'" she replied curtly and looked away.

"Don't play games with me, Liss," he said through gritted teeth. "You won't win."

Her head snapped back to scowl at him as he parked in the hotel's secured car park. "Says the man who one moment gives me the greatest kiss of my life and the next is shouting at me like I'm a child."

She threw open the door and ran for the stairwell on her shaky legs. She wouldn't get the lift with Bear. She pushed open the door to the stairs and ran up them, but he wasn't far behind, and with his long legs, he was taking them two or three at once.

Suddenly, he caught up as she turned between flights of stairs. He walked her backwards until her shoulders hit the wall. Cold air breezed through the stairwell, but her body burnt against the fire radiating from him. Her limbs shook as he stood in front of her. Their toes touched, and he held his hand out, desperate to touch her but too scared to do it.

"What did you mean about that kiss being the greatest of your life? I thought you said it was a mistake," he growled.

Suddenly, Bear's phone rang, and his eye twitched. The tune was familiar. It was a song by Mazdy.

Liss set her jaw and replied between gritted teeth as Luke's words returned to her like lava from a volcano, "It doesn't matter. It was a mistake. I'm not another client who you fuck with."

Chapter Eighteen

Bear recoiled at Liss's comment as if slapped. His brow furrowed as he stared at her, and he stepped away like she'd accused him of something hideous.

The temperature change left Liss shivering. He turned and walked down the stairs, slower this time. He grabbed his phone and cancelled the call. Silence filled the stairwell.

"Why are you going down the stairs?" she stuttered.

"Because we can't get directly to the suite via the main stairs, and the lift is safer." Bear didn't hold the door open for her at the bottom, although he waited for her to get in the lift before he joined her.

As the lift rose to their floor, she uttered, "I went to the pub because I thought something had happened. I messaged Isla earlier as I needed to talk to someone. She didn't reply, but Steve messaged and said something had happened at the pub." She didn't owe him anything, yet the need to stop him from hating her was like a banshee wailing in her stomach. She couldn't ignore it.

Bear kept his back to her as she talked. At Steve's name, he bristled, but he remained silent. "I got Isla's number by calling the pub. I wasn't trying to risk my safety, but I needed to check everything was okay."

"But you did," he replied flatly.

"I did what?"

"You did risk your safety."

The lift pinged, and the doors opened into the suite. Bear walked out, and she followed behind him. Liss kicked off her shoes and let the carpet squidge around her toes. It was the only comfort she was going to get. Bear strode around the suite. His hands shook as he checked all the rooms and any place considered a safety risk.

"Could you strap up my arm now?" she asked when he turned on the television and flicked through the channels, eventually picking a music one.

He stared at her blankly, and she prepared to fight him, but instead, he walked across the room and grabbed a green box. "Sit," he barked toward the chair in the corner. The fight was leaving her, and she sat obediently. It seemed like a lifetime ago when she was starting her last shift in the pub, and since then, everything had transformed, including her attraction to Bear. It came from nowhere, and she couldn't control it.

He knelt beside her and fashioned the sling to fit her arm.

"I risked it for my family," she said quietly.

His face was unreadable, but his words cut her with the edge. "Steve isn't your family."

"Everyone at the pub is my family. They're the only family I have," she justified, wincing when he touched her arm. "When my mum got ill, I had to leave university and care for her. But I needed to pay for food and bills, so Hugo, the owner, let me have a job. He even gave me shifts that fit around caring for my mum."

She spun her ring as Bear continued to work on her sling. He tested the knot at her neck and worked it more. "And then your mum died," he said. Not "then you lost her" or "when she passed" or the other things she hated people saying if they said anything at all.

"Yes. And suddenly, the pub was all I had. I threw myself into my work. I was productive, and I had value, and the place improved too. Eventually, I became deputy manager and then manager. It doesn't compare to having a real family, but it was like filler that you put in cracks on a wall. It doesn't fix them, not really."

This was the longest she'd been away from the pub since her mum died. Without the place filling her days, the pub meant less to her.

Bear's words distracted her from her thoughts. "It's like the cracks are still there, but you can't see them, and they're not as damaging," he replied, his hand covering hers to still her spinning ring. It wasn't like he was trying to counsel or give her space to speak. It was as if he knew and understood what being alone meant. His eyes appeared glassy, and he blinked several times before clearing his throat. "I was worried when I found you at the bottom of the stairs. I know our kiss was a mistake, but, but…please don't do anything like that again, because I can't bear anything happening to you." He wasn't talking about her from a professional standpoint anymore. "And if you need to rescue someone, let me know, and we can go together. Deal?"

Liss nodded as she stared into his deep brown eyes. "Deal."

"Thank you for telling me about your mum. I can't imagine how painful it was to go through her death and the years since, especially as you were alone. But you're not alone now. You have me and Strike. I'm not going anywhere." He squeezed her hand like he had in the cellar.

It filled her entire body with a glowing warmth. "How did you fall down the stairs?"

Liss explained the lights going off in the corridor and that she'd heard something in the cellar as Bear worked on her sling.

"Does it hurt anywhere else?" He was softer now, but she debated mentioning the hand pushing her. He wouldn't believe her anyway.

"My knees," she replied as if that would divert his other questions.

His hands brushed her legs as he rolled up her leggings. Blood caked at her knees, but the sting was a welcome distraction.

"It's a surface wound from when you fell, but I'll clean it up for you." He left the room and returned with a bowl of hot water and a flannel.

"What aren't you telling me?" he asked, resuming his place below her. His eyelashes framed his eyes, which shone with concern. His relentless touch and genuine care were too much, especially after everything. "Did something else happen in the cellar?"

She contemplated her answer as he squeezed the flannel in the water.

"This will sting, but you're strong enough to deal with it."

At the hot cloth against her wounds, her breath hitched.

"It's okay," he soothed. "Now tell me what you're not telling me." Bear cleaned her wounds and carefully wiped the blood away.

"Someone pushed me," she relented, confident that his human lie-detector skills would get to the truth eventually. "A hand was at my back at the top of the stairs.

I can't prove it, and you guys didn't see anyone, but... Maybe I'm imagining it."

"Or maybe you should trust yourself." He sat back on his feet. "We'll get to the bottom of this."

He dried her skin with a second cloth and added plasters to her knees. "And I'm sorry again for earlier. I shouldn't have gotten angry. I know what it's like to want a family."

Liss held her breath. Bear was sharing a rare moment of vulnerability, and although it only added to her questions, she kept her mouth firmly shut for fear of scaring him.

"Are we friends again?" he asked as his hands squeezed her calves.

"Yeah, we're friends." She twisted her mouth to the side, unable to smile.

At that point, his phone rang. It was the same Madzy ringtone as before. Bear turned and cancelled it. The muscles in his back flexed as he took deep breaths.

"Luke said you were her...bodyguard," she said, her voice going up at the last word. She counted to ten while waiting for him to shut the conversation down.

"Yes."

"And?" she replied, elongating the word.

Still, he didn't turn. "And there's nothing else to say about it except it's not what you think. And Luke shouldn't be talking about clients. It's private."

She huffed under her breath. "That's not what I heard."

As he turned, his face was blank, but the twitch of his eye was a giveaway. "Things aren't always as they seem. You can choose to believe me or not." His eye twitched again. "But you can't trust every person, even those you've known for years."

He shoved his hands in his pockets and walked towards the kitchen part of the suite.

"Bear." Liss jumped up and banged her arm in the process. Her howl brought him back to her immediately.

"Bloody hell, woman." He held her tenderly. Her heart ached, but it was pointless. He was her bodyguard and nothing more. Maybe his way of getting in her head was part of his appeal. She'd meant what she said about the kiss. But she barely knew him. Maybe he was purely her coping mechanism for the new drama in her life. "Have you caused more damage, Liss?"

She shook her head as he investigated. He ran his thumb gently over her wrist. Her breath hitched. She followed his touch with her gaze and revelled in the burn it left. Was it so wrong to embrace her attraction if it helped and gave her a bit of calm?

"Maybe you should kiss it better," she stammered, blinking in surprise at her words. He wasn't a good guy, but his actions suggested she had him wrong. She was probably just another horny woman overwhelmed by her emotions and unable to resist Bear's seduction.

He looked up at her. His eyes crackled with intent. Bear bowed his head, but his gaze refused to leave her eyes as he brushed his lips across the pulse point of her inner wrist.

"Your heartbeat is frantic, Princess. Should I be worried about you?" His chest rose with every deep breath.

Her words caught in her throat.

"Is there something wrong with your mouth? Do I need to kiss that better too?" His voice was deep and gruff.

She tried to hide her smile, but it pulled at the corners of her mouth. She licked her lips as Bear tipped her chin with his finger. "These lips could do with some attention."

Anticipation and arousal owned her body, and her head swam, threatening her balance. She held onto his bicep, careful not to squeeze it like an inexperienced teenager, as he leaned in.

"Hold on tight," he taunted her. She'd read in love stories about the heroine's knees going weak, but she'd thought writers overplayed it for dramatic effect. Yet her legs trembled, and Liss gripped him harder.

She closed her eyes, and her tongue teased her lower lip.

RING RING.

At the hotel intercom, Bear leant his forehead against hers. His lips brushed hers as delicately as if he'd used a feather to tease her.

"Saved by the bell," she whispered against him.

"Anyone would think you were relieved," Bear replied as he headed to the hotel phone. "We need to stop doing that."

He was unreadable as he flipped to his professional mode when answering the call. "Describe her," he grunted. The person on the other end must have passed whatever the test was because he followed with a "Send her up."

"Have you eaten?" he asked Liss.

She shook her head. "But I'm not really hungry."

He stared her down as he told reception, "And send up four burgers, fries, and all the puddings."

He replaced the phone in its cradle as she protested, "I said I'm not hungry."

"As far as I know, you've barely eaten today and are

about to take painkillers. You're eating."

She glared back at him. But the way he told her what to do made that heat between her legs continue to burn. She'd spent her life with independence forced upon her and unable to trust anyone, yet she was putty in Bear's hands after four days.

"I can't eat four burgers and all the puddings," she pouted with narrowed eyes.

"You keep pouting like that, and I won't call you good girl again." His eyes darkened, and a flush heated her cheeks. He'd not mentioned it since the night he slept in her room. Why did that do something to her, and what filthy thoughts would he give her next? In subtle ways that probably meant nothing to him, he was teaching her about her wants in a way she hadn't experienced before. She glanced at his hands and imagined them sliding into her leggings. "Interesting. And for your information, two of the burgers are for me, and I got an extra one because Isla is on her way up. Now be a good girl and get ready for our guest."

"I hate you."

"You tell your rosy cheeks that," he said with lips so full she wanted to slap them off his face.

"I will fuck you up."

The lift dinged, announcing Isla's arrival. "Save that for later when your arm's healed. I look forward to being fucked up by you," he said, although he shook his head and face-palmed as soon as he spoke.

Returning to banter rather than sharing painfully personal things was almost a relief. Liss liked both Bear's sweet and naughty sides, even though they had the power to destroy her.

Isla jumped out of the lift, oblivious to the cage of

sexual tension she'd walked in on.

"Liss, oh my god, your arm. What happened? Steve called me and told me you were hurt at the pub. What were you doing there?"

Bear shook his head. "I need to make a couple of private calls. Would it be okay if you two went into the bedroom?" He was unexpectedly polite. "I'll bring the food in when it arrives."

"And painkillers."

"I wouldn't forget those, Princess. I never forget pain relief," he replied before rubbing a hand down his face and mouthing, "For fucks sake, Bear."

If her supposed attacker didn't kill her first, then Bear would be the death of her. She let out a slow breath. What a way to go, in the sexiest blaze of glory imaginable.

Chapter Nineteen

"Tell me everything," Isla demanded as she closed the door to the bedroom.

Liss stared out the window, giving her burning cheeks the time to cool. Tall buildings crowded the small space of the city, and in the distance, sports grounds and local landmarks littered the area. She bit the inside of her mouth as she focused on the tiny people-shaped spots below.

"Hey, Liss," Isla called out as if she'd been talking for a while. "What is going on between you two? I can't tell if you hate each other or want to fuck each other, but either way, it's the hottest thing I've seen in ages. I'm guessing the book helped."

Liss turned to find Isla with her hands on her hips. Thank god her best friend was here after everything. "Coming from the woman who's screwed Ewan in the last six months, and I'm ignoring the book comment." Liss chuckled. Isla smirked and flicked her hair. "Could you help me get changed? I want something soft and cuddly to wear."

Isla slowly helped Liss out of the sling and her leggings, vest, and bra before putting her in fluffy pyjama bottoms and T shirt while discussing the enigma that was Ewan.

"Do you shout ballbags when you come?" Liss asked, resting against the bed's headboard.

Isla burst into laughter. "Is that what he said? The cheeky twat." Tears ran down her cheeks, and she gasped for breath.

A knock came at the door.

"Enter," Liss shouted. Smells of burgers and freshly cooked chips wafted through the door. It mixed with the scents of caramel, chocolates, and raspberries. Her belly rumbled louder than Isla's laughter.

A bemused Bear lifted the food as he stood at the doorway's threshold. "Is she okay?" he asked as Isla gasped for breath.

"No first aid needed here," Liss replied as drool collected in her mouth. "We're talking about Isla's eventful sex life."

"Hey." Isla threw a pillow. Liss ducked, and it hit the headboard.

"I'll go," he said, popping the food on the bed and backing away.

Isla and Liss shouted for him to stay and eat with them.

The hint of a smile crossed his face before disappearing as quickly. "Okay, but then I have other work." He pulled painkillers out of his pocket before leaving the room and returning with drinks from the fridge. "No alcohol while you're on these. Not that you two need it," he added under his breath before sitting in the chair at the edge of the bedroom.

Liss ripped her burger apart with the ferocity of a panther. She moaned orgasmically as the sauce filled her mouth and the melted cheese covered her tongue. As she groaned a second time, she sensed attention. Bear tracked her hunger with licking lips and a shift in his seat.

Liss's blush remained as she gulped down her pills and drink. Bear continued to watch her, only this time, her throat held his attention.

"Ummm, yeah, where were we?" Liss asked as heat climbed her chest. "Oh yeah. You shout 'ballbags' when you come."

Isla grinned around a chip. "I do not," she replied. "I say it when a man comes, and I don't. And when he offers me no release yet thinks he's done. Arsehole."

Bear winced. Occasionally, his gaze would flick up to Liss before returning to his food.

Liss wiped the sauce off her lips with the back of her hand.

"The most depressing thing is that it's not unusual," Isla added before taking a huge bite of her burger.

"I should go," Bear mumbled. "I'm not sure I need to be here for this."

"We might need a male perspective," Liss added. She didn't want him to go. His presence grounded her after everything that had happened that day.

Bear scowled at his second burger. "Fine, but I'm leaving when I've finished eating," he said between bites.

Liss popped a chip in her smirking mouth as if she'd won an hour of verbal sparring rather than get him to stay a little longer. "What were you saying, Isla? What do you mean it's not unusual?" Liss asked with her mouth still full of chips. From years working in the pub, she learnt you can't stop for anything, including eating. She covered her mouth with her hand to attempt a slither of etiquette; she might be a princess, after all. She might have to have behaviour classes!

"I miss fucking," Isla grumbled.

"But you've slept with at least four guys this year," Liss

commented, licking the sauce off her fingers. Bear shifted in his seat again.

Isla reeled off a list of names while tapping her fingers as she counted them. "It's more like six. But that's not the point. I miss fucking. That moment when you're desperate for someone in that animalistic way. When you rip their clothes off or, even better, when you leave the clothes on because you want them inside you that second. You know what I mean. A really hard fuck."

Liss pondered briefly. "I've had sex, so I guess I get what you mean. I've had kisses like that." She refused to look at Bear, but her gaze drifted that way when she added, "But not in sex. Like I've experienced nice sex."

Bear raised his eyebrows as he took another bite of his burger.

"Kisses and nice sex are not fucking, Liss. Sex shouldn't be nice. It can be sweet and gentle and loving but never nice. You've slept with several guys."

Liss shrugged and gave a noncommittal, "I guess."

"From what you've said about the guys you've slept with, especially that one where everything needed to be clean and planned, I can't imagine that was hard fucking." Liss nodded in agreement. "But what about the guy at university you picked up a month before you left? Wasn't that fucking?"

Bear's burger held his attention, but his eyes widened every time Liss spoke.

"His name was Bryan," Liss replied. "Or was it Ryan? We didn't have sex. I gave him a blow job, and he said it was the best he'd had."

Bear coughed loudly. "The chip went the wrong way," he mumbled before sipping his drink.

Liss sighed as she shook her head. "But there wasn't anyone like you describe."

"You must have had a good fuck though?" Isla demanded incredulously. "Why didn't I know this before?"

Liss eyed the puddings. "The guy from a couple of years ago was okay. But the two times we did it, his cat scratched at the door, and he kept getting texts. It was never that passionate, desperate for each other sex. And with the other one, it was more like a cup of tea at the end of a long day."

"Fucking hell." Isla blew out a breath. "So it was like nice sex then. Not the other kind?"

Liss shrugged. "I'm not sure. It wasn't bad sex."

"This isn't right. 'Not bad sex' isn't even good sex, let alone the fucking I'm talking about. Help me out here, Bear. I bet you've experienced hard, mind-blowing fucks in your time."

"Don't involve me," Bear grunted, but he continued to peek at Liss from beneath his eyelashes.

"Seriously, Bear. Don't you think Liss needs a good fucking? You need bending over furniture and being fucked until you scream." It might have been Isla saying the words, but Bear's eyes widened as he gave Liss his full attention.

Sweat beaded his forehead, and he rubbed the back of his neck. His ears developed that familiar pink tinge.

"Bear, you okay?" Liss asked.

He swallowed loudly before jumping up. "You've got your puddings, and I've got work to do," he replied, fumbling for his drink as he bolted from the room.

Liss was wide-eyed as he reached the door. She wanted him to stay, yet he was her bodyguard with a reputation as a player. *I need to get a grip.* Her cheeks burnt hot, and she finished her drink and snapped up the pudding. The freezing ice cream on her tongue highlighted rather than quelled the heat of her attraction for him.

"So all this time, I've missed out on great sex?" Liss stuttered as the ice cream slid down her throat. Do you think Bear ran out of here because he was embarrassed for me?"

"Honey, based on what was going on in his trousers, I don't think so."

"Oh," Liss replied. Her face burnt hotter. "Ummm, let's talk about anything else instead."

"If you're sure." Isla's eyebrows were high as if she was expecting more, but when Liss didn't speak, she carried on. "And you can tell me why Steve was still losing his shit with worry when he called me."

"Steve? Bear had a word with him as we left. They don't like each other."

"I'm not surprised."

Liss eyeballed her friend. "What do you mean?"

"You haven't worked out why Steve still works at the pub? Why he'll always work at the pub as long as you're there?" Isla sighed. "I thought you knew."

"Knew what?" Liss asked, still hauling ice cream into her mouth.

Isla ran a hand slowly down her face. "It's not for me to tell you. He needs to, or I must create a situation where he can." Before Liss could ask what she meant, Isla changed the subject. "Now, tell me about the fall. Did one of the ghosts trip you?"

Chapter Twenty

An hour later, there was a loud knock at the door. Maybe Bear had decided he wanted to continue the earlier conversation. Liss shouted, "You can only come in to eat chocolate and talk sex." She and Isla giggled.

The door flew open, and Strike strode through it. "I'd like a word with Liss, Isla."

Liss winced. She wasn't in the mood for another Strike lecture. She glanced at Isla for support, but she was checking her phone.

Isla jumped up and collected her stuff. "Shit. I should have met with my brother half an hour ago." She grabbed the apple crumble. "I'm taking this. If you need me, give me a call. Make sure you sleep well tonight, as you've been through too much recently and need rest."

Liss nodded as Strike glowered at both of them.

Isla hugged Liss quickly and whispered, "Don't let that one bully you. I bet his bark is worse than his bite." She waved to Strike, he ignored her, and she ran to the lift.

Liss wetted her finger and stabbed at the remaining crumbs of the strawberry cheesecake. It was the only pudding left, bar the chocolate torte she'd saved to share with Bear. She needed to stop fangirling over him, especially considering the Mazdy thing.

Strike cracked his neck before grunting his reason for being there. "The palace gave instructions for you to be there tomorrow first thing. I'm guessing the results are in." If Bear was closed off, Strike was locked in a prison cell on a deserted island. The guy was stoic and unfeeling. Didn't he realise how significant a piece of news that might be to her?

Bear would have tried to soften the blow by leading into it. She chased another crumb around the bowl before stabbing it with her finger. It clung to her like she was a life raft before falling off and joining its crumb friends.

"I expect you ready by nine a.m. Bear and I will take you." It was like a military command rather than a trip to the palace to determine if she was a princess. Tomorrow could change her life forever.

"Where is Bear?" She kept her head down and focused on the crumbs, concerned what she might reveal. Strike might release Bear from duty if he knew her feelings. She wasn't ready for him to be gone from her life yet. She ground her teeth. She barely knew him, yet seeing Strike walk through the door rather than Bear, the ball of hope that grew every second she was with him shattered into smithereens, filling every vein with despondency.

"He's with our other client." Maybe he was treating that client with the same mixture of care and seduction he gave Liss. "And then he's on an overnight break. I'll be here to ensure you don't leave like you did before."

"I'm not a prisoner," she snapped. But hurt ruled her angering heart more than being trapped. Bear had made her promises. When he'd rescued her at the pub, he'd promised he wouldn't leave her side. She gritted her teeth, remembering the vulnerable story she'd shared with him.

No one saw that side of her, and shame filled her that she couldn't take it back. She was a silly girl with a crush.

Strike scowled. "We're trying our best to keep you safe. You saw what happened when you didn't listen to instructions. Do as we say, and you'll live." He cracked his neck again. "This business is important to us, and we have a reputation to uphold. You're not helping that."

Liss squeezed her lips. If they spoke to them like this, it was a surprise they'd any clients.

He let out a breath infused with contempt. "And another thing. Stop dicking around with Bear."

"Dicking around?"

"This business is important to both of us, and he can't have a distraction like you." Her face stung. "He's more vulnerable than he lets on. If you respect or care about him—a virtual stranger, I might add—back off and treat him as professionally as he's trying to treat you."

Like the moment he kissed me like I've never been kissed before?

Strike's lips were pinched. Briefly, he and Liss remained like this, neither of them giving an inch.

Finally, Strike snarled, "You wouldn't be the first client to try and seduce your bodyguard, and you won't be the last. Bear doesn't need that shit, so cut it out."

"Are we done here?" she snapped.

Strike slammed the bedroom door. Liss threw a pillow at it. The loud thud garnered no response. So Bear was off-limits. That was fine because he'd not stayed as he promised. He was probably fucking Mazdy, and that was fine too. Everything was fucking fine. Liss was used to being alone, so nothing changed. Her ears pounded as she gripped the duvet.

Chapter Twenty-One

"Wake up, Princess. We've got to go in ten minutes," someone shouted. It was like she was flailing at the bottom of a well full of water and couldn't bring herself out. A hand touched her cheek, slowly coaxing her awake.

Eventually, she opened her eyes. She rubbed the exhaustion away from them and yawned loudly. "Ouch. *Motherfucker*." Suddenly, the last week came flooding back: the meeting with royalty, the fall at the pub, and Bear. Her sleep had been so deep.

"How many painkillers did you take last night?" Bear asked as his thumb brushed her cheek. His face was close, and he furrowed his brow as he touched her. She remembered Strike's warning to stay away from Bear and recoiled from his touch. As much as she didn't respect Strike's words, she didn't want to cause problems for Bear or have anything to do with him.

He stepped back, and his face momentarily dropped before he replaced it with a mask of ambivalence. "You needed rest, but that means we've only got ten minutes. I'll leave you to get dressed and see you by the lift ASAP."

He strode out of the room before she could explain her flinch. Not that she owed him that.

It was her DNA test results day, and she didn't have

time to shower. They should have roused her sooner.

Liss braved the mirror and blanched. Dark circles settled under her eyes, and her hair desperately attempted to leave her scalp at multiple angles. A quick smell of her underarms made her reel. She couldn't go to the palace smelling like off cheese.

Everything hurt as she moved around the room. With the pain in her arm and a time limit, she'd only manage a sink shower. Isla had named it that during university when she dramatically threw water at herself and practically flooded the shared bathroom.

Liss smiled at the memory until Bear bellowed, "Eight minutes!" from the other room.

She quickly cleaned her teeth, tossed water at herself, and dressed. She paraded into the room with one minute to spare.

"You okay?" Bear asked as they stepped into the lift. Liss caught her reflection. She resembled a hungover ghost.

"I'm fine," she replied curtly.

"You seem off." He side-eyed her, and she shrugged. If he was waiting for an explanation, he was out of luck. Strike's warning replayed as the plinky-plonky lift music encroached on her thoughts. Maybe Bear woke her late because he'd only just returned from seeing Mazdy or another fuck buddy. She stared anywhere but at him as jealousy pinched her belly. Liss grimaced as she shifted her arm in the sling. The painkillers hadn't kicked in, but it was a little better. "Is your arm okay? Are you nervous about today?"

"I said I'm fine, Bear." She winced at her tone.

"Right." He released a huff of air.

The wounds in Liss's heart opened deeper. Liss kicked herself at her teen behaviour.

The lift doors opened at the parking garage, and Bear led her to the four-by-four where Strike waited.

He offered to help her in. "Because of your arm." But Liss shrugged him off and struggled into the car by herself.

Again, he huffed but didn't say anything. Liss caught Strike's reflection in the rear-view mirror. He gave her a nod. *I didn't do it for you.* The words teased the tip of her tongue, but she stared out the window.

The car was silent, but Liss reflected on her future as the green parks turned into skyscrapers and the vivid spring colours became muted greys and concrete shelters with no spaces between them. Everything would change after this meeting. Today, she'd learn if she was royalty and part of an establishment. Maybe the test would be negative, and she'd return to her life, pulling pints and laughing with punters about the royals by the evening.

Her nana was adamant she was the King's granddaughter. What would it mean to have a family? Growing up without money and struggling for every meal was okay. She and her mum were a force against the world and made the best of all they had, but there was something else. Liss had always missed having siblings or cousins to play with. Her dad had disappeared before her birth. He didn't want children and made that clear by avoiding all contact. She'd tried to find him when her mum was ill, but either he'd left the country or changed his name, because he remained incommunicado. That's when the pub and the strangers in it became her family.

But today, all that might change. Liss couldn't ignore ties to the royal family and their history anymore. She twisted her hair with trembling fingers, and her teeth quietly chattered. The situation was epic. Bigger than epic.

I can't do this.

She'd been confident and rude when she'd met with them last time, but her nana had been with her, and Liss hadn't understood the moment's importance. Everything with Bear over the previous days was a distraction, but today, she was alone. The King or his family might talk her into making a decision she didn't want. She could destroy her whole life in one meeting.

"Are you okay, Liss?" Bear's eyes were like saucers.

Her mouth turned down, and she squeezed her lips together. She tried to keep it together on the surface. She wasn't ready to change her life forever. She fisted her hands. *I don't know if I want this.*

"She's fine," Strike snapped. "She's a big girl who can handle her own problems."

A look of confusion and annoyance passed between Bear and Strike. But the conflict between the two of them couldn't stop her rapid breathing.

"We're here," Strike announced, nodding to the gatekeeper. The car rolled down a long driveway. They were in a different place this time. "It's St. Peter's Palace."

Her trembles turned to shakes and traversed her body. Her shoulders wouldn't keep still.

Bear slid his hand back and held it out to her. She reached for it and held it tightly. His skin was warm against hers.

"Bear," Strike warned.

Bear swatted his hand. "Fuck off, Strike. She's freaking out, and I won't watch it happen when I can help."

"And that's exactly the problem when it comes to you."

"Don't," Bear snapped before fixing his attention on Liss. "You've got this, Liss. You're safe. Today is a meeting, and you're not committing to anything."

His thumb stroked the pulse point inside her wrist, and she recalled his lips brushing against it the day before.

"I'm going to ask you to let go of me," he said. Liss's pulse increased further. Her vision blurred at the edges as if the world was closing in on her. "But then put your good hand on your heart instead. It will help your breathing." She stared at him with wide eyes. Lines covered his forehead, but he continued to run his thumb around her pulse point. "Trust me," he said, showing her what he meant with his spare hand. He did the same the day before in the basement.

She removed her hand from his caress. Instantly, she missed the warmth of his touch. She copied his action while ensuring she didn't strain her arm again.

"It's a simple technique to relieve stress. You can do it anywhere, no matter what is happening around you. It helps you focus on your heart or breathing. I don't know how it works, but I learnt it years ago, and it works for me."

Liss focused on the connection between her hand and her heart. She gulped down air, and her breathing slowed. Bear's voice was deep and soothing as he counted her breathing in and out. Liss closed her eyes as her body calmed, and when she opened them again, the blurriness was gone.

"You okay?" Bear asked, his eyes wide with concern.

She nodded and mouthed a "thank you" as Strike parked the car.

"You got this, Princess. We'll be in the room with you the whole time, and no matter what happens, you have a say in this," he said. His voice kept that softness that got her through her panic. It flowed through her and brought confidence with it. She could do this. She had to do it. "Ready?"

Liss offered a tentative smile, and Bear reflected it before his face entered bodyguard mode. She recognised it now. It was like the second before a fighter went into the ring. He was centring himself and preparing for battle. She glanced at Strike, who did the same. Liss prepared herself as the men had. She took a deep breath and erased emotion from her face. She set her chin and let coldness reflect in her eyes.

"Let's do this," she said as Bear helped her out of the car and led them into the palace.

Chapter Twenty-Two

"Felicity," the King called from the entrance of the palace. The archway he stood beneath glinted like the stone was infused with royal jewels. But the rest of the building carried a coldness, from the straight lines of architecture to the shadows under the other archways lining it. The windows lining the building were tiny; all she spied was black inside the framed white holes. It was like a prison.

"Welcome," he said as she neared him. His eyes wore the same dark circles as hers, and there was exhaustion she hadn't recognised before. She felt a pull to care for him. His mysterious illness was destroying him. All the money and influence in the world couldn't stop death once it knocked on the door.

Liss recalled the searing pain that twisted her mum's body in her final days and the nights she sat and watched her breathing, wondering if it would be their last moments together. The deterioration was fast at the end, and although the nurses were excellent, in those early hours after they went home, Liss remembered the sensation of her chest crushed by force. The only person Liss loved was gone; she'd never have her mum back. Maybe money and influence could have provided better pain relief and given her hope. Would they be standing here together, her mum learning if she was the King's daughter?

The King embraced Liss gently to avoid squashing her arm, and as much as it felt like she was being unfaithful to her mum's memory, she allowed the hug. He held her for a few seconds, and she relaxed, wrapping her good arm around his body. He was skinnier than she expected and smelt of antiseptic.

As he released her, his face shone with a grin wide enough to surround her in love. She didn't need test results to tell her what that smile meant. She was a princess.

Fucking hell.

"I'd like to talk in private if that's okay," he said, leading her into a drawing room like the one she'd sat in at the other palace. Where that was red and gold, this was royal blue and wood. Emerald green added accents to the edges of carpets and high-backed chairs. It wasn't to her taste, but it wasn't her house. A comfy corner sofa would have worked wonders. Suddenly, she focused on the other two things she wouldn't want in her house.

Marianne, who sat in one of the wooden and, no doubt, hand-crafted side chairs, spied her like a bird ready to peck a bug to death. Standing stiffly next to her, with his hand resting on Marianne's chair, was Prince Alex, and his gaze, although guarded, betrayed a contempt that surprised her. Their faces read "How can we bury you without anyone knowing?" rather than "Welcome to the family."

Red roses sat on the tables in crystal vases, and Liss teetered on the edge of smelling them to rid the antiseptic scent from her nostrils, but a red and blue porcelain pheasant caught her eye. Liss sensed Marianne and Alex's eyes burning a hole into her neck. Maybe they thought she was hoping to steal the bird. As if she'd want anything that gaudy.

Liss turned to see the King smiling at her. "I'd rather have my bodyguards in the room, King Archibald." Bear and Strike nodded and stood at the side. Bear's eyes softened when he glanced at her, and she remembered what it was like to have her hand on her heart. She took a breath and raised her body before sitting. Maybe great posture would help her confidence too. It worked for Marianne.

"If you're sure, then that's fine," he replied, although his stuttered response suggested it went against protocol. "And you can call me grandfather if you wish."

"Spoiler alert," Liss replied with a smile.

Alex grumbled something under his breath. Bear glared in his direction before resuming his blank stare.

"Oh yes. I haven't explained, have I? Before I do, please tell me you were okay after your fall." His smile made his eyes crinkle, and she fought the temptation to forget the worries about her future and embrace that she had a family now. "I heard that something happened in your pub."

"You're well informed," she replied. "I sprained my wrist, but it's healing quickly. The painkillers worked their magic on my sleep last night, but I didn't have the opportunity to put more effort into my appearance today."

"We'd noticed," Marianne replied with puckered pink lips. She looked like a cat's anus.

Liss sucked her lower lip into her mouth. The urge to fight back clawed at her skin, but her mum taught her to ignore bullies.

"Don't worry at all. That you're here is more than we can ask for. Besides, there will be plenty of opportunities for you to dress up, including tomorrow night," the King replied, clapping his hands together.

"Don't forget to take your tea," Marianne said, nodding at the cup on the King's coffee table. Or was it a side table? Princesses should know the difference.

The King's voice was raspy as he said, "These two are good to me. They've flown in the best doctor in the world to help me. Their caring is more than I could ask for."

They didn't seem caring, but Liss had infiltrated the family. She wanted to learn more about his illness but needed to ease the tension with Alex and Marianne. There would be time to talk to the King. "That is lovely. But did you say something about me dressing up tomorrow?"

"We're having a party in your honour. It's mostly for close friends and family. We will announce that you are part of our family and a princess." Dread crept into Liss's belly. "It won't be a big affair but a way to celebrate you. Isn't it wonderful?"

"I'm not sure I..." Liss stammered. "I haven't decided if I'll accept the role of princess yet."

"This party isn't you announcing what you want, although I'm sure we will consider that fact," Alex said, rolling his eyes to Marianne as if Liss wasn't there. "This is the opportunity for my father to recognise your place in the family."

"Exactly," the King rushed to add. Liss dropped her chin. The King wanted to do something nice for her. "It's my way of welcoming you. Whatever you decide, you will always be family."

"Is it because you think you're better than us? Or are you one of those lower-class fools against royalty? How bloody imbecilic," Marianne muttered.

The audacity of a stranger to say that to her. She

should have graciously welcomed the King's idea, which was her fault, but Marianne didn't need to be offensive. Her mum would have told her to hold her tongue. Bear cleared his throat, and his chin hardened.

"Oh, she's spinning her ring again. Watch out," Marianne quipped before chortling.

Liss was thrown back to her last visit to the palace when they'd questioned her royal status, and now they expected her to welcome it with open arms. Her stomach burned, forcing words from her mouth. "You're hardly making me want to participate in this family if you're an example of it." The corner of Bear's mouth raised slightly. It only hinted at his amusement but allowed her gumption to flourish. "It's a lot to take in, and I don't want to enter into something rashly. I need to learn more about what it entails and what I will agree to first. My mum didn't bring me up to avoid hard graft. Not that I'm saying that's what—"

"How dare you?" Marianne snapped. Liss hadn't meant for it to sound like that. Her pulse quickened, and her ears pounded. "Do you understand how humiliating it is for this family to have someone brought up like you associated with it? And you don't think you want to be part of it?"

"Aren't you marrying into this family? So you're not technically part of it yet either," Liss replied, butting heads. Words continued to tumble out of her mouth. "Besides, before I was rudely interrupted, I was trying to show my due diligence by ensuring I had all the information. It's not like I want to let the name down. I want to be able to help people and not just cut ribbons."

Bear cleared his throat loudly, and she took a breath.

She went too far with the ribbons bit. She needed to be kinder.

Marianne's eyes blazed, and Liss pressed her fingers against her lips, but at the King's laugh, everyone stared at him.

"She's disrespectful, sir," Marianne fumed as she repeatedly smoothed her pleated skirt.

Between guffaws, he replied, "She has a point. You cut a ribbon yesterday." His laughter became coughs that were like a dog's barks. He winced, and tears leaked from his eyes.

Suddenly, a man dressed in white appeared. "Let's pop you on a ventilator. You want to be at your best for tomorrow night," he said in an accent Liss couldn't place. The King gave Liss a brief hug before leaving the room. It was all so quick that she didn't have the opportunity to thank him or ask how he was.

"The ribbon cutting was a hospital." Marianne stood and stamped her foot. "I don't have time for this, because instead of planning my wedding, I have a party for a pleb to organise. The utter disgrace."

Marianne stormed out of the room, leaving a wide-eyed Alex in her wake. Liss stared at the gilt-edged mirror covering a wall. She saw both bodyguards and the rest of the room through it. Bear made brief eye contact and winked at her. Flutters filled her belly. She was supposed to be avoiding him.

Eventually, Alex sat close to Liss. "I'm sorry about that. She's not normally so rude." Liss bit her tongue at her retort. It seemed unlikely that Marianne was sweetness and light. But maybe it was time to give the family the benefit of the doubt, as they were her family now, and that was all she'd ever longed for. "But the wedding is in six months, and she's found the organising stressful. This announcement about you has stolen some of her thunder too."

That was fair. No one wanted their wedding ruined by a usurper, especially a reluctant, bratty one like Liss.

"But I should apologise for myself too. I was rude when you were here before and today too. It's a lot to come to terms with. My father explained after he made the live announcement that learning he had another daughter he'd never meet and couldn't be there for as she died nearly destroyed him. Our relationship is strained, but that's not your fault. Will you forgive me?"

Liss nodded and took his hand in her good one. "Of course. It's been a rollercoaster for all of us, and it must be painful to see your dad grieving and ill. I'm sorry that your mum died before you knew her."

Alex nodded. "It is." Liss expected him to share more; after all, they'd both lost their mums, but Alex moved to business. "Let's discuss what being part of this family and an official princess will involve. I'll get my secretary to make notes as it's a lot to absorb. Then, you'll have up to a week to consider it before we officially announce you to the press. You must sign documents and be given a new residence."

"Okay," Liss replied, fiddling with her ponytail. She wanted to be there for Alex, and maybe this was the best way to support the family and to give something back to the King, but it was all so fast.

"While I summon my secretary, I will leave you to decide who you will bring as your date tomorrow." Liss's eyes flicked to Bear, who looked anywhere but at her. "And what you're going to wear. You must be excited."

Her heart raced, and her mouth dried up. What was she getting herself into?

Chapter Twenty-Three

Bear's smile tickled the corner of his mouth as he passed her Isla's phone number in the car. "In case you want to invite her as your date. I wasn't sure if you'd kept her number after you used it yesterday."

Liss returned his smile as she fumbled with the mobile. "Thanks." Prince Alex agreed she could bring her bodyguards and three others to the party. She needed strength in numbers.

He turned away again. Liss had learnt enough at the palace to understand that her new bodyguards would be from the royal household once she accepted her role within the family. She'd have a secretary and team to help her with appointments, outfits, and behaviours. Protocol informed what her days entailed, and the palace would develop an identity for her. Bile burnt her throat. She'd spent years carving out her life after her mum died. She'd re-written her future and designed her life around the pub, but now she could have what she wanted. It had to be a good thing.

She crossed and uncrossed her arms repeatedly.

Bear tapped at his mobile as he hummed a faintly familiar tune. She needed to stop thinking about him. He was off-limits. Besides, today was Tuesday, and by the end of next week, she'd give the King an answer on officially becoming a serving member of the royal family or renouncing her throne. Although Archibald said it wouldn't change her place with them as a family, she didn't believe it. Alex would become king and lead a busy life; her grandad only had months to live. She'd never see Bear again, but all these changes must be better than her current life.

The bile continued to rise; it sat in her mouth, taunting her as she toyed with the hem of the shorts she'd thrown on before they left the hotel.

Strike and Bear glanced at each other again.

Bear stopped humming, and his mouth twisted to the side. "You've got a lot on your mind." He turned to look at her between the gap in the seats. With a body his size, it was an uncomfortable movement. He forced himself into an awkward space to check up on her. "Anything you want to talk about?"

She shook her head and glanced warily at Strike, remembering his warning. "It's nothing."

"Never trust a woman who says it's nothing," Strike grunted.

"It doesn't matter. I'm not sure I could explain it to you two anyway." Liss bit the inside of her mouth.

"Try us, Liss. We've got another ten minutes left of this journey, so you might as well talk about something," Bear pressed as Strike spied her through the rear-view mirror. "If you can't trust your bodyguards, who can you trust?"

Liss looked between the guards before staring at her shorts. The pink was garish and clashed with her peeling nail varnish.

"Oi." She glanced up. Bear's eyes narrowed. He was doing his human lie-detector look again. "Would it help if

Strike apologised for his behaviour so far?"

"My what?" Strike thundered.

"You've been a dick, mate," Bear said matter-of-factly. Liss's eyes felt like they might pop out of her head.

"I don't know what you mean," Strike grunted.

"'She's a big girl who can handle her own problems,'" Bear replied. His impression of Strike and the line he'd given as they got to the palace was spot on. Strike pursed his lips.

Liss smiled at their back-and-forth. They sounded like they could have been brothers. Visually, they weren't alike, but there was something special between them, and she longed for similar. She was close to Isla, but the connection between the lads was another level. Occasionally, the car stopped at traffic lights, and she glimpsed strangers smiling or going about their business. She'd never be able to do that again.

Strike remained quiet. After a couple of minutes, she stared at the reflection of his furrowed brow and flitting gaze through the rear-view mirror.

Bear grinned at her. "Give it a moment. Strike takes a while to process when he knows he's done wrong."

Strike grunted before saying, "Fine. I've been a dick to you, Liss. You've not made any of this easy, but our previous client was hard work. I've been taking it out on you."

"Well, fuck me," Bear said slowly before clapping his hands together. "Liss, what you don't know is that a Strike apology is rarer than a total eclipse. And that one was golden. It was an absolute beauty of an apology. I'd call your mum and tell her, but she won't believe me."

"Fuck you, Bear."

"Fuck you too, brother," he replied, and they smiled at each other and squeezed each other's hands in a handshake as Strike continued to drive. Liss's heart ached again for that closeness with someone. The loss of freedom was worth it for the family. Alex was okay, and Marianne would come around.

"So now we've heard Strike's apology, you have to tell us what you're thinking," Bear said, his big brown eyes giving Liss no room to escape his questioning.

Liss squeezed her lips together before blurting, "I've spent too long having no one. I can't rely on myself alone anymore and don't want to."

Bear's mouth twisted to the side, and Strike glanced at her again. His eyes repeatedly flicked to the road, but they continued to return to her.

"So, are you officially going to join the royal family?" Bear asked.

She took slow breaths. It was a relief to talk to someone. Isla and Steve would be biased, and Nana would speak about parties and money but not the essential things. Although, Nana wouldn't have coped with the lack of freedom either.

"I don't want to. But it's the opportunity to have a family, something I've searched for until I settled on the pub. There will be staff and duties, but since Mum died, all I have is Nana, and you've seen how messed up that relationship is. You guys wouldn't get it." Liss twisted her hair as she processed.

"You're right. I've always had my family. Two parents who did everything for me, and then when I joined the army, I got another family. But Bear knows."

Bear looked down and then back at her. His eyelashes fluttered softly. He took a deep breath before responding,

"Yes, although—" A phone rang with the Mazdy ringtone. "Shit. That's a certain agent."

"Fucking hate that woman," Strike snarled.

Bear looked from Strike to Liss. "It's about our last job. They're talking to a newspaper about us." So it was the agent who'd called when they were in the stairwell yesterday. Maybe Mazdy wasn't Bear's significant something.

"Is it something I can help with?" Liss asked as her fingers tingled, and she tapped her feet.

Bear shook his head as the car's speaker phone rang.

"No," Strike grunted before adding to Bear, "We can't do this with her in the back."

"For fuck sake, Strike," Liss replied as the phone continued to ring. "You guys have more on me, a future princess, than I'll get from this call. I won't share anything I hear, and I'll keep my mouth shut." Liss motioned zipping her mouth shut before locking it with a fake key that she threw over her shoulder.

Bear smiled until he accepted the call.

"Janice, what is this?" Strike asked, pulling over to a parking spot.

"Hi, guys." The American accent was breezy. Bear's eye twitched. "How are you both?"

"We're busy. What is this?" Strike repeated.

Liss rolled her eyes. If Janice hadn't intended to cause them trouble before, she would now. They needed to practice their phone manner.

"Mazdy has spoken," Janice announced. Strike mumbled something, and Bear side-eyed Liss as best he could in his passenger seat. "She wants to tell the *Daily Mail* everything about her illicit night with the bodyguard."

Liss's eyebrows jumped up.

"There was no night, and you have no proof," Strike hissed. His eyes blazed, and his knuckles were white as he gripped the steering wheel.

"Because you deleted the photos of Bear kissing her," Janice replied.

Bear fisted his hands as he growled. "She kissed me, and I stepped away, as you know. She forced herself on me, and I remained professional and stopped it instantly."

So he didn't have a thing for all his female clients? Liss hid the smile that threatened to dance across her face.

"That's not what the photos suggested."

"That's why there are no longer any photos. You know the truth, and you know Mazdy forced herself on Bear and that he did the right thing." Strike let panic slip into his voice. Janice had them against a wall. Bear inched forward as the seatbelt pulled him back.

"I know that, Mazdy knows that, and you guys know that, but it doesn't matter. I don't need to give the truth, because a story like this will sell even though it's a lie." Janice chuckled before continuing, "Lads, at the end of the day, I don't need photos, because no one cares about proof. All I need is for Mazdy to sell this story to the papers, which she will because it will do wonders for her publicity and career, especially with the tour coming up. I'm kindly giving you a heads up. Shall I give the writer your number for a quote?" she added. Her cruelty dripped through the car's speakers.

Strike's face burned red. He was seconds away from ripping the phone from the holder and hurling it out of the window.

"Excuse me, Janice, is it?" Liss slid forward. Strike tried to end the call, but Liss slapped the back of his head.

"Yes, darling, and who might you be?" she replied with an emphasised drawl.

"I'm the lawyer for the 'lads' here, and I have been recording this entire conversation, darling," Liss added cockily.

"I didn't agree to be recorded," she exclaimed.

Liss unclicked her seatbelt and leaned closer to the phone. "What was it you said on my recording? Oh yes, 'a story like this will sell even though it's a lie.' She forced herself on Mr. Bear." What was his surname? She sped on so that Janice wouldn't realise she was lying. "Which, in itself, is sexual assault and a crime she could be arrested for. But with fraudulent claims too? She'd be looking at serious jail time."

Strike's and Bear's mouths dropped wide open.

"Hold on—" Janice shouted.

Liss smirked. "You see, Janice, Mazdy has very lucrative contracts and relationships with brands and charities. How many would you say there are? Twenty, maybe twenty-five?"

"She's got forty contracts with extra endorsements nearly signed off," Janice stuttered.

"That's impressive. You must be a fantastic agent," Liss replied.

Janice's smugness at being so obviously flattered came out in a girlish voice. "I am the—"

"Well, all that's about to change," Liss cut in like a panther, gripping Strike's headrest with her good hand. "Because when Mazdy is arrested, and this recording is released, it won't just affect all those contracts, but you will lose her as a client, then your other clients will follow, and as a final insult, the industry will ostracise you. No money coming in and having to retrain as a bartender. God forbid."

Bear covered his mouth, but his eyes twinkled. She gave him a wink.

Give me your phone. I need voice notes, Liss mouthed to Strike as Bear's phone sat in the cradle.

"Tell me that you won't let this story go to the press and that you and Mazdy will never discuss it again."

"Well, I—"

"Fuck me. You must love being poor and working in shit places. You know, you could be charged with fraud as well? How does a criminal record sit with you, Janice, and what about a couple of nights in a prison cell? I bet—"

"Fine," Janice shouted. Liss hit record on the voice note app. "This is a non-story. I will never put it out on any media, and we won't ever go to the papers."

"And no book deals or sneaky anonymous social media posts either."

Janice repeated the sentence, adding between what sounded like gritted teeth, "And we'll never talk to anyone about it again."

"And you will never call my clients again." Liss shouted "never," freezing the bodyguards to their seats. "Because if you do, we will chat with others and see if Mazdy has a history of forcing herself on other members of her staff. Word will get around about her behaviour, and no bodyguards will work with her again."

"Fine. You have my word."

"I'm not sure I can trust that, but I have my recordings." Liss flicked her ponytail.

"Okay, okay," Janice relented.

"Right, we're done here. Goodbye." Liss hit end on the phone and then the recording.

Bear whooped, and Strike sang her praises as Liss sat back in her seat.

"I could fucking kiss you," Strike shouted, throwing his hands in the air.

Liss rolled her eyes. "That's what got you two into this situation in the first place."

"Good point. Where did you learn all of that? Could she be arrested?" Strike's grin was so broad that she wanted to cheer.

Liss stretched her good arm and rested in the seat like it was her throne. "As if I know. When Mum was ill, I watched loads of law shows. I bullshitted my way through that entire call. But you have a recording now, you'll never hear from them again."

Strike laughed, but it was Bear that caught her attention.

Bear turned his body so far in the seat that he was fully facing her. After a heartbeat of locking his eyes with hers, he rubbed his chin and said quietly, "I can't ever repay you for that."

Liss smiled sheepishly, although her belly fluttered under his gaze. "Get me back to the hotel. And be quiet when Isla visits. I need a shower and to get a fancy dress for tomorrow."

Bear's big brown eyes didn't leave her face as Strike eased them back into traffic and took them towards the hotel.

Chapter Twenty-Four

"**S**trike, where are we going?" Liss waggled her hash brown at him.

It was the day of the party, and the bodyguards had woken her early, although they refused to explain why. Strike was driving, and Bear sat in the front passenger seat. Neither were talking. "Bear, it's eight in the morning, and as much as I'm enjoying my McDonald's breakfast, I don't think I should be out and about. I still haven't got a dress."

"This is the perfect day to be out and about. Now eat up and enjoy the view," Bear replied, turning in his seat. "If you don't want to eat that hash brown, I'll take it off you."

Liss licked it. "If I lick it, then it's mine."

Bear's pupils dilated as he swallowed loudly. "I'll keep that saying in mind."

He winked, causing her face to flush. Liss looked warily to Strike, waiting for a lecture, but instead, he smiled and shook his head. Since the call yesterday, they'd all relaxed. The night before, they'd watched a movie in the hotel together. Luke had joined them, and aside from the popcorn fight that ended with boxing techniques between the bodyguards, it was like friends hanging out.

The breakthrough with Strike was monumental, but occasionally, she'd caught Bear staring at her. Even now, the memory of his gaze from the night before sat inside her. *As if I was someone to care about.* Liss pinched her skin. This life wasn't forever, and in little over a week, both men would be memories.

"Alright," Strike said to Bear. "We're nearly at the drop-off. Message your friend."

"Do I get to know the plan? If you tell me, then I'm less likely to fuck up," Liss grumbled.

"She's got a point," Strike said, smirking. "She does like to fuck up our plans."

She wanted to laugh and shout. Being part of this dynamic filled the holes in her heart. Isla, Steve, and the pub had done that, too, but there was something about these guys.

Strike parked. His eyes were wide as he checked the windows and mirrors. "Safe," he said, and Bear nodded.

"Hello!" Liss shouted.

"You're so demanding, Princess," Bear cheeked. "Strike is going to drop me off. I'll do a quick ground check, and then you and I will get out and go through that side door. Strike will pick us up in just under an hour."

Bear jumped out of the vehicle.

Liss stretched her still sore arm restlessly. "But what's through the side door?"

"A surprise," Strike said flatly. Bear nodded, and Strike moved the car to the side door. As much as she knew this was their job, the way they focused on her safety eased her anxiety. "Bear wanted to do something special for you as a thank you for yesterday. My thank you was the McDonald's."

A smiling Bear opening her door ceased her questions. "I'll call you when we're ready."

Strike nodded.

Bear grabbed her hand and coaxed her through the side door as Strike drove off.

They were in a corridor littered with boxes. Liss wanted to make their job easier as she'd promised, but the secrets were getting to her. She gritted her teeth as Bear's hand touched her lower back, and he guided her forward and up some stairs.

Suddenly, they were outside a thick fire door. Even as the warmth from Bear's hand filled her, her arms shook with anxiety. "Bear, please tell me what's going on. I'm scared."

"Princess," he replied, turning to her and cupping her face. "Today is your last day before the press gets even wilder due to tonight's party. I wanted to say thank you for everything and give you a bit of the freedom you deserved. I called in a favour, and here we are."

Her forehead hurt from her knotted brows.

The door opened, and a stunning woman stared at them. Her tailored blouse and high-waisted trousers made her look like a Victoria's Secret model on a business trip. Her accent was pure Essex. "Welcome to Harrods, Felicity. I'm Nina, and we've got an hour to find you the perfect outfit for tonight."

Liss gasped and stared back at a beaming Bear. "How's this for *Princess Diaries*, Liss?" He chuckled at his joke. The joy before her made her stomach flop even as her heart swelled. "You'd best hurry up. We need to be out of here before the shop opens. Buy all you need. We'll call it a business expense."

Nina took her hand and led her towards dresses that shone and glittered, but nothing compared to the sparkle in her heart that Bear had given her this gift.

Even as they returned to the car, Bear couldn't stop beaming. He'd been like that the entire time they were in the shop.

During the hour, Liss chatted to Nina as she tried on outfits. The pain in her arm hadn't helped, but the woman was gentle. She was another one of Bear's hookups who became a friend. Well, as close as he got to friends.

"How was it?" Strike asked as he eased the car into traffic.

Liss clutched her new purchases tightly as she fought to find the right words to express her gratitude. "No one has done anything like that for me before."

Bear grinned. "And you're not angry with us for making you get up early?"

She held her breath. What he'd done for her was epic, but she couldn't overthink it. He was saying thank you for the tight spot she'd got the lads out of.

"Not even after our late night watching movies," she replied. "And your boxing showcase."

Bear pulled on the back of his neck. "Yeah, that tends to happen when we're chilling."

"And how often do the three of you watch movies together?"

"Never," Strike replied. "Our downtime is normally spent in the gym or sleeping. But it was a good idea, although I had to work off the extra calories at six this morning."

"I shall take that to mean that I'm a good influence on the both of you." Strike grumbled in response. "So are we watching *Princess Diaries* sequel next?"

Bear and Strike chuckled.

"That's one of Bear's favourites. He can't get enough of that romcom shit."

Bear glared at Strike. That nugget added to her joy.

Tonight was going to be amazing.

Liss couldn't wait to show off her dress that was now hidden in a fancy black bag. She messaged Isla about the evening. Isla, Steve, and Steve's brother were attending the party as a four. She should tell Bear.

She nibbled her lip as the four-by-four meandered towards the hotel.

"Shit," Bear grunted and mumbled something to Strike while pointing at his phone.

Liss leaned forward, but she was a ghost to them. A pressure formed in her head. She caught the odd word between the men, but it didn't mean anything to her.

"Do we let her go tonight?" Strike asked. Bear's hunched shoulders and relentless finger-tapping on the dashboard told her it was serious.

"There will be a lot of security there, and she'll have both of us. We can do an extra sweep before the night starts and ensure the vehicle is always ready. Our hotel is safe if we have to get her back quickly. They wouldn't have sent the threat to The Bell if they knew that Liss was at the hotel," Bear replied with business-like efficiency, yet he rolled his broad shoulders and his eye twitched. Liss's heartbeat thundered. "We need to let the palace know so that everyone is aware. If they say it's okay, then we go ahead."

Strike nodded.

"If this concerns me, I should know," Liss snapped, drawing a turn from Bear. Strike dead-eyed her in the rear-view mirror. "What happened to the pub? Is anyone hurt?"

Bear sighed. "Nothing has happened. It was a note,

and no one got hurt." He turned back.

"A threat aimed at me?"

Bear's eyes continued twitching, and Strike sucked his cheeks in hard.

Bear shrugged, but she tapped him until he looked at her through squinting eyes. "Yes. Are you sure you want to know? Because it doesn't change anything."

Horns beeped outside the car as Strike flitted through traffic, but the juddering movement didn't stop Liss as she folded her arms in a challenge. "It made you two question whether I should go tonight."

Strike grunted, "Tell her. She needs to understand the things that might happen in her future."

Bear huffed before reading from his phone. "'That little bitch better watch herself. She's a dead princess walking.'" Bear refused to look up. "It was addressed to you."

Air escaped from between her nearly closed lips. "Do I have any reason to be worried?" she asked as if it was a note about who was swapping a pub shift.

"No," Strike replied while side-eyeing Bear.

"And I can go to the party? I want to go to the party." Liss gazed at Bear, who continued to stare at the phone as if it were a treasure map.

"You can go to the party," Strike spoke again for the two of them. "There's nothing special about this threat, and we're both in agreement."

But she wasn't interested in Strike's opinion. Bear turned his phone over repeatedly in his hand. "Can I go to the party?"

"Yes." It was like the grunt of a stroppy teenager forced to finish their homework.

Liss occasionally gazed out the window at the strangers whose lives no longer resembled hers. Her earlier happiness was gone. Surely, a future of threats was worth it for a family. And of course, the party would be safe. It had to be, right?

Chapter Twenty-Five

Darkness surrounded her.

Hands reached for her from the walls. They called out her name as they grabbed and pulled at her clothes. One hand gripped her around the throat. "You're alone," it rasped. "You'll die alone with no one to save you."

"Get away," she cried, but another hand forced itself over her mouth.

The entity behind her was pushing her towards the stairs of the pub. They wanted to throw her down them.

"No one will save you." The voice left an icy chill that filled her bones even as her body burnt with fire. "You're already dead. No one cares that you exist. You have no one."

Hands held her at the top of the pub stairs. She cried out, but no one came for her.

"Princess Felicity," the voice said before cackling. "You'll be dead before you take that name."

Fingers dug into her shoulders as hands shook her.

She gasped as she woke to find Bear leaning over her with his hands holding her shoulders. He wasn't piercing her skin with his fingers like the monster in her dream. His large body filled the space beside her bed, his presence like a foreboding creature who could crush her with one hand, but his touch remained gentle and his face full of concern.

"Liss?" he whispered. The room was a strange mixture of light and dark. The only light in the room glowed from her open bedroom door. "Are you okay?"

"Fine," Liss rasped as if glass was embedded in her throat.

"You were screaming." Bear eased himself onto the bed and opened his arms. Liss filled the gap, and he held her close. His leg bobbed, and his pulse thrummed in his throat.

The bedding was damp, and sweat drenched her T-shirt. Liss's shivers grew with each second. The terror from her nightmare wouldn't leave her. She may have been awake, but it was as if her body kept the horror. It flowed through her blood and threatened to take her under once more; her limbs continued to tense. *I'm going to die alone.* It didn't matter that she'd have blood relatives close. The heat and care in Bear's embrace weren't enough to obliterate the nightmare.

Tears rolled down her cheeks.

"Sit closer, Princess. I need to get you warm."

She climbed into his lap, and he cocooned her with his arms. She hissed as she moved her sore arm. Bear held it gently as if it were a treasure worth more than gold as he rocked her slowly, and she wept against his chest.

"I don't know what that nightmare was about, but Strike and I won't let anything happen to you. He's fought against bigger enemies than this joker writing you notes."

His voice was low and soothing, but his rapid heartbeat betrayed him. Liss focused on how his accent rounded words. He smelt of wood and citrus, and she breathed him in.

He continued, "And I might not be a former soldier,

but I've fought beasts in my time. We've got this, and we've certainly got you."

Liss wrapped her good arm around him. He was pure muscle yet still soft in the way she needed. "Then why is your heart beating so fast?" Liss croaked against his shirt.

He didn't reply, but his heartbeat slowed as he rocked her. Liss breathed in time with him. His shirt was crisp enough to leave creases on her face, and she'd probably soaked it with her sweat and tears, but she didn't let go. His hands rubbed her back, the heat penetrating her cotton top. He brushed her hair with kisses and hummed an unfamiliar tune. Eventually, her eyelids drooped, and her body pulled her to sleep, but she shook herself awake.

"I smell bad," she griped, ruining the moment.

"I know," he teased.

She giggled, which was a relief after everything. This man relaxed her, no matter her emotions. "I need a shower."

A movement in Bear's groin surprised her.

"Right," he said with a cough. His awkwardness made Liss smile again. "I'll leave you to it."

"I can't do it alone." Liss hurried her words. He twitched beneath her, and she blushed. She forced her shoulders to relax. "I need help because of my arm. I was hoping Isla would be here by now to help."

"She can't be much longer. You don't want me helping you while you're..." He didn't finish his sentence and instead cleared his throat. Was saying naked too much for the burly bodyguard? "And you suggested it was hurting less."

But Liss didn't want to jar it before the evening. She wanted to dance in the beautiful dress Bear paid for at her party. Still, that meant being naked with Bear.

"Pass me my phone," Liss said, chewing at her cuticles. Maybe Isla could rescue her. Bear leaned back and grabbed the phone while holding her close.

"There's a message," Liss said with shaky laughter. Bear let out a breath. "But it says she can't be here until five, and that will only give us enough time to do my hair and make-up. We'll need to leave straight after that. I need to shower now."

Even Bear's deliciously citrus smell wasn't enough to mask the scent of her stale sweat, and she needed to look incredible for the party. It was a big deal, and she was desperate to show Marianne she was worthy of joining the family. It made the prospect of being naked in front of Bear a minor problem, but it was still a problem. She trembled. Maybe if she took painkillers before she showered, it would be okay.

Bear looked at his watch, but she didn't need him to confirm it was only three. She must get in the shower.

"Okay," Bear said gruffly, shaking his head. "What do you need me to do?"

A zip of excitement filled her body. "I can undress by myself." It would be difficult, but she'd do it to make the moment easier. "But I'll need you to wash my hair and ensure I don't slip when I get out. That's all."

"That's all," he repeated gruffly and nodded slowly.

"You can close your eyes as you do it. And remember that guy I sent a sexy picture to? He didn't reply, so my body can't be that good," she reasoned for him. Bear pursed his lips. "For all you know, I have boils and blotches on my bum."

"Don't say bum," he replied, easing her off his lap. Liss worried her lip as he fumbled with words. "And I'm sure it's...." Bear sighed loudly. "It doesn't matter. Just get undressed." He cleared his throat. "I'll get you a towel and help you into the shower with my eyes closed."

"Cool, thank you," Liss replied.

The situation was anything but cool.

Bear shuffled across the room and retrieved a towel. Even as she meandered to the bathroom, he wouldn't meet her eyes. She shivered as her damp T-shirt caught the air. She turned, and he shoved a towel at her, his gaze still firmly on the floor. "Shout when you need me. I'll be on the other side of the door."

"Okay."

He remained in the bedroom as Liss stepped into the bathroom. She unsnapped her shorts and caught Bear's eye in the mirror's reflection. He sat motionless on the bed and did a double take when she accidentally made eye contact. Liss smirked when the phone that he was turning toppled out of his hand. Bear's ears bloomed bright red as he dropped his head to the floor and turned to face the wall before remembering the phone. Liss giggled as she attempted to get her shorts down.

"Stop giggling. I didn't realise I could see you in the mirror," Bear grunted, but his voice was raspy and dry.

"Sorry," she said, giggling again as she waggled her bum in a clumsy attempt at getting her shorts off without hurting her arm. As they touched the floor, she announced, "Shorts down. I'm getting there."

"I don't need you to commentate," Bear grumbled. Liss rechecked the mirror. He was tapping his hand restlessly against his thigh. His trousers appeared tented.

"Focus," she whispered, pulling at her T-shirt with her right hand. She winced as she attempted to lift the hem of the top up and over her head, but she couldn't get the angle without twisting her injured wrist. Liss took a deep breath and pressed her lips together as she counted to five. She tried again, but the pain was so sharp every time she got close, it ripped through her body. Liss didn't want to make it worse before the party. She tried again.

"Fuck," she cried out.

"What happened?" Bear shouted.

"Nothing."

"Princess," Bear warned, "I'm coming in the bathroom unless you say otherwise."

"Fine," she snapped, still standing awkwardly. The pain was nothing compared to the arousal pulsating through her. Goose pimples rose on her skin at the sight of an awkward Bear pulling on the back of his neck, with his sleeves rolled up, revealing his forearms and a little of his tattoos. All she wore were knickers and a T-shirt. She'd removed her bra one-handed before her nap.

His eyes locked with hers as if looking anywhere else would be dangerous. He swallowed repeatedly and hunched his shoulders.

"I can't take the rest of my clothes off without pain, and I want to rest my arm before tonight. I did my shorts," she murmured. Her hands hung limply by her side.

"Great," he replied, but his eyes didn't leave hers.

"But I need you to remove my T-shirt."

"Fuck. I mean, sure, okay," Bear stuttered.

"Slowly. Not slow in a sexual way, but gentle. You know what I mean," she said, fiddling with the hem.

"Yes, I know. I really fucking know. I'm going to close my eyes while I do this," he grunted.

"But what if you touch my boobs or something else?"

He swallowed loudly, drawing her attention to his

bobbing Adam's apple.

"Good point." He pulled on the back of his neck while keeping his gaze high. "I'll squint."

Liss licked her lips.

"Don't lick your lips like that," he grumbled.

"Sorry." His eyes resembled little pillar boxes with a tiny bit of pupil showing. Her body burned with fire as she attempted to quell her desire.

She subconsciously rolled her hips as he reached for the hem of her T-shirt. "Fuck," he grumbled.

"Can I help in any way?" she replied huskily.

"No." Sweat beaded his brow, and she smiled at how her badass bodyguard was coming undone over the simple removal of a T-shirt. "But stop smiling, stop moving your hips, and stop that tongue doing anything that will get both of us into trouble. I'm being respectful."

"What if I don't want you to be?" she whispered louder than intended.

Bear huffed and grumbled as he lifted her T-shirt. As his hands and the hem reached her breasts, he swore under his breath and closed his eyes before squinting again. She sneaked a look at his crotch. Liss bit her lip at the prospect of pulling down his zipper and revelling in his length and thickness.

"No lip biting either." He stepped a little closer to lift the T-shirt fully off her head, and her nipples, now slightly erect, threatened to brush against his chest. "Shit, Princess. This moment is going to kill me."

He pulled the T-shirt over her face. The collar caught on her neck, and he stepped closer to unhook it. His chest pressed into her breasts, and his hand skimmed her hip as he held her against him to stop her from wobbling.

Liss held her breath. His body against hers caused little electric shock sensations. The heat from their skin-on-skin touch made the ache between her legs burn hotter. She was like a furnace as he pulled the top off her head. He didn't move back. They locked eyes. He swallowed again.

"You should get in that shower." His voice was hoarse. She'd have to shower with her knickers on. She couldn't ask him to remove them. His erection pushed against her, and she wrapped her good arm around his neck. Her arousal climbed higher. His body set a fire inside her.

"I'm a mess and want to look pretty for the party." Her voice was so quiet.

"You're beautiful, so you won't need long to get ready." He gulped loudly. Liss licked her lips as the sparks under her skin went off like fireworks. "I want you so fucking much, Liss."

The intercom buzzed as Liss's phone rang from the bedroom.

"Are you fucking kidding me?" She grimaced as he leant his head against hers briefly. Her whole body cried in disappointment.

"Saved by the bell yet again." But based on his clenched jaw and uncomfortable walk to pass her the phone before he shuffled to the intercom, his body disagreed.

"I finished work early, and I'm on my way up," Isla shouted on speakerphone. "I can't wait to see your dress. Tonight is going to be spectacular."

Liss covered herself with a towel as Bear confirmed the guest was allowed up.

Bear focused on the floor as they waited for the lift. She could offer him the promise of another time. They only had a week left together. She ground her teeth and held her towel tightly against her nearly naked body.

"Babe," Isla shouted as the lift door opened. She dragged a suitcase with her and threw a rucksack on the floor. "I couldn't decide what to wear."

She was a whirlwind, but even a whirlwind couldn't temper Liss's desire for Bear. She gritted her teeth and forced her best fake smile.

"That's awesome. You're just in time because I need a shower. Please help."

Liss did her utmost not to look at Bear. Cock-blocked by her best friend and with no opportunity to work him out of her system. Maybe he was relieved by Isla's interruption.

"Let's get your smelly ass in there," Isla shouted, her hair bouncing as she dragged her stuff towards the bedroom. "You're going to look gorgeous for our men tonight."

Liss froze. She'd not told Bear Steve was coming. The bomb threat had filled their focus.

"After all these months of Steve promising to hook me up with his brother Ollie, I might finally get my hands on him. And Steve is so excited about going with you," Isla joked.

"But—" Liss turned to Bear, but his hunched shoulders and broad back faced her. It made her thirsty just looking at the strength in his flexing muscles. She shook her head at Isla. They were going as a group of four, not as couples.

Isla walked into the bedroom, leaving Liss to explain the joke to Bear, but he was already heading towards the lift.

"Make sure you and your men are ready in two hours," he grumbled, overemphasising the words "your men." "I've got to make things safe for you."

He slipped into the lift. As the doors closed, he gave her a dead-eyed stare.

CHAPTER TWENTY-SIX

An upbeat song by Harry Styles played in the background as if they were getting ready for a night on the town and not a dignified party at the palace.

Isla hummed as she applied the flush pink lipstick to Liss's lips. Butterflies fluttered in her belly, although an inexplicable dread snapped at the edges of their wings. Someone wanted her dead, Bear was acting weird, and she was about to be announced as a princess.

What next?

The room smelt of honeysuckle and jasmine moisturiser. Liss wriggled her nose and lifted her hands to squeeze her nostrils, but Isla slapped them away. "You'll ruin your make-up."

Isla instructed that Liss wasn't allowed to see her transformation until the last minute, and a blanket covered the mirror on the other side of the room due to Liss attempting sneaky looks. The glow-up was already ninety minutes in. Liss crossed and uncrossed her arms.

"I can't believe I might finally get to kiss Ollie. Maybe you'll kiss someone too," Isla added.

Liss furrowed her brows and opened her mouth to argue.

"Don't move your lips," Isla rebuked.

Liss sighed and rolled her eyes. During the glow-up,

they'd giggled over the make-up and outlandish hairstyles Isla found on funny TikTok videos. The rest of the suite was eerily quiet.

It was nearly like the old days when Isla gossiped about her recent conquests, but the prospect of Liss's future loomed over them. It could end their friendship. Either way, it was nice to talk about anything but the prospect of the announcement until Isla mentioned kissing.

Isla stuck a tissue between Liss's lips. "Press your lips together."

Liss did as asked before Isla added another layer of lipstick. This could be the last time they did this. Once Liss gave up her life for royalty, she'd have stylists. She kept reminding herself it was to have a family. Her mum hadn't wanted her to be alone.

Suddenly, a thud at the door infiltrated the safe space.

"You have two minutes," Bear grumped through the wood. "And your men are on the way up."

"Don't let them in," Isla shouted back.

"I'm not your bloody servant."

"What's got up his arse?" Isla commented before announcing to Liss, "You're done. Stand in front of the mirror."

Liss tentatively approached the mirror, but the blanket still hid her glow-up.

"Are you ready?" Isla asked.

Liss nodded. Her mouth was dry, and her tongue stuck to the roof of her mouth. When she was a teenager, her mum would take one evening off every three weeks, and they'd spend it watching movies or catching up on school news. But a couple of times, her mum did her make-up. It wasn't as professional as Isla's. It was often the garish things they found in the bargain bin, but those nights were special. Liss's mum would complement Liss's hazel eyes or high cheekbones as she swept brushes across her cheeks or applicators on her eyes. Her mum knew she struggled with confidence, especially compared to the girls at school, so her mum would build her up emotionally, mentally, and physically whenever she got the chance. Memories of popcorn and bright blue eyeshadow with pink eyeliner caused a tear in Liss's eyes. Her mum would be happy she was joining the rest of her family.

Isla beamed as she whipped the blanket off. Her eyes sparkled, but all Liss saw was the stranger in her reflection. Liss's hazel eyes somehow appeared golden and shone brightly. Thick dark waves cascaded down her shoulders, framing her face and mirroring her eyelashes that fluttered when she blinked in admiration at Isla's creation. She tilted her head as she curled the waves around her fingers. They resembled her mum's. The waves were stiff with hairspray, but Liss couldn't resist touching and bouncing them. Liss pressed her lips together and then beamed at how plump they looked.

"I look like a princess," she whispered.

Isla smiled. "You've always been one, beautiful. Pop on those sparkly heels, and we'll get going. We should leave the guys waiting for a few minutes.

"I can't believe your bodyguards did all that for you. They must like you," Isla said, referring to Liss's outfit as she added a couple of flicks of eyeliner and hairspray. Liss fumbled with the straps of the heels. "It's a shame you won't see them once you're officially part of the royal family."

Liss mumbled her agreement. Her purple floor-length dress fluttered as she bent. It shone under the lights of the hotel bedroom. Liss never wore anything expensive or showy. It clung to her curves perfectly. Liss slipped her heart talisman into her glittery clutch bag. She needed her mum with her in some way that night.

As they stepped out the door, it wasn't Steve's beaming smile that caught her eye but Bear's jaw that dropped briefly before he mumbled something that looked a lot like "Fucking hell" under his breath. Even with all his training and professionalism, he couldn't keep his eyes off her. Her cheeks flushed under the intensity of his gaze. He shook his head and grinned. It was the dream reaction, and she stepped closer to him.

"You're beautiful," Steve whispered, pulling her attention from Bear. He held out his hand as Isla walked towards Ollie. Liss pursed her lips, gazing at Bear, who still stared at her in wonderment. "We look good together. Don't you think, Liss?"

"I don't k—" she mumbled, wobbling on her heels. Steve slipped his hand around her waist.

"Lean on me, Liss. I promise not to let you fall," he said as she attempted to right herself.

Bear stood. His eyes narrowed. "If all the lovey-dovey crap is done, we'll—"

"What's your problem?" Steve asked, but Bear ignored him.

Strike appeared from the lift and quickly gave instructions to ensure their safety. There was a lot about what they couldn't do and how the bodyguards would always watch Liss and those around her. She glanced at Bear, but he was busy packing bags and checking equipment. He tapped his earpiece and nodded to himself before grabbing his phone and swiping through it. But his eye twitched.

"I'm blown away by you, Liss. I'm used to seeing you every day, but tonight you're an even better you," Steve whispered, causing her to bristle at the sentiment behind his words. It was just make-up and a dress. She was still her underneath.

"I'll get the car," Bear grunted. "And make sure you listen to the briefing. It's for your safety." Bear stared directly at her.

"But the King was sending a limousine," Steve crowed.

Bear bristled as he stared at Steve. "Liss will be in the car with me for safety. Strike will be in the limo with you, your brother, and Isla."

"Hold on, mate," Steve snapped. Bear's mouth wore a blunt edge. "I'm going in the car with Liss. I know how anxious she gets, and I want to be close."

"I'm not your mate." His jaw was tight, and his eyes were like pinchers. Her pulse was rapid. Steve had helped her anxiety in the past, but this was making her worse. "Liss?"

Liss shivered. Although she often told people off or showed attitude in the pub she didn't do difficult conversations in her personal life. When she left university to care for her mum, she'd sent an email rather than having a conversation.

"Yeah, sure, whatever. Steve can come with us." Anything to stop the confrontation.

Bear rolled his eyes. "Fine. Do what you want."

He strode into the lift and banged the close door button.

Chapter Twenty-Seven

The car journey was as awkward as Liss expected. Tension brewed between Bear and Steve. Bear refused to answer any of his questions, and every time Steve stared at him, his face pinched.

"We're five minutes away," Bear grunted through the speakerphone connected to Strike, who travelled in the limo with Isla and Ollie.

"Good. I've had word that the sweep of the venue raised no concerns, but we must be on our guard. My senses have left me on edge," Strike replied. Liss's stomach churned. Everything about this night was alien to her, from her fancy dress to her date beside her who tried to hold her hand. Suppose the strangers all stared and judged her like Marianne? She bit her lips before remembering Isla's threats about ruining her make-up.

"Noted," Bear replied. "I trust your gut, bud."

"Ever since Pickle Park." Strike chuckled through the car speakers. A smile tickled Bear's lips.

There was no point asking what Pickle Park was, but curiosity still danced across her skin, causing her to shiver.

"Cold?" Bear asked, his focus on her even when looking out the window.

"No," Liss replied. Tension snapped at her chest, tightening as they neared the palace gates. She gripped her clutch bag as if holding it was like touching the heart talisman.

"Anxious?" he asked, and his eyes softened as he gazed at her through the rear-view mirror.

As she nodded, Steve nudged her. "You need this." He fumbled in his pocket and got out a vodka miniature. "It will calm your nerves."

"Is that wise?" Bear growled. "She needs to be at her best, and she's on painkillers."

Steve's face soured as he rolled his eyes. "It's two shots. Give her a break." He squeezed Liss's good hand. "It's worked all those times before, eh?"

On the rare nights when Steve joined Liss and Isla on a night out, their ritual was to down a double vodka. It took the edge off the nerves. Tonight was just another night out, albeit at a palace surrounded by royalty and their friends. She reached for the bottle.

"I'd rather she's alert for tonight." Bear glared at her. "Don't drink that."

Fear and anger threatened to turn her trembles into shakes. She downed the vodka. As the spirit burnt her throat and fired her insides, she prayed for relief.

Bear brought the car to a stop and jumped out as Strike pulled up behind them.

"It's okay, Liss. You're so beautiful that everyone will want to speak to you. But don't worry. I won't let you out of my sight," Steve added. Bear yanked open the door, reached for her bag, and offered his hand to help her.

"Next time I advise you not to do something, don't do it. I'm trying to keep you safe," Bear said in Liss's ear as her shoes hit the red carpet.

"Don't tell me what to do," she replied between

clenched teeth. Bear's demands and Steve's intensity added to the tension that resembled pins stabbing her belly.

Bear muttered, "Fine. I'll keep you safe, but if you want to make a tit of yourself, go ahead, Princess."

"Let's have some fun," Steve proclaimed as he jumped out of the car. Bear dropped her arm and gave her her bag as Steve grabbed her other hand. She'd gone sling-free, but it still hurt from the fall, even after the painkillers. She winced, but Steve didn't notice as he waltzed her up the carpet to the palace with a laugh.

"There you are," Marianne said brusquely beneath the dancing lights of the silver chandelier. It was bigger than Liss's shower cubicle at home. Crystal dripped from each holder. Similar structures of beaming lights hung delicately throughout the room. Paintings of cherubs and boats daubed the ceiling.

"Yep," Liss replied. Marianne's mouth twisted sourly, but Bear held Liss's attention. He'd positioned himself so no matter which stranger she spoke to, he was in her eyeline. Even with Bear's professional stance, his clenched jaw suggested he was seething. They'd only been at the event for twenty minutes, and he'd grimaced each time she'd sipped her champagne. It was the only way to get through the night.

Her mum barely touched alcohol, apart from the odd glass of prosecco at Christmas, but Nana swore by it. Her nana would have been at home here, so maybe it was time to emulate the confidence and attitude that served her well at her soirées.

"You're not listening," Marianne huffed.

Liss hadn't realised the future queen was talking, so distracted by Bear's glare as she lifted her thin, stemmed glass to her lips. Bubbles danced against her nose as Steve gave her a nudge. He hadn't left her side, which she should have appreciated, but she wanted space. She was never the centre of attention and didn't want to be. Usually, at parties, she'd watch people from a corner or find a job to do, so she faded into the background, but this party was for her.

Liss stared at Marianne over the top of a glass that probably cost more than a month worth of takings at the pub. "Sorry," Liss mumbled. Not that she meant it.

Marianne snorted, and Liss pushed down the giggle that rose in her throat. The combination of strong painkillers and a lack of food meant the alcohol hit harder, especially with anxiety owning her body. She tucked her bag under her arm, reminding herself why she was there.

"As I said, the first hour tonight will involve Alexander or me introducing you to guests."

"How many guests are there?"

"Two hundred," Steve announced.

"At least someone was listening." Marianne nodded to Steve, who smiled back. Liss was nearly a foot shorter than the rest of the group, and they talked over her.

"Why are you so distracted, Liss?" he asked, squeezing her hip. Liss chanced a glance at Bear. His jaw twitched.

"Who are these two hundred people?" Liss asked before taking another sip of her champagne. It was slipping down so easily that she was nearing the end of her glass. "The King said it was close friends and family tonight."

"Steve, please catch your girlfriend up," Marianne guffawed.

Steve clapped his hands and laughed as Liss replied, "I'm not his girlfriend."

Liss gripped her glass as Steve puffed out his chest. "The two hundred are friends or relatives of the family. They've come to meet you and celebrate you joining the family. You don't need to know their background, as when you officially become a princess, you'll have someone to do that, but you must remain respectful."

This was the desperate to impress side of Steve she saw when he was with his parents and Hugo, the pub owner. Maybe she'd speak with him later when they were away from people.

"Right." Liss finished her glass. She raised an eyebrow at Marianne. "And what if someone is disrespectful to me?"

"As if that would occur here. This isn't your pub," Marianne said sharply. Liss's version of people being disrespectful must be different from theirs because she hadn't met anyone friendly yet. A waiter with a tray of drinks walked by, and Liss nodded at him to get his attention. Within seconds, he'd taken her empty glass and given her a fresh one. "We'll have to make a rule book for princess dummies at this rate."

Liss stared at the ceiling, trying to decipher the action in the pictures, but the blinding lights forced white spots to appear in her vision. She sipped her drink and smiled as the bubbles danced in her throat. Bear was pursing his lips and shaking his head. She fought the temptation to stick her tongue out at him. Princesses didn't stick their tongues out.

"Later, the King will announce you as his granddaughter."

"But I haven't accepted the throne yet," Liss replied, retucking her bag under her arm.

"But you're still his granddaughter." Marianne muttered something under her breath before adding, "There will be guests tonight who will be very interested in you, as you've usurped their line to the throne."

"But I—"

"Anyway." Marianne raised her voice before smoothing her hair and painting a smile. "Before we sit for dinner, the King will announce you as his granddaughter."

"Where is the King?"

Marianne blinked rapidly, but before she replied, Prince Alex appeared with an older couple. "He's not feeling well. He apologised but said he would be down before his speech. The illness is taking its toll." The older couple nodded.

"What illness is it, if you don't mind me asking?" Steve probed.

"I do mind. Stephen, isn't it?" Alex replied, pulling himself up taller.

Steve nodded before bowing.

"Should I be curtsying?" Liss yawned. She hadn't meant to, but the painkillers were making her sleepy.

"Not today, but refrain from yawning in my face," Alex huffed. Alex's suit fitted him well. He would have someone to cater to him for every aspect of his life, including what he wore on any given evening.

"I'm even more convinced that you need a 'being a princess for dummies' book." Marianne's laugh resembled the screech of a dying bird. Did she repeat her joke for Alex's benefit or Liss's double humiliation? Their combined laughter was loud enough to draw the attention of other guests. "I'm going to have a lot of fun watching you make mistakes at dinner," Marianne added with a throaty chuckle that made Liss want to crawl away until the night was over. Liss's hands sweated, making her glass slippery.

"She's going to make lots of mistakes," the woman with diamonds dripping from her ears crowed. "Don't worry, dear. As soon as dinner is over, there will be dancing. You do know how to waltz, don't you? I'm sure you've watched enough Strictly Come Dancing."

The group's laughter increased until a shadow descended over the group.

Bear loomed above all of them. He turned to Liss and spoke loud enough for the group to hear, "Miss Felicity, could I add something to the earlier safety briefing?"

Even his tightened lips were kissable. Liss nodded and followed him out of the ballroom.

Steve stayed with Marianne and laughed at more of the clucking that followed her out of the room. Hopefully, the briefing would last the rest of the night. Suddenly, she found herself in a side room. More chandeliers lit up every corner, although these gave a golden hue to the historical busts that framed the space. Paintings of old kings filled every wall. Was any part of the palace homely?

Liss faced Bear, who folded his arms and stared back at her.

"Well?" she asked, putting her bag and glass on the ground before rubbing her wrist gently.

"What?" he grunted, eyeing her movements.

"What do you want to add to the briefing?"

"Nothing," Bear said, shaking his head. "I thought you might want space from your family's behaviour. And maybe five minutes to sober up."

He was right about needing space, but he didn't need

to get in a dig.

"They're not my family. I don't have a family. I don't have anyone on my side." Did she mean that? After all, the reason she was there was to have a family.

"You have a boyfriend," he hit back before refolding his arms and raising an eyebrow.

"I don't. I have a man who is a friend, not that it's any of your business." She downed her drink in defiance.

"He's not acting like a friend," Bear replied, walking away.

"And how should a friend act? Please share your wisdom, Bear." She followed him. Her heels tapped against the marble floor. "All I've seen from you tonight is a grumpy man who wants everyone to do as he says. You're a guy with emotional walls up who just has hookups. It's not like you'd know how to be anyone's boyfriend." The alcohol was loosening her tongue.

Bear stopped suddenly. He seemed to grow another foot as he turned. Liss froze as he stepped closer. His hands were in fists, and his jaw was stiff. His body burnt against hers as he said in a tone laden with depths that made her limbs quiver, "Princess, if I were your boyfriend, I wouldn't stand for anyone talking to you like Marianne and Alex did tonight. I wouldn't care if they were royalty or the fucking president. If I were your boyfriend, I would have destroyed this place and all those in it because of the lack of respect they gave you. No one would ever laugh in your face or call you a dummy again. Nothing would be more important than respecting and caring for you."

He turned on his heel and walked away again.

Liss threw her hands in the air. She kept her wince internal. "Is that what Steve should have done? How would that help this situation?"

He stopped sharply and turned. "It wouldn't help the situation, but it would prove to all those who aren't even good enough to kiss your fucking shoes that you are the most incredible woman in the world. You deserve daily adoration, not humiliation, whether dressed like you're on a catwalk or lounging in your pyjamas," he growled.

Liss sucked in the air. His eyes bored into hers. No man had called her incredible before. He added before she asked him to repeat himself, "I'm going to walk the building and ask Strike to watch you. In the meantime, stop drinking before you do something you regret."

It was as if his previous words meant nothing. He was telling her what to do again. Why did everyone insist on telling her what or who she should be? Liss's head swam. It was too late for his warning. The alcohol was in control, and the only thing stopping her from doing something foolish was food and sleep, and neither were on offer any time soon.

CHAPTER TWENTY-EIGHT

Liss counted to ten and walked back towards the ballroom, but slow footsteps behind her made her pause.

At a croaking sound, she whipped around, lifting her fists to protect herself.

"Felicity." It was the King. His steps were shaky, and his hands trembled as Liss rushed to his aid, tucking her arm through his.

"King Archibald—" she gasped. His eyes sunk in his head, and his skin wore a yellow tinge.

"Felicity, you're beautiful. That shade of purple suits you," he replied between coughs. The antiseptic smell surrounded them, and close up, she spied his wrinkles even under the corridor's glittering lights. He'd deteriorated so quickly.

"Should I ask someone to bring a chair?" she asked, rubbing his back. His suit was soft against her palm. "Or maybe you should return to bed?"

"No, I am fine." He pulled himself up and puffed out his chest, but it didn't hide the quake of his hands or the weariness that flowed from him with each shallow breath. "I've got to introduce everyone to my new granddaughter. The King can't be anything but at his best."

She winced a smile at the reminder that she was

entering a life that wasn't for her. People shouldn't always be at their best, no matter who they are. Suddenly, the King launched into a story of being in a battle when he was in the air force. "And as fifty fighters closed in on my platoon, we held our nerve. I didn't lose any men that day. The battle saved a village." She wrinkled her nose, and her now genuine smile grew as his hands danced. This was the King she recognised on television. If she rejected the throne, he wouldn't want to spend time with her anyway.

"King Archibald—" she uttered, attempting to broach the subject of her future.

"Grandad," he cut in gently. "Please call me grandad."

"Grandad." His eyes lit up, and creases appeared in the corners of his smile. A warmth filled her chest. This man seemed to accept her for who she was in a way her nana never had. "I was wondering what happens next."

"Tonight?"

"No, I—"

Marianne and Alex rushed through the door. "There you are. We're ready for your speech. You're going to be late," Alex chastised his father as if he were a small child caught playing in the toy aisle at a supermarket.

As her head fuzzed and her gaze swam, she held the King tightly.

"I've told you before, Alex. The King is never late." He stopped to whisper to Liss, "Everyone else is merely early." He chuckled, and Liss joined in. His laugh was melodic until his barking cough replaced it.

Marianne elbowed Liss out of the way. Liss attempted to speak, but Marianne held a hand in her face to quiet her. Her diamond ring glinted under the lights, nearly blinding her. "Have you taken your medication, sir?"

"Of course. And I've got the rest right here in case I

need a top-up." The King fumbled in his pocket. His hands shook, and he dropped a foil packet of pills. Alex crossed his arms and tsked. Liss glimpsed the label as she reached for them, but Marianne nudged her aside and retrieved them. Something was familiar about the pack. Liss pressed a hand against her mouth, but the alcohol made it trickier to reach her memories.

"Good, but don't show everyone. The pills are experimental, remember?" Marianne added, shoving them back in the King's pocket.

"But—" Liss attempted. Her stomach was lurching now.

"Come on, Father." Alex shoved Liss to one side and grabbed the King's elbow.

"It's your big moment, future Princess. Don't do anything stupid and trip up," Marianne whispered in Liss's ear, giving her a quick push once the King was out of earshot. She laughed before joining the King and Alex. Liss stood in the hallway, fighting her thoughts as Marianne's pink dress swung with every step she took.

She'd seen similar pills before. She closed one eye tightly as if that might help her remember where, but that made her vision blurrier.

She wasn't sure how long she'd been standing there, but suddenly, Steve was by her side, holding her hand and moving her towards the ballroom. "I've been searching for you. They're calling your name."

"My granddaughter and, I hope, future Princess of this country, Felicity." The King's voice boomed across the golden ballroom. Strangers applauded her as she rocked on her heels.

"I can't believe I'm here with a princess," Steve

commented, taking her bag and hurrying her forward. "You're so beautiful."

She turned to Steve to request her bag but saw a fixed-jawed Bear over his shoulder, standing near the doorway. He'd stood there the whole time, ensuring her safety as she chatted with the King. That was his job, and it didn't mean more than that. His cold, hard stare towards her and Steve suggested he'd heard Steve's words. But Steve was just excited by the night. He was still her caring friend.

"Come on, Princess." Marianne was by her side, jostling her. Liss wanted her bag; she needed the talisman. "The King is waiting."

The crowd eyeballed her as she tottered towards the King. She'd drunk too much. Sweat beaded the back of her neck, and her mouth was desert dry. She was embarrassing herself and the King. He believed in her. He wouldn't want her in his family now.

But his beaming smile suggested otherwise. Liss reached his outstretched arms and let him envelop her in a hug. "You're going to be fine. Don't worry. I'm right beside you."

Liss took a deep breath and faced the strangers. The sparkling jewels dripping from the ladies dazzled her. She squinted as she caught Alex sneering, but when she looked again, he smiled.

The silence was like a courtroom waiting for the judge's verdict, and rows of expectant faces stared.

Marianne looked her up and down and smirked. There was an ugly twist to her mouth. Liss wobbled on her heels as she attempted to grasp the microphone. Righting herself caused her to stand on the edge of her toe, and she tripped and fell to the floor. She thudded to the ground with a bang that made everyone gasp.

I can't do this.

Somehow, she'd not made her arm worse, but the humiliation was like bruises tattooing her skin. Liss dragged her sore body up and attempted to stand. She dropped her head as she smoothed her waves and hid her face, but the hairspray made it immovable. She needed her mum to give her the confidence to do this.

Taunts from playground bullies echoed in her head as she returned to the microphone. She wrapped her good arm across her body. She should run from the building and never look back like she had when asked to present at school. She didn't fit in. This wasn't her. She couldn't speak to groups of people. Vomit climbed up the back of her throat, and she looked wildly around the room.

Even through the crowds, Bear's presence was all-powerful. His eyes lit electricity in her limbs, reminding her of the power she found in their self-defence class and her attitude when confronted by royal expectations. Her beefy bodyguard had his thumbs up and was nodding his encouragement. The action appeared uncomfortable for a man who spent his life stoic and revealing nothing. If he could do that, then she could do this. "You got this," he mouthed. "You're the best woman here. *Princess Diaries* attitude on."

Then, a smiling Isla caught her eye. Lipstick-red marks on Ollie's collar hinted at where she'd been all night. Isla mouthed, "Remember, you're amazing."

Liss took a deep breath, fisted her hands, cleared her rattling throat briefly, and said, "Sorry about that. I couldn't compare to the King's speech, so I had to make my mark differently. Literally on the floor. Sorry, Grandad."

The King smiled, and everyone laughed as he hugged her again. He didn't tell her off for embarrassing him. Her nana would have.

Bear smiled and nodded. A glow filled her belly as she swept her gaze across the room. "I'm not used to public speaking, attending beautiful parties, or being surrounded by strangers, some of whom are now my family. But I hope to make my grandad proud and learn all about him and his past while embracing my new life as a granddaughter. I know there's speculation on my future, but for now, it must be my secret."

The uncomfortable smiles hadn't deterred her from speaking the truth. The King started a round of applause, and people joined in. Marianne folded her arms and gave her a death stare as she whispered something to Alex. He shook his head before replying, but suddenly, guests surrounded her, blocking her view. The King introduced her to cousins and close friends. There were former nannies, secretaries, and the King's best friend.

Even as exhaustion buckled her knees and played with her focus, she forced a shaky smile, recognising the comedown that accompanied sobering up. The shock of the fall had helped. Conversations flowed around her, but as she admired the guests' cacophony of outfit styles, her stomach rumbled. Why hadn't anyone served dinner yet? She scanned the crowd, but Bear and Strike were missing. More bodyguards crossed the room, their strides harried as they pressed their earpieces tightly into their ears.

The King's army friend shared stories of his penchant for a nip of whisky. He shoved one in her hand and toasted her. Liss sipped the measure as the King nodded his encouragement. It was like a furnace in her mouth before it seared her throat. It wasn't what she needed to fill her empty stomach.

"That will put hairs on your chest," the former colonel laughed. "Drink up." She knocked the rest back, resulting in the moustached old gent thrusting another in her hand.

"I'd like you to meet your cousin, Gable," the King said, introducing her to Prince Gable and his wife, Beatrice. "You've stolen their place for the throne, and they're incensed."

Liss gulped the fresh glass of whisky. It went down easier than the first one. She turned and was pleasantly surprised by the beautiful couple. They held each other's hands and smiled broadly. Gable resembled an adult version of a cherub from one of the ceiling paintings, and Beatrice's red hair shone under the golden lights. Her emerald gown gathered at the waist before blooming across her legs. Gable's bowtie matched his wife's delicate green ensemble. They were like a Hollywood couple. The glittering purse in Beatrice's hand reminded Liss of her bag. Her eyes flickered across the room as she searched for Steve and her bag, but he was missing too.

"I've never been more angry." Prince Gable laughed, drawing Liss's attention to the group.

Beatrice elbowed him as her laugh carried like a gentle song across the group. "Ignore him. He's such a trickster. On our first date, he told me to dress in my most formal ball gown for the finest meal I'd known. Then he drove me to a drive-thru before taking me to the local park, where we sat on the bench in the dark." Her Scottish accent was a beautiful lilt.

"Were you annoyed?" Liss asked, glancing at a twinkling-eyed Gable.

"It was the best date I'd ever had. As I sat on dirty

swings in a beautiful navy gown, I knew I was already in love and must marry him." Beatrice's smile danced.

"Something I'd known from the moment I first saw her in the university corridors." Gable took Beatrice's hand and kissed the back of it. The love between them poured out and surrounded the group like the steam from a hot chocolate. Yet something wasn't quite right about Beatrice. Her make-up was darker than her complexion required, and she repeatedly pressed a hand to her lips. Maybe she was pushing through sickness for duty too.

"Don't forget we're celebrating tonight," the King chimed as a waiter holding a silver tray aloft paused beside them. He gifted them glasses of champagne. Gable's gaze flickered repeatedly to Beatrice as she gripped the glass tightly.

Suddenly, a woman in a black suit whispered in the King's ear. She wore an earpiece like Bear's.

Liss's eyebrows knitted in confusion.

"Nothing to worry about, darling Felicity. It's just a bit of royal business," he exclaimed. Yet he worried his hands, squeezing them together as he said it. "I'll be back in a moment. And I shall bring you another glass of champagne. We're celebrating tonight. Drink up. Drink up."

Beatrice's smile didn't reach her eyes as she nodded back. Gable rolled his shoulders as he watched the King leave. Liss glanced at Beatrice, who smoothed a hand over her stomach as if stroking her belly. Of course. All the signs were there. Pale faced, on the cusp of sickness, worried husband, and avoiding alcohol. Liss had served enough baby showers at the pub.

Liss whispered in her ear as Beatrice brushed a hand over her stomach again. "Are you?" Liss left the question hanging in the air in case Beatrice was sick rather than pregnant.

"Pregnant, yes, but only eleven weeks. I've been sick for a couple of weeks. But we can't tell anyone. We don't want to get them excited until the first scan. A royal baby is huge news. If the papers hear before the King…" Beatrice's voice trembled.

"Your secret is safe with me," Liss whispered and was gifted a hand squeeze from Beatrice. "Let me finish this and then we'll swap glasses,"

Beatrice nodded.

She downed the champagne in two gulps. She'd regret it, but it was a necessity. Beatrice quickly swapped her full one for Liss's empty flute.

"You're a breath of fresh air."

There was something endearing about Beatrice, but Liss shrugged, unused to compliments, especially from strangers. "I'll have a breath of a brewery by the end of tonight."

Beatrice giggled.

"Lissy," Steve bellowed as he bounded up to the group. "I can't wait to tell you about all the fancy people I've met."

Her introductions were quick as she reached for her bag. She took a breath and gripped it so tightly that one of its sequins fell to the ground.

"I kept the bag safe for you." Suddenly, Steve slipped a hand around her waist in a gesture too familiar for their friendship. "I hope you were okay after you fell earlier."

She nodded and eased out of his hold. He wasn't acting himself tonight, but then neither was she. She glanced at him as Gable and Beatrice politely listened to his stories about the guests he'd met.

A pale King rejoined the group. "Everything okay?" Gable asked.

"All is well." But his eyes darted around the room, and he rocked slightly on his heels. "Drink up, Felicity. You too, Gable. Beatrice is setting a fine example for us all with her empty glass. My granddaughter is home, and I only want joy here tonight."

Liss downed her drink and regretted it instantly. Her stomach lurched as Steve thrust another glass of champagne into her hand.

Gable expressed concern for the King's health, but Liss only caught the odd word. The stress of the last days and the adrenaline from her speech combined to overwhelm her. She gripped the only thing close: Steve's hand.

"Thank you for bringing me tonight," Steve whispered. "Being here with you means everything." Her stomach lurched again.

"Do you want to powder your nose?" Beatrice asked. "We can chat as we walk."

Liss nodded quickly as her hunched shoulders eased.

The men smiled as Liss and Beatrice excused themselves.

"You don't look well," Beatrice said, standing close enough to keep Liss upright but without drawing suspicion. Beatrice sneaked their drinks onto a passing tray before they stepped out of the room. Security staff hurried past. Liss struggled on her heels, clutching the doorway to stop from falling. Her feet ached more than a night shift at the pub, but princesses didn't ditch their heels.

"Beatrice, can I have a moment?" Marianne crowed as they walked through the corridor. "It's about the wedding."

Beatrice's eyes narrowed as she spoke. "I'm showing Liss where the bathroom is, although I want to talk to you about the King. I'm worried about his health. He's deteriorating too quickly. Isn't there any treatment available for him?"

Marianne swiped the question away with her hand. "The man is dying."

Liss cocked her head. "But didn't—"

"Run along to the toilets, Felicity. You look like you'll be sick, which is hardly the behaviour of royalty. Drink too much of the champagne, did we? I suppose you're not used to such fine pleasures. It's that way." Marianne pointed to a corridor.

"I'll catch you up," Beatrice said softly, her eyes crinkling in care. She squeezed her hand before Liss tottered down the corridor. Beatrice's comment to Marianne made her pause. "Don't you speak to her like that. She's part of our family now."

"Don't forget who you're speaking to, Beatrice. I will be your Queen before the end of the year, and I will have your respect," Marianne snapped.

Liss pressed her fingers against her mouth and waited, but the voices disappeared. They must have walked towards the ballroom.

Liss turned the corner. There were stairs here. An open window blasted fresh air, and she gulped it down. After a few minutes, the vomit subsided, and a joyous, easy feeling replaced it. Liss walked up the stairs until a grunt behind her made her turn.

A grumpy Bear tapped at his leg and occasionally touched his earpiece.

"What do you want now?" she huffed, fighting the attraction that made her mouth dry and a heat rise between her legs. Alcohol always made her horny, or maybe it increased her confidence and freed her. Bear continued to inspect her as if she was under his microscope.

He handed her an open bottle of water. "Drink this." She dropped her bag and downed the water, rolling her eyes at him. "I need to get you out of here."

"Why? I haven't eaten dinner yet." She attempted to walk down the stairs towards him but toppled against his body. She pressed her hands against his solid chest, and he held her arms, keeping her safe. Muscles rippled against her fingers.

"You're very strong," she said, staring at his mouth. She licked her lips slowly.

"We have to go. Strike will bring the other three, including Steve, who's been whispering in your ear and trying to touch you all night," he said. His eye twitched, and his jaw moved as if he was chewing gum. "You could do better, by the way."

"Someone like you?" Liss's hands slid down his chest as she winked at him suggestively. "You're not even my type."

"I didn't mean me." He rolled his eyes. His chest rumbled against her hands, and she squeezed gently.

Liss pushed against him and righted herself.

"It doesn't bother me. I'm not into princesses." He shrugged, but his eyes grazed her body as he spoke. "So Steve is your type?"

Liss thrust her hands to her hips. "No." Did he smile? "I like slim men, but not skinny." Her words were jumbled. "I like swimmer bodies and men without bulk."

Bear bristled, and he continued to chew. "I can outrun any guy in that room and any swimmer jock you've been with. I could easily outrun Steve."

"I don't care about that. That's not why I like them."

He smelt of fresh mint. Liss's eyes dropped, and she licked her lips again. Her hands returned to stroke his chest as she professed she didn't want a body like his.

His urgency disappeared. "Then enlighten me. What is it about?"

Liss cleared her throat as she grabbed Bear's hips. The stairs cancelled their height difference, and her body flushed at the opportunity to be at eye and mouth height with him. She dropped her voice, forcing him closer. "Because I'm tiny and can't straddle big men."

Her vision swam, but the way his eyes locked onto hers was unmistakable. His heat filled her, yet goose pimples covered her arms as he replied, "I guarantee you'd have no problems wrapping your legs around me. And if it didn't risk everything Strike and I worked for, and if you weren't drunker than a student at fresher's week, I'd insist on lifting you, pushing you against the wall, and proving it right here."

"But someone could walk past?" She gripped his waist tighter. He was like a wall of fire, and she wanted to combust in him.

"I'd give you the fuck of your life right here, and I wouldn't care who saw. Maybe I'd want them to watch how I own your pleasure when you scream my name. And I can finally admit that because you won't remember what I said in the morning." But she never forgot the things she heard when drunk. It was her superpower. Bear tucked a wave of hair behind her ear and brushed her forehead with his lips. "Now we need to get you out of here and then get you to bed with water and paracetamol, Princess."

"Stop calling me that." She pushed against him again

and fell back to sit on the stairs. She wasn't acting like a princess, and she didn't care what people thought. Fuck everyone who wanted to judge her. Liss folded her arms and glared at him.

"Stop pouting. Somehow, it makes you even sexier. And like it or not, you're a princess, and I have a job to do." His gaze flicked around the stairway. "My instincts tell me we don't want to stay here much longer, so let's grab your bag and go."

Liss pushed him away as he tried to grab her hand to help her up. "Nope." She stood and sashayed further up the stairs. The slit of her dress revealed her thigh. "This is my party, and I will have fun."

"Don't make me chase you." She froze to the spot. Why did that sound so fucking hot? "I've done this the nice way, so now the hard way," he growled. The sound vibrated in her pussy.

"I'd like to see your hard way," Liss sassed, hiding how her hands shook.

"I'm giving you to the count of five," he growled.

She imagined him counting to five before slamming her against the wall and fucking her into submission. Liss looked over her shoulder and found Bear staring at her bottom. She grinned, wiggled her eyebrows, and jiggled her bum. "My eyes are up here," she replied. "And FYI, you don't get to tell me what to do. You're not the boss of me."

"That's where you're wrong. I'm not only your boss, but I also own you for the next week. Now be a good girl, or I'll put you over my knee," he replied, his tongue darting to lick his lips. She ran up the stairs, but he climbed the stairs in strides and was quickly right behind her. He grabbed and tossed her over his shoulder before handing her her bag and walking her back down the stairs. "I'm taking you safely to bed."

"You wish," she said, wiggling against him.

There was a sound at his earpiece. "I'm on my way," he replied.

"Where are we going?" she asked as he stepped through an unfamiliar corridor. It was rudimentary compared to the others she'd seen that night, with no fancy lighting or paintings on the wall. She gripped her clutch bag tightly as he pushed open the doors.

"We're heading to the servant's exit. It's secure."

The split above her leg was getting wider and was close to revealing her underwear. She tried to grab the material, but it caused Bear to huff as he held her tightly against his shoulder.

She rolled her eyes.

"Less sass from you," he grunted.

"But—"

"I've got eyes in the back of my head, and I saw your reflection in the glass door we passed through," he conceded. All the corridors merged as she languished against him. They passed through another door. Smells of roasted meat and creamy dishes filled this corridor.

"I like it up here," she announced. "It's a new perspective, and I don't have to walk. My feet hurt, although I adore the fancy shoes. Thank you for buying them; they are beautiful."

They'd reached an entranceway now. "My pleasure." Bear pulled Liss off him and placed her in the corner of the cramped space.

"We're here. Bring the car," he said into his earpiece as Liss shouted, "Feet! Sore feet!" She dropped her bag to use both hands to unsnap her shoes.

"I'm not picking you up again, so you'll have to put them back on." He stared daggers at her.

Liss parted her lips, but he pressed against the earpiece again. His shoulders tensed. Mentally, he wasn't in the same space as her, and the low chatter she picked up from his ear turned into a frantic blasting. She couldn't distinguish the words, but his eyes darted around the small space, and his hand went under his jacket.

"A threat? We knew something was off. The car is arriving now. I'll bring her straight there."

Liss tucked her bag under her arm and grabbed her shoes, but unceremoniously, Bear flung her back over his shoulder. Her handbag hit the floor.

"My bag," she shouted as he pushed through the doors.

"There isn't time. You can replace everything in there." He strode across the asphalt. Darkness surrounded them in the back of the palace. Gone were the ladies and gentlemen in all their finery.

"But it's important!" Bear was still professional, but his body was more rigid beneath her than before. He'd raised his shoulders and was primed for action. "Bear, please."

She didn't care if she was bought all the jewels in the world if she didn't have her keepsake.

"For fuck sake," he grumbled. It was fast becoming his catchphrase. He kept Liss tight to him as he returned to her bag, grabbed it off the floor, and held it close. Bear rushed them back outside. He reached a new black four-by-four. He quickly looked around it, careful not to swing her around, before dropping her and her bag in the front seat and clicking in her seatbelt. Within minutes, they were speeding out of the palace grounds by a secret exit that avoided the long driveway.

With his fixed expression and mouth set in a thin line, she didn't ask questions. He handed her another water bottle and a chocolate bar, and she thanked him before consuming both. Liss sneaked a look in her bag and found the heart talisman. She gripped it and stared out of the window.

The city's lights flashed by, but soon, they were less frequent. Her eyes drooped, and her heart slowed after the frantic escape. Eventually, when she couldn't fight the tiredness any longer, her eyes fluttered closed.

Chapter Twenty-Nine

Liss woke in an unfamiliar space.

Light slipped through an open doorway, softly filling the room. Pink flowers bloomed up the walls, reminding her of her neighbours, Helen and Ted, who kept an eye on her when she was home from school.

Once a month, if her mum wasn't working, they invited Liss and her mum for dinner. Ted was the grandad she didn't have. He'd sip a glass of whisky at the end of the day but top it up when Helen wasn't watching, although she always was. Liss shucked in bed, smelling the faint scent of lavender, wishing to return to the time before her mum lost contact with the couple. Liss's throat thickened. They were another reminder that she was alone unless she accepted joining the royal family. But the cost was growing.

Suddenly, a photo caught her eye. It was of a couple around their late fifties standing with Strike and Bear. The couple beamed, and the bodyguards, in jumpers and jeans, smiled too. Were Bear and Strike brothers after all?

Liss threw on the jumper that sat at the end of the bed over her dress and crept around the room. There were more photos of the couple. Liss watched the passage of time as she spied a chuckling blond baby on the beach with a bucket and spade that was too big for him.

As she sneaked out of the room, she saw a photo of the same blond boy still young and in his school uniform. Although there were no massive muscles or telltale glare, the blond hair, beauty spot near his ear, and slightly off-centre smile reminded her of Strike. Liss continued down the corridor, spying another photo of Strike in a rugby kit. He couldn't be more than eight but was larger than the other children.

There was a photo of the couple before the grey hair pushed through the light brown, with Strike outside Buckingham Palace. With travel guides in hand and a camera hanging around the older guy's neck, they were the epitome of tourists. More images were taken at famous UK holiday hotspots before the wall transformed into photos of a slightly sour-faced Strike in a different school uniform.

Liss wrapped her arms around her body. The relief that her arm was healed couldn't replace the knowledge that her grandma had ditched all her photos of Liss. There were only so many times her nana could say, "She looks like a munchkin," before her mum gave up. Liss didn't belong to anyone, and since her mum died, no one celebrated her life as Strike's family celebrated his.

Liss paused on the stairs. Where was Bear in the photos? One of the images of Strike with Bear appeared as if on command. They both looked like older teenagers, but Strike carried a little more of his adult bulk. Strike was smiling broadly, as were the couple, but Bear stood to the side, out of place. Liss leant closer to study him. His hands were covered by his sleeves as if he'd dragged them down to hide something, and a bruise peeked out of the collar of his shirt.

Voices from a room at the bottom of the stairs

couldn't distract Liss from the bodyguard memorabilia. There was a collection of winner trophies with a boxer on top. The name Drew Chambers was etched on each one. Next to the awards was a certificate for Caleb Moorcroft for graduating from school.

Liss eased herself down the stairs. In bare feet, she was as silent as a mouse. A photo on the wall showed a proud Strike with the same certificate, and below that photo was another where he wore military dress. She reflected the smile of the proud soldier with her own.

She froze at the next picture. Bear held his arms aloft. He was bloody and bruised, but his grin suggested he'd won the biggest fight of his life. He probably had, based on his baggy red striped shorts and naked chest. So he was Drew, and he boxed. At least that explained the weird boxing he and Strike did on movie night.

"They still can't find them?" Bear asked from the side room, distracting her from the photos.

"No."

Bear and Strike stood by a rustic kitchen table topped by two empty cups and the phone on speaker that they talked into. The bodyguards wore their smart clothes from the party, although they'd undone their shirt collars and draped their jackets on chairs. Bear paced, but Strike was like stone.

"They have to be together somewhere," Strike said, pushing the chair back with a scrape against the floor.

"Check with Liss," Steve shouted through the speaker. "Where are you anyway? I should be with her."

Bear suddenly stopped and hunched his shoulders, but he relaxed at a brief shake of Strike's head. "Liss is asleep, and you don't need to know where we are."

Steve's voice pitched. "Let me guess. It's confidential

except for jumped-up bodyguards who think they know best when they've fucked up and don't know shit. How could you let Liss go to the palace when you suspected something? And now my brother and Isla are missing—"

Liss jumped into the room. With reflexes that made more sense after seeing the soldier photo, Strike grabbed the phone and turned it off the speaker.

"I'm on my way. I'll find them," Strike said and hung up as Bear grabbed Liss.

"What the hell is going on? Someone tell me before I fuck everyone up." She knew how ludicrous it seemed, a five-foot woman threatening two men who towered above her and could toss her into a bin.

"We can't find Isla and Steve's brother. The royal guards are checking the palace for a bomb, and a guard we've worked with is at the hotel, as we got a threat there too. The bomb threat was for you, and we presume she's safe, but in the meantime, we'll continue searching for her as if she's at risk," Bear explained as Strike grabbed his jacket and slipped out of the room. "I'll be back in two minutes, okay? But could you make us a coffee while I speak to Strike?"

Liss nodded, the wind yanked out of her from the lack of fight and how simply Bear shared the news. She busied herself at the kettle before opening cupboards and drawers. Someone wanted her dead. She rattled a biscuit tin, but it was empty. She grabbed a milk jug from the fridge. It was nearly empty. If Isla was hurt, it would be Liss's fault. The jug slipped from her hand as she bumped into a chair. Glass smashed across the floor. The dregs of milk flowed over the hardwood floor, and glass spread to the far reaches of the room.

She cried as she imagined Isla trapped by an invisible force. She shouldn't have gone to the party or drunk alcohol. She might have noticed what was happening. Liss reached for a chunk of broken glass, but Bear grabbed her hand.

"There's no point crying over spilt milk," he whispered in her ear. She spun on her toes and went to hit him, but he caught her hand in his and held her still as she wept against him.

"It's all my fault," she gasped between sobs.

"No, it's the fault of some psycho who has an agenda that we're still trying to understand. Let me pick you up so you don't cut your feet on the glass."

"But the coffees," she cried.

"I'll sort those." He sat her on the table and ripped open a chocolate bar. "You need sugar."

"Are you a chocolate magician? You always have one of these to hand."

Bear shrugged as she placed a square of chocolate in her mouth.

Bear brushed a broom softly against the floor while explaining that the bomb threats had come in after she spoke on stage. They'd checked the building, and while Bear got her out, they'd learnt the hotel was at risk.

Liss pulled her hair like butterfly wings to tighten her ponytail. Dark waves cascaded down her back. He watched every movement.

"Strike found a suspicious guy in the palace cellar during one of his sweeps, and security is interviewing him now."

Bear sunk to the chair in front of where she remained on the table and wrapped his hands around her calves before pulling her closer to him. She sighed as she stared into his eyes.

"So what now?" she asked, her eyes dropping to his creased shirt. "What can I do?"

"Nothing," Bear replied. His hands remained on her calves, warming her skin. "We have to wait and see what everyone finds. My aim is always to keep you safe. So we brought you here, which is a first for this house. No one will find you here, and we trust you to keep this place secret when this is over."

Bear closed his eyes and puffed out a breath. He was weary too. She shifted closer, and inadvertently, his hands slid to her thighs under her dress.

"It's been a long day," she said.

He nodded slowly, looking back up at her. "That it has, Liss."

"And I'm sorry for shouting at you in the palace." His brows knitted together. "When I said you had your walls up and wouldn't know how to be anyone's boyfriend."

Bear shrugged. "I've had worse."

"But not from me. Not like that."

"It's okay. Last night was a lot for you. And I was being overprotective. I'm sorry. I wanted to keep you safe, but I didn't need to be a controlling dick about it." They smiled softly at each other. They'd survived their first proper argument. "How's your arm?"

She waggled it. "Better."

He raised an eyebrow. Liss fought the temptation to flatten it. "And how is your head?"

Her gaze soured. "I wish I hadn't drunk so much."

His fingers stroked her thighs as he smiled. "You were sozzled."

Liss pulled away in an attempt to kick him, but Bear

held firm. Her belly ached at his touch. "Will Strike bring Isla here if he finds her?"

Bear looked away. "Probably not. We want to keep her safe, but you're our priority."

The clock above the oven drew her attention. All they could do was wait. Bear continued his strokes, and her legs trembled under his palms. Liss had been selfish at the palace, only caring about herself, and Bear was right. She was drunk.

"You're thinking too hard," he uttered as he squeezed her thighs.

She glared. "I need a distraction. I can't keep sitting here when my friend may be injured and while that guy is interviewed." She pulled herself out of Bear's grasp and jumped off the table. She strode back and forth across the kitchen floor, her dress dancing around her legs.

"There might still be shards of glass," Bear shouted, but Liss continued to pace and wring her hands together.

She might be trapped forever. Her future couldn't involve friends because her choices put them at risk.

Bear reached to still her, but she ducked away. She scratched at her arms. "There's no point holding me still. If I stop pacing, then I'll fall apart. I can't believe someone wants me and my friends dead. I don't want to cry anymore. I need to know if Isla is safe. Please distract me, Bear." Her shakes were uncontrollable now, and her throat was closing.

Bear wrapped his arm around her waist to hold her still. He chewed at his lips. Her pulse was rising. "I can only think of one way, but you won't like it."

She narrowed her eyes. "You're going to try to kiss me while my friend is missing?"

"Of course not. I don't need to touch you to distract

you." The depth of his voice tickled her skin like his thumbs had earlier. But his furrowed brow betrayed an uncertainty. "I want to ask you a question."

Liss shrugged. How distracting could a question be? Was it a maths quiz? "Only if I get to ask you one," she countered.

He locked her gaze. Even in a cosy family kitchen, he transformed her shakes into shivers. "Okay." Crinkles appeared around his eyes. "You've never been fucked."

"That's not a question," she snapped. "And people need to stop saying it."

"Why?" he grunted.

"Why what?"

"Why have you never been fucked?"

Liss pushed his hands away and walked around the table to create a barrier. She shoved her hands on her hips. "I've had sex. It was fine." She raised her voice. His distraction worked, which made her angrier because he'd done as she asked. "I don't understand the obsession with it. And what does getting fucked mean anyway?"

"Sex should never be fine," Bear replied.

Liss raised an eyebrow and bared her teeth.

"Remember the sex you had," he continued as he walked around the table to meet her. "Was it hard, fast passion that made your body sore but left every limb buzzing with adrenaline? Did you think about it for days? When you sat at your desk, did you have flashbacks to how he made you scream as he thrust inside you? Fucking is an addiction. When you're properly fucked, it's all you can think about. You touch yourself, desperate to feel it again."

She froze as he closed in on her. Their stares locked. Liss couldn't form words, not that she knew what to say.

Her skin blistered with anticipation, and she rolled her hips as his words teased her. His hand brushed her ponytail, making it swing.

"Have you experienced a moment where you relive the build-up to the climax and you find yourself biting your lip or unable to continue a conversation because all you want is to ride him again or have him inside you? You're desperate for your skin to be touched because it will spark a memory and a sensation. You don't get sex like that with everyone, and there is a place for the loving kind, too, but there's something irresistible..." His lips were on the cusp of brushing hers. "...something life-transforming about a fuck that makes your soul ache as you touch yourself and relive it."

His breath rasped as she leaned in for that touch.

"I thought you said we shouldn't do this," she replied as shivers criss-crossed up and down her legs, and she quivered under his heady gaze.

"I say a lot of things, and most of them are bullshit."

She laughed despite the intensity of the moment. "You're a dick, an irresistible one, but a dick nonetheless."

"You're distracted, though."

She pulled her lips into her mouth. "Maybe you should check in with Strike."

As if on cue, Bear's phone rang. He answered immediately, his stare never leaving her.

"Good. I'll tell her," he replied to a male voice that sounded like Strike. He hung up the phone and said, "Isla's safe. Strike found her and Steve's brother doing something similar to what we were talking about. She didn't know about the bomb."

"Cool."

"Cool."

"And thank you for distracting me. You're very good at faking desire."

"Yep, I'm like fucking Tom Hardy with my acting skills," he grunted as he fisted his hands. "I'm going to do a perimeter check, and you should probably get back to bed. Strike will bring your clothes as soon as the hotel is secured. We'll stay here until you move to the palace and take up your place with new security."

Bear walked with a wider gait than usual and banged the kitchen door. "Fuck," he grunted from the other side. And then he was gone.

Chapter Thirty

Liss stretched out in bed. Sleep was a waste of time, and she'd rested enough.

With the curtains tightly closed and her burner phone and watch in her bag, time lost meaning. She needed to make a decision about accepting the throne. The King suggested the family would be there for her, but his health was rapidly deteriorating.

And then there was Bear. They barely knew each other, yet she couldn't deny her attraction. Maybe it was just the connection of two people in an intense situation.

Yet she couldn't stop thinking about him and his past. Even now, she wanted to be sitting near him as he worked.

Liss huffed loudly. Her mum used to say that a cup of tea and a biscuit solved everything. Maybe she was right. Yet again, Liss walked down the hall of memories dedicated to Strike's family. She paused briefly at the photo of Bear, his arms raised in glory. He was majestic.

A ringing phone in the kitchen drew her closer, but Bear wasn't there. Papers littered the countertop and table she'd sat on earlier.

The ringing from beneath the messy stack of papers wasn't stopping. Liss untied and retied her ponytail, but the delay didn't prevent the phone from ringing. Bear would be angry if she answered it, but Strike might need him urgently. She pushed the stack to the side, sat, stood, and sat several times, holding the phone.

The name on the screen said, "The Big Cheese." Was that an inside joke and another name for Strike? She poked her head out the door, but there was no Bear.

Liss pressed answer.

"Hello, Bear's phone," she said with a fake clear-cut accent. She'd turned into her nana. "Can I help?"

"I need to speak to Bear immediately. Strike isn't answering his phone. What sort of half-assessed operation are you running over there?" a snooty man shouted.

The drama of the previous evening and all the events following took their toll. This guy was wasting time when Strike might have been calling about the bomber.

"We're running a company that doesn't need your attitude or business." Her pub persona kicked in. It was the personality she brought when someone drank too much and vomited on her pub floor. "The men are in a highly confidential and imperative meeting, and you don't get to make demands from them just because you shout the loudest."

"But—"

"But nothing, sir," she cut in. Maybe dickheads were the distraction she needed. The tension of the last days came out in force against the unsuspecting arsehole. "If you'd like to leave a message for Bear, I'll ensure he gets it as soon as his meeting finishes, but if you'd rather rant without reason, I'll happily tell you where you can shove your business. They are busy men with enough business to avoid dealing with people like you. Are we clear?" Liss paced the kitchen as she fisted her hand.

"Fine," he stuttered. "Can you get them to call me as I need to book them?"

Was she speaking to the minion for a cheese company? The Big Cheese wasn't a brand she recognised. "Certainly. Can I take a name? Presumably, the number to call is the one you called Bear on."

"You want my name?" the caller's voice pitched.

Liss snapped, "Unless you'd like Bear to speak to a psychic before he calls you, it would be helpful." Somewhere in the house, the toilet flushed. What would Bear say if he caught her on his phone? Liss ran around the room, searching for a pen, but there was nothing. She yanked open the fridge and grabbed the first thing to hand: a can of squirty cream. "When you're ready."

"The name is Brian Fellowfeather," was the curt reply.

Of course it was something impossibly long. Hopefully, there was enough cream in the can.

"Thank you. I shall let Bear know when he comes out of his meeting."

"Make sure he does, as I want him and Strike in two weeks."

"Have a lovely day," Liss replied, returning to her polite phone voice as she swept the papers on the table to the side. Brian grumbled the same before hanging up.

With the phone still in her hand, she sprayed the name on the table as Bear walked in and leaned against the doorway.

"So many questions," he said smirking. "But the first is what are you doing on my phone?"

"It rang, and I answered. Don't get pissy about it." He opened his mouth and closed it again. "You look like a fish."

He puffed out his chest. "A sexy fish?"

"Obviously," she sassed.

"The phone, Liss," he replied, his voice low and his arms folded.

"Is that the way to talk to the woman who got you a job with The Big Cheese?" she replied, adding a swirly line beneath the name Brian Fellowfeather and staring proudly at her work.

Bear strode to the table. His eyebrows were nearly touching his hairline. "Are you kidding me? You spoke to Brian?"

Liss shrugged. "The guy is a dick, but I put him in his place. Stop staring at me like that."

"You have no clue who he is, do you?" Bear's face went slack. "Did you give him attitude?"

"Maybe." She winced. "How important is this cheese factory owner?"

"For fucks sake, Liss. You spoke to the Prime Minister's director of operations. He's a client we've tried to land for years. He expects people to lick his boots."

"Well, I didn't do that. I may have suggested we didn't need Brian's attitude or business." Bear's mouth dropped open, so she promptly added, "But I told him you'd call back when you were out of your meeting. And I'm quoting him word for word. He said, 'I want him and Strike in two weeks.' I guess I got you a job. I accept thanks in money or chocolate."

She squeezed a glob of cream directly from the can into her mouth as she grinned at Bear. Sugar coated her tongue.

"We can't do then," he replied in a high-pitched voice. A panicked Bear was a surprise. "Once you're done with us, we've got invoices and reports to complete for previous clients, and Luke is too busy with IT, not that he can type reports, but then neither can we and—"

Liss sprayed a glob of cream onto his nose to quieten him. He rolled his eyes but calmed slightly, especially when she wiped off a blob with her finger and pressed it between her lips. She sucked hard as he raised his eyebrow and shook his head.

As the cream languished on her tongue, she said, "I'll deal with that. I've done things like it for the pub, and I can touch type. It's the distraction I need." Bear's eyes were wide as she managed his concerns. "But you've only got me for a week because…we won't discuss what's happening then. In the meantime, start thinking about getting an office manager, because you need to sort out your admin, bookings, and everything else."

Strike arrived within the hour with a bag of clothes for Liss.

As soon as she was make-up–free and in her joggers and strappy top, she relocated to the living room, where she spread notes scribbled on serviettes and every other scrap of paper across chairs and the surrounding floor. It was another photo-filled room. She placed the information in piles and developed a system as the smiling couple from their wedding photo gazed back at her.

Strike and Bear mumbled outside the room, but she demanded the speaker play Taylor Swift as she immersed herself in the mess. It looked like no one had touched their paperwork in ages. It was a surprise they'd survived this long with their inability to match invoices to half-written reports.

Liss sang along with Taylor until she became aware of the two bodyguards staring at her from the doorway. Strike worried his lip while Bear's brows knotted together.

"My singing isn't that bad," she joked before demanding Alexa pause.

"We need to talk to you about something," Bear mumbled, striding into the room.

"Don't mess up my piles," she shouted, forcing Bear into the nearest rosy pink sofa chair and Strike to perch on its arm. Their massive bodies looked hilarious in the furniture made for smaller people, but at their pensive faces, her smile froze. "What now?"

"We need to tell you about the bomb threats," Strike said slowly.

Bear rubbed his stubbly chin absentmindedly. He filled the chair to the point that it could burst. All it would take was one of his stretches.

"Stop pussy footing around me. Tell me so I can get back to the tunes," she snapped.

Bear raised his eyebrow, but the rest of his face didn't change.

"There were no bombs. We checked everywhere, so you don't need to worry about that." Liss made a wind-up finger movement as he spoke. Strike usually faced everything head-on like a bull. "But it came with a threat."

"And?" she replied, drawing out the word and getting a wide-eyed stare from Strike. "There's no point sugar-coating it anymore. I'm getting used to being at risk."

"Yeah, sure," Strike replied edgily as he wrung his hands together. "So the threat came in."

"Spit it out."

Bear's eye twitched as he spoke. "They said they'll kill

you if you don't renounce the throne."

Liss sat back on her feet and lowered her head. The fear was there, but there was something about this house, being overseen by Strike's family photos, that made that fear manageable. Maybe she was numb, or the last days had taken their toll.

"Liss?" And there was something about Bear and Strike too. They made her feel safe. She'd spent her adult life searching for something and now she might have found it in her bodyguards. She sighed loudly. Maybe she was training herself to become used to the drama because she would take the throne. She didn't know anymore.

From the corner of her eye, Strike shrugged helplessly at Bear, who mouthed, "Is she okay?"

"Guys, chill the fuck out. I'm fine, but I dunno. I thought it would be bigger." They stared at her like she'd grown a spare head from her shoulder. "Will you continue to keep me safe?"

"Of course." Bear nodded like a dog desperate for a treat.

"But aren't you scared?" Strike asked. "Especially as you want to be a princess."

"Yes, but I'm managing it." Liss watched the men, who looked more like little boys asking the grumpy neighbour for their ball back than bad ass bodyguards. "I'm not sure what I want—"

"But you said an hour ago that I—I mean, we—only had you for a week," Bear cut in before clearing his throat.

"Yes, because I might take up the throne, but either way, things are changing." Bear opened his mouth, but she set her jaw and continued. "Whatever this bomb threat is about, it's out of my control, and my decision about taking the throne is the thing I can control. As long as my friends are safe and I have you two, then I'll make my decision with consideration. Being a princess makes sense because maybe it's my calling. I've never been good at anything else, but for now, I'll stay here and do your filing, type up your reports, and enjoy my last days of trapped freedom. Is that okay?"

They paused and nodded synchronously but continued to twist their lips.

"If that's everything, can one of you make dinner as I'm starving?"

They nodded again before tiptoeing out of the room.

Chapter Thirty-One

The scent of pasta sauce wafted through to the living room.

The growl from Liss's belly echoed her sentiment that it was the best thing she'd smelt in days, apart from Bear. The rumbles turned to flutters as she reached the kitchen and witnessed the man who would destroy her enemies humming to classic pop playing from the radio while stirring something on the stove. A pink apron hung around his neck, although he'd left the tie strings undone.

There was a softness to his face that she'd only seen in one of the family photos, and as she stared in a dreamy trance, she vowed to know more of this carefree Bear if he let her. This version of him was like a new song. And the way he talked to her about fucking earlier was liquid arousal. The combination of the two versions was irresistible.

He spun on his toes as the singer hit her high notes. His spoon was his microphone as he belted out the Whitney Houston classic. Suddenly, he froze as he saw Liss.

"You okay there, Mr. Bear?" she replied with a smile. "I thought you had eyes in the back of your head."

He blushed as he laughed with a throaty sound. "Even bodyguards are allowed a break to murder the classics."

Bear was more likely to murder her heart. But as he

kicked out one of the chairs for her to sit, she went to him. "Let me do this up first. I'm worried you'll trip, and I can't have my karaoke king upended on the floor." She stroked his body unnecessarily as she reached for the strings, and he leaned into her, wrapping his arms around her waist from behind. They stayed like that for a second. With his arms around her, her heart rate slowed even as goose pimples rose on her arms. It was a different kind of intimacy from all the sexual touches they'd had. Did the prospect of the following week being their last together mean they were letting their barriers down? It made sense, as it was something her mum had once told her when she was dying. Suddenly, the rules didn't matter when your fate was decided. This week was their now or never. But maybe he was like this because of the house. It was a special place for the guys. Perhaps it was his safe space to be the real him.

Liss's heart slowed as she basked in the connection. This man, a stranger, was someone significant. She couldn't tell him she wanted more because it was impossible to have more.

Her stomach rumbled again, breaking the moment, and he resumed stirring the sauce as she tied his apron in a knot before patting his bottom.

"What are we having?" she asked breezily.

"My signature dish is pasta bolognese with garlic bread. All homemade, of course," Bear replied as she sat at the table. Her limbs were lighter than they'd been in days, maybe years. Bear flipped the oven door and pulled out the bread with one hand while stirring the pasta with another. Domesticated Bear was a revelation.

"I didn't know you were a chef." She briefly closed her

eyes and breathed the scent of freshly cooked garlic bread. A moan slipped from her lips.

Bear pulled on the back of his neck as he reached for the plates. He was so endearing.

"To be honest," he said over his shoulder, "I can't cook many things. Strike's mum taught me before I left home, as she said a man should be able to cook at least one dish in case someone special visits. I'm still unsure if she referred to herself or a future partner."

These nuggets about his past were more valuable than gold, and she held tightly to every one.

"There's wine in the rack over there. Pour a glass if your head can handle it."

Liss ignored his tease as she poured herself a drink. It wasn't the time to revisit the conversation before he'd carried her to safety. She went to pour him one, too, but he shook his head. Still on duty.

"So you use this dish to woo the ladies?"

Bear stopped, and his brow knitted together as he stared at the ceiling. "I don't think I've cooked this for anyone but Jeanette and Cliff, Strike's parents. I guess there isn't much kitchen time when I'm with women. Unless you count when they're screaming from the countertop while I lick—"

Liss covered her ears. "La la la," she sang. "I don't need to hear about your sex life."

He placed the food in front of her. Bear knelt before her, taking her hands off her ears before holding them still. His hands were rough, and she resisted the urge to run her fingers across each bump and healing cut.

"Princess, I don't need to say anything for you to imagine me naked. I can see it on your face whenever you bite your lip or squeeze your eyes tightly closed. But remember: you're the only woman, other than Ma, that I've cooked for, and yet I've still not been between your beautiful thighs. Now eat your food like a good girl, and maybe I'll let you have pudding."

She shoved him away as he beamed at her. Her desire ramped up from PG-13 to rated R within a few sentences. Taking a slow sip of wine, she regrouped as he chuckled while grating parmesan onto her dinner before sitting opposite her.

"I didn't get to ask my question earlier, by the way."

"Go on then," he replied before popping a piece of butterfly pasta between his rosy lips.

"You said Ma and talked about leaving home. Are you and Strike brothers?" Bear shook his head as he chewed. "You're in loads of photos, but there's none of you until you're a teenager."

"I've said that Strike was my family. I know what it's like when those closest to you by blood aren't there for you. My parents weren't my biggest fans when I was growing up. I was hard work. Most weeks, the head dragged my parents to school to sort out one mess or another. I was a difficult kid who became a difficult teenager and ran with a bad crowd. You know the sort, getting into fights, shoplifting, and being dicks. But Ma and Pa, my jokey name for Jeannette and Cliff, took me in when I needed somewhere to live, and they treated me like a son. We became a makeshift family, although not here. They live here now when they're not travelling the world."

There was a lot of information, and she had more questions, but as her mum used to say, don't empty the jar all at once in case you can't handle the contents. "And where are they now, or are they due home tonight?"

"They're in Thailand. You can't keep them still for long; they're always off to parts of the world they've not seen. It's for the best they're not back tonight, as there's only three bedrooms, and you and me would need to share a bed," he said with a wink. It was as if he couldn't do truth for long. "That's your question over with," he added.

"Okay, that's fair. I won't press you anymore for now, but I have more questions," Liss said, tapping her knife on the table.

"I don't doubt it, but I'd be happy for you to press me later," he added with a head tilt.

This guy.

The following days passed in a mixture of paperwork, movie nights, and meals. Liss spoke to Isla on the phone daily and managed a call with Steve and her grandad too. Her life was slowly changing, yet she and Bear found innocent ways to touch each other constantly. But it never went further. Strike's presence was a constant reminder that this was their job, not some pre-royalty fling. Yet her heart was investing in Bear, and it was getting harder to control.

"House check, done," Bear announced as he entered the living room, where Liss finished a report. "We've got more alarms around this place than the palace, but a visual check of the equipment and space doesn't hurt. Have you spoken to the King?"

"I spoke to him briefly," Liss replied, stretching her neck from side to side. The paperwork was a great distraction and allowed her to do something she could master, but sitting on the floor was playing havoc with her body. "It's weird to have a day without Strike. I've got used to having you two around all the time and Luke on speed dial. I'm going to miss you three when everything changes."

The last three days they'd become a little family, working around each other, eating meals together and dialling Luke in during the evenings to watch movies with them. She winced as her shoulders clicked. Bar work was a nightmare for her body, and it wasn't unusual for her to be soaking her weary limbs in the bath after a shift so she could sleep. She missed the pub, but with time away, she admitted she'd been hiding there since her mum died.

She sucked in a breath as Bear's hands rested against her shoulders. "Is it okay if I help you? I've experienced enough pains to know it's best to deal with them when you can."

Liss nodded as her mouth dried up.

"Where does it hurt? Direct me." Such a simple request made her body thrum.

Bear smoothed his thumbs over her shoulders, working down her back. She made noises of appreciation. It was good, but it wasn't enough. She could take her top off…

"It might be easier if you remove your jumper so I can get to your muscles," he said, reading her thoughts.

Liss held her breath as she eased off her jumper, leaving her in a tight, strappy top. His fingers got to work immediately. Occasionally, he'd find a knot and push his thumbs against it until it popped. His hands manipulated her body. She shivered, and he paused. "My hair," she said as if in explanation, and he swept her ponytail to the side.

His breath touched her neck, and she shivered again.

They wouldn't dare do this with Strike around, but he'd been gone all day preparing for the next job.

"So, the King," she managed to say, although, with a mouth as dry as sandpaper, it came out as a croak. "I'm worried about his health. He's deteriorating all the time. I only managed a brief conversation with him alone. I'm worried that all isn't as it seems."

His hands travelled lower until they were pressing against her lower back. She let out a deep moan. "What can you do about it? Is there anyone else you can speak to, maybe his doctor?" His woody and fruity scent filled her, and at his proximity, an extra scent of something else in his aftershave reminded her of trips to the sea. Liss eased back against him and immersed herself in his touch.

"I don't have access to him, but maybe Beatrice does. I liked her, and she'd be a great person on my side, but I don't have her number." She stumbled over her words. Bear worked back and forth on a knot below her shoulder blades.

"Strike will get it. He knew her brother in the forces. Leave it with me," he added, his voice slow and deep. "And so you know, we've got a plan for the rest of the week. We'll spend a few more days here, and on Thursday evening, we'll return to town. Friday is the big announcement."

Her sigh was deeper than the arousal sneaking through her bones. "When I take the throne or renounce it?"

"Yep."

She was on the cusp of asking what he thought she should do when he worked out a knot she'd never reached. She let out a throaty moan, and his body juddered behind her. "Cool. I think we're good," he said, clearing his throat. "What do you want to do tonight?"

Liss looked over her shoulder and smiled at his blushing face. Liss licked her lips before parting them seductively.

"Shush, you," he grumbled. "I meant, which movie do you want to watch? I don't want to risk more chatting, as you keep getting my secrets."

Liss chuckled. She'd learnt much about him over the last few days, which only worsened her attachment. Less chatting was a good idea. "Whatever movie you want to watch. It's your choice, but no more romcoms. I need a break."

"It's just us tonight. Luke is sorting out tech for the next job. Strike's back at some point, but probably not until the early hours," he said, shifting his trousers. "I'll get the snacks."

He'd reached the doorway as she shouted, "And get into something more comfortable. Those trousers seem to be frustrating you, and I'd hate for you to feel restrained."

He grunted a nonsensical response as he left the room. The relaxed version of him was too easy to tease.

Chapter Thirty-Two

Bear's second favourite movie genre played on the tiny television in the semi-dark room. *Die Hard* was everything she was expecting an action movie to be: gritty life-or-death situations with a damaged hero trying his best. She was basically watching Bear's life.

Without Strike keeping an eye on them, they'd sat against each other. Bear's body was warm, and as Liss fought sleep, she rested her head on his shoulder and curled up against him. When he wrapped an arm around her and his hand stroked her back gently, she reminded herself they were just friends hanging out. Since they'd met, her life had brimmed with stress, distraction, and exhaustion, and tonight was no different. But within the safety of Bear, her limbs lightened, and her breathing slowed.

His lips brushed her head, and she slid her hand under his top and stroked his chest. His muscles quivered, and she remembered all he'd said in the kitchen about what it was like to be properly fucked.

"Liss," he grunted as she leaned against his chest. "I don't get involved with clients."

His heart beat rapidly. Usually, she'd take the rejection and leave, but there was something in how he said it, like a grain of hope rested on his tongue.

"I won't be a client soon, and then we'll never see each other again. I'll have guards and be locked away from the world," she replied, biting the inside of her mouth. "You don't get involved with clients. But I won't use anything against you. You don't have to invest in this or me, so don't worry that I'll text you all the time. I get what this is."

He paused the film and faced her. He tracked her tongue as she ran it across her lips. "You deserve to have someone invested in you," he said as he tucked a strand of hair behind her ear. She closed her eyes, remembering his lips brushing her forehead in the palace. "Look at me, baby."

Liss opened her eyes to find Bear worrying his lip as he stared at her. "You don't do hookups."

"I don't do good sex either, apparently." Liss attempted to lighten the moment but resigned herself to the truth at Bear's intensity. "Next week, I won't be able to have casual sex or fun dates. We both have a lot to lose. If I sleep with some random guy, the media will be all over it. There's so much I've missed out on, and I'm scared I won't ever have it."

She dropped her head, but he tucked his finger under her chin and eased it back up. "I don't want to hurt you, Liss, but this will be a one-off—well, three-off—once I discover how to make you come hard. I'm not relationship material. But I'd be lying if I said I hadn't thought about you naked and moaning my name since the second you cheeked me in the Bentley. Are you sure you can do this without feelings?"

She brushed the pad of her finger across his lower lip. His nostrils flared as she dipped her head to kiss him. He eased his mouth open, and their tongues explored each other. His fingers threaded into her hair, pulling out the elastic that held her ponytail, and she leaned into the kiss. She stroked his stubble with the back of her knuckles. Shivers slid up and down her back as she took the kiss deeper, pushed him against the sofa, and climbed onto his lap. His hands gripped her thighs as she ground against him.

"Princess," he uttered against her lips. "Don't stress. I want this, but you didn't answer my question. Are you sure you can do this without feelings?"

Of course she couldn't, but she needed it. Her pulse quickened as she took one of his hands and pressed it against her breast.

"We only have a few days left, so how many feelings can I get?" She struggled to catch her breath as he thumbed her nipple. "Please show me what it is to be well and truly fucked. I can't spend the rest of my life never knowing. What if you're my only chance?"

She slid his hand down to between her thighs and pressed it against her clothed pussy. To her, it was like she was on fire.

He ran his knuckles across her joggers. "You're already wet for me, Liss." She clenched her jaw and moaned with pleasure. "You're fucking soaking for me," he growled.

He brushed his lips against her neck, and his left hand moved from her thighs to slide inside her joggers. "I'm not going to ask if you're sure again, though my instincts demand I do. I trust you know what's best for you. From what I've learnt about you, you've been through a life that some can't imagine. But if you want to stop or change your mind, you say so, because you always have an out with me."

Liss nodded. She held his hand against her as she ground against him, moaning every time a knuckle grazed her pussy. "That's my good girl. Take control and own my hand."

She met his heavy-lidded eyes.

"I love how much you need this, need me." His lips returned to her neck. "Strike could return when we least expect it."

The heat between her thighs was building, and it was getting trickier to concentrate on his words. Her fingers trembled as she gripped his shoulders. His kisses on her skin were like fuel on flames.

"And you're nervous." Her skin flushed against his breath. It might have been part of his job to read her, but he didn't have to be so good at it. "I'm taking you to your room."

His eyes shone as he stood and threw her over his shoulder. "I liked carrying you through the palace this way. You've got a gorgeous, curvaceous bum. At this angle, I can enjoy my endless fantasies of spanking it."

Her stomach rolled with arousal. Damn, she wanted Bear to spank her one day.

"Be gentle with me, baby," he added.

Was he teasing her again, or was she projecting her invested heart onto him? The feels were there no matter what, but she needed this. "I'd hate to damage your ego."

"If anyone can, then it's you." Was that a hint of vulnerability?

He pushed open the bedroom door and tossed her on the bed. As she bounced on the mattress, she basked in his control of her needs. His biceps rippled even as every muscle seemed to go taut. He was so fucking beautiful. His wide-eyed gaze travelled up her body with awe and desire. "What have guys done in the past that really turns you on?"

Her mouth twisted to the side as she wracked her memories. Her previous experiences were interesting, but they merged as mediocre moments.

"Fuck, baby, I'm going to have to put all my skills into you," he growled, rubbing his chin. "When you fantasise or when you dream, what do you imagine? And don't tell me you don't, because I've seen you drunk and heard you moan in your sleep." He licked his lips achingly slowly. "Anyone can build up passion with choice words and the odd movement, but it takes investment to seduce someone's mind. I want to make your mind ache with untapped arousal when I'm the first to give you a good fucking."

She rolled her shoulders back, and air escaped her lips.

"Close your eyes, baby." Her brow furrowed again. Bear raised an eyebrow and waited until she'd submitted to his request.

"I'm not going to touch you." At her grumble, he chuckled. It was a throaty sound that reached inside her belly. "I should have said that I won't touch you yet."

She squeezed her legs together at all he offered her.

Wood scraped, and hinges squeaked. "What are you doing?"

"I kept something here that you might like."

She pressed her fingers together to stop them trembling.

The bed depressed a little. Bear must have joined her. His lips returned to tickle and caress her neck. Liss moaned loudly.

"You like that," he murmured against her skin. Bear

fingered one of the straps on her top before pushing it down. He replaced the sliver of material with his lips. He lifted the hem of her top and blew air across her skin, causing her to shiver. Suddenly, he brushed something soft, like a feather, across her stomach. Everywhere the feather went, his lips quickly followed.

He pulled her top off while whispering filthy promises in her ear.

"My joggers too."

"I was going to make you wait, but that's for next time." He slipped his fingers inside the material before easing them down her legs. Liss squeezed her eyes tightly, gripping each moment for her memories, as waves of anticipation threatened to thwart her attempt. "Yes, baby, feel every sensation." His murmurs were like pure arousal.

His voice dropped impossibly lower, and heat flooded her body. "Fucking gorgeous. I could worship your body all day and never get tired. You're beautiful."

His feather stroked the inside of her legs. She opened them wider as his lips followed the trail of the feather. He kissed up and down her shivering legs, pausing at the knees. She reached for his head to make him move higher.

"I'm so fucking hard for you already," he mumbled before ignoring her demands and easing down the cups of her bra. Her nipples were hard, and as the softness of the feather grazed her skin, her back bowed, and she gritted her teeth. It was too good already. Wetness collected in her knickers as he controlled her pleasure. The sensuality overwhelmed her, and yet she demanded more. Liss knew what was coming next, and her body craved it. Instead of a kiss, this time, his tongue swirled around her nipple.

She cried out, "Bear."

"Yes, Princess?"

She grabbed him and kissed him hard on the mouth. He settled between her legs as they made out. It was the slow dance of two people tempering their arousal but unable to completely control it. She scratched his back as she fumbled for the hem of his T-shirt.

She pulled it up and over his head.

"Open your eyes, Liss." The tattoos spiralling up his arms that had intrigued her before were barely a distraction as she ran her fingers through his chest hair. He held his body above her as she explored him. She toyed with his nipples. He winced a little.

"Not a fan?"

"I fucking love it, but they're sensitive as hell right now," he grunted as she repeated the touch. He swooped down and kissed her hard. His covered erection jumped against her as she bit his lip. "You fucking menace," he whispered against her mouth.

His hand slid down her body, and he briefly stroked his knuckles across her pussy. She ground against him, but he removed his hand quickly.

She opened her mouth to argue, but his hand slid inside her knickers. Her breath caught in her throat. "Fucking soaking for me."

She kissed the devilish grin off his face as he ran circles around her clit with his fingertip. She ground herself against him as he continued to play with her. With one hand, she held onto his shoulder as he varied his movements, sliding wetness from her pussy onto her clit and speeding up. With her other hand, she held him tightly to her pussy.

He murmured his satisfaction between kisses, "So bloody sexy."

"Inside me," she begged breathlessly.

Without question, he slid a finger inside her. Nothing else mattered as he thrust one, then two, fingers inside her. She dug her nails into his shoulder and moaned his name as he took her higher.

The vibration of his phone on the bedside table threatened to distract her until he ducked his head and licked her nipple before biting it gently. Her back bowed again.

"Don't stop," she cried out.

"Never," he growled back at her.

He licked and sucked her neck as his fingers continued to push inside her, and his thumb circled her clit. As his phone vibrated, his lips pressed harder against her neck, and he rubbed her clit. It was impossible to grip the thoughts that spiralled around her consciousness as he finger fucked her. She wanted this forever. She was drunk on him.

His fingers pushed in and out of her as he praised her body and reactions. His words were like breaths of adoration, and as she thrust her hips in time with his fingers, he told her that he couldn't wait for her to ride his face and that her body was perfection.

She hung onto him like she might drown in the pleasure forcing her under. Each second took her higher until every sense was filled with arousal and anticipation. Bear owned her with his touch. His mouth lavished her body as he thrust his fingers. Each spark of lust ignited and joined to create an out-of-control blaze, and her body tipped over the edge.

"I'm coming," she cried out.

"That's my good girl. Come for me." He kissed his

praises against her skin. Lights burst, and the world exploded as she orgasmed. Her chest heaved with each breath, and she shook against his hand. His lips barely left her body as he kissed her neck and breasts and travelled down.

"No," she bellowed. Bear lifted his head suddenly.

"You want me to stop?" he replied, shifting his erection in his trousers. It was weird how caring that move was. The guy was harder than a rock, but he'd stop at any moment if she asked.

"Bear, your phone has gone off twice, and I'm not doing anything to get in the way of your job. Even if it didn't involve my safety, I wouldn't," she replied, yet she pulled him back up to kiss his neck as he'd kissed hers.

He reached for his phone. "Fine, but I wanted you riding my face, Princess," he huffed, but the hair's breadth of a smile confirmed she'd made a good decision. It didn't thwart the lust still owning her. No guy had made her come like that before.

"Strike's texted that he's on his way. Fuck." Bear shook his head.

"How long have we got?"

Bear dropped the phone on the nightstand before ensuring she was staring deep into his eyes. "We need hours for what I want to do with you. I want to make this so good for you. You deserve at least the whole night. I've spent the last few days fantasising about twenty positions I want to try with you. I'm desperate to know which makes you come the loudest and which turns you feral. I want to know all your different moans and—"

"Baby," she replied, using the name he used for her on him, "I want your lips on my pussy and your tongue inside me before I suck your cock."

His eyebrows arched nearly as high as the top of his forehead. "Dirty-mouthed, brat," he smirked, making Liss grin. And now she liked that name, too, when said from between his flushed lips.

She shook herself briefly. "But if this is our only chance, I want to know what it's like to come while your dick is inside me. I want to ride you." She'd found her filthy voice, and there was no going back now. "Take your joggers off."

He swallowed loudly. "Filthy-tongued sassy women are a massive turn-on for me."

Her smile teased the corners of her lips. "On your back and get that cock out. Please tell me you've got a condom?"

"Yeah."

She didn't want to remember that she was another conquest. When their days together were up, she wanted to be the one Bear couldn't stop thinking about being inside of.

Bear was naked and on his back within seconds. His cock pointed at her, and she licked her lips as she wrapped her hand around it. Pre-cum beaded the tip, and his eyes never left her face as she stroked down his length. His cock thrust itself into her hand as she palmed it.

"You're fucking everything." Bear's eyelashes fluttered. She smirked as she ripped open the condom wrapper with her teeth and then sheathed his cock. His erection juddered and jumped as if she was its puppeteer. "I want to make this good for you, but it's been a while."

She raised an eyebrow. "But your fuck buddies?"

Bear shrugged. "I haven't had one for a couple of years. Work, life, you know."

This guy was such a mind fuck. She shook her head and pushed away the pressure to perform.

"Lay back, because you're about to be fucked by a princess for the first time."

He made a weird sound under his breath.

"I'm not your first princess?" she teased as she lined up his cock and eased herself onto the head.

"Technically, no, but—"

She grabbed his wrists and shoved them against the pillow. "Then I'd best make sure I'm the best princess you've ever had." She slid onto him and ground on his dick before leaning back and bouncing, ripping the smart-ass response from his mouth.

He still managed to get out "No contest" as she rode him with an intensity she'd never experienced in sex before. His hands gripped her bum and ensured their rhythms merged. She was like a woman possessed as she threw her head back. His cock went so deep.

His moan was guttural as she leveraged herself higher before slamming down onto him repeatedly. A smile tugged at her lips as he fought to keep his eyes open. A mixture of agony and pleasure was emblazoned across his face as he watched her. His head fell back.

Arousal filled her body, sparking every inch of skin against his to life. Sweat beaded her chest, and her limbs quivered as he pulled his nails across her body. His abs rippled beneath her, tightening and loosening as she thrust her body forward. Suddenly, Liss remembered his turn-on.

"You like fucking me, baby? Do you like the idea of your cock inside me, filling my pussy, or is it the way my breasts bounce as you watch? My nipples are so close to your mouth. Do you need to control my pleasure? You're such a sexy fucking bastard."

His eyes snapped fully open then, and he made a choking sound. "Don't make me come yet," he growled.

"Is that a challenge or a dare?" she said with a grin that felt like it covered her face before leaning close enough for his lips to graze her chest.

"Princess…"

"Do you worst, Bear," she replied. "Fuck me in whatever position you want."

"But—" Caution filled his word as much as desire.

"Fuck me like you need me. Fuck me like you fantasised."

He lifted her off him and flipped her. "Get on all fours," he demanded. He was so desperate, and yet she was the one with the power.

Liss leant on her hands and knees, arching her back as she waited for him. He slipped a finger in her pussy and mumbled, "Still so wet for me."

His skin burnt as he pressed his body against hers and eased himself into her. Power and restraint rippled through him as his hands gripped her waist. Liss looked over her shoulder to witness the awe-filled face he made as he pressed deep inside her. Her heart jumped even as she willed it to chill.

"Own me, Bear," she replied. Their time was running out. Strike could arrive any second.

Bear gripped her tightly as he pulled back and thrust inside her again. "Fucking beautiful," he grunted as he repeated the action.

She moaned as he deepened his penetration. This was fucking. It was the raw, animalistic pleasure she'd never experienced, and now she understood all that Isla said.

Bear was strong enough to push her off the bed,

especially with the height difference between them, but he held her tightly the entire time, his fingers digging into her flesh. He fucked her deep and hard. Her thoughts on what she'd missed out on until now were brief as his dick filled her repeatedly. He was relentless in his pursuit of her orgasm. "Rub your clit as I do this. Next time, you're riding me, and I'm rubbing it myself," he growled between pants.

She did as instructed, and instantly, her arousal jumped higher. Their moans unified as Bear continued to thrust inside her. Sounds of his body slamming into hers as they cried out filled the room. Liss's body wobbled as she tried to pleasure her clit as Bear slammed into her. It made him grip her tighter. Her skin would carry marks of his ownership.

"Fucking come inside me, Bear," she commanded with a power she'd never harnessed in sex. "I can't get enough of your dick, but I want you to come first."

"Not before you, Princess. I want you coming around my cock," he grunted. The dirty talk as they raced to who could make the other come first during their forbidden sex session would have been a lot more satisfying if a car hadn't come down the driveway at that point. Wheels against stones made her rub harder, and Bear upped up a gear with his pounding. "Come now, baby."

She opened her mouth to argue, but then he added her kryptonite. "Come like my fucking good girl."

She screamed her orgasm as he praised her. He held tight as arousal flooded her system, and her arms tried to give out beneath her. Her shouts of "yes!" filled the room.

Heat filled her body. "I'm coming," Bear grunted between gasps of breath. With one last thrust, he held himself inside her. Her arms folded, and he leaned against her.

"Fuck," he said in a voice so gravelly it was like he'd never sing a tune again.

The car stopped. Bear hesitated behind her.

"Go," she whispered, turning over and hunkering down against the bedding. Bear disposed of the condom before pulling on his clothes and shoving his phone in his pocket. Basking in the glorious after-glow of orgasm, she watched him reach for the door handle before running back and kissing her hard on the mouth. His hands held her face as he deepened the kiss and massaged her tongue with his.

The front door banged.

She dusted a kiss on his lips. "Go."

Bear ran to the door. "You're everything," he whispered, staring at her before darting out the door

.

Chapter Thirty-Three

A bump outside Liss's room woke her several hours later.

It was a little past two a.m. Bear had left three hours earlier, and after tidying herself up, she'd drifted off to sleep. The after-glow lasted long enough to quash any regrets her sexual exploration might have brought, but now the anxiety was tightly winding around her belly and ripping it in two.

She didn't want to consider that she was a meaningless conquest Bear would forget by sunrise, but how would he be after this? Liss covered her face with the pillow and screamed into it. Isla would chalk up the experience to a fun night and not let it stop her from doing whatever else she wanted. But Liss couldn't. Liss screamed again. At a tap on her bedroom door, she returned the pillow underneath her head and readjusted the bedding.

"Come in," she whispered in a sleepy voice.

Light filled the edge of the doorway, revealing Bear still in his grey joggers and T-shirt. His stance was casual, yet fluttering butterflies replaced the pins that tried to stab her belly. His T-shirt strained against his tattooed biceps, and his muscley forearms had her aching for a repeat performance.

"You awake?" he asked so softly that her heart

swelled in her chest.

She couldn't get the feels. But the belly butterflies were out of control.

"Yeah."

"Can I come in? I wanted to check you were okay after…"

"Sure."

Bear stood awkwardly by the side of the bed. He pulled on his neck. Liss winced at her need to ensure he was okay. "You can sit on the bed with me." He looked cautiously at the bed, as if it might become a gun-slinging enemy, before perching on the edge. "Is Strike still here?"

His head bobbed. "I mean, no. He left half an hour ago. I've finished a perimeter check. I was heading to bed when I heard you." He refused to meet her eyes.

"I must have been making noises in my sleep again." He glanced at her with a raised eyebrow. Bear tapped his forearms before resuming his stare of every part of the room but where she lay. "Are you cold? Because there's room under the duvet for you." It sounded like a desperate chat-up line.

"I don't get cold. Ma jokes that my blood is always boiling, but I'll join you under the duvet. I feel a bit weird sitting on the edge like you're sick and I'm your nurse."

As his body touched hers, goose pimples danced across her skin. Damn feels.

"Cuddle?" he asked. His eye twitched in the light still coming from the door.

"Sure," she replied as some tension slipped out of the room. She snuggled against Bear's chest, their legs tangling as he held her close. He radiated a warmth that made her want to hum in satisfaction. "Does Strike know?"

"He probably suspects, but I didn't tell him. I wanted to check that you're okay."

"You already said that."

He cleared his throat. "I don't normally fuck and run unless we've agreed that's the plan. I would have cuddled, especially as this was a thing for you." Just her? It was a weird way to describe it, but she let him talk. "You were amazing, by the way. I don't say that because you need to hear it. The guys from your past were dicks."

She held her breath at his mixture of cursing, caring, and vulnerability. This side of Bear was unnerving, and yet she wanted more. Undeniably, he made her come as no one had before. It was one hell of a fuck. But he intrigued her too. It was a dangerous combination.

"I guess."

He pulled her a little higher to look at her. "Seriously, Liss. They must have been the biggest wankers."

She swallowed loudly before stuttering, "Maybe I didn't want to fuck them like I wanted to fuck you. Maybe the heat wasn't there."

His mouth scrunched to the side as he studied her. "I get that. When someone really does it for you, it's amazing. Nothing compares to that."

She nodded before stroking one of his tattooed biceps. "Do I get to find out about your tattoos?" she said, changing the subject. She didn't want to discuss if she was catching feelings for him, and that was exactly where this conversation would go.

Liss slunk a little down the bed and cuddled back up to him. It was weird to feel so changed by what they'd done and yet be this close to someone who didn't. Bear stroked her hair, causing nips of electricity to travel through her scalp. Even his soft side was addictive. Maybe he'd changed a little. "You know how I told you the other day that I was trouble as a teenager and used to get in loads of fights?"

"Yes." Liss stilled as he continued to hold her close. Her breath synchronised with the movements of his chest, and she relaxed into him. "Did you get hurt?"

"Yeah, too much. I got known for being reckless, and my friends, who were all older, encouraged me to start street fighting for money. I was desperate to fight the biggest guy. I wish I could explain why I was like that. Maybe it was the arguments at home and being unable to meet my parent's expectations. I was the stupid son of academics who made me feel like I wasn't enough. I never achieved at school because it didn't make sense to me. The worse I did, the more their affection and attention seemed to wane. I couldn't impress them no matter what. But the bad crowd thought I was awesome. So I went to them. I felt like I fit in, kind of. But then it all went wrong."

Liss ran her fingertips across his tattoo. The room's silence and the Bear's heat were like a blanket that kept her safe. The house was worlds away from their problems or past. It was like anything was possible, even the truth and being completely open with someone. She relaxed into him and let his calm slow her pulse. "Do you remember when I freaked out about grabbing your throat during self-defence?"

Liss murmured yes as her finger followed the swirls forming a boxing club emblem.

"That happened to me." Liss waited, willing him to speak. "My parents had kicked me out for stealing from them. I owed some nasty people money for losing street fights, and my friends ditched me." Even with the threats to her life and the knowledge that her world was changing, she felt safe in this house and knew that one of the reasons Bear shared his story was because he did too. The decisions about her future had faded, and as much as she knew his story would be painful, she wanted him to speak it. His woody citrus smell enveloped her. "I shouldn't have stolen. After everything I had done and being excluded from school, it was the last straw, so they washed their hands of me."

"I'm sorry," she whispered.

He brushed and kissed her hair. "I know you are, baby. But it's like I'm telling someone else's story. I'm safe now."

"But then?"

"But then I was fifteen years old, scared and needing somewhere to stay. I ended up in the territory of this hardass drug dealer from another town. I learned then what absolute terror was, and I've never felt anything like it since. He grabbed me by the throat and squeezed as his gang jeered. For a long time, I could hear their shouts as I slept. It was as if they were always there, waiting in my nightmares to get me."

Liss gasped. "What happened?"

"The police turned up. If they hadn't, I'd be dead." Liss held her breath until Bear brushed a kiss against her forehead. The sweetness of his touch softened the shock at his story.

"It's okay, Princess. I survived. I was such a punk to those coppers even though they'd saved my life. I refused to give them any information about me, and I wasn't telling them about my parents and giving them a chance to reject me again. So they dumped me in a cell overnight while they decided what to do with me."

She gripped his chest and held him. Even now, she

wanted to hold him forever and keep this badass man safe. "But what does this have to do with Strike's parents?"

"Earlier that day, I'd bumped into one of the kids from my old school who was handing out flyers for a boxing club in town. He was a little older than me and owned anyone who messed with him, even me once in the playground when I gave him lip. He was gentle but still smacked me down. He said that he remembered me putting up a good fight that day and should join a boxing club. I laughed at him, but he wrote his number on the back and told me that if I changed my mind, I should call."

"That was Strike?" Liss asked, putting the clues together.

"That was Strike." Bear's hands continued to caress her skin. His fingertips stroked her back, and her stomach flushed. She pushed away the awareness that, for her, this wasn't just sex. "The police went through my stuff and called the only number available. Strike used to hand his mobile to his parents at night so that he'd sleep. Ma ruled with an iron fist and the best brownies in the world."

Liss chuckled. Bear and his chocolate addiction.

"Anyway, Ma answered the phone. By the morning, I was living with her and Pa. They paid my debts and sorted out a new school for me. I never returned to the streets and never had to be scared again. I joined Strike's boxing club, and I was good. Strike left school a few years later and then went into the army, but we were best friends from the moment I came to the house and shared his room. Imagine the two of us in bunk beds."

"Like two giants in a doll's house?"

"Exactly." He chuckled. "They cleared out the garage for me eventually. They gave me a home."

"And what happened to your parents?"

Bear sighed. There were so many emotions in that sigh, and all were heartbreaking. "Ma and Pa spoke to them and told them they were missing out on a relationship with me, but they didn't care. According to them, I'd already burnt my bridges."

"And now?" Liss asked, her voice wavering.

Bear trembled, and his voice cracked briefly. "I heard they'd moved north. My contacts check them occasionally. They're less spritely and still miserable, but they're alive. I considered visiting them, but I'd know if they wanted anything to do with me. I told you before that you find your own family. I hoped it was my parents, then I thought it was the gang. But the only place I could truly be me, where I could push the boundaries and safely discover my identity, was with Strike, Ma, and Pa. I found my family—well, they found me."

Liss closed her eyes. "I guess."

"Don't get me wrong. A part of me will always be alone because that's who I am. I don't let people in," Bear said. His voice was light, but truth filled the space between them.

"I've kinda noticed," she replied without judgement.

"And I've no idea how you've managed to get in, because no one knows this stuff about me except my adoptive family." He took a quick breath. "But I let Ma, Pa, and Strike in over time, and now they're my world, and I'm theirs."

"Do you still box?" Liss avoided any reference to her family. She must decide her future, and this wasn't the time to do it.

"I've boxed in a couple of charity matches and pop to my old gym once a month, but that's it. It's a young man's game, and although I'm only twenty-six, it's not for me. I boxed while working as a doorman, but when Strike came out of the army, we started this, and that's all the adrenaline I need."

"And you don't miss it?"

Bear stroked his thumb across her lips. His intimacy didn't surprise her anymore, but sadness attached to the moment like little Velcro balls. It might be the last time she saw this side of him again. He cleared his throat. "I miss boxing a little, but I love this job and don't want to do anything else again. Besides, I don't find my adrenaline just through work." He leaned closer and kissed her tentatively before settling back against the pillows. "Sex with you was more intense than any fight, job, or shootout."

She ached to hold him, to feel his touch and submerge herself in their connection. Everything he shared made her care about him more. It was as if they were two ends of a piece of string that now bound them to each other no matter what. His eyes shone with their shared connection, and with a quivering heart, Liss kissed him back. It was the gentle kissing of two people entirely comfortable with each other and living in the moment. Tentatively, he lifted the hem of her T-shirt with raised eyebrows. She helped him pull it up and over her head. He tossed it to the side of the room, and she positioned herself under him. It wasn't smooth, but it didn't need to be. Bear rested above her before kissing down her body. His mouth brushed her skin, and his tongue pressed against her breasts. She opened her legs as he travelled lower. Before, it was a fraught fight of sexual desperation, but this was the opposite. His lips touched her belly, and she froze.

He raked her body with pure desire. "You're beautiful,

Liss. Every part of you turns me on, and your stomach is one of the things I fancy about you. It gives you these sexy hips, and we both know your ass makes me hard. But if you want me to avoid it, I will."

Her lips parted, and she whispered, "Don't stop."

"That's my girl," he said against her skin. He growled more names as he explored her body, avoiding where she wanted him the most. He pressed his mouth to the inside of her thighs, and she sucked her lower lip into her mouth. He had skills for days. Each touch heightened her desire more than the last, and as he climbed her thighs to her pussy, she held her breath.

"Don't forget to breathe," he whispered before blowing across her clit. She jolted against the bed, but it didn't deter him. With a flat tongue, he licked her pussy in one stroke. A shot of desire coursed through her veins.

With his forearm against Liss's belly, he licked and sucked her clit. The way he'd pinned her gave him control against the tremors and shakes that owned her body. He swirled the tip of his tongue around her clit before sucking on it hard. Each time she moaned, his efforts doubled. He understood her body quickly, and as she cried out, he ran circles around her clit before dipping his tongue inside her. Liss held his head against her in an attempt to direct him, but it was unnecessary, as he was attuned to all of her reactions.

His movements sped up as he feasted on her. Her eyes fell back into her head when he licked harder. His lips caressed her clit, while he slid a finger inside her, hooking it slightly. He was the master of her body, and he repeatedly pushed two fingers inside her. The scent of her arousal accompanied his movements. It was heady and intense, yet there was more to it than that. *Don't invest your emotions.*

But it was already too late. Bear seduced her body—and then her heart.

Her wetness against his skin and his licks on her clit were the soundtrack to his endeavours. He coaxed her climax closer. Their friendship was sass and fight, but in the near silence of the room, he made her come apart. Her pants and gasps spurred him on, and as he pushed her arousal higher, the deep burn in her stomach signalled how close she was. His teeth grazed her clit, and her trembles turned to shakes against the arm that kept her pinned to the bed. He didn't relent for a second as every limb clenched tightly before releasing in an orgasm that exploded behind her tightly closed eyes. Her heart was out of control. For a second, she feared it would explode in sparks of little lights. As his licks slowed and his fingers eased out from her, she gasped for deeper breaths. He peppered kisses to her skin and repeated his earlier movements but in reverse.

"You're fucking everything, Liss," he regaled. His lips were wet from her juices, and he swiped the water from her nightstand. "Now go to sleep so we can repeat that in the morning."

He wiped his mouth before kissing her hard on the lips. She turned over, and he brushed her shoulders with his lips. "Goodnight, beautiful," he whispered as she fell asleep.

Chapter Thirty-Four

Liss opened her eyes gradually. She was butt naked with the duvet tightly tucked under her chin. Her body ached every time she moved.

Her night with Bear wasn't a dream.

She glanced over her shoulder, confirming her fears. The bed was empty. A check of her watch told her it was still early—well, early for a pub landlady.

The scent of bacon and fried eggs teased her nose, and her belly rumbled angrily as if forgotten. It deserved a hearty feed based on last night's flips and aches. Liss slipped joggers and her T-shirt on before creeping down the hallway towards the stairs. The familiar photos shared new things with her now that she understood their backstory. She thanked Strike's mum and dad as she passed their photo for taking care of Bear.

Bear's naked back greeted her as he sang at the oven. With joggers hanging off his toned hips, heat filled her limbs. With guys from her past, she'd never experienced wanting sex so close to having had it. Yet with Bear, she was drooling at what they could get up to that day.

"Morning," she said breathlessly, brushing her lips against his rippling back. Every part of him was muscle, and she leant into him and slid her hands to his chest.

"Morning, Liss," Strike said behind her. She whipped

around and was confronted with a smirking Strike sitting at the table, although his eyes remained buried in his phone screen.

"Fuck," she shouted. Bear threw his head back and laughed. Her pulse quickened, and she attempted to bolt from the room, but Bear threw her over his shoulder. His body rumbled with laughter beneath her.

"That's hardly the polite morning greeting I expected from a princess," Strike chuckled.

"Leave her be." Bear popped her onto the chair. "She needs feeding. This princess deserves to be waited on."

Bear attempted to kiss her, but she slapped him away. "I'm sorry, Strike. This isn't good for the business and—"

Strike interjected as she tied her tongue in knots. "I'm okay with it…ish." He pointed at a smug Bear. "Not that I want the details. I like you, Liss. You've done good things for the business and were a great movie buddy this week. I'm not condoning this, because, as we know, I'm a grumpy bastard who doesn't like to see people having fun." He smirked as Liss covered her mouth with her hand. She'd never said it aloud but thought it several times. "But I like how Bear sings, and he hasn't sung in years. Just don't let it detract from the job."

"You're being weird," Bear said with a raised eyebrow.

Strike shrugged, but they were missing something. Being with the men only increased her curiosity about their history, and learning about Bear pushed her to learn more about those he cared about.

"Just feed me. I've only got an hour before heading out to investigate the bomb threats. Something is off about this whole thing." Questions rested on the tip of Liss's tongue, but Bear placed a bacon bap before her. Her belly growled, causing both men to laugh.

She covered her blushes with the giant bacon roll and chomped as the men discussed future jobs and Strike's plans for the day. She licked the ketchup off her fingers, drawing a hungry gaze from Bear that she pretended not to see.

"I'm chatting to Steve today too. I don't like the guy," Strike replied between mouthfuls.

Bear slapped his hand loudly on the table, causing it to shake and coffee to spill. "Finally, you've come around to my viewpoint."

Liss's shoulders froze. "What's this about Steve?"

"Before you freak out," Strike said, placing a hand on Bear's shoulder, "Steve's acting weirdly. We looked at CCTV around the pub after your incident, and he was at the pub, but afterwards, he sneaked out of a back alley."

Liss stilled. "He must have had a reason."

"I didn't like his behaviour at the palace party," Bear grunted, but at one look from Strike, he squeezed his lips together in a stern line.

"True. I'm not saying Steve's a bad guy or has anything to do with the threats, but we've been in this job a while, and when our instincts say someone is behaving unusually, nine times out of ten, there's a reason."

Liss was silent, which drew wary stares from the bodyguards. But Steve wouldn't try to hurt her. She didn't have many people on her side, and if she couldn't trust Steve, then she barely had anyone left. She was truly alone.

Bear's eyes pinched. "Don't defend him." Her silence didn't mean she didn't believe them. She couldn't deny the facts they'd shared. That he'd sneaked out of the pub didn't make sense.

"But he's my friend. I've known him for years, and you

two have known him ten days," she said, reaching for her mug. Confusion replaced her earlier happiness. The men were good at their job. But Steve couldn't be a bad guy. "I need to think about this."

Strike held Bear back as she rambled out of the room.

She needed to call Isla and discover Steve's secret that she'd hinted at the week before.

Liss returned to the paperwork she'd ditched in the lounge as she called Isla.

"Hey."

"Hey, you," Isla replied. The sound of her best friend's voice calmed her. "Do you still promise to call me when you're living in a palace?"

Liss smiled. She'd do everything to keep their friendship. "Maybe."

Isla laughed. "You'd better. You're a bit early for our daily call though. Everything okay?"

"I can't hide anything from you," Liss replied, moving papers out of her way to sit.

"Not since you fell over a chair during university induction week and jumped up pretending you were okay. I saw you."

"I know you did because you remind me about it monthly."

Isla's cackles carried down the phone. "Thank you for never finding me too much hard work. Steve said the other day that I was lucky to have the both of you."

"You're not hard work. I've never thought that about you. But as you've mentioned Steve, I have a question."

Liss took a deep breath. "You said when we were in the hotel bedroom last week that there was a reason he continued to work at the pub and hinted it was related to me. What did you mean?"

Isla made noises like she was deliberating her reply. "It's not my place to say."

"But?"

"After the way he was at the party, I'm guessing he'll never tell you himself." Isla paused, and Liss fought the temptation to jump into the conversation. "Steve likes you. I don't know if it's just a crush or more, but he's liked you since the early days."

"Oh." Liss ground her teeth. But that didn't make sense with what the guys said. He wouldn't push her down the stairs even if he had unrequited feelings for her. "Did you think he was acting weird at the party?"

"Super weird, even his brother was concerned. I'm sorry I wasn't around to take care of you. Ollie's beautiful blue eyes distracted me," Isla joked. "And I thought it was time for Steve to shoot his shot before we lost you for good."

"But you won't lose me. I'll still be around."

"Not like before. Your world is about to change if you decide to take the throne. And you should because you need that family you've spent years searching for. I watched what happened to you after your mum died. I was busy with my degree but still saw your desperation for a purpose."

"I guess," Liss replied. They'd never had a conversation about that time. But everything was coming out now.

"The pub became your world, and I get it because you needed something to care about and something to care about you. But you can have a real family, who are there for you and..." Isla tailed off. Liss spun her ring.

"And?"

"And I didn't want to be the one to tell you, but Steve said yesterday that Hugo has signed the contract with the pub chain. Having a princess work there previously has raised its value. It won't be here for you if you return, so you need to find a different purpose."

"Like taking the throne," Liss replied, resigned to her future. Her home was gone, and one of her closest friends was not who she thought. Then there was Bear. Her words slipped out. "I slept with Bear last night."

"What?" Isla shouted. "Tell me everything."

Liss spent the next half hour giving Isla the highlights. They talked a little more about Steve and his crush, but Liss didn't spill that the bodyguards were investigating him.

"I'm guessing you've got the feels for Bear," Isla said just as Liss was about to hang up. "What are you going to do when you take the throne?"

Isla was talking about it like it was a done deal, as were her bodyguards and yet she was still undecided even though it would give her everything she wanted. "I'll get over him. He doesn't do relationships, and I can't trust the feelings I have for him. We've not even known each other for two weeks. We've been thrown together by trauma, nothing more. I need to embrace my future and the chance at a family. I can't have both."

"That sounds like a pre-prepared speech you're using to convince yourself. Are you sure?"

"I have to be. There's no future for us."

"Then hold on to that, and don't let his awesome dick or grumpy charm distract you from what you know you have to do." He did have a fantastic dick. "Catch you later, Liss."

Chapter Thirty-Five

It only took another hour of graft, but with an indie pop station playing at full blast, Liss managed to shut most of her thoughts out. Occasionally, she'd find herself mumbling about a fated future and friends she couldn't work out as she filed notes and reports that the guys must have bunched together in one big disorganised pile at the end of a job.

The radio presenter suddenly announced her favourite song. There was a rule in the pub that when "Feel So Close" by Calvin Harris played from the speakers, you must turn it on full volume and dance like no one was watching.

Liss jumped up and tossed herself about the room as the first bars played, desperately holding onto memories of her favourite nights at the pub, nights she'd never get again. She bounced on her feet and threw her arms in the air as the song climbed higher. The beat filled her body as Liss stood on the tips of her toes and let her hips shift back and forth. It was as if she was on a rollercoaster as she spun around and around.

Why had Steve kept his crush quiet all this time? There was no chance she'd date him because she'd never had that attraction to him, but they could have talked it out.

She climbed on the sofa before touching the sky and

projected herself off it. As she twisted in circles, she caught a familiar hunched bodyguard watching her. But his inspection didn't deter her, and she continued to dance until she couldn't breathe. Panting, Liss turned off the radio and waited.

"I could watch you do that for hours," he said, levelling her with a stare.

Her chest slowed as she regained her breath.

"I'm sorry for what I said about Steve," he said as he leaned against the rustic doorway. The grey joggers still hung from his hips, and the scruff on his chin had her fingers tapping against her body. "I'm sorry. You're right. I haven't known him for as long as you."

"But?"

Bear held out his hands. "Steve set off my bodyguard senses. All of us bodyguards have instincts. We've learnt a lot from mistakes and being around people. Some of mine are from being part of that dangerous crowd when I was younger and recognising people's behaviour, especially when they're trying to hide what they're really up to."

"Like when I'm at the pub, and I'm wary of someone, but I can't always understand why."

"Exactly. I'm always vetting people, deciphering their motives and behaviours."

"And something about Steve seems off." Liss sighed as Bear stood closer. Surely, Steve's crush meant he wouldn't try to hurt her, and yet Strike and Bear's thoughts reminded her that you never really knew someone's motives. She hadn't known he had a crush even after being friends with him for years.

"I don't apologise often and know my feelings about Steve are biased—"

"Because of your instincts?"

"And because I'm jealous."

Liss stared in disbelief. "Of Steve?"

"Yes." Bear stepped closer. His scent reached her even as he stood several arm lengths away. She tasted his woody smell on her tongue. The only sound was a ticking clock as they eyeballed each other. It was as if she stood on the edge of a cliff, waiting for a moment to change her life forever. "I'm jealous because I fancy you. God, I sound like a teenager. I like you, Liss, more than I've liked any woman. I don't get jealous, and I don't get invested, but then there's you."

"But what's so special about me?" she said, her voice wavering.

"Everything. You came into my world with your ability to care about everyone: pregnant strangers who you get drunk for, old men from your local pub with grumpy dogs, Luke who opens up to no one but told you about his One Direction love—don't worry, he doesn't know I know. You even care about Strike."

Liss's smile was tentative. Bear bit his lips as he stared at her. "And then there's me. No one cares about me or has ever cared about me as you do. You make me laugh, whether it's because you're giving me attitude or because you want to beat me at self-defence, which isn't even a competitive sport. You listen to everyone and want the best for all of them. You challenge me and cuddle me. You make it possible for me to close my eyes and sleep without fear that someone from my past is going to attack me. You make me feel whole. You've changed all my rules in less than two weeks. Do you get how ridiculous that is? I haven't let anyone in for years, maybe forever, but you're under my skin."

He held a hand out and waited. His whole body trembled as Liss offered him her hand. He pressed it against his chest. His heartbeat was rapid, and his body was fire even through his T-shirt.

"Fuck. I sound unhinged. I don't know if it's because this can only be a short-term thing or if maybe there is a connection between us due to who we are and our pasts. I spent all this time thinking there was no point searching for the thing that was missing in my life."

"Why?"

He shook his head. "Because I was lucky enough to find Strike, Ma, and Pa. I thought that was all the luck I deserved, and I honestly thought nothing could fill the hole left by whatever I was longing for."

"What are you saying, Bear?" Her fingers gripped his T-shirt tightly as fear filled her.

"You're lonely." Liss stared but didn't answer. They both knew the answer. "I see the same loneliness in you I carry daily."

"But you have Strike and Ma and Pa." Her voice was barely a whisper.

"And you have your friends and your nana," he said, making her scoff. "Okay, well, you have your friends. But don't you still feel alone all the time? It's like there's this weird longing, and something is missing, and as much as you search, you can't find it. What if you're what I've been looking for?"

Liss pulled away from his chest but continued to hold his hand. She willed her limbs not to tremble from the fear of losing control. He made her feel hope, but it was false, and it would only lead to their getting hurt. Theirs was just a fling, and he knew that. "Bear, in a couple of days, I'll—" She fought with the word "probably." There was no room for that in this conversation. Maybe the connection she'd felt with her grandad since the party was holding her back too. He'd shown her a chance at love and acceptance, and they were family. "I'll take the throne because my old life no longer exists. I learnt today that they're selling the pub, my home. I've spent my life searching for a real home, a purpose, and a family, and now I have that opportunity. You can't get feelings after you told me not to."

"But you did, anyway, didn't you?"

"We barely know each other."

"You know more about me than anyone but the three people who've been in my life since I was fifteen, and I know you've told me things you've not told anyone." Tears brimmed her eyes. She couldn't deny it.

"I need a solid future, and we'd be a mess together. You don't do relationships."

She'd hurt him. But it was the truth.

"I know. Maybe being cooped up in this house makes me think differently. But you're right. You have to get on with your life. I want you to get on with it and be the incredible princess I know you can be. And I have work and a relationship-free life to return to." His laugh sounded hollow. "Look at me, Mr. No Emotion. Did I ever tell you that when I was a doorman, the police called me the nicest, nastiest bastard they'd met?" The crumb of humour was a relief.

She offered him a tentative smile as Bear brushed her lips with his. "No, you didn't, but I believe it."

He chuckled. "I'm going to get some air and regroup. I'll be back soon."

"Okay," she replied, letting him go. It had to be the right decision. But why did it hurt so damn much?

Bear made good on his promises and returned an hour later.

He yawned wide enough to suck in the entire room as he walked through the doorway. Liss grabbed his hand as he neared her and pulled him down on the sofa beside her. He needed rest. She continued to tap away at the laptop Luke had sent her as he sat close. She searched for the invoices folder and filled in the details from the loose papers she'd spent the last hour organising.

She chuckled at one of the reports she'd finished with. In it, Strike had talked about a civi who'd caused a "cluster fuck." After a bit of googling, she'd realise it was army slang.

"Why did Strike join the army? Was it a lifelong ambition?" Liss asked. It was a relief to be back to the every day with him.

"Not really. Strike shocked the whole family when he left to join the army weeks before he was supposed to leave for university. We thought he was happy, but he just disappeared, and he barely returned when he had leave. He shouldn't have been able to join that easily, but Pa's brother is high up in the forces, and Pa suspected he'd pulled strings. It was a weird time, and he never explained it." Liss nodded as she tapped. These men had more secrets than the Pentagon. "What are you doing?"

"Sending invoices. Luke sorted out encryption software for me, and now I can send all the invoices and reports that have been hanging around for months. Promise me that you'll sort out your processes and make this easier in the future. I'll do what I can before Friday, but you should get someone in. You could build your business easily with the right stuff in place, but you're wasting your time on admin," she explained as she emailed a minor celebrity they'd taken care of in Dubai. "And you can book cheaper flights and hotels than you use."

"How do you know all of this?"

"When you have a nana like mine, you're used to sorting out other people's lives. I may not be social media savvy or able to kick a ninja's ass"—Bear side-eyed her, making her chuckle—"but I can do this in my sleep."

"I wish I had your skills. Strike, Luke, and me are like toddlers distracted by toy dinosaurs with this stuff. Maybe we should take someone on." Bear sat back and yawned.

Liss glanced at him from beneath her thick lashes. "You're tired."

"I'm blaming the emotional bomb I threw at you earlier. I'm not used to all this stuff in my head. Get in and get out, and no one gets hurt," he added with a mirthless laugh.

Liss licked her lips as she deliberated her response. Some issues were best left alone. "We're cool. It's a good way to be, I guess. But I was thinking about the Steve thing. I want to speak to him if possible. Maybe I can get out of him what he was doing at the pub that day."

"Strike and I were talking about that. We'll head back to town on Thursday morning in a couple of days. You can chat to Isla, get your stuff together for your next steps, and speak to Steve, too, if you want." He was playing it casually, but out of the corner of her eye, she witnessed his hunched shoulders. "And I promise to not be a dick to him. Scout's honour."

She elbowed him, although it didn't ripple a muscle. "As if you were a scout."

He huffed as he turned on the television.

Two invoices down, eighteen more to go. They could add another bodyguard to their team if they didn't spend all their time on this. After five minutes, Bear still hadn't moved. His back was straight, and his shoulders tensed. There was no sign that he was watching the sitcom.

"You okay?" she asked as she sent another email.

"Yeah, all good," he said with a higher voice than usual.

"High voice means lie voice," she replied without thinking. "Sorry, that's something my mum used to say when I came home from school tattered."

"Tattered?" He faced her, but she buried her nose in the laptop. He turned off the television. Seconds ticked by, but he wasn't filling the silence.

"I was bullied a lot at school." His stare was like an insect on her skin. "We were poor and moved around a lot. My lack of confidence and being a poor kid meant I was easy pickings."

"I would have destroyed them if I'd been your friend then," Bear declared, causing her to roll her eyes as a smile tickled her lips.

"And got into more trouble for it." Liss shared stories of the worst things they did to her, including locking her in the school. "It's weird to think how different life would have been if the King knew about us sooner. Maybe Mum would have got the medical help she needed. Maybe she'd still be here." She'd give anything to have her mum close, even for one more minute.

A tear slid down her cheek, and she turned away to hide it, but there was no fooling Bear, who slipped the laptop on the floor and lifted her onto his lap. She sighed as he enveloped her and held her against his chest. If anyone else had done it, she'd have pushed away their support, but with him, everything was different. He was right earlier. Maybe he was under her skin as much as she was under his.

"Tell me about your mum." Bear dusted her forehead with a kiss.

His heartbeat was like a comfort blanket, and she counted the rhythm before speaking. "She was funny but didn't mean to be. She worked a lot, but the system was against us, and she never saved enough to buy a house because she was always renting. But even when she was exhausted from working three jobs, she'd help me with my homework or sit and watch movies with me. I got my business mind from her, not that she used it how she wanted."

"A clever woman."

Liss hummed her agreement as she leaned against his chest.

"Super intelligent. One of her jobs was on the production line at a car factory. She'd explain how to improve processes and write proposals for changes that saved the company thousands."

"Did she take the proposals to her bosses?" Bear asked. His woody citrus scent was like fresh air for her soul.

"Yes, but they didn't listen. They told Mum they knew better than a factory worker, but then they'd steal her ideas and pass them off as their own. One of them received an award for the cost savings and transformation of the paint shop."

"Bastards," Bear mumbled under his breath. Her heart

threatened to burst from her chest from that minor word of support. These feelings for a virtual stranger hit hard and fast.

"Exactly. Mum wasn't always serious and work-focused. My favourite memories are our trips to the city to find random tat for the fancy dress box from the market and eat fish and chips while seagulls attempted to dive bomb us." Liss giggled to herself.

"Fancy dress box?"

"Once a month, we'd dress up in items from the box and have a themed meal. One night, we dressed like Nana and had to speak like her. On another night, we dressed up as if we were in an eighties high school film, and on another, the theme was how aliens might see us. Our clothes made no sense, and we talked backwards and ate weird food concoctions. It was hilarious." Her mum was an incredible woman with a creative mind that rivalled her business brain, but life kicked her repeatedly. Liss sighed sadly. "How's this for irony? We wore plastic tiaras and old curtains one night and pretended to be royalty. We drank from cheap chipped china cups and ate teeny cucumber sandwiches."

Liss glanced at Bear, whose gaze softened. A tear slid down her cheek. Most people weren't allowed to see her vulnerable. Somehow, he'd become her safe space and a friend she didn't want to lose. "I miss her so much."

Bear hugged her tight.

"When she died, it was the two of us. She avoided pain medication or anything that made life a little easier for a long time. She punished herself because she was leaving me alone. I never did anything to make her feel that way, but throughout her life, she carried guilt from her relationship with my dad and for not giving me the life she wanted. She'd hate that I was alone. I must accept my royal title for her and live the life she couldn't. And to have that chance to have a real grandad."

Bear remained silent, which was the wisest thing he could do, but it wasn't what she wanted. He should tell her not to join the royals and remind her of her other options. "You'll be a fantastic royal and make a massive difference. Your mum would be proud, and I'm sorry for her suffering. I'd do anything to take that away from you. Did she take the painkillers in the end?"

"Yeah. Eventually, Mum relented. The doctor gave her various things, including one that gave her hallucinations and nearly damaged her liver before they realised she was on the wrong meds. Shit!"

Liss jumped out of Bear's arms and paced the living room. Wrong drugs. It triggered a memory. She stopped in the middle of the room and squeezed her eyes tightly. There was something about medicine from the party at the palace.

"What's going on?" Bear's mouth gaped, and his eyes darted.

She shushed him and closed her eyes again. She placed her hand over her heart like he'd taught her, trying to fix the jumbled thoughts competing for attention. The memory was on the tip of her mind, like when a forgotten word rested on the tongue. Medicine, King, and lies.

"Something fucked up is happening with the King's meds," she exclaimed as the memory of Marianne telling the King to take his experimental medication and the separate one of Marianne telling Beatrice that nothing could be done for the King. A wide-eyed Bear was still too scared to speak. The combination of the stress of the party, the alcohol, trying to fit in, and then that bomb had thrown her. No wonder she hadn't remembered until now.

Liss explained the foggy memories from the party before adding, "It might be nothing, but I don't like it. I can't do anything though. I'm not part of the family yet, and no one will listen to me above Marianne and Alex. And with them close to him, they're the most obvious ones to be poisoning him," she said, putting all the pieces together. "But they wouldn't try to hurt the King. He's Alex's dad! No one could do that to their dad." She was rambling. "What can I do?"

Bear reached into his pocket and held out a piece of paper. "This is from Strike. He got Beatrice's number from her brother. Maybe she can help."

"It's worth a shot." Liss's body shook. "You believe I could be right then?"

"Without a doubt. We all know something is off, and you're more perceptive than you realise." She was so relieved that he didn't laugh at her or make her think she was losing it. "Call Beatrice on my mobile. Your burner should be fine, but mine is encrypted as hell. Luke's hacker friends couldn't track it, and they got into the Government Comms HQ."

Liss cocked her eyebrow as Bear unlocked the phone and handed it over. Its wallpaper was of a lake at sunset. It wasn't a generic screensaver, and she didn't recognise it.

"My real safe space," he murmured. "Maybe I'll take you there one day."

"In the parallel universe where I'm not a princess and you're not a bodyguard," she replied absentmindedly as she copied the number from the paper into the phone.

"Yeah, I guess." She glanced up. He stared blankly into space, his mouth downturned before he quickly fixed his jaw. "I'll leave you be while you call her."

"You trust me not to check your texts?" she teased, hitting the green button to connect.

"There haven't been any texts to check for a while, and anything from the past wouldn't compare to what we did last night," he replied, raising his eyebrows a couple of times as his eyes sparkled.

Heat flooded her body. A royal conspiracy and the possible murder of the King, yet all she wanted was his retreating body, naked and beneath her again. *I'm the worst.* Liss bit the inside of her mouth as Beatrice's phone rang twice before going to voicemail.

Chapter Thirty-Six

A couple of hours later, Beatrice still hadn't returned Liss's call, and neither had the King. They'd promised to speak today, and she had questions she needed to ask him.

"You okay?" Bear asked from the doorway. When he leaned against it with his furrowed brows and arms folded, she wanted to jump him. How many tugs would it take to make those joggers go from hanging off his hips to pooling at his feet?

"Yeah, I guess," she replied, her skin flushing as she moved the laptop aside. She'd sent all the invoices and accompanying reports. There was nothing left to do.

"I could hear you grumbling from the kitchen. You were louder than the music," he teased.

She tapped her foot restlessly against the carpet. "I'm overthinking this stuff with Grandad. Over a few days, he's deteriorated beyond reason. He has access to the greatest medics available, which means Marianne and Alex can't do anything."

"What do you know about these medics?"

"I don't even know their names. He's gone downhill, even since I met him. I've googled photos of him from the last couple of months, and he's a bit tired, but nothing like the last couple of days. If how he was at the party is any sign, he might die before Friday. Something is going on, but it can't be." Bear crossed the room in three strides and enveloped her in a hug. "I don't want to lose him."

"You're doing well, Liss," he replied. "Your life has transformed quickly, and you're keeping your head above water. You're so fucking strong."

"Life didn't give me a choice. I was strong because I didn't have other options."

He smoothed kisses against her forehead. "I get that."

"Talk me through the plan again."

"Only over treats because you've been in this room too long, and everyone needs chocolate chip cookies." Liss followed him and the smell of sugary goodness to the kitchen.

"Oven fresh and ready to make a princess smile," he said as he popped on a pair of oven gloves and pulled out a couple of trays of white chocolate chip and raspberry cookies. The kettle boiled as he placed two cookies on a plate before her.

Drool lingered in her mouth as the scent of baked treats filled the space.

"I don't want you to burn your mouth, so be sure to blow," he said as he moved around the room like it was his sanctuary.

"Yes, baby," she replied with a wink that made him chuckle as he continued to prepare the drinks. She broke the cookie into pieces and took a bite. The white chocolate coated her mouth, and she groaned in ecstasy. "You made these?"

His beaming smile was endearing. "Ma taught me to make them. I have a bit of a chocolate addiction," he confessed.

"That explains a lot. No wonder you always have a bar of it in your pocket."

Bear shrugged. "Got to be prepared, right? I work out a lot to keep these hips trim. Ma said if I was going to eat chocolate all the time, then I should learn to make something good rather than get my fix on the rubbish stuff."

"She's a wise woman." The sweetness of the raspberry hit her tongue.

"She'd love you. You've got the right amount of feistiness combined with kindness. You should meet her when…." Bear tailed off.

This thing between them wouldn't include meeting families or nights out with their friends. They'd agreed their lives needed to go in different directions, which meant they only had days left together. Liss gritted her teeth. She was making this decision for her mum and the life she never had. Liss needed to have that family too. Besides, Bear had been explicit; there wasn't space for Liss in his future. He could only act like they were a couple because they'd agreed it was for days, not forever.

Her mobile rang loudly. "It's my grandad."

She swiped another cookie as she returned to the living room.

The King barely spoke between hacking coughs and agonising groans. Surely, it was a blip. She couldn't lose him. Her future was rearing closer, yet even aware of how happy it would make him, something held her back from confirming her position in the royal family.

"Will you visit me on Thursday before the big press conference on Friday? I'd love to speak to you and have a proper chat before the circus begins," he rasped.

"Of course, Grandad," she said as Bear placed a cup of

coffee on the table and left the room.

She couldn't admit that the hope of a future with Bear might be holding her back. There was a connection between her and Archibald. He was caring. It was something she hadn't had in a family member since her mum, but maybe that would change if she renounced the throne. Liss shook her head. "What are your doctors saying about your condition? I'm sure, as royal medics, they've seen a lot—"

"They're not the royal medics," her grandad replied between coughs. "They're specialists that Marianne found. When my doctors couldn't decipher what was wrong with me, she made a stand."

As the fine hairs rose on Liss's arms, she sipped her coffee and considered her next question. "So it's not cancer?"

"No. Sadly, no one knows what it is, including the medics who arrived two months ago."

"Is that when you started taking the medication? The pills you carried at the party reminded me of the ones Mum took when she was dying."

"I feel your care, dear Felicity, and I'm so grateful for it. If I'd known about your mum, my beautiful daughter, I wouldn't have rested if there was treatment or support anywhere in the world available to her. Around six months ago, I was relatively healthy, but I started to take a vitamin drink due to being "beyond my health peak," as Marianne and Alex called it. I remember it well because it was the day after their engagement, and she said she wanted me to be well enough to make speeches at the wedding." He paused to cough so loudly that she closed her eyes and pressed a fist to her lips. His illness was breaking her heart.

"But I started to get ill about three months ago. My tests drew no answers, so darling Marianne brought me those medics, but there's nothing they can do. When the death toll chimes your name, then you go. I'm glad to have met you and to see you carry on the royal name."

Heat filled Liss's cheeks. He wasn't trying to blackmail her, but guilt rested inside her. She needed to accept her lineage for him and her mum. But that didn't take away from his illness and her suspicions. "And those pills you're taking, what's their name?"

"I'm taking a couple of pills for different things. But the ones you saw are experimental painkillers that are supposed to bolster my immune system and kill any infections. They're such a blessing. I'm unsure of their name, but they have eased the pain."

"Who told you they did that?"

"I can't remember. I must go. Marianne's on her way back and likes to be around when I have calls or see visitors, but I wanted to speak to you alone and say that it will be lovely if you decide to take the throne. I will see you Thursday before the big press conference on Friday, my beautiful granddaughter."

The phone went dead.

Liss ran to the door before turning back. She knew precisely what pills he was taking. The image of them at the party was fixed in her brain. They were a form of morphine given to her mum in her last weeks for pain relief. They didn't do anything he said and weren't experimental. That might be the only treatment he'd had. Liss laboured over her worries, shaking violently enough to make her teeth chatter. Even Marianne wouldn't kill her future husband's dad and Alex wouldn't be party to that. The timing of the vitamin drink made her body sweat even as she shivered. She needed to stop what was happening to the King before it was too late, but she was nobody compared to Marianne and Alex.

"Bear," she squeaked. She couldn't do it alone. The shakes filled her entire body. Was this a panic attack? She attempted to call him again, but her mouth wouldn't open. Her heart thudded. She was always alone. It was the same panic that controlled her after her mum had died. Suddenly, Bear appeared. He walked her to the sofa and sat her down before grabbing a blanket and covering her lap.

"What's happening, Princess?" he asked, wrapping her legs tightly. "What did the King say?"

If Marianne heard them talking about the pills she might escalate his death. Liss opened her mouth, but words stuck to her tongue like someone had poured glue into her. As the thoughts clouded her brain, her body refused to stop trembling.

"Liss, you're scaring me."

Liss shook her head to reset herself, but her heart pounded harder and harder.

Chapter Thirty-Seven

Bear pushed her hand against her heart. "Breathe, Liss. Please close your eyes and focus on your breathing."

Liss did as instructed, but her pulse was uncontrollable. Marianne was killing the King, and there was nothing she could do. The idea was ludicrous. Liss shook, and her teeth clamped down so tightly on her tongue that she tasted blood.

Suddenly, Bear disappeared. *I'm alone.* He couldn't deal with her like this. The King would die. Marianne would destroy Liss next. She couldn't trust Steve. Her new life risked the safety of those around her, like Isla. Her grandma didn't care and—

Suddenly, items clattered onto her lap from the handbag she took to the palace party. Bear tossed everything out.

"You made us go back for this for something. I don't know what, but this bag or its contents must be important." Bear searched through the items but was as dumbstruck as when he pushed her hand against her heart.

Liss nodded in the direction of the plastic heart. He grabbed it and opened her hand. Bear placed the heart in her palm and wrapped his hand around hers and the heart. "Count to ten with me, Liss. Please."

The combination of his touch, his soft albeit strained voice, and the heart from her mum forced the distraction she needed. As Bear reached six, she mumbled with him. The tension in his shoulders eased and her heart slowed. By ten, she was exhausted but calmer.

Bear pulled Liss against him and repeated his count from one to ten. The gaps between the numbers got longer as she breathed. They counted together until her breath was under control and her chest unrestricted.

Before she could explain, Bear's phone rang. She passed it to him, but he returned it. "It's Beatrice. Do you want me to go?" Liss shook her head. She needed him by her side. Hopefully, she wouldn't have to repeat her thoughts if she could explain them at all.

Liss turned the call to speakerphone as she answered.

"Hello, Felicity. How are you holding up? I'm so sorry I didn't get to speak to you at the end of the party." Beatrice's Scottish lilt warmed her. They shared niceties, although Liss fisted her hands as she struggled not to blurt out her fears. But catastrophising wouldn't help if she was going to get Beatrice onside.

Bear squeezed Liss, and her shoulders relaxed with her escaping breath.

"Have you seen much of Grandad?" Liss asked.

"Not yet, sadly, but we're visiting him later this evening. I spoke to him a few days ago, and I'm worried about him."

"I've spoken to him several times and just got off the phone with him."

"How did he sound to you?"

"He had a new hacking cough. I can't believe how many new symptoms he has each time I speak to him. I told him I'd see him Thursday, but he's going downhill so rapidly. He said himself that it's only been in the last six months. How can someone get ill that quickly without anyone knowing what's wrong? I'm scared for him."

"I am too." Beatrice's voice wavered slightly. "He seemed fine six months ago, and then things just changed. I'm baffled. Will you talk to him about accepting a royal role when you see him on Thursday?"

"Yes. That's my plan. I would have talked about it more with Grandad today, but..." She couldn't tell her the truth.

"But?"

"He said he had to go. He'd wanted to speak to me privately but said that Marianne was on her way back and liked to be around when he spoke to people or had visitors."

Beatrice was silent. Maybe Liss sounded like a gossip. Her mouth twisted to the side as she waited. "That explains why she insisted on being there tonight. I was happy to hear it because Gable and I wanted to speak to her about her behaviour to you at the party."

"Oh?"

"I was disgusted. You were given a bad impression of our family. Where you should have been welcomed, you were mistreated. I'm so sorry."

Liss sighed. "Thank you. I thought maybe I was being silly, but it did hurt."

"You were so kind to secretly drink on my behalf and for not telling anyone about the baby."

"It goes without saying. It's yours and Gable's secret to share when it's right."

"Well, I will be having a word with Marianne. Alex should have behaved better too. Before Marianne, he didn't even want to be king. He liked organising parties and enjoyed the operations side of being a royal. He wanted to stay in the background. I don't recognise him anymore."

"I wasn't a big royal watcher in the past. But I thought he would be a little kinder," Liss replied, squeezing her eyes shut briefly. She continued to tremble. She wasn't skilled at diplomacy unless faced with a drunk punter. "It must have been a shock for him. Are Gable and Alex close?"

Bear took her hand and squeezed it. The panic attack had exhausted her and now she didn't know how to broach the prospect of attempted murder. Bear handed her a cookie, and she breathed the sugary goodness in deep. She could do this.

"They were close, but Alex pushed Gable aside after he met Marianne at a party. The couple quickly became inseparable."

"But you think he wants to be king now?" The cautious approach was agonising. She wanted to yell about her fears for the King.

"Yes. He's asked Archie several times to give up the throne since the engagement, especially as at that time Archie struggled more with energy and focus." Liss shared a glance with Bear. "And now he's getting his way but losing his dad." He can't want that.

"That's so sad, especially since losing his mum at such an early age. It must be difficult to grieve his dad's sickness and deterioration when he's in the public eye."

The clock ticked slowly as she waited for Beatrice's reply. "Yes and no. The thing is—no, I shouldn't say."

"Say what?"

"It's just that you said that you were worried about Archie's condition. Something you don't know about me is that I was training to be a doctor before I met Gable, but I put a hold on my studies when we married. Relationships and jobs are hard when you have royal family duties, but I will return to it one day."

Liss stored away that nugget, although even if Bear's job merged with her royal life, their relationship wouldn't last.

"Have you spoken to Grandad's medics? They might talk to you due to your training."

"I tried, but Marianne made me leave the room. And to be honest, he's deteriorated even more since those new medics arrived. There should have been scans and investigations, but there hasn't been anything."

"And the medication they're giving him doesn't seem right either."

"They're not medicating him."

"But they are," Liss blurted. Her heart beat rapidly. "I saw Marianne ask him if he was taking his pills. I recognised them as similar to what my mum took in her final days. They're pain meds at best. I think they're giving him something else, too, but I don't know what." She steeled herself and squeezed Bear's hand tightly. Her next words might destroy her relationships with her family or worse. Liss took a deep breath. "It sounds like something out of a movie, but Marianne, and maybe Alex, are trying to do something to Archibald."

"I agree," Beatrice whispered. Liss pressed her hand to her mouth. "I mentioned something similar to Gable. He won't agree, possibly because Alex is his family."

"I hadn't considered the added betrayal for Gable. When I spoke to the King today, he said the pills were painkillers that bolster immune systems and kill infections."

Marianne gasped. "That sort of technology doesn't

exist. Those pills might be damaging him."

Liss stuttered, "We need to get all his pills tested. Gable might believe the proof then."

"Even with my suspicions, I can't believe Marianne and Alex would try and hurt him. Archie is his father." Her shock suddenly transformed, and her voice slowed. Liss imagined the purpose in Beatrice's stance. "I shall get hold of a couple of pills tonight when we visit him."

"And Strike can get them tested," Bear jumped in. "He has a friend who works in a lab. I don't know if we can get a result before the press conference, but we must try."

"Exactly," Beatrice replied. "Glad to have such an excellent team on our side. It's Bear, isn't it, from Bodyguard Corp?"

Bear puffed his chest. "Nice to make your acquaintance, Princess Beatrice. If you can get them to your brother tonight after seeing the king, then Strike will pick them up from him. If anyone is following you, there will be no connection to us. Strike and your brother were on the same platoon in the army. Not that we're allowed to talk about it."

"Of course, top secret," Beatrice replied. "And that's an excellent plan."

"But with your pregnancy. You need to look after yourself," Liss interjected with a puff of air from her mouth.

"But I have to do this for my country and Archibald. He is a good man, and I love him dearly. I must do this for Gable and our future baby too."

"If you're sure," Liss replied, holding her breath.

"I'll be safe, Felicity, I promise. Let's chat again tomorrow," Beatrice instructed.

Bear added, "In the meantime, speak to your brother, and I'll contact Strike. We'll sort this."

"Take care, Beatrice," Liss whispered as her heart jumped up to her throat. This could be a wild goose chase where she'd risked the safety of others for her silly ideas.

"You too, Felicity. And Bear?"

"Yes, ma'am?"

"Protect Liss and convince her she has keen instincts. It's taken me weeks to believe something is occurring. She's a great addition to the family, and we're lucky to have her. Take care, both of you."

Beatrice ended the call, leaving Liss and Bear in silence.

Chapter Thirty-Eight

With Beatrice's words and the team's plan ringing in her ears, Liss took to her bed.

Time passed quickly, and she fought sleep. She barely had time left in this sanctuary. But as she grappled with memories of her mum and what she'd say, the exhaustion from her earlier anxiety attack overwhelmed her, and she fell into a deep sleep.

It felt like minutes later when she woke to the smell of childhood Sundays during cold winters. Bear poked his head around the door with his latest offering, bringing the scent of freshly baked bread mixed with stewed beef and winter vegetables.

"You awake?" he asked as she rubbed her eyes.

Liss nodded and pulled herself to sit before he placed the lap tray on her and let her feast.

In one spoonful, she knew it was the best stew she'd ever eaten. She languished in the taste before her belly rumbled at her to hurry. Bear sat on the edge of the bed and beamed while she ate.

"I call this Bear stew." Liss eyed him warily as he chuckled. "No bears were harmed in making this stew except when I dropped a ladle on my foot. But there's a secret ingredient, and I'll only tell you if you're nice to me."

Liss gave him a wink. "How nice are we talking?"

Bear's Adam's apple bobbed as he swallowed. "Not that nice yet. Strike said he'd pop in when you woke."

"Shame." She licked her lips and delighted in the blush covering his cheeks.

"Fine. I'll tell you." He beckoned her closer with a crooked finger. Instead of telling her his secrets, he kissed her neck and brushed his lips across her earlobe. She shivered against his smiling mouth. "The secret is one slice of teddy bear ham. Everyone needs a bit of Bear inside them, especially you."

She slapped him on the arm as he licked her spoon with a satisfied grin. "You think you're hilarious."

His eyebrows danced as he grinned.

"You're not eating too?" She ripped the bread in half with her teeth and dipped it into the juices at the bottom of her bowl.

He reached for some of her bread. "This was for us to share, but—"

She slapped his hand away. "Get lost. This is all mine. And I want more cookies too."

"You're feral," he teased before reaching into his pocket and retrieving two cookies wrapped in a piece of kitchen roll. "And if you play your cards right, there's more where these came from." His charm was the light she needed after the earlier phone conversations. But soon he'd be out of her life. "I've already eaten with Strike. We chatted through the plans. He's heading to Beatrice's brother, who has the pills."

As if on cue, there was a knock at the door. "Everyone decent?"

"For now," Bear replied.

"Come in, you dickhead," Liss called. "The only thing raising my temperature is this stew. It does more for me than Bear ever could."

Bear grumbled as Strike entered. "It's so good. Bear may be a massive bell end, but his kitchen skills nearly rival Mum's."

"Don't let Ma hear you say that," Bear replied, standing. "I'll get more cookies for this lady because I love how delicate and princess-like she is when she eats."

He jumped away as she swiped him, although he returned to kiss her and grab the tray.

"How are you doing, Liss?" Strike asked as Bear slipped out the door with a bouncing step.

A long breath pushed out from between her lips. "Confused, exhausted, and freaking out with stress, but also…weirdly happy."

Strike hung around at the edge of the room. Maybe he was like Bear and only comfortable in women's rooms if he was having sex in them.

"A bit different to your life a couple of weeks ago?" Where Bear was to the point with a cheek that made her want to fuck him and laugh with him, Strike was serious and soft. He was often business, but there was more under the surface.

"Definitely. How do you deal with a life where one minute you're in one place and the next in a different country?" Liss asked, nibbling one of the cookies.

Strike folded his arms. "The army trained me well. It helped me deal with unpredictability at a level I'll hopefully never have to live through again. This business gives me control. We don't have to accept every job offer, and soon, we'll be able to pick and choose clients and countries much more easily."

"Bear told me you went into the army suddenly. How

come?"

Strike shrugged, stepping closer as if he were more comfortable than seconds earlier. "For the same reasons you're thinking of not taking the princess role."

She tilted her head. "So Bear didn't tell you I'm going to take it because of my mum?"

"He told me. But I know you're still thinking of not doing it." Bear must have guessed.

"Because of my confidence," she replied.

"Because of love."

"Whoa, hold on. I don't love Bear, and he certainly doesn't love me. We've just met, and I can't love him, because that doesn't happen. It's the thing of TV dramas," she blustered.

"The same dramas where a woman finds out she's a princess at the age of twenty-four before learning her half-uncle might be trying to kill her grandad?" Strike was unsmiling. "I've known Bear years, and the man you see right now is the person he rarely is. He doesn't let his barriers down and refuses to let people close, apart from me and my parents. Even then, he's not as gentle and caring as he is with you. You've brought that side out."

Liss nibbled the cookie and kept her head down.

Strike continued, "I mean this in the nicest way, but when you go, which you will because you feel you owe it to your mum"—she gritted her teeth—"it will crush him, and I'm scared I'll never see the Bear that's lived here over the last few days again. So when you leave him, you make sure he knows it's over between you two, because he needs a future, not a life spent wondering what could've been while he hopes you'll return to him."

Someone hurt Strike. As much as his request stung, there was pain behind it, and it was Strike's pain, not

Bear's.

"I'll take your words on board," she replied with a glare as Bear returned to the room.

"What words?"

Strike shrugged. "I was saying that if we prove Alex and Marianne have attempted to murder the King, then Liss has quite the future. Her life is going to be an *epic* TV drama." He stared at Bear and cocked his head out of the room. "A word."

So Strike's cold demeanour returned. What a fucking joy. But he had a point. Whatever Bear felt for her, she didn't want to ruin his life because she was honouring her mum's memory. But she couldn't be a bitch to him either.

Instead of energising her, the stew and cookies brought waves of exhaustion. Liss settled back against the pillow, grabbed the book Isla gave her the week before and waited for Bear to return and explain what Strike meant about her life becoming an epic TV drama.

Chapter Thirty-Nine

"**P**rincess," Bear's whisper from outside the dark room was enough to stir her from the book.

Liss eased her head from the pillow. Stretching her arms and neck was tricky. She'd had too much rest and not enough exercise, and her grogginess was a side effect.

"Hey," she replied as he stepped into the room.

"Can I sleep in the bed with you? I didn't want to assume," he replied. Opening one eye, she watched him wait by the side of the bed. His boxers rested on his hips like a tantalising tease. Bear stepped from side to side like a teenage boy asking a girl to dance. His vulnerability stabbed at her chest, and she pulled back the duvet and beckoned him in.

He jumped into the bed. His bulk tested its strength. "Sorry," he said sheepishly with a grin.

Liss turned out her lamp and stretched against him. "What time is it?"

"About three in the morning. Strike's dropped the pills at the lab, and he's staying in town tonight. He wants us to have time together." They lay on the bed and stared at each other like two best friends on their first sleepover.

"Are you sure that's what he wants?" Liss remembered Strike's warning. It wasn't fair to drop that bomb on Bear and cause problems in their friendship before she walked.

"I think so. Strike said he hadn't seen me this happy. I can't imagine what has brought on the change to my personality though." His eyebrows danced with amusement. He held her hand and brushed the inside of her wrist with his mouth. "In case you were ever in doubt, this is all you, Liss. We don't have long together, but I want these days to be special, which is the least you deserve. I can't take you on a date, and I can't romance you like…"

"Like?"

"I've never romanced anyone." His eyes flitted upwards.

"You just fuck them, eh?" she joked.

"Oi." He scooted closer so their lips were nearly touching. He smelt of chocolate cookies, and Liss held the memory tight. "I give them the best hours of their lives."

She didn't doubt it. The time they'd spent with each other's bodies were life-changing. The moments wound around Bear's heart were just as significant.

"Tell me something you've never told anyone," Liss whispered. In the darkness of the early hour, they were under a spell, and she didn't want to break it with loud voices.

His brow knitted together as he wrapped his arm around her and pulled her body as close as their faces were. "Once, when I worked on the door of this rough club, I was chatting to the DJ. I was giddy because he'd promised to play my favourite song. It was a Spice Girls track, but that's between you and me."

"My lips are sealed."

"They'd better not be," he replied, causing her to roll

her eyes. "Anyway, in my excitement and because I was nineteen years old and trying to show off, I tried to jump the DJ booth, but I caught my foot and hit the floor. I was jumping up to face my humiliation when the cry went out to the other door staff. The DJ thought someone hit me. Suddenly, we had five hyped-up, massive security guys lumbering onto the dancefloor, and all these drunk dancers jostled to see what was happening. By the time I'd stood, there was a massive punch-up. One of the security guys decided who took me down and tried to drag him out. Everyone was throwing punches. It was carnage. In the end, the police arrived and broke it up."

Liss's giggles were out of control.

"Oi, you." Bear pouted. "Right, I'll have to stop you from laughing then."

He kissed her gently on the mouth and tangled his fingers in her hair. Liss wrapped her legs around him. The heat was there. It never left, but like lovers in it for the long haul, they embraced the opportunity to be in each other's arms. His lips were tender, and his hands gentle as he caressed the strands of her hair. Occasionally, one of his hands held her thigh against him, but neither pushed it further. Instead, they revelled in the intimacy, as if through kisses and caresses, they created a future in each other's arms where royalty and expectations didn't exist. Bear became her world, and as her body offered him its most intimate secrets, he protected them with his entire being while gifting her his own.

As the sunrise streamed through the window, Bear jumped out of bed. He yanked open the windows before returning to her bed. Her lips were sore and her heart full as he sat up and pulled her to sit between his legs and gaze out of the window.

"The best bit about this room is the view of the sunrise," he whispered in her ear, cradling her between his legs. She shivered against his breath as it tickled her neck. They held hands in front of her body as the sun rose.

The hills that peaked above the river outside her bay window glowed with a sunrise more beautiful than she'd ever seen. It was as if the world was aflame with a promise of a future. In the silence of the early hour, the impossible felt possible. "Somewhere in our parallel universe, we're waking up to this. We have two dogs—"

"And a feral cat," she cut in.

"We have two dogs and a feral cat," he conceded, brushing kisses against her ear, "on the bed with us, and we're sipping coffee and nibbling on cookies as we watch the sunset."

She faked a gasp. "Cookies for breakfast?"

"Trust me, we'll find a way to work it off, and I don't mean long dog walks." Tingles ran the length of her spine, and she reached for his hand and caressed his knuckles with kisses. He hummed as he sighed. "What are our dogs and feral cat called?"

"The cat's called Zorro because he's a fighter," she replied as he stroked up and down her arm with his fingertips.

"And the dogs?"

"Jeff and Roy, like old-school football pundits because human names for dogs is funny."

He squeezed her tightly. "You'll get no argument from me."

"I like the sound of this parallel universe." She turned to kneel in front of him. She peppered his lips with kisses. "I presume you'll cook a roast dinner for me every

Sunday."

He tucked a loose wave behind her ear. "Whatever my princess wants."

"But I won't be a princess in this world."

Bear smoothed the lines on her forehead away with his thumb. "You'll always be my princess," he replied softly. Bear laid her down on the bed and eased her T-shirt away before worshipping her body and making love to her under the light of the rising sun.

After a breakfast, Liss returned to organising the business while Bear planned Bodyguard Corp's work for the next month.

Somehow, the day passed without incident. They lived like a couple going about their everyday lives. Strike called to let them know that they'd probably have the results of the tests by Friday. The King might refuse to believe them, but she needed to try and save her grandad even if she tore her new family apart.

Several beeps from the laptop distracted her. It was a bunch of receipts of payments from the invoices and reports she'd sent out, and there were requests for repeat business.

"More business than these guys can cope with," Liss mumbled to herself. There must be a process for these situations.

She listened out for Bear, but he was busy on a call.

Liss video called Luke.

"Hey, Liss." One Direction played in the background. "How's it going? Not long now for you, I guess."

"Don't remind me." His ears tinged pink as if she'd

told him off, and she smiled quickly to relax him. They chatted daily about the business, and he came out of his shell each time. "Tell me, what happens when you guys have too much protection work for Strike and Bear?"

Luke fiddled with his wristband. "We have a bank of people that the lads trust, and we contact them. Some clients prefer a female bodyguard; others want someone who can be with them in like Australia when both Strike and Bear might be working in Europe. There's a database of names I can get you access to, but why do you ask?"

"I'm getting emails about jobs, and Strike and Bear have little availability, not that you can tell from their calendars. I wonder what more they could do to ensure loyal clients." She rapped a pen against the laptop. Her stomach grumbled.

"You sound like an operations manager, with talk like that," he quipped. Liss reached for her water that sat on the coffee table. She didn't have the skills for that sort of job. "But sadly, you'll have to be Queen instead."

The glass toppled, and Liss caught it, although not before water slopped onto the carpet. "I'm never going to be Queen. I'm not next in line to the throne."

Luke cocked his head. "But Strike told me about Marianne and Prince Alex and how they should be arrested. If anything happens to the King, you could be Queen by Friday."

"No, no, no," Liss mumbled, pushing the laptop to the sofa and pacing.

"Didn't you realise?" Luke's ears were pink all over now. "It's the lineage thing. Strike explained it to me."

"I didn't, I... It was what Strike meant last night by epic TV drama. I can't do this. I can't be Queen and lose my grandad...this isn't my life. I ran a pub. I'm not a queen," she ranted.

"I thought you knew. I'm calling Bear," Luke shouted down the camera. "Calm down, Liss, please. You might not be Queen by Friday. It could be months or years in the future."

"You're not helping," she cried before resuming her pace. Her feet pounded the carpet.

Within minutes, Bear rushed into the room. "I'll leave you two be," Luke shouted before ending the video call.

Bear narrowed his eyes. "Princess, what's going on?"

"Don't call me that. I'm not a princess. Fuck, I might be Queen soon, Bear. I can't be Queen! I can't talk confidently to a group of people. You saw me on that stage the other night, and that will be nothing if I end up ruling this country. I can't rule this country," she bellowed.

Bear grabbed her to hold her still. She shook in his arms. He held her against him until her body calmed, but it didn't stop her thoughts from spiralling. She sat on the sofa and dropped her head to her hands. She didn't even want to be a princess. She was only doing it because she wanted a family and to live the life her mum never had the chance to.

"Overthinking isn't helping, and you're not going to resolve anything that way," Bear mumbled helplessly.

"Then what do you suggest?" she crowed against her hands.

Bear knelt in front of her and eased her hands from her face. His skin was hot. "You've not been outside for days, and it wouldn't surprise me if you have cabin fever. We need to distract you." He pressed the laptop's lid down and moved the table out of her way.

"You want to get sexy at a time like this?" Although

incredulous at his suggestion, it eased the tension from her shoulders. She gave his crotch a pointed look.

His deep, sensual laugh eased her anxiety further. "I didn't mean that. How about exercise?"

"Stop saying filthy things," she joked, forcing humour to distract her from the destructive thoughts. "How about a jog? Can you run with me and ensure I'm safe?"

"Don't let this fine yet muscly body deceive you. I can run. But you have to promise me one thing," Bear said as his hands slid into her waves.

Liss locked eyes with his. "Go on."

"I can watch you stretch and run behind you to enjoy the view of your fantastic arse."

Liss laughed against his mouth as he kissed her hard. It was what she needed. Maybe he'd taken her lead of being rude to push past the stress. It'd worked for them before. Her tongue eased his lips apart as he fisted her hair. She slipped a hand into his joggers. His cock pulsed in her hand, and he groaned into her mouth as she kissed him with unspent energy. She closed her eyes and stroked him until he was hard against her palm. Her legs clenched as he lifted her by the thighs and backed her against the wall. They should do this instead of running.

Eventually, Bear pulled back. "Those weren't the stretches I meant. We need fresh air before it gets dark. It will be safer in the light."

She pouted her reply.

"Later, I promise," he grumbled, shifting his dick in his boxers. "I must be a masochist, because I've never wanted to fuck you more. You're my addiction. I can't stop thinking about you whenever I'm not with you. Now, change out of those wet knickers, and I'll meet you at the door in ten minutes."

"Who said they were wet?" she replied breathlessly.

He looked pointedly at the front of them. "The sweet spot at the front of your joggers is a dead giveaway," he replied with a strained chuckle. He raked his eyes over her body again before limping out of the room.

CHAPTER FORTY

The gentle wind lifted the strands of her hair that had already fallen like ribbons from her ponytail.

Sun flushed her skin with heat, warming her as she tipped from side to side to stretch her back. Most of her stretches were in the house, away from prying stares, but as she breathed in the scent of spring flowers, she closed her eyes and pushed her hands high. The taste of freedom was more than she had hoped for. Green fields surrounded the long private road that led to the remote house owned by Strike's parents.

"Come on, Slowcoach," Bear shouted as he led Liss down the driveway onto a bridlepath.

Birds flew high above the trees. They appeared carefree and Liss longed for the same from her future. She breathed the fir-filled air. Bear was right. She needed this. She only ran a few times a month when her shifts and energy allowed. Because she couldn't afford a gym membership, she ran outdoors in the concrete jungle with diesel fumes.

She overtook Bear, slapping him on the arse. His response was a gruff swear word. Liss waved at the sheep as she sped past them. The breeze continued to tousle her hair.

Bear shouted directions as they jogged further into the countryside. The ground was unsteady, and a couple of times, he grabbed her hips to stop her falling. Little did he know how much that turned her on. Thoughts about never seeing him again competed with fears of the future and questions about the King.

"Left," he shouted, directing her into a forest. Liss usually ran wearing headphones, often obliterating her thoughts for thirty minutes. With her tiny legs competing against his long ones, their noisy steps were out of time.

"Stop," he shouted as she reached a smaller path.

Liss froze. "What's wrong?" Her words were barely audible between her pants. Hair strands stuck to the sweat covering her skin.

Birds crowed, and leaves rustled in the trees. "You're thinking too hard."

Liss leant against a tree as she attempted to fill her lungs. She sensed his eyes on her chest as she panted.

"I'm terrified I'll fall and snap an ankle." But at least it would mean she'd be in his arms again. Maybe he'd carry her to her bed to release even more endorphins. Flashbacks from their morning left her aching.

"I wouldn't let that happen to you." Leaves crunched as he stepped closer. "You're a good runner."

"This helped, although nothing stops the overthinking." Although now that he was in front of her, she knew what might temporarily stop her overthinking. In his grey joggers and T-shirt that gripped his muscles, Bear was sex in sportswear. But this was about running, not her need to have him.

"Then I guess we'd better keep going. I don't want you to get cramps." His eyes dropped to her calves as she flexed them. His Adam's apple bobbed as he swallowed, and he shifted himself in his joggers. She wanted to feel his dick again.

"You don't want to help me work out a cramp?" She positioned her foot on a low horizontal branch and stretched. Sweat dripped down her chest, and he licked his lips.

"You're a tease," he said, his voice gruff. He tracked Liss's movements.

"Am I distracting you, Bear?" Heat crept between her thighs due to his primal stare. His eyes were dark enough to lose herself in and never return. "Have you ever done it in a forest?"

"Yes."

"I haven't." Liss stood and pressed Bear against a tree. He went willingly. Branches cracked beneath his large feet. Liss stepped on a handily placed stump, allowing her to be on his level. She bit her lip as she stared into his eyes. "But there's a first for everything."

"What sort of bodyguard would I be to have sex in the open where anything could happen?" he rasped.

"A horny one?"

The arousal coursing through her from when he came inside her that morning wanted release. The kiss and palming of his dick was only the beginning.

"Liss," he warned.

"Chambers," she replied, remembering his surname from the boxing trophy in the house.

He swallowed hard. "No one in my life knows that name except Strike's family. It sounds fucking glorious on your lips. Say it again," he demanded.

"Chambers," she replied, drawing out the name.

His lips hit hers hard and fast, and he gripped Liss's

hips tightly. Their tongues tangled, and he pulled her against him. The frenetic thoughts that had dogged her all day slipped away as she immersed herself in Bear. He slid his hands underneath her joggers and knickers and squeezed her bum. His hands were big enough to hold all of her. Bear trailed kisses down her neck. His lips were hot on her skin, and she moaned and whimpered his surname, writhing against him the entire time.

He crowded her body, and she revelled in him. Her hand slipped beneath his joggers and palmed his dick as she had earlier. Foreplay was better than running. His mouth reached her strappy top, and he pulled it down and wrapped his lips around her nipple.

Liss whimpered loudly.

"I know, baby," he replied. He shoved her joggers and underwear to the ground, and she kicked them off. His joggers and T-shirt quickly followed after he retrieved a condom from the pocket.

"I thought you weren't the sort of bodyguard who had sex in the open," she teased between gasps that made her thrust against him even as he tried to sheath himself.

"I'm the sort of bodyguard who's always prepared," he replied, grabbing her thighs and pulling her against him. Her chuckle stuck in her throat as arousal dripped around her body like he'd injected it into her blood. "And I'm always fucking horny for you."

He pushed her against a tree before lining his dick up and thrusting into her.

"Again," she cried as he eased out and pushed back in. Some moments were for making love, and others were for the sort of sex Liss had missed all her adult years. Pure, wanton fucking. She'd be touching herself for days, remembering his cock inside her body and his words in her head.

Bark scratched her back. A princess shouldn't have evidence of the feral fuck she had with her bodyguard, but she didn't care. The pain branded the moment to her soul.

His lips continued to caress her neck and breasts as goosebumps exploded across her skin. Her hands cradled his head against her body as she cried her pleasure. Her thighs were tight against his hips, and she held onto him like he could save her from the storms of her life.

"Vocal, aren't you?" Bear said between kisses. His smile blessed her flesh.

"I want everyone to know how fucking needy and dirty you make me," she said before screaming as he thrust into her deeply.

"Fucking hell, you're going to destroy me."

"Just a matter of time, Chambers," she said between pants as he continued pushing her orgasm higher.

Her use of his surname was a catalyst, and he kissed and sucked while pounding her relentlessly. Bear offered her the endorphins she needed to break her thoughts. Suddenly, her orgasm exploded. She held on to him, digging her nails into his shoulders as her arms shuddered. Liss repeated his surname. His climax carried her deeper into ecstasy, and his body shook into hers.

She kissed his lips and neck and sucked on his ear lobe between gasps. Sweat covered the hairs of his chest, dampening her top.

"Bloody hell," he said between pants that made him quiver nearly as much as his climax had. "Sex with you is just—it's everything."

Eventually, he carried her back to her stump and eased away from her once he was sure she stood on her own. Liss shivered in the cool air as he helped her put her joggers back on before dressing himself. They stared at each other, eye to eye, once more. She swallowed as he appraised her body. In the stillness of the forest, it was as if the words flooding their mouths were too impossible to share.

Bear bit at her lips and stroked her cheek with his palm. She closed her eyes and breathed in their shared moment. After minutes of immersing themselves in each other, they headed back to the house hand in hand.

Bear's phone rang as they walked. "Strike, what's up?" The words on the other end were brief. "Fucking hell. I guess we'd best get home. We'll pack up and be on the road soon. I'll call you when we're close."

Strike's voice wasn't loud enough for Liss to understand, but Bear's response was clear. "They're escalating if they're willing to plant a bomb in the pub. There's no point hiding anymore. It's safer for everyone if they think they know where to find her."

Chapter Forty-One

Everything took longer than planned, with Bear insisting they ate and showered before returning home.

Liss thumbed the heart talisman as they drifted through the countryside in the four-by-four. Shapes leered through the darkness. They were trees and nothing more, yet every figure represented a threat or enemy that didn't exist two weeks ago.

Someone had planted a bomb at her pub. They found it before anything happened. But she fixated on the realisation that she and Bear had lost their last night together.

And there was her new family. She wasn't ready to lose her grandad.

Liss tapped restlessly against her chair. There was much to learn about the past and questions she wanted to ask on behalf of her mum. A title couldn't be enough for Alex to kill his dad. Sickness filled her belly as if she'd ingested poison. That she could be Queen in days loomed like a spectre. Liss gritted her teeth to ward off panic.

"You're overthinking." Bear's gravelly voice cut into her thoughts. "Talk to me, Princess."

His hand rested on her bobbing thigh. "Shouldn't you call me Queen now?" she snapped.

"That explains why you're overthinking."

"What do you expect?" she shouted. The panic hit thick and fast, and she took it out on her closest ally.

Bear spoke so quietly that she leaned closer to hear him. "I don't know. I'm overthinking, too, and that isn't me. I'm rational and make decisions based on realistic threats and planning. But with you..."

"With me what?"

Liss turned in her seat to face him. He said nothing more, and she pushed his hand from her thigh as she stared. Occasionally, headlamps from other cars lit his face. His lips were tight, and there were too many lines on his forehead. Her gaze dropped to his hands. His knuckles were white, and he gripped the steering wheel.

Bear's eye twitched as he said, "With you, I'm scared. I don't know what I'd do if something happened to you. I'm selfish because you're going through this shit. But, Liss, soon we'll never see each other again, and the only thing that gets me through that is knowing you're safe. You don't deserve any of this. You're a good person."

"Am I?" She wanted to hurt him like she was hurting, but those glimpses of his body language proved he was in pain too. Instead, she returned to her humour defence. "I once put pepper in a punter's dinner rather than salt."

Bear threw his head back and laughed. Liss nearly grabbed the steering wheel as the car wobbled across the road. Tears sprung from his eyes. "I bet he deserved it though."

"He pinched my arse," Liss replied. "I dropped his ham on the floor three times before smothering it with pepper. The dickhead said it was the best ham sandwich he'd ever had."

Tears rolled down Bear's cheeks, and his whole body

shook with laughter. "Is that really the worst thing you've ever done?"

Liss shrugged, and her smile was tentative. She grabbed Bear's shaking hand and placed it back on her knee. "I used clean toilet water in another guy's drink."

"What did he do? Because I know he did something to deserve it."

"He stole my phone on the way to the palace and told me that he didn't want to see the photo I'd sent to a guy of me in my underwear because it must have been bad."

His chuckle was short-lived. "Whoa. That was me! Although, I got off lightly. I was a dick to you when we first met."

"And several times after." Liss leaned over and kissed his cheek. "You're worried about me, Bear, but I worry about you too. Your job is dangerous, and a part of me wonders if one day I'll read an article telling me you're dead."

"If anything happened to me, you'd never read about it." She shivered at the emotionless way he said it. "I'm going to miss you. If the prospect is this painful, I don't think I'll cope."

"You will. You can do anything." Bear lifted her hand to his lips and kissed the inside of her wrist. A tear slipped down her cheek, but she swiped it away before he saw it.

"My job is to notice things," he said as he turned the car with one hand. "But I'll pretend I didn't see that." She huffed as pain cracked her heart. "I'm worried about you too. Those bastards planted a bomb in the pub you managed. Things are escalating from idle threats."

"Do you think it's Marianne? As much as I hate her, I can't believe anyone would do this for a royal title," Liss replied. She stretched her legs. They'd been on the road for hours, and she wasn't sure where they were, when they'd be home or where home would be that night.

"Power makes people do crazy things. I suspect she's after money too. The escalation suggests that she knows Beatrice has taken away some of your grandad's pills. Strike asked her brother to watch over Gable and Beatrice. Everyone is at risk until we get the results."

"This is my fault. I wanted a family. I didn't want to be alone anymore, but if my link to the royal family had remained a secret, none of this would be happening."

Bear moved her hand to his thigh so he could use both of his on the steering wheel. Streetlights, houses, and public buildings hinted that they were in the suburbs now. Liss glimpsed a pub that Isla had dragged her to once while hunting for the single guy from her course that she wanted to "accidentally" bump into. It was a failed stakeout fuelled by tequila slammers. Liss sighed. She wouldn't have adventures like that again. She'd see the world but without her friends. She didn't want any of this.

Guilt covered her body like a rash. But she remembered all those days her mum had dragged her tired body back from work after being overlooked and used. She had more skills and intelligence than all those executives. Her mum should have received respect and a chance to live and change the world. She had to do it for her. It was the best way to honour her memory. Liss had spent years hiding in the pub, but this was her time to make the world know her mum's name. Her mum would have done this, so Liss had to take her place. Yet her terror and sadness sickened her.

"None of this is your fault, so don't think that." Lights flashed across his weary face. "You didn't ask for any of this, and you're a victim here."

"So how do I stop feeling like this? What can I do to fight this situation?"

"You hide."

Liss pulled her hand away, but Bear grabbed it and held it against his heart. "I can't protect you when the threats are unknown. I'm terrified you'll get hurt, and I'll break if something happens to you. We're going to a safe place."

"No fucking way. I have to get to the pub. I know the bomb didn't go off, but I must check that the place is okay."

"Liss," he pleaded.

"The pub used to be my home. I might never visit again, but it was my family, my safe space, and where I made some of my happiest memories. At the very least, I need to check it and say goodbye. And don't Liss me, the person you've cared about and had feelings for over the last couple of days—"

"The last twelve days. I've cared about you and had feelings for you since the first day I met you," Bear interjected.

Liss closed her eyes and lowered her head as she allowed herself a moment to reflect on his admission. She wanted to relax into his declaration, but she couldn't. She looked up and caught his eye. A streetlight flashing across his face made them look watery.

"Finish your sentence, Liss."

He was changing the subject because she hadn't commented on his declaration.

She forced saliva into her dry mouth and spoke slower now. "That person, me, is the same one who needs to do this. I need to care for the thing that saved me after Mum's death. Please let me return there and check on it one last time."

Bear remained silent as he drove. Liss rapped her nails against the door handle. She'd fight him if she must.

Suddenly, he swung the car and made a U-turn in the middle of the road. "Fine," he shouted. "I know what it is to have that safe space, and I'd be the same. But I'm still going to be a grumpy dick about it."

"I wouldn't have you any other way." She kissed her angry Bear on his cheek.

He bristled. "This doesn't mean you've won this one, so don't think that you can win anything in the future with your impassioned speeches about my feelings."

"I wouldn't dare," she replied with a satisfied smile, but sadness still turned the crack in her heart into a crevice. Strike's words about leaving Bear with no doubt that they weren't an item flashed. She couldn't hurt him. Another tear slipped down, but she looked out the window, adamant that he wouldn't see it.

Bear parked at the pub.

Liss glanced at her dark and empty flat. She needed to make her heart empty to get through the following months. Liss waited for Bear to tell her it was safe as she considered who'd live in her flat next. After Friday, she'd get her possessions.

There wasn't a place in the palace for her corner sofa where she and Isla could watch movies while throwing popcorn at each other and laughing over Isla's conquests. She dragged herself to it when she had a hangover or period pain, hunkered under blankets, and watched crappy reality television. Liss's sofa reminded her of early mornings when she was a poorly child and her mum stroked her hair as she cried or struggled through a fitful sleep.

I have to do this for you, Mum. You deserve your moment.

After calling Strike with their location and performing a visual check, Bear helped her from the car. Her limbs clenched, and her gaze darted around the space. Bear was the same. Although he'd made it clear it wasn't his choice to come to the pub, he'd ensure she was safe and not be a brat about it. But maybe a fight would make it easier to walk away.

Several lights glowed from the pub windows. The flat was Liss's base, but this was her safe space. When no one else employed her because she cared for her mum, Hugo let her work whatever shifts she could. Liss hadn't worked in a pub before, and it was a miracle she was allowed to stay after her first shift, which involved broken glasses and chaotic drink orders. But as she got to know the punters, it became her home. With her unexpected skills in operations, she made it a successful business. Liss's heart rattled at what could have happened if the bomb had gone off. Bear said it wasn't set and couldn't have, but bile climbed her throat at the idea that her people would have died because of her choices.

"Are the lights on a timer?" Bear asked as they stepped to the main door.

"No, everything goes off after closing."

"Which is usually by now?"

Liss glanced at her watch and nodded. It was a little

after midnight. Everyone was gone way before now on a Wednesday night, and finding a bomb would've closed the place early. Hairs rose on her neck as Bear pulled her closer.

"I don't like this. We should go or at least wait for Strike." He was wide-eyed as the pub's front door opened.

Steve glared with hollow eyes and pinched lips. "I thought you'd turn up eventually. You'd best come in."

Liss held her breath and stepped over the pub's threshold before Bear grabbed her.

Chapter Forty-Two

Steve's pupils were huge, and his eyes darted around the pub as he pointed at the seats.

Liss hadn't seen him like this before, and as she stared at his worn appearance and shaking body, she gripped Bear. She bit the inside of her mouth to stop panic from claiming her. Bear attempted to stand in front of Liss, but she stepped away.

"Aren't you going to sit?" Steve commanded rather than requested. The lights that hung from the walls glowed. As shadows danced up the walls every time he moved, his features wavered, an eery spectacle.

"What's going on, Steve?" Bear asked, refusing to sit.

Bear surreptitiously surveyed the area. From spending time with him, Liss knew the dangers he was searching for. Steve was jittery and unable to keep still, but there was no sign of a weapon. The bar was empty except for a glass filled with a neat spirit. Liss's stomach turned. The only spirit Steve drank like that was gin, and that was rare because it made him unpredictable.

"Sit down, Liss. I need to talk to you," Steve said grimly, refusing to look at Bear.

"Look, mate," Bear replied casually as if his calm would rub off onto Steve.

"I'm not your mate, remember?"

"Good point. Sorry, Steve." Bear held his hands in the air, but he wasn't surrendering. He'd faced worse situations than this. He had her back, and everything he did would be to protect her. She was certain. "Liss and I will sit, won't we, Princess?" He gently took her hand to convince her to follow his lead.

"Don't call her that," Steve screamed. "And don't hold her hand. She's not yours."

Liss froze.

"She's not yours, Steve," Bear grunted.

"Are you saying that she wants you? Is that where you've been, Liss, hanging out with him while your friends worried about you?" Spittle flew from Steve's mouth.

"She was safe with me. I've protected her and ensured she was happy, which is more than I can say for you," Bear growled between gritted teeth. "You should have treated her better at the party."

Steve's nostrils flared, and he pushed his hands over his ears.

"Bear," Liss whispered. "Please stop. This isn't helping."

Bear held her gaze briefly. His vulnerability was evident from the slight twitch of his eye. She squeezed his hand before letting go and nodding at the chair. "Sit, please," she whispered.

Bear raised his eyebrow defiantly, even as he sat on a wooden bar stool. Liss edged nearer Steve like he was a baby deer. She eased his hands from his ears. "Steve, I want you to sit too. I'll get you water. I suspect you've had a long night. We're going to chat."

Steve sat as she filled a glass with water and handed it to him. "I know I acted weird at the party."

Bear grumbled, and she shushed him with a glare. He

rolled his eyes but remained silent. The scent of chips and pies, the pub staple on Wednesday nights, lingered. A swell of sadness filled Liss at how much she'd miss the place, even as she held Steve's hands.

"I was like that because I love you. I've always loved you."

Liss chewed the inside of her mouth to mask her shock. She'd thought from what Isla said it was just a crush. "Why didn't you tell me before?" she whispered.

"I didn't know how. And when we found out you were a princess, I was petrified I'd lose you. I thought if people saw us as a cute couple, like at the party, you'd see it too." He squeezed her hands. "And I know you, Liss. I know you wouldn't want to be a princess. That's why I did what I did. I had to help you."

"What do you mean 'help me'?"

Steve shook his head, refusing to meet her stare.

"Steve, did you make the bomb threats?" Betrayal pierced her soul. "Did you bring a bomb into my pub, my home?"

"No!" He jumped, sending his chair clattering to the floor. Bear shot up too. Although he was behind her, she sensed him as clearly as if he'd brushed kisses to her skin. She pushed her hand down to remind him to sit. The chair scraping across the hardwood floor convinced her that he'd obeyed. He was her feral wolf to contain.

"Please sit, Steve. You're too tall, and it's easier to have this conversation if you're sitting." She'd used the tactic when dealing with some of the beefiest punters. Even the threatening men didn't usually want to terrify a woman. Their anger was rarely on her. As Steve sat, she eased out a breath. "When you said you did something, what were you talking about?"

Steve held his head in his hands. "I pushed you down the stairs when you came to the pub."

Liss covered her mouth. Bear grumbled something.

"But I didn't mean to." Steve lifted his head and fixed her with his big blue eyes. "I wanted to tell you how I felt. I found you at the top of the stairs, but I was nervous. I wanted your attention but pressed your shoulder harder than I meant to. You slipped and fell. So I ran."

"You left me hurt at the bottom of the stairs?" Sadness stung the back of her throat. He should have helped her. Bear helped her.

"I'm sorry. I'm so sorry. I panicked, but then you invited me to the party. That was my chance to help you say no to being a princess."

He wasn't a villain, but this wasn't the act of a true friend. He thought his actions were helping her, but he'd destroyed her trust, possibly forever. "So you didn't plant the bomb?"

"No. I wouldn't, I couldn't. Marianne wanted you to renounce the throne. We chatted at the party, and I told her you didn't want to be a princess."

"You've been working with Marianne to terrorise me?" she cried, her eyes teary. It was another knife in her back. He was stopping her from making her own decisions and emotionally attacking her in the process.

His speech sped up. "It wasn't about terrorising you but setting you free."

Liss's jaw fell.

"It's always been about making you renounce the throne, because that's what you want." He'd never asked her if that's what she wanted. Maybe it wasn't what was in her heart, but it wasn't his decision. It was hers. "Marianne has called every day to find out where you are. The bomb was to stop you, hitting what you loved so you'd make the right decision."

Liss stepped back, her thighs hitting Bear's legs behind her as Steve wept. She needed to feel Bear's presence.

"You've got this," he said so quietly she wondered if she'd imagined it. His belief filled her, and his touch centred her. "You're strong and confident, and you're incredible."

Liss said, "But the bomb couldn't go off."

"That wasn't part of the plan. Marianne told me to call Isla and find a way to get you here, and then once you were, you'd find the bomb. You'd go into hiding and never accept the throne, but I couldn't do it. I called the police instead."

"Steve, what you did was beyond wrong. You don't get to force me into decisions. It doesn't matter what you thought you knew. You didn't speak to me or check what I wanted. What you did wasn't an act of love; you underestimated me. You tried to control me. I didn't think you were like that," she said, her voice breaking.

Bear touched the back of her leg, grounding her. She took a deep breath.

"I'm not. I was scared. I regret everything, Liss. You have to believe me," he said tearily.

"You should have spoken to me, but instead, you betrayed me when I needed the people I believed I could trust. And you did this with Marianne. How could you?"

Steve's head dropped, and he wept. It broke her to see him like that. He'd gotten mixed up in a situation for the right reasons and yet did the worst thing imaginable.

"I'm sorry. I'm so sorry." His blond curls jumped with

each crying breath.

Liss grabbed a chair and pulled it next to him. "I don't know if we can come back from this."

"I'll do anything to make it better. I need to get your trust back."

"I don't know if you can," she said, resigning.

He lifted his head. "I could give a statement to the police about what I did and Marianne's part in it. I've got messages I could show them." He fumbled with his phone. "Will it help?"

Liss shrugged. "Maybe. But you should have already done it."

Steve nodded, although tears streamed down his face as Liss stroked his back.

Suddenly, Strike crashed through the door. Confronted by the scene of a seated Bear, a gentle Liss, and a weeping, defeated Steve, he let out the only thing he could. "What the actual fuck is going on here?

Before anyone could answer, he added, "It's like I've walked into an episode of bloody *EastEnders*. Get me a whisky, Liss, before I lose my mind."

"Nice to see you too, Strike," Liss said with a roll of the eyes. "You do love the dramatics."

"Whatever," Strike announced. "The test results are in, and we've got a rich witch to confront. But whisky first. I've had a fuck of a day."

Chapter Forty-Three

Within an hour, they were back on the road.

They'd left Steve at the police station with Luke for updates. The confession should be enough to ensure Marianne was held to account for her criminality. Combined with the test results, King Archibald must believe them. But what if he didn't?

By the time the sun started to rise over the city streets, they were like a rogue gang high on coffee as they headed to the palace with the test results. Strike's scientist friend did them a massive favour by testing the tablets and providing results in about a day.

It was impossible to believe that the last time the sun rose, Liss was in the warmth of Bear's arms before they'd made love. As the car skidded to a stop, Liss checked her watch. It was six a.m. Bear touched her leg from the front passenger seat. It was brief and yet comforting. She wasn't alone yet.

"Why haven't the gates opened?" Liss demanded as her heart rate rose and her fingers trembled. "Is it because they didn't know we were coming?"

"It's because they *did know* we were coming," Strike replied between gritted teeth. "But we're ready for anything. We'll find a way in."

"All for one and one for all," she replied half-heartedly.

"We're not the three musketeers." But Strike's smile and Bear's chuckle made her smirk. There was nothing like a little light humour with your bodyguards before bringing hell to the royal palace. "Right. Let's do battle."

"Does he always sound like a Ghostbuster?" Liss asked a still laughing Bear.

"If only you knew." Bear chuckled.

The men left the car and helped her out after they checked for safety.

The three of them barrelled up to the security as a unit. "We need to see the King," Strike shouted, drawing the attention of the odd passer-by from the street. If the sudden braking of their massive four-by-four wasn't dramatic enough, their behaviour might get them arrested before they saved anyone.

The guard eyeballed Liss. "You're not seeing the King. We've been given strict instructions not to let anyone in."

"I'm his granddaughter," she protested, adrenaline soaring.

"We know who you are." Another guard walked from around the corner. "You're the one we definitely can't let in. The King is too sick to have visitors. We're following orders."

"Call Alex now," Liss snapped. "And before you tell me what time it is, remember that I will be living here soon, and I can make your life a nightmare. Call him."

Liss couldn't make their lives a nightmare even if she wanted to, but the threat worked. The guard stepped away and mumbled to whoever answered his call. He hung up quickly.

"They said you can't see the King. They added that if

you don't renounce your title, you're putting yourself and all those you care about at 'deathly risk.'" The guard winced. "Don't shoot the messenger. Marianne is a witch. But you didn't hear that from me."

Liss's mouth twisted as she considered her options.

"I'm not backing down no matter what happens to me now or in the future," she whispered between gritted teeth to Bear and Strike. "I'm not letting my grandad die because someone's obsessed with power and status. Not ever."

"I've got you," Bear grunted.

"What do you want to do?" Strike's nostrils flared.

"This is fucking ridiculous," Liss raged, throwing her hands in the air. Strangers stared.

Bear grimaced. "Princess, chill."

"Shout 'Princess, chill' to me loudly. I have a plan."

Bear's brows furrowed, and Strike shook his head.

"Trust me, okay? Remember, I'm the woman who saved you from Mazdy's agent. I've sorted out your invoices and paperwork, put the Prime Minister's operations director in his place, and got you more work." Her pulse was out of control. "So trust me."

"You might as well." Strike shrugged. "We're running out of things to lose anyway."

"And I need your most dramatic ways. Think falling doorman who trips on a DJ booth," she cheeked Bear.

He glared at her but still hollered, "Princess Felicity, I need you to please chill the hell out. If Marianne and Prince Alex won't let you see the King, there's nothing we can do."

"I fucking adore you," she whispered to Bear before jumping up and down and shouting, "But I need to see my grandad. He's dying, and I need to talk to him about whether I should renounce my title tomorrow."

Passers-by pulled out their phones to record her, but she needed the press. Liss shoved her hands high and screamed as loud as she could, "I have secrets I need to tell my grandad, the King. Shameful things for a future princess. I need to confess."

She covered her smile with her hand as more people stopped. Her ranting continued until the press flooded the street, quickly followed by a car with blacked-out windows.

"Beatrice and Gable." Strike nodded towards the vehicle. "I called them from the lab."

"Clever man," she said, shoving Strike playfully.

He beamed as he pretended to jolt from the power of her hit.

Journalists and strangers wielding cameras surrounded Liss before Gable and Beatrice reached them.

"What's going on, Princess Felicity? Has the King locked you out the gates already?"

"Has there been another bomb threat?"

"Have you decided what you're gonna do 'bout the title?"

That question smarted more than the others, but Liss confronted the press with Strike and Bear flanking her. With their height differences, they were a funny trio, but she loved having them close.

Her body shook with adrenaline as she announced to hungry photographers, "Marianne and Alex won't let me in the palace because I know what they've been doing to the King. We have proof that they've been poisoning him."

The gasps of the crowd momentarily stunned her. Bear squeezed her hand and nodded his support while Strike whispered his words of encouragement. The press's shock was short-lived, and the questions were suddenly thick and fast.

Gable and Beatrice's security pushed through a gap in the crowd while television presenters recorded live pieces to cameras. Strike handed the results of the tests to Gable as Beatrice rushed towards Liss and enveloped her in a hug. "I'm so proud of you."

Liss instantly returned the sentiment as Gable announced to the baying crowd, "Thank you for joining us at such an early hour. We didn't want to go on record with this before speaking to the King, but he is a prisoner in the palace. The prince and his fiancée won't allow him to see us. Marianne and Alex removed his professional medical care." The attentive group gave angry shouts. "Due to their suspicious behaviour with the King's medication, we tested it this week, and the results are damning." He waved the paper with the results on them in the air.

The crowd froze. At the clattering footsteps behind Liss, she turned. Marianne ran to the gate. Alex was behind her, his eyes steely and his hands in fists.

"She's lying. Felicity is a lowlife. We regret allowing scum into our family," Marianne shouted.

There were more gasps, and Bear tensed beside her, but Beatrice cried out, "And yet you threw me out of the King's bedroom the other evening, Marianne, when I spoke to the King's medics. When did you become the one who makes the decisions in the family?"

Alex interrupted with a roar, but the crowd was silent again. A hunched-over figure appeared from the palace steps and wandered towards the gates. It was the King. Marianne attempted to help him, but he waved her away. Liss ran to the gate as the King demanded the guards open it.

The King embraced Liss, and then Beatrice, as soon as the gates were open. When he reached Gable, they conversed quietly, and Gable handed him the test results. They studied them together as Liss turned to Bear and Strike, who shrugged. She bit her tongue as everyone watched. Gable's bodyguards cornered Marianne and Alex.

After the brief conversation, Archibald cleared his throat. He announced to the press, his voice gravelly from the toll of his illness, "What a morning. I bet some of you aren't used to rushing to a story at such an early hour. Especially you, George," he joked pointing at the national television company's royal correspondent, who laughed. Archibald's charisma was undeniable, even when everything significant to him crumbled. *I'll never have that skill.* "As you're aware, we deal with family matters privately. However, confidentiality hasn't been our friend in recent times. I was private for too long about the woman I once loved, and if I'd been honest, I might have had the opportunity to meet my daughter before she died. Now, my son and his future wife have used privacy against me, ensuring I hid the news of the medication they insisted my medics prescribed."

The crows that hung around the palace were louder than the stunned crowd.

"I will need to speak to my family, as I have also learnt that the recent bomb threats and the unexploded bomb left in Liss's pub were Marianne's doing."

Alex drew a loud breath as he stared at Marianne.

"As you can imagine, it's a lot to comprehend." Archibald stilled temporarily, and Liss's heart ached at the hollow circles beneath his eyes and his weary form. "However, I ask for your respect as we decide our next steps. The police will be involved, and there will be criminal proceedings against all perpetrators. In the meantime, I shall undergo urgent medical treatment. As always, we have a duty to this country and its people. We will have our announcement with Felicity tomorrow. Thank you for your time."

The palace guards shooed the press and bystanders away as bodyguards held Marianne and Alex in place. The King walked Gable, Beatrice, Liss, Strike, and Bear towards the palace. Archibald took Liss's hands in his. His skin was cold and his hands frail. Tears brimmed her eyes at what his family had done. "I'm so sorry," Liss murmured as she shook against him.

"Darling Felicity, you have nothing to be sorry for. I am sorry for everything my family has forced you to endure. I welcomed you into my world, and they hurt you. Please forgive me."

"Of course, you did nothing wrong." She embraced him in a gentle hug. He was thinner than when they'd first met, but his eyes still sparkled. There was hope.

"Thank you. I wanted to speak to you this morning about the future and learn your decision, but I expect you will require more time to decide. As a result of today, you will be next in line to the throne. If and when something happens to me, you will be Queen. That is a lot to comprehend." His posture was stiff, but he made firm eye contact.

Liss's mouth was sandpaper dry.

"However, I must deal with my son and Marianne and see what can be done regarding my health. The police will arrive shortly; the less you have to do with them as you reflect, the better. I shall see you tomorrow, but in the meantime, consider your future wisely. You have proved yourself beyond understanding, and I would love you to be a princess, and then Queen, but it has to be your decision."

He kissed her on the cheek and hugged her. This man had accepted her in a way her nana never had. She wanted to explore this connection and love, but it came at a cost.

He turned to Bear and Strike. "Gentlemen, thank you for keeping her safe. You have done a commendable job, and I will ensure you get my family's highest recommendation. Please keep her safe until tomorrow."

"Certainly, sir." Strike pulled his chest high. "I'll stay a little longer to give you the test results and discuss our witness. Bear will take Liss to a safe place."

The King nodded. Liss offered Gable and Beatrice a quick hug before returning to the car. As the adrenaline faded, exhaustion filled every part of her body. Bear strapped her into her seat, and the gentle motion of the vehicle ensured her eyes fluttered closed in minutes.

Chapter Forty-Four

Liss opened her eyes slowly, rubbing sleep from the corners.

The room was bathed in darkness except for the light radiating from a chrome lamp on the cupboard beside her. One wall held a large painting of a lake. She'd seen that image before.

She lifted her head off a marshmallow-soft pillow and stepped to the window. It was a grey suburban street with cars lining the road and light pooling from the dirty streetlights. It was like someone had painted a plain English city side street.

Liss inspected her room for a clue to where she was. The wardrobe and chest of drawers had a high finish, and boxing glove cufflinks sat in a pot on top of it next to a couple of bottles of aftershave, but it was without photos or homely touches.

Suddenly, footsteps padded outside the bedroom door, and she rushed back into bed. Briefly, she breathed in the scent that lingered on the duvet. It smelt of wood and citrus. This was Bear's apartment. The lake image on his wall matched his screensaver.

The door creaked open, and Bear's face, covered with stubble from the last couple of days, appeared through a gap in the doorway.

"How do you always know when I'm awake?"

Bear's chuckle made her heart swell. "Must be my superpower." The bed dipped as he sat. "Did you sleep okay?"

She stretched like a starfish and yawned. "Deeper than I thought possible. I must have been out of it. What time is it?"

"It's nearly midnight. You slept all day." The edge of his lips turned down briefly, but he returned to a non-committal smile. "Are you hungry? Because I can make you something."

Liss held her hand to her mouth and closed her eyes. Regret tainted her breath. "I slept through our last day together. I'm so sorry."

Bear reached for her and hugged her tightly. Once more, she smelt warm wood and citrus. She squeezed her eyes even tighter and attempted to write an unforgettable memory.

"Liss, you've been through a hell of a lot. Two weeks ago today, you were opening up the pub for the last time. Your body can only sustain the trauma for so long. But I love that you felt safe enough to sleep soundly here. You needed it." The heat of his body made her flush through the long T-shirt. It smelt of him. A car bumbled up the road outside. Its exhaust sputtered as it passed. These were their last hours together. Sadness tore her heart as he rested his chin on her head. "I'll bring you food. I cooked a roast for whenever you woke up, but I'm guessing you'd rather toast or cereal?"

Her stomach growled as if disagreeing.

Bear pulled away to meet her eyes, and his face lit up with laughter. "Roast dinner with all the trimmings, then?"

She nodded enthusiastically.

"And how many potatoes? Because I feel you're a roast potato kind of woman."

"Six?" she replied with a wince, expecting him to tease her.

"That's my girl," he replied with a smile. "Six it is. I made seven in case." She forced a smile until he'd left the room. Her face drooped, reflecting her heart. She wasn't his girl and never would be. She'd tell the world she was a princess in twelve hours.

And I'll never see him again.

Her whole body ached with the sadness that consumed her soul. The King needed her, but becoming a royal meant giving up her old life. But aside from Isla, she had no one else and nothing to stay in her current life for. Her two weeks with Bear had been incredible, but they couldn't be together, even if she didn't accept her royal title. They only worked because it was short-term. He didn't do relationships, and nothing would change that. And it was the right thing for him. She didn't want to get in the way of his work or be something else for him to worry about. Their lives were heading in different directions.

Liss stared at the lakeside image on his wall. He'd said she'd changed his rules in less than two weeks. But he'd regret that his life had to change to accommodate her. Becoming a royal was a complication he couldn't add to his life of control and planning. And there were positives to her taking the throne too. She'd spend more time with Gable, Beatrice, and, hopefully, her grandad. There would be parties and trips as well.

She breathed in the scent of his pillow. As much as she tried to convince herself it was for the right reason, she couldn't deny that without Bear, her happiness would always be tainted by the loneliness he saw in her. And she'd know that somewhere in the world, a man held her heart.

"Here it is," he announced as he returned. He grinned as he held aloft a plate of heated roast beef, vegetables, Yorkshire pudding, and six roast potatoes. Bear popped it on a tray on her lap before raising his eyebrows at the question he didn't need to ask.

"Yes, you can get under the duvet with me." She smiled as she used food to push down her emotions.

He tucked himself in beside her.

"Aren't you going to eat?" she asked as she sliced a roast potato and swooshed it through the gravy.

"I already ate," he replied. "Besides, now I get to watch you eat. Bugger, that sounds creepy." He winced. "But I don't cook normally, and I get a weird pride from how much you like my food."

Liss's chuckles turned into delighted groans as a roast potato dripping in homemade gravy touched her tongue. She hummed as she popped a bit of Yorkshire in too. Bear nodded with a beaming smile.

"My god, you're amazing," she replied, unashamed at her full mouth. Liss refused to linger on what the royal household would say if they saw her talking with her mouth full. She had a night of freedom left.

Bear updated her with family news while she gorged on his cooking. Strike had handed over all the necessary evidence and would return to Bear's flat in the morning to take Liss to the palace, where Gable and Beatrice would support her for the big announcement. The police had Marianne and Alex in custody, although Alex's hand in everything was less than they initially thought. He didn't realise the pills contained poison but believed his dad was getting old and they were denying him the full support to help him pass on.

"Do you believe that?"

"I don't know," Bear conceded. "But it's not up to us to decide."

The King was in the care of world-class toxicologists flown in within hours of the revelations. He was receiving the best treatment, but no one was willing to make a prognosis until they saw how he responded.

"So that's it. All sorted and with a big red bow," she said, sagging against the bed as Bear took away her tray before scooting back under the duvet.

Liss rested her head against his chest. His warmth and the regular pound of his heart comforted her. The next time the sun set, she'd be alone, scared, and desperate for his care. They sat like this in silence, safe together. Liss closed her eyes and breathed slowly. A happiness that she'd never felt before swelled in her heart at just being close to this guy who made her think she could conquer anything.

Time passed, and the quiet of the house lingered. His breathing was slower, as if he was sleeping. She languished in his safety and let him rest. He hadn't had enough recently. After a while, maybe even hours, he stirred.

His words echoed in his chest. "I was just thinking about you. Are you doing okay about your decision and announcement?"

"Kind of. It's my duty and my way to honour Mum. I need to live the life and take the opportunity she didn't have. But then there's you."

"Me?" Bear's voice cracked.

Liss closed her eyes and willed herself to be honest. "I

don't want to say goodbye to you. I'm not good at goodbyes, but after only two weeks with you, I can't imagine a life without you by my side. We can't have a future, you don't do relationships, and I have a duty, but we'll never spend time together again."

Bear leant back and lifted her face to his. "I don't do goodbyes either. We can stay up to watch the sunrise and then nap, and then I'll slip out so we don't have to say goodbye."

He made it sound so easy. Maybe it was for him.

Liss nodded as tears brimmed her eyes. She was stupid to hope he'd tell her they'd make it work.

"Don't cry, Liss. You'll be a fantastic princess and an epic queen. People will write songs about you and perform shows in your honour." He didn't understand the real reason for her tears. "And whenever you see the sunrise, you can remember our time together."

Liss smiled half-heartedly as he brushed the tears away from her cheeks. He kissed her softly, but as his hands cupped her cheeks, she deepened it, easing his lips open. Her fingers danced across his stubbled chin, but nothing was gentle about how his mouth opened to hers. Liss pulled his bottom lip between her teeth before meeting his tongue with hers. Warmth fused with need, and his hands fisted in her hair. His tongue massaged hers as she climbed on top of him. He stroked her skin beneath her T-shirt as she ground herself against him. He reached for the hem and pulled it over her head. She was naked and ready for him.

Turmoil unravelled in her stomach at her acceptance that it was their last time together. But she pushed the pain down as he stared at her in awe. Arousal scorched them as they quickly pushed his joggers down and off. They became a mess of limbs and lips in the frenzy of their lust. Liss cried out as he kissed and sucked at her neck. Heat controlled them. Her pussy burnt with desire, and she panted loudly as Bear's thumb grazed and rubbed circles across her clit. His cock was hard between her thighs, and the sensations made her cry out for more.

"I want you good and wet for me." His voice was low and thrummed through her body. She writhed against him.

"I want you inside of me."

She was frantic as he attempted to increase foreplay. But as much as she should have made it last, she needed him deep inside her. She bit his skin and whispered the dirtiest words into his ear before licking and sucking the lobe. Her nails scratched his nipples, making him hiss. She was desperate for their bodies to fuse as they owned each other one last time.

"I wanted this to be slow and dirty, but you're fucking impossible. I need you riding me, baby," he groaned. Bear reached for a condom, and she ripped the wrapper open and slid it onto him. His eyes rolled in the back of his head. He made everything sexy.

She lined him up against her and gritted her teeth as she pressed down onto him. His cock filled her easily as if their bodies were designed for each other. Liss flattened her palms against his chest, running her fingers through his chest hair and revelling in how he tightened his pecs even as he hissed and clenched his thighs.

Back at the palace party, he'd said she wouldn't have a problem straddling him, and he was right. He was hard in all the right places.

Liss threw her head back as she rode him. Their lovemaking was intimate yet fed her cravings. She desperately tried to clutch the moment forever. Her hands slipped to either side of his head, gripping the pillow as she rode him. He stared at her with something more than awe. She glowed under his stare. She bucked her hips and stretched her thighs as he lifted his pelvis to thrust inside her. Bear's nostrils flared as she forced him deeper. Her heart thudded as they fucked.

Her fingers slid to her clit to send her pleasure higher, but he slapped her hand away and thumbed it for it himself. It was swollen from the coarseness of his fingers, and she leant down to kiss him hard as he continued to rub and stroke her. She kissed and sucked his searing skin before biting his shoulder. His body jumped beneath her.

"Fucking hell," he grunted and gripped her butt with one hand to force her into riding him quicker. Her moans were wicked as his hands caressed and squeezed while they fought for pleasure.

"Fuck me harder," she growled, and he flipped her to her back and thrust inside her.

The lovemaking lasted for hours as they changed positions, and both climaxed several times. As the sun rose, Bear held her tightly and whispered how much she meant to him and that she'd changed his life in ways he never expected. She'd taught him that he wasn't truly alone and that he would have endless memories of her no matter what happened.

"In our parallel universe, we're living by the lake in that picture," he said, pointing at the painting on the wall. "And we're fighting and making love in our beautiful cabin."

"Don't forget Jeff, Roy, and Zorro. We need our dogs and feral cat." She drew her bottom lip between her teeth as tiredness swept over her.

"I'll never forget them, and I will never forget you, beautiful Liss."

She fell asleep to her name on his lips.

Chapter Forty-Five

The bed moved once the sun climbed higher in the sky.

Liss let Bear leave without telling him she was awake. It was what he wanted. The sadness that captured her heart streamed down her cheeks as soon as the door closed.

He was gone forever.

She sobbed without sound for fear that he might hear. She couldn't stomach that he'd regret their last hours together.

By eight a.m., she'd tossed some clothes on, but her eyes were red and raw, and her heart broken. The knock on the bedroom door was heavier than Bear's.

"I'll be out in a second," she shouted. Strike's familiar grunt reverberated through the wood.

Bear made good on his promise and was absent from the breakfast, but she had no stomach to eat. As Strike drove her, he attempted to make conversation with information about Steve but gave up at her lack of response.

Liss's heart sped as they neared the palace, thudding frantically. It was like the second time she'd visited, except there was no one to comfort or keep her calm. *Because I'm all alone.* She'd started this because she'd wanted a family, yet it took the last week to realise that the family available to her wasn't in blood but in those she chose to be around. Bear was right.

Liss's pulse continued to climb, and her limbs shook. She couldn't breathe. She gripped her throat tightly. She needed her mum's heart talisman. It must still be in Strike's parents' house. Princesses probably weren't allowed such momentos anyway.

I can't do this.

The sun glinted off the tears caught in her eyelashes, blinding her.

Strike yanked the steering wheel and pulled the car to a stop.

"You're panicking."

"No shit," she snapped as she gasped for breath. The car didn't smell like Bear anymore. She'd already lost him. Strike's scent of spice, oranges and musk radiated around her.

"What would Bear do?"

Liss closed her eyes and tried to imagine Bear's face even though it ripped at her chest. "He'd tell me to put my hand on my heart."

Strike helped move her hand and put his own to his heart. Her rapid heartbeat eased a little as she did the breathing exercise Bear taught her. Her breathing slowly returned to her control. It was inevitable that it would happen again, maybe throughout her future.

The palace loomed in the distance like something out of a dark fairy tale. She was getting every young girl's dream, yet it was her nightmare.

"I wanted to say sorry," Strike suddenly said, staring out the front windscreen.

She fixed her chin. "For...?"

Strike dropped his head before turning in his seat. "For the way I treated you. I've been a dick in numerous ways, and you've tolerated my shit and Bear's too."

"There was nothing to tolerate," she mumbled.

"Yes, there was. Don't let me off. I've got baggage from my past that Bear doesn't know about, and I treated you like crap because I haven't dealt with it." He closed his eyes briefly. "I'm sorry for trying to keep you apart and then telling you to break his heart as your final goodbye."

"But I didn't break—"

Strike held a fist to his lips. "He's heartbroken, Liss. You may not have done it, but it happened anyway. I've never seen him like that before. Bear doesn't let people in. His parents mistreated him, and he refused to trust a soul again, apart from me and my parents. But he let you in and showed you his vulnerable side."

Liss let out a long breath. "But it's all been too quick and based on drama. It's not real. And it doesn't matter because if I could be with him, which I can't, he doesn't do relationships."

Strike huffed. "*Didn't* do relationships. What the hell do you think you two have been doing? And so what if it's been quick? Some people exist in long relationships without feelings and tolerate each other every day, and some relationships have the passion that lasts forever through the arguments and daily bullshit."

Liss stared out the window at the palace's turrets, but the blue flags swishing in the breeze made her feel sick. They should have put them at half-mast.

"You don't have to do this," Strike added with a grunt.

"If not me, then who?" Liss glared at him. "And I have to honour my mum."

"Would this make her happy?" he snapped.

Liss returned to look out the window. Strike eased the car back onto the road. "I'd best get you to the palace. You can't be late today, of all days."

As she exited the car at the palace, she hugged him and whispered in his ear, "Love hurts us all. You too, Strike. I hope one day you can be happy."

Strike shrugged. "I hope you can be too. Take care of yourself. Thank you for everything."

Liss gave him one last wave before skulking through the palace doors.

Liss sat in the chair, waiting for the highly sought-after make-up artist to finish her final touches. But Liss preferred Isla telling her to press her lipsticked lips together. They'd giggled for ages, applying make-up on the evening of the palace party.

That same evening, Bear had looked at her like she was worth more than all the gold in the world. Would she have flashes of him and how he made her feel forever?

"How are you, Liss?" Beatrice must have entered the room silently, or maybe Liss was too distracted. Beatrice's hair was in an intricate low bun, and her natural make-up made her skin shine. Her teal dress, which gathered at the waist before the pleated fabric finished at the hem, highlighted her red hair. She was the picture of elegance in the semi-formal dress and would surpass Marianne as a style icon. Liss couldn't emulate it even if she wanted to.

Liss shrugged as she caught the reflection of Beatrice's eyes in the mirror. "I'm okay," she replied, devoid of genuine emotion. In an attempt to get through the speech and the next hours, she'd attempted to shut down her emotions. But with each minute, her body was more difficult to regulate. She wouldn't be able to keep her heart calm without bodyguards, without Bear. "At least I look okay."

"What an understatement," Beatrice quipped. Liss's dark waves were pinned up, and her skin was without blemish. The make-up artist gave her smokey eyes and honeyed lips. "You're beautiful."

Liss offered a fake smile. "Thank you. How are you doing with everything?" She hoped the raise of her perfectly shaped eyebrows would convey her real question. After the drama, Beatrice's pregnancy left her anxious.

"Can you give us a moment, please?" Beatrice asked the make-up artist.

Once alone, Liss exclaimed, "Are you and the baby alright?"

"The baby is fine." Beatrice smiled softly. "And I spoke with Archibald this morning, and he's jubilant about our news."

Liss smiled genuinely, although it didn't last long as the fears of giving her speech and spending the rest of her life on duty caused bile to fill her throat. Her head dropped, and she fisted her dress.

"Liss, I'm worried about you. You've been through so much recently, and although we don't know each other well yet, your anxiety is streaming out of you. Is it the speech? I can tell Archibald to keep your moment brief."

"It's the speech, my future, and the realisation that I'll be Queen one day. I'm not ready for any of this." And to top it off, she'd lost the only man she felt something for.

Beatrice turned Liss's rotating chair to the side to face her. She held her hands gently in hers. Her perfect French manicure reminded Liss of the shock of the make-up artist when she viewed Liss's bitten and peeled nails. "You don't have to be ready yet; being scared is okay. I was terrified when I married Gable with people watching and inevitable comments about how I wasn't from an aristocratic background."

Liss raised her head.

"Gable and I spent years preparing for our part in this family and learning how to behave. We know all the right things to say and do, but we don't always get it right. I once ate what I thought was a delicacy, but it was a table dressing. We're here for you, and we'll help you. When we were prepared for duty, we expected we might be King and Queen one day because Alex didn't want to be, but it means we can help you better. You have us no matter what, and we will be by your side when you need us."

Liss forced a smile. It was a kind offer, and she would rely on both of them. But there was no sugar-coating it because, ultimately, Liss would serve alone. Her experience with Steve made her doubt her friends' motives in a way she never believed possible.

"Do you want this, Liss? If you could pick your future out of all the possible futures, is this what you imagine for yourself?" Parallel universes filled with dogs and feral cats on the edge of a beautiful lake distracted her, as did the memory of Bear's face as he held her in the early hours.

"What I want isn't an option. It's for my mum."

"Your mum would want you to be happy. How would she feel, seeing you right now? Everyone has a calling and purpose; some people know theirs early on, and some learn later, but you shouldn't be unhappy because of expectations. I feel expectation, too, but I love meeting people and being a face for this family."

Liss shrugged off the comments about her mum. It was easy for Beatrice to say what should be, but it didn't stop the pull on Liss's heart to do the right thing. "I have to do it for this country. It's what I must do."

The conversation stopped short as the King entered the room. His skin wore a little more colour, and although he wobbled against his stick, he carried more energy than the day before. The whispered talk in the palace was that the doctors were increasingly confident.

"Felicity, darling, you're beautiful. Have you made your decision about our future? I'm delighted to introduce you to the world—well, those who didn't see you in yesterday's adventure."

Liss nodded, keen to hide her emotions before the King.

"Capital news. I won't ask you what you'll say, because this is your decision, and I don't want to bias you. But whatever you decide, you'll always be part of my family."

Liss waited for more. Surely, he didn't mean that? Maybe if she'd been able to spend more time with him recently, she'd know for sure.

"Speaking of which," he continued, oblivious to her concerns, "your grandma is here. She'd love to see you, but remember, you only have a few minutes together." Liss attempted to curtsy, but the King stopped her with a hug. "You don't have to curtsy in private for me."

"So much to learn," Liss whispered.

"And lots to enjoy," he said with a smile. "Beatrice, walk with me."

"Of course." She squeezed Liss's hands before

departing.

The make-up artist darted in and gave Liss her finishing touches before leaving. Liss was alone again with thoughts that speared her mind like demons who wouldn't let her rest.

Her heart was like an avalanche, unstoppable and increasing with every passing second. She stepped out of the room and collided with her grandma.

Chapter Forty-Six

"Look at you," Liss's nana said loud enough to draw attention from the new bodyguards who watched the awkward family hug. She'd dressed in a baby pink suit like she was auditioning for Legally Blonde, the Grandma Edition. And yet, as always, she carried an air of style and sophistication.

Those genes must have missed Liss.

The palace assistant assigned to Liss hovered nearby, pointing down the corridor and mouthing two minutes.

"Hello, Nana," Liss replied with a sigh. The last thing she needed was a kick to her confidence, but maybe it would be a temporary distraction. "Shall we walk this way? I've got to be in the press room in two minutes."

"Certainly, darling. Isn't this exciting?" her nana asked. "Who knew that my little granddaughter would one day be queen?"

"Indeed." The speech was at the forefront of Liss's mind. How would she say she dreamed of being a princess when it was the last thing she wanted? If only she had her mum's heart talisman. Maybe that would give her the courage she needed. "It's a shame Mum didn't get to be part of it."

She hadn't said it to guilt her nana. It was pointless to

push that opinion now.

"Oh no, she would have hated it," her grandma crowed.

Liss stopped short, which drew a panicked face from the assistant. Liss's life would now forever be part of a schedule.

Her nana continued walking down the corridor, oblivious to Liss's surprise.

"What do you mean?" Liss cried.

Her nana turned. "Your mum was always happy in the background. If the King had told her she was part of a royal family and to perform duties and meet people worldwide, she'd have hated every second. It was one of the reasons I never told her." Liss stepped closer to her grandma, who rambled, oblivious to Liss's confusion, "Her life was impossibly hard, and I didn't always help that." That was an understatement. "But she loved her life with you. You made her happy, and the life you're about to enter would have destroyed that. That wasn't her world. You were."

Liss's lower lip trembled. "But—"

Her grandma touched her shoulder. "Every day, I regret not getting her the right support when she was dying. I thought it was a simple illness, and by the time word got to me on my travels that it was cancer, it was too late. If I'd known, I would have fought every member of the royal family and every stranger to get the best treatment for her, but I didn't know. She sent me a letter, but I didn't get it until after she died. She spent her life trying to protect me, trying to protect all of us, from the worst life threw at us. And I don't know why she did. I should have protected her. She was my little girl."

Her grandma's eyes reddened, and Liss cuddled her.

There was so much Liss hadn't considered, and she had many questions, but an increasingly anxious assistant pointed to her wristwatch and the press room. Liss wanted to shout that there was always time for hugs, but maybe there wasn't. She was a princess with obligations now.

"But this life wasn't right for your mum. She struggled and worked many jobs, but all she wanted was for you to be safe and reach your dreams. She wanted you to be happy, which she dedicated her life to."

"Felicity, I need you to take your place in the press room," the assistant said. "Ms. Granger, Barnaby here will take you to your seat."

Liss's heart raced, and her limbs shook. She tried to put her hand over her heart, but as the assistant nudged her into a room the size of a ballroom, with hundreds of people tracking her movements, sweat dripped down her back and onto her uncomfortable white lace dress. They'd dressed her as a debutant. Sick rose into her throat, and tears brimmed her eyes as she stepped onto the platform.

I can't do this.

Suddenly, Beatrice slipped something into her hand and whispered, "From your bodyguard."

Liss gripped her mum's plastic heart tightly. Strike must have guessed. As she stood on the stage with her heart racing, she stared at the blurry figures in the crowd. She recognised a couple from the party, but most were strangers. Everyone stared at her. The weight of their expectation was like rocks tied to her feet, pulling her under the swells of her panic. Vomit filled her mouth.

Even as she held the heart in her fist, her breath was ragged, and another drop of sweat slipped down her dress. Then, she caught the bright brown eyes and soft gaze of Bear. It wasn't a hallucination. It was actually him. He stood at the back of the room, his hand lifted to his heart, and he took deep, slow breaths. Liss followed his lead, and he mouthed, "You got this, baby."

Liss counted to ten as she pressed the talisman heart against her own. Her breath regulated, and her body stopped shaking. Familiar faces caught her eye, including Strike, her grandma, and Isla. They gave smiles of encouragement as she opened her mouth.

"Good afternoon, ladies and gentlemen." Silence descended, and once more, she met Bear's gaze. He nodded and smiled his encouragement. He said he didn't do goodbyes. Why was he here? "Thank you for coming to meet me. I don't see myself as anything that special, and I've never seen so many people in one room before, so excuse me if I stutter. I'll try not to fall over like I did when I spoke at the party."

Some of the group laughed at the memory. Bear beamed.

"As you know, it's been an interesting couple of weeks." Again, there was laughter in the crowd. "I guess that's an understatement. It's been a rollercoaster, but it's had its joys, too, as I met my family and made friends that have changed my life forever." At Bear's grin, she swallowed slowly. Words threatened to rush from her mouth, but she had time. They were here for her, after all. "I came here today, certain that I would take my place as princess and one day as Queen of this country. I adore this country and have seen so many parts of it, from the inner streets of this city, where I've thrown several people out of the pub, to the beautiful countryside and beaches that my mum and I visited on our family holidays. My mum loved this country, too, and she would have been excited to meet her dad and all you lovely people. She would have been nervous, too, because, like me, this role wouldn't have been right for her."

There were gasps in the crowd. Liss looked at the King, who smiled in encouragement. There was no dismay or annoyance on his face. Liss continued slowly, allowing everyone to catch up with her decision. "You deserve rulers who adore publicly serving you. Some people have trained for it and long to do just that rather than hide in the background and focus on the operations side. I'm still looking for my role and purpose, but this role isn't it." She fixed Bear with her stare as if he was the only person in the room. "I know where my heart belongs, and these weeks have taught me that I have to follow my heart, whatever the cost."

Bear inspected her, his face unreadable. Damn his ability to hide emotions.

"However." She glanced around the room again. "I've met the people who adore this country and want to serve it with all they have. I won't be your Queen in the future, but I have met your future King and Queen. The country is lucky to have them; they will rightly serve you. Gable and Beatrice are those people, and I'm lucky to call them and King Archibald my family, if they'll still have me after today's announcement."

The King, Gable, and Beatrice stepped onto the stage and hugged her, full of the love she needed. "Thank you for allowing me to have this experience for a short time."

"Felicity, you will always be my granddaughter; nothing can change that. Thank you for your honesty and respect for this country and the family." The King's eyes shone with tears. "And thank you for saving my life."

Liss nodded and allowed King Archibald and the future

rulers to field questions as the press went wild. She stepped off the stage and returned to the corridor, confident she might finally have the peace she craved.

CHAPTER FORTY-SEVEN

Liss breathed a sigh of relief as she stepped into the corridor where she'd bumped into her grandma before the big speech. It was empty except for a suited palace bodyguard in the shadows at the end.

She sat on the floor against the wall and brought her knees to her chest, hugging them tightly. "What now?" she mumbled to herself. Alone again, the press would hound her, and she wouldn't have a bodyguard to rescue her. She cradled the heart between her hands. "I want to make you proud, Mum. I need to work out how."

"Your mum would be proud of you," the bodyguard replied. Bear stepped out of the shadows.

Of course it was him. His face was unreadable as he stepped closer and stood before her.

"I thought you weren't coming today."

"I wanted to make sure you had your mum's heart. But what now, Princess?" Her heart swelled. He was the most beautiful being she'd ever seen.

Liss's hands trembled, but not from adrenaline, anxiety, or fear. It was from her joy at taking control of her future. "I was asking myself that same thing. I can't return to the pub. It's not mine anymore. Maybe I should go travelling. Others my age have, and I didn't get the chance before. But with everything that has happened, the press won't leave me alone, and others want a piece of me. I've seen what happens to royals in other countries who ask to have their titles removed. And that's another point. You can't keep calling me princess; I'm not a princess anymore. I don't think anyway."

"You're still my princess." Bear's hulking form was out of place as he sat beside her. The sumptuous red carpet and brocade wallpaper suggested the corridor was too fancy for grown adults to sit on the floor, but she wasn't moving except to face him. Their legs touched. They both appeared uncomfortable in their professional clothes. She preferred his T-shirt that she'd sneaked into her bag after he left. He was sexier in grey joggers. "If you want to travel, I can use my contacts to ensure your safety. I know bodyguards in most countries."

She shook her head. "I don't really want to go travelling. I've always been a homebody, and I'm happy here. But I don't know what to do. I've searched for my forever career for years and never found it. I don't have any skills."

Bear reached for her hands and held them tightly. "Bloody hell, Liss. You're clueless. You've transformed my company, made Luke feel like it's okay to be himself, saved the team's reputation from a lawsuit, and brought out Strike's kind side, which Luke was adamant he didn't have." His smile was soft as he sighed long and hard. "In all seriousness, there's a protection company that requires an operations manager with your skills and understanding. You're incredible, and the business needs you. And there's nowhere safer for you than with us."

"But the guys won't want that."

"They've already voted you Employee of the Month. I disagreed, as I wanted the award, but they insisted you'd earned it."

His hands were warm. "You don't have an Employee of the Month award."

"You're the first. Honestly, it was their idea."

Liss cocked her head and stared at him. He raised his eyebrows at her inspection. "Bear, I'm not sure I can work with you. I like you way too fucking much."

"Did you swear in the palace?" he teased.

"That's how much I like you," she joked. "You heard what I said about where my heart belongs."

His eyes sparkled, and suddenly, he kissed her hard. He tasted of mint and sunshine. Her lips zipped with electricity as they made out in the palace corridors. The current carried through every cell until it rose goosebumps on her arms and tingled each strand of her perfectly styled hair.

He pulled back, and air escaped from between his lips. His brow furrowed, and he looked down before catching her eye. "Liss, I'm not good at words. I'm not good at anything involving emotion, and yet, with you, I am. With you, I'm finally home. I grew up believing I didn't deserve love and would never have that home. I thought life needed to be adrenaline and screwing around, and then I met you, and I found my safe space." His cheeks flushed. "When I look at you, I get more adrenaline than when a guy comes at me with a knife, and the fucking is beyond my fantasies. But I got something else. It's this feeling of being home and loved. And it's like nothing I could have imagined."

"Bear—"

"Yes, Princess?"

"What are you saying?"

"I'm saying, in the sappiest way I can, that I'm pretty sure I'm in love with you. I know it's only been a couple of weeks, and I don't want to scare you with the big declaration. But I know that I'm not good enough even to sit next to you, let alone be loved by you. You're intelligent and savvy, a member of the royal family, but more than that, you make me laugh, you make me sing and, well, you rock my fucking world. I want to be someone who does relationships, but only with you. I know it's been two weeks, but you're it for me, Liss."

She stared at him. He licked his lips slowly, and she gripped the heart talisman so tightly that it would leave an imprint on her hand.

"Could you love a badass bodyguard?"

The corners of her mouth crept up as he unpinned the waves of her hair. "What are you doing?"

He cleared his throat loudly. "You make me nervous, and I need to keep my hands busy. This is what you do to me."

Liss stilled his trembling hands in hers. "I'm in love with you too. It terrifies me as much as doing a speech in front of the world's press. But you're everything I've been looking for. I was hiding at the pub, but with you, I don't need to hide who I am, and I can do things I didn't think possible. You were right when you said I'd carried loneliness. But I make sense when I'm with you." She brushed kisses against his forehead, coaxing him closer until they made out. She hummed against his lips as he pressed his hands into her hair. "But wait. I need you to promise me something."

"I'm listening, although I'd rather be kissing."

Liss forced her face into a serious, regal stare. "You must promise me that you'll cook me food and sing to me every day."

Bear cocked his head and raised his eyebrows. "Is that all?" He pulled her into his lap.

"And I want lots and lots of mind-blowing sex in all sorts of places."

He twisted his mouth to hide his smile, but even he wasn't that good, and soon, he was throwing his head back and roaring with laughter. "Yes, baby. I can give you that daily. It will be a sacrifice, but I'm undeniably committed."

"You're it, Chambers," she sighed.

"And you're my princess," he growled as he cupped her face and kissed her hard enough to make her toes curl.

Epilogue

"It's not going to be perfect enough," Bear shouted from the kitchen as Liss stepped through the front door. Jeff and Roy barked their hello to Bear as they traipsed mud through the hallway. "You better not be getting the hallway messy.

How did he know her this well? The curse of living with a bodyguard.

"Nope, all good," she shouted back before drying the dog's feet and wiping down the hallway's hardwood floor. Within minutes, the dogs were racing around the house, chased by Zorro, who lived up to his name. If he wasn't terrorizing the dogs, he was driving down the local bird population.

Liss giggled as she stepped up to Bear's naked back and brushed kisses against his shoulders. "The food doesn't need to be perfect, although I'm sure it will be. However, they probably won't notice it if you're still in your black boxers. I don't mind a naked chef, but they probably don't want to watch me making 'please fuck me' eyes throughout dinner."

Bear's shoulders tensed as he stirred the sauce with one hand and squeezed stuffing balls with another. "I didn't want to get food or oil on my clothes," he said, grabbing a spoon and lifting a little sauce out of the pan.

"Taste this. Is it too herby?"

He pressed his lips together and blew across the sauce before offering it to Liss. He was so fuckable. Even cooking Bear was irresistible. How many hours did they have before everyone arrived? She needed him to blow on her clit with those beautiful lips.

She licked the sauce while fixing him with her gaze. The smells radiating from the food reminded her of the night he'd made her a roast dinner on what they thought would be their last hours together.

"Stop trying to seduce me with your filthy eyes and tell me about the sauce," he growled. "Too salty?"

"Something in here is too salty, and it's not the sauce," she sassed. "It tastes so good that I'm considering covering the man I love in it before licking it off."

She licked her lips slowly, and he dropped the spoon in the pan before taking her in his arms. "I adore you, baby." He kissed her hard and grabbed her bum. His erection was perfect, and she ground against him. It pressed against her as it throbbed.

"No, we can't." Bear released her, and she sighed against him. "Sorry, Princess. I want this to be perfect. I've not cooked for someone's family before, and when that family includes the fucking royals, the pressure gets to me."

"Bear, they'll love you as much as you love me."

"Impossible. Nothing can get close. I love you more than I ever thought possible, and I'll tell you that every day until you can't stand to hear it."

He turned down the dials on the cooking and kissed her hard again before walking her towards the bedroom. He pressed her palms against the window and fitted his body behind her. They'd watched the sunrise above the hills and lake that morning. He once promised to show her his safe space, and now they lived in it together.

From behind, he pulled open the snap of her jeans and lowered her zip. He slipped a hand in the front of her knickers. "Already wet for me." He brushed his lips against her neck and rubbed circles around her clit. She moaned and whimpered as the doorbell rang.

"Fuck," he shouted, suddenly jumping around the room. Liss would be horny all day now. "They're already here."

"It's just Strike. He must be here early to sneak food," she joked. "Put your fancy clothes on, and I'll let him in."

"But you're not dressed for visitors either," he replied, running around the room and picking up various items of clothing before dropping them again.

"Bear, chill, or I'll make you hold Mum's plastic heart." Bear stopped suddenly and shook his head. "Now you get dressed and come and chat with Strike, and then I'll rush and get changed. It's Christmas Day, and we're enjoying ourselves."

"Sorry, baby." He grabbed her and kissed her hard as the doorbell rang again.

"Fucking Strike," she shouted as she ran to the door while zipping her jeans back up.

The dogs rushed him as she opened the door. They barked and jumped at him, desperate for his cuddles. "You could train them, you know," he grumbled as he crossed the threshold.

"Happy Christmas to you, too, you grumpy fucker," she replied, and he rolled his eyes playfully before hugging her.

"Are the King, Gable, Beatrice and the baby here yet?"

"No, because you're an hour early. You made us miss quality time," Liss replied as he handed her a bottle of wine. "I have no idea how you cock-block Bear and me even now we live together."

"Just skilful, I guess." He shrugged.

Liss led him to the kitchen. "By the way, your mum's trying to get hold of you. Are you ignoring her calls? They're thinking about selling the house you grew up in. At some point they want you to clear it out."

Strike glared and ground his teeth.

"She said you wouldn't want to do it." Strike blinked slowly. Liss swallowed but pushed on with the rest of the message. "She said the neighbour whose daughter you used to hang out with still owns the house, and imagine the fond memories you'll have staring at their house as you pack." Liss poured him a hot chocolate, his secret favourite drink on days he wasn't working. She loved the boy's mum, but she hated giving these messages, especially as they were due for food later.

Strike grumbled.

"I guess Bear and I could do it and the place probably won't be sold until later this year. But you're always owed a lot of holiday and the two new bodyguards you're training will have been with us for months and be well established. You might as well spend your holidays doing something. No one needs a break as much as you."

"Fine, I'll do it," he snapped. "Typical that my mother has you on the case when the place hasn't even been sold."

"So tell me more about the neighbours. Your mum said their daughter was called Millie." His cheeks were flush, and his jaw was tight as if he was gritting his teeth hard enough to break them. Suddenly, Bear walked into the kitchen, halting the forming questions.

"My potatoes. Please don't burn my potatoes," Bear shouted.

"Nice to see you, too, buddy. Happy fucking Christmas," Strike grumbled.

"Oh shut up, you grumpy bastard. You always were extra grumpy at Christmas. Did I hear Liss say something about Millie, our neighbour?"

Strike shrugged, but his jaw got impossibly tighter. It was like he was auditioning to be a brooding Hollywood hero.

"Enough of this Christmas joy. I've got to get changed. I can't believe on our first Christmas together, we'll watch Grandad on the television making his speech while he sits with us. It's going to be so random."

"I'm glad he recovered after all that business. He's got a couple of years left in him yet." Bear pushed up his sleeves, revealing a hint of his tattoo. Liss's belly flipped with lust.

"I don't suppose you could help me with something in the bedroom, Chambers." Liss sucked on her lower lip as she fixed Bear with her stare. She couldn't be Bear-free all day.

"I don't know," he stuttered as she stretched her head from side to side, revealing the expanse of her neck to him. "I...err."

"Fuck off upstairs, the pair of you. I'll look after dinner," Strike grumbled. "I haven't bought you a present."

"I'll make sure he gets two," Liss shouted as Bear chased her up the stairs.

REGALLY BINDING

THERE'S MORE…

I hope you enjoyed the first novel in my Closest Protection Series featuring the men of Bodyguard Corp.

Sign up to my newsletter to get updates on my book releases, as well as access to giveaways and exclusive bonus content including a bonus scene between Liss and Bear, which is free to everyone who signs up.

You can sign up via: https://tinyurl.com/Rebecca-Chase

Or via my website: www.rebeccahchase.com

In the meantime, keep reading for the Regally Binding playlist and information about the other books I'm releasing in the next two years. And here's a peek of **Head Over Feels**, an enemies-to-lovers steamy sports romance and the first book in my rugby romance series.

If you like spicy, humorous British romance with a bad boy book boyfriend then you need to give Aidan a try.

Chapter One

Beads of sweat slid down Sophia's chest. She stilled her trembling fingers long enough to pull down her skin-tight dress to a respectable length. The hem slipped from her hands. The scarlet material clung to her curves, daring her to accept its challenge and wear it beyond the confines of her bedroom.

She cringed at her reflection in the mirror. Graham would smirk when she wore anything revealing. Maybe her ex-boyfriend had been right, she wasn't sexy, and the dress wasn't her style. But her job meant the world to her, and Sophia refused to risk the wrath of her boss over a dress. Why did she have to dress up for the art exhibition anyway? She was never required to wear more than jeans and a jumper while running activity sessions with bereaved children.

She loved working for The Jameson Foundation, and the work she did, the charity changed lives, but the essential fundraising events tested her limits. They ensured major donors saw the importance of their donations and gave a little more. But Sophia was a support worker, not a fundraiser, and these nights left her empty.

But the demands from her boss still rang in her ears,

"You will be serving food to funders and giving a speech. Wear something smart but demure. It's an art exhibition, not a formal dinner. There will be creative types whose money matters to this charity. Don't wear that ugly brown thing again."

There hadn't been time to buy a new dress. The red dress, borrowed from her housemate, caught her eye in the mirror.

I look like I'm trying to get laid. Not that anyone would want to sleep with me, or that I'd let any guy get close enough to try.

The dress did something special to her body. Sophia admired her boobs in the mirror. The scarlet material stretched comfortably across them, cutting below the flush of a fading summer tan. She rarely showed her body off, but the plunging neckline made her want to arch her back while puffing out her chest, and the scarlet colour brought out the natural red highlights in her brown hair.

Her pulse thrummed, and her breath caught in her lungs. Sophia reached for the hem again.

"What's up?" Nicky, her housemate, poked her head around Sophia's bedroom door.

Sophia yanked at the scarlet fabric, but it continued to grip her upper thighs like the hands of a horny man on a crap date. Sheer willpower wasn't enough to make the dress, that had moulded itself to her curves, move lower on her legs. Would Olympic class tugging help?

"Don't you dare ruin my dress. I never fail to get laid when I wear it," Nicky exclaimed, striding into the room, her blonde bob bouncing as she walked. She appeared in the reflection in the mirror. "You look fantastic. The funders will be eating out of your hand. Your arse looks amazing." Nicky gave Sophia's bum a quick pat.

Sophia's face creased in annoyance at her inability to allow even her best friend to touch her. She stared at their reflection, remembering how unlikely it was that they became friends on the first day at Bristol University seven years earlier. Nicky was a firecracker; slim, petite and feisty as hell. She was everything Sophia wasn't, but their friendship had never been stronger. They were lucky to have each other.

"I know she's your boss, but I don't see why Tasha decides who wears what. If you're going to wear a dress at least pick one that makes a statement," Nicky said, but Sophia was distracted by her globe like boobs.

"I look like a sixteen-year-old desperately attempting to dress to impress the bouncers so they can get into a club," Sophia smirked.

"Are you saying I have no class?" Nicky jested.

"No," Sophia sighed. "You're shorter than me and slimmer, it doesn't look indecent on you. The trashy dress suits you," she teased.

"Thanks. Maybe I shouldn't let you borrow my dress." Nicky rolled her eyes, but there was a grin on her face. "You can attend the exhibition in that hideous polyester thing your mum gave you years ago for graduation instead."

"Sorry, Nicky. I'm an awful friend. I throw myself at your feet, begging for your mercy. Can you ever forgive me?" Sophia attempted an awkward bow.

Nicky straightened the wide shoulder straps that came down to form the suggestive neckline. "Stop flashing those Bambi eyes at me. I can't be angry when you look at me like that. You look beautiful and not cheap or trashy. But let's ask a man's opinion. Oi, Ryan!" she hollered in the direction of the corridor. "Come here; we need you."

Before Sophia could protest, Ryan swaggered into the room. He'd styled his blond hair in surfer waves. Sun-kissed skin shone from his naked chest, and baggy shorts rested casually on hips that drew her eyes to his perfect V lines. Nicky's fuck buddy was the sort of guy who starred in your fantasies yet possessed the intelligence of a Labradoodle puppy.

Ryan was the first guy she'd had in her bedroom in years. Sophia shrunk, shy in her outfit as he shrugged. "I'd do her but lose the underwear. You don't need anything under that dress if I remember correctly." He winked at Nicky

Sophia winced. *I can't go commando.* But before she could protest audibly, Ryan seized Nicky and swept her over his shoulder. Nicky laughed and squirmed as they headed out the door. Jealousy and embarrassment heated Sophia's face.

It wasn't that she fancied Ryan, more that he was a reminder of the things she wanted; a gorgeous guy slinging her over his shoulder and anywhere else he wanted. *And yet I won't let guys get close.* Nicky regularly told her she was beautiful, but she couldn't believe it. The blame for that lay with Graham.

What had her colleague, Jack, and the only male she had in her life said? "If you want to be confident, then do something that scares you." He'd struggled to come out to his conservative parents until he was in his late twenties and they'd refused to accept him as part of the family ever since. He'd understood what it was to be scared.

"This scares me," she whispered to her reflection. But Ryan was right; her underwear made the dress bunch at her hips. She would look better without it, and maybe going commando would boost her confidence and make her feel sexier. *It's worth a try.*

Nicky's bedroom door slammed shut. Within moments the laughter turned into declarations of need.

Sophia sighed as she raked up the hem of the dress, reaching underneath to grab her black cotton underwear. No one had come close to making her moan like that. Even when she'd had fun with her favourite vibrator, she hadn't uttered a peep.

There's something wrong with me. Sophia's ex-boyfriend, Graham, had suggested as much, reminding her constantly of her faults.

He would hate this.

The rarely released rebel in her rose angrily. Graham could piss off, along with his controlling behaviour that she knew damaged her self-worth. *S*he yanked down her underwear and tossed it in the wash basket.

Sophia headed out her room and padded down the corridor, heels hanging from her fingers. Muffled offers of pleasure accompanied moans from Nicky's room; they were promises that Sophia had never experienced first-hand. Ryan's words resonated through her as she drove to the art exhibition, sexual acts she'd only imagined filled her. "I'm going to taste every part of you tonight, and I'm not going to stop licking you until you're screaming this place down."

Sophia avoided the sharp elbows and handbags worth more than her salary as she moved through the crowd of guests, a silver tray of hors d'oeuvre between her hands. Art wasn't her thing, and the pieces paled into comparison when she could watch those attending the exhibition instead. They barely noticed her as she handed out food, swiping bite-sized pastry parcels with their veiny hands while boasting about their importance and achievements. Portly men who chanced a canapé from the serving plate, while eyeing their unimpressed wives, spoke loudly, "I really shouldn't. According to my wife, I'm supposed to be watching my weight." They followed up their reasoning by ramming a third and then fourth spinach and feta parcel into their gobs.

Force a smile and get on with it.

At least the venue was stunning, albeit chilly. The grand cathedral stood in the centre of town. Its beauty took Sophia's breath away. If it hadn't been for the event, she would have been investigating every nook and cranny or better yet, at home in her fleece pyjamas.

"Aren't you a sexy minx?" A man with ruddy cheeks and a throbbing nose wedged himself between her and the exit to the busier cloisters. Hidden from her view was the grand entryway into the spectacle that was the central part of the church. Sophia imagined the gentry, centuries ago, bowing in worship as they continued their debauched lives in private. The cloisters were off to one side, arranged as a square with a garden situated in the middle. In the summer, the smell of herbs and well-tended plants ruminated around the maze of paths. Rumours told of bodies hidden below the cloisters. No one had found the door to the crypt. It was probably a way to make money from tours, but Sophia had been fascinated with the building since she'd first visited it.

Tonight, there was no opportunity for adventure. The cathedral beckoned her to discover more of its mysteries, but she couldn't escape the irritating stranger.

"Would you like something to eat?" Thrusting the plate in front of him, she attempted to divert his attention.

He ignored the canapés and leaned closer.

Bloodshot eyes loitered on her chest. "Is everything here on offer tonight?" Alcohol wafted from his breath into her face.

She pursed her lips, swallowing the bile, and hid the grimace threatening to replace the plastic smile that had served her so well that evening. Even guys she was attracted to weren't allowed in her personal space, let alone men like this. Nicky said her barriers to physical contact were too high, but it was the only thing that stopped her getting hurt again.

"I'd pay handsomely for the right item," he said. His sausage-like fingers moved closer to the tray and what was beyond it.

She recoiled, searching for an escape. What was wrong with this guy? The other guests were mostly polite, and some were great champions of the charity's work. At the other end of the corridor, Tasha stared her down with a warning look. In the briefing before the event, Tasha had demanded that she keep the guests entertained at all costs, but Sophia wasn't about to sell her morals for a quick buck. *She shouldn't push me like this.* But Tasha had never liked Sophia. *She'll make my life hell if I disobey her.*

Drool gathered in the corners of the letch's mouth. Sophia's muscles primed in fight or flight as he moved in.

*****

Why did I come here alone? Aidan's stomach knotted, but he kept his pace to the cathedral. A mesmerising and foreboding sight, the gothic building loomed through the dusk like a warning. It was as if something was going to happen tonight that he couldn't predict or prepare for.

He shook it off. The evening was a promise to John, a friend and a former mentor who saved him from a life of anger and sadness. Unfortunately, it was also another night going stag. A woman on his arm would have eased the obligation.

Bianca was the last significant woman in his life. She loved to hang off his arm at events. He reminisced their explosive bedroom antics and the flick of her tongue across her lips. Once upon a time, the memory of what else she did with her lips would have required a not-so-subtle shift of his trousers, but now it left him cold. Unfortunately, he couldn't trust Bianca Tandy. While her impulsiveness was attractive, over time, it became dangerous. She forced her position in his life, attempting to drive everything and everyone out.

Inside the building, the cold numbed his face, but it couldn't dull the memories of her. He'd executed their break-up in public and away from valuable things. He'd feared her taking a golf club to his car or manhood. If anyone questioned him, he'd said it ended because they weren't compatible. In truth, the nail in the coffin of their fling was the day he discovered Bianca was lying about being on the pill, desperate to hogtie him for good. Babies weren't something he wanted, and it had cemented his decision to finish with her. Despite all that, Aidan didn't hate her. He didn't even know her. That she hid most of her true identity worked well for both of them. Aidan had no intention of sharing his true self with anyone, especially not a woman. *You can't commit to long term.*

Don't think about it. But the emotional scars of his possible illness were there every day. He hadn't had a diagnosis of the hereditary Huntington's disease yet, but only because he refused the tests. *I don't want to know my future.* Huntington's was a death sentence. He'd watched his dad die from it and knew the suffering that would come from testing positive. *I want to live for now, enjoy my life, enjoy women.* Long term relationships weren't for him, and as a result, it was easier not to let anyone in. No one should have to suffer because of him.

Aidan shook himself. *Don't do this to yourself. Get through this event and then go to a bar and see what the night brings.*

Taking a deep breath, he turned full circle to admire the beauty around him. The architecture displayed a mixture of violence and grace that spoke to his past and soul. Today, he was an artist showcasing his work, but by the weekend, he'd be an artist of a different kind. He'd use every ounce of strength and aggression in his muscles as he battled adversaries. Power, adrenaline and brutality would roar through him as he sprinted around a rugby pitch to the chants of thousands of fans singing his name.

A cackle of laughter drew his attention. His eyes caught those of a perky blonde woman at the end of one of the corridors. The make-up caking her face didn't hide that she was a little older than his thirty-five years. If she was trying to catch his attention with the bounce to her walk, it worked. *Maybe she can make the night interesting for you.*

"Hey there, sexy. I'm Tasha." A giggle sprang from her ruby red lips. "You are hot! I bet you get that a lot."

"Umm..."

"I get it a lot, too."

Confident women were usually a turn-on, but she was off the scale. Her intensity was like kryptonite to his flirting skills. Wild eyes were upon him, and briefly, she reminded him of Bianca. It wasn't a good thing.

"Fancy a date sometime? Unless you don't think I'm attractive," she squealed.

"I err…" He stumbled through his words, trying to keep up with her machine gun comments and questions.

Bottle blonde hair was flipped in his direction, whipping him in the eyes.

"You think I'm ugly, don't you?" she said with a pout.

"Actually, I was—" he attempted.

"Oh, you're Irish. I love Irish men," she moaned. He got that a lot, his accent was impossible to hide. Seduction dripped from every pore as she slithered closer. "I can prove to you that I'm beautiful all over, although it's my bedroom skills that you really need to experience."

Aidan remained silent. He had the chat-up lines, he always did, but there was something about her that made him nervous to say them. What would he be talking himself into? He didn't want to lead her on.

"Call me. You don't want to make me angry now, do you?" the woman growled, slipping what he presumed was her business card into his trouser pocket and attempting to stroke his crotch at the same time. Aidan flinched at her unwelcome advances. She'd made his penis jump back inside his body. *You need to find safer people to talk to.*

Tasha's spiked heels barely made a noise as she departed. He turned in the opposite direction, ramming into a soft woman's form. *Watch where you're going, Aidan, you fool.* Scarlet flashed in front of his eyes and he accidentally hip barged her away.

With quick, strong reflexes, he wrapped one arm around the front of her waist and stopped her hitting the floor. The dress clung to her curves as she hung like a rag doll in his arms, her legs flailing in mid-air. The tray she'd been carrying clattered to the floor, muted by the dull roar of chattering guests.

Everything turned to slow motion as the hem of her dress slid up her thighs. Aidan's crotch stirred. The awkward angle was a bonus as it offered him the best view of her clothed bum. It was a struggle not to stroke his free hand along one perfectly formed cheek. Did it feel as good as it looked? An outraged voice cut through his imaginings.

"For fuck sake. Will you put me down?" The scarlet beauty wriggled in his hands, the waves of her chestnut hair cascaded down her shoulders. He held her firmly against him. The scent of coconut filled his lungs, and his stirrings increased.

"I think what you mean to say is 'thank you'," he whispered in soft Irish tones. The woman in his hands froze momentarily before resuming her bid for freedom. What was the safest way to put her down without her falling? Her efforts gave him an unexpected thrill as she tried to wrestle herself free. Her skin-tight dress climbed higher.

I want to see her face.

Aidan stood straight, forcing her vertically against his chest. She squealed enough to make him pull back. She stumbled.

His adrenalin surged as she spun, glaring at him. He admired the defiant way she lifted her chin to meet him. Her dark eyes narrowed.

His responding arousal was intoxicating. He shifted uncomfortably, hoping it didn't show through his chinos. It pulsed with every flutter of her eyelashes.

Flushed cheeks and red, moist lips caught his attention. The spotlights in the cathedral highlighted the gold strands of her hair, matching the flecks dancing in her eyes. She struggled with the hem of her dress while reaching for the plate that was still on the floor. Flustered, she tripped and nearly fell off her heels.

His reputation with women was well earnt. Friends and foes had bandied about the word shameless alongside his name on more than one occasion. She wasn't like his other women though, her shoulders slumped forward, and she repeatedly fiddled with her clothes as if uncertain of herself.

"Why would I thank you?" Her hiss was barely a whisper. "Your massive body was in the way."

There was something about her that turned him devilish and ready to tease. Maybe she could make his evening less of a chore. He would gladly take her home that night. He'd enjoy bringing out more of that fierce attitude and obliterating her shyness in the bedroom. "You noticed my body then?"

"It's impossible to miss." Her tone was laced with exasperation, but the hint of a smile teased the corners of her mouth. His grin stretched further. What was it about her that appealed to him so much? She was the opposite of ladies like Tasha; dignified, funny and not forcing an agenda on him. *I'm actually having fun.*

Her gaze dipped, looking down his body and pausing at his crotch. Did she know she was staring? Her eyes widened, and her mouth dropped open in surprise before transforming into a small smile. What did her reactions mean? He was hooked on working her out.

"I have eyes as well, although I wonder which of us is admiring the view more," he replied with a wink.

"I don't know what you mean," she stuttered, but her eyes flicked back to his crotch, and she blushed as red as her scarlet dress.

He forced his laugh down. Laughing wouldn't help him seal the deal, and he wanted her. There was a beauty radiating from her, but it was more than that. She'd sparked his interest. Was it the way she'd attempted to hide her cute freckles with make-up or her awkwardness at their interaction? She was a challenge that made him want to play his best game. She would be in his bed by the end of the night. He'd bet his rugby career on it.

REGALLY BLINDING PLAYLIST

Royals – Lorde

Kissing Strangers – USHER

Jealous – Nick Jonas, Tinashe

Best Song Ever – One Direction

Quit – Cashmere Cat, Ariana Grande

Only You – Cheat Codes, Little Mix

All You Ever Wanted – Rag'n'Bone Man

Coffee – beabadoobee

Feel So Close – Calvin Harris

How Will I Know – Whitney Houston

Jealous – Labrinth

Who Do You Think You Are – Spice Girls

Lose Control – Teddy Swims

Pounding – Doves

Wildest Dreams – Taylor Swift

Try Sleeping with a Broken Heart – Alicia Keys

Let Forever Be – The Chemical Brothers

Strange - Celeste

Like I'm Gonna Lose You – Jasmine Thompson

Run Away With Me – Carly Rae Jepsen

Acknowledgements

My great-great-grandma, a ballet dancer who allegedly had an affair with an English Prince and gave birth to a son who resembled the prince, deserves the first mention. Thank you for inspiring me.

I'm very lucky to have Elizabeth Holland, Kathryn Kincaid, and Sarah Smith as brilliant beta readers who take the time to decipher the thinking behind my words and whose suggestions and thoughts push me to improve my stories. Thank you for always taking the time to listen to my questions. All three of them have beautiful romance books you need to read if you haven't—a special mention to Kathryn, who copes admirably with the multitude of DMs I send her.

Thank you to Joanne Machin, a lovely human and world-class editor. Her notes are incredibly helpful, and they often make me smile, too.

My husband deserves a lot of my gratitude. You put up with a lot. I couldn't survive book releases without you and your patience.

The biggest thank you to the readers who've taken a gamble

on an unknown indie author, especially those who've been with me since the beginning and watched my writing develop. Your reviews, likes, and comments keep me going.

To seajart who designed my book cover, you have skills for days, and somehow, you're able to create beauty from my ramblings.

Thank you to the friend who inspired one of my favourite ever characters. I'm sorry I couldn't include your love of Johnny Cash or your mum. I could definitely imagine you dancing to pop hits, though.

All of those at my day job who allow me to keep my writing secrets while also banging on about books. You make me laugh and cry, and I will miss you.

Finally, a massive thank you to my friends 'in real life' and the ones I've met online. You make these stories possible. Thank you for being there even when I have hyperfocus. You always ensure I'm cared for, even when I forget to care for myself.

ALSO BY REBECCA CHASE

Head Over Feels: An enemies to lovers steamy sports romance (The Bulls Rugby Series Book 1)

Stalling in Love: A steamy opposites attract romance (The Bulls Rugby Series Book 2)

Occupational Hazard: An Anthology of Spicy Workplace Stories

Keep in Touch: A sweet coming-of-age love story

Rebecca Chase is featured in the following anthologies

Best Women's Erotica of the Year, Volume 4

Erotic Teasers: a Cleis anthology

COMING SOON

Go Cook Yourself: A spicy grumpy v sunshine enemies to lovers romance (Cloud Cookery School Series Book 1) – dual POV, 1st person. **Out 5th November 2024.**

After catching her boyfriend cheating with her best friend, Ruby returns to her family's business, the Cloud Cookery School. It's been six years since she turned her back on her family.

Gareth Kelsey has lost his restaurant, his livelihood, and, worst of all, his dog to Clive, his ex-business partner. Just when he thinks life can't get any worse, Ruby turns up at work, insists she's in charge and asks him to help her win Clive's competition.

But the more time Ruby and Gareth spend working together, the more they start to like each other and an irresistible attraction forms. But they must fight their feelings because Gareth is moving away, and Ruby is determined to make the school a success. Plus, Gareth is keeping a huge secret that could ruin everything between them. Can they endure it all, or are they destined to break each other's hearts?

Start Your Engines: A brother's best friend enemies to lovers sports romance (Coulter Formula One Racing Team Series Book 1)

Fake A Chance On Me: A fake dating sports romance (The Bulls Rugby Series Book 3)

Bodyguard book 2 - Strike's and Millie (Title TBC): A second chance, friends to enemies to lovers bodyguard romance (Closer Protection Series Book 2)

ABOUT REBECCA CHASE

Rebecca Chase is an English rose and a pocket rocket with a taste for drama, romance, spice and love. She adores writing, whether it's a short story with unexpected passion or a novel that takes you through the ups and downs of a blossoming relationship. She's always looking for everyone's next book boyfriend. When it comes to her stories, you can guarantee there will be romance, there will be mind-blowing sex, and, most of all, there will be love that lasts a lifetime. You'll be desperate for more while aching for a happy ever after.

CONNECT WITH REBECCA

Website - www.rebeccahchase.com

Twitter - twitter.com/rebeccahchase

Facebook - www.facebook.com/RebeccaHChaseAuthor

Tiktok - @rebeccachaseauthor

Instagram and Threads – rebeccahchase

Goodreads - 15019280.Rebecca_Chase

Printed in Great Britain
by Amazon

43483299R00229